MY
MOTHER'S
Daughter

MY
MOTHER'S
Daughter

Ann O'Loughlin

ORION

First published in Great Britain in 2018 by Orion Books,
an imprint of The Orion Publishing Group Ltd
Carmelite House, 50 Victoria Embankment
London EC4Y 0DZ

An Hachette UK Company

3 5 7 9 10 8 6 4

A CIP catalogue record for this book is
available from the British Library.

ISBN (Export Trade Paperback) 978 1 4091 8333 4

Typeset at The Spartan Press Ltd,
Lymington, Hants

Printed and bound in Great Britain by Clays Ltd,
Elcograf S.p.A.

www.orionbooks.co.uk

To John, Roshan and Zia. With love. xxx

Part One

Chapter One

Rathmoney, County Wicklow.

Hours passed. Margo sat in her favourite wingback velvet armchair by the window. The rain sheeted down outside, balls of water creating their own symphony on the galvanised roof of the big shed out the back. Wind squealed around the house, whipping in from the sea, across the fields, hitting against the building, driving the worst of the weather against the glass panes, whistling between the loose bits of wood at the top of the bay window, a loud gatecrasher into her thoughts.

Her body was stiff, her mind racing; in her hand a letter. She did not need to read it, she knew every line off by heart. Margo scrunched the letter into a tight ball, letting it roll over the palm of her hand, dropping to the floor. Decisions made in the dark may never last, but she had no choice. Her daughter was sleeping, her husband dead.

Conor's funeral had been the day before. Crowds shuffling forward to offer their condolences: Conor's name uttered with a reverence, mumblings that he was a good man; big rough hands laid gently on Elsa's head, regrets expressed she would have to grow up without a father. Trays of sandwiches were passed through the house, bottles of whiskey unscrewed and poured;

3

beers uncapped, pots of strong tea brewed, music filling the big rooms as night closed in.

She had sat in her black suit, three strings of pearls at her neck; elegant, aloof, polite, a shy smile wavering on her face, a grateful nod for anybody who leaned in with pre-prepared murmurs of consolation. Somebody fended off the most chatty, steering them into the kitchen, so they did not bother her with unnecessary talk.

Jack Roper from across the road, wearing a fresh shirt and zip-up fleece, his trousers neatly creased, had offered to tend to the animals. She was grateful, she did not even know where to start.

'I can help out until you find your feet, decide if you are going to keep on the old place,' he said, tugging at the collar of his shirt which was making his neck itch, causing a rash to creep upwards.

Margo had stood up, clumps of tissues on her lap cascading to the floor. 'This is our home; there is nowhere else we would want to be, especially now.'

Jack Roper's face deepened red with embarrassment. 'I wasn't insinuating anything else; I had a great respect for Conor; I just want to help.'

Repentant, she'd leaned towards Jack, rubbing his arm gently. 'I know. Conor loved your chats and advice; he said he could not have made a go of it without your guiding hand.'

The farmer beamed with delight as his wife pressed through, a huge lasagne dish in her hands. 'Don't be giving this to the hordes of Genghis Khan; keep it for yourself and Elsa. When everyone is gone and all the ...' she hesitated, '... all the fuss has died down, you won't want to be cooking.'

She made to give the dish to Margo, but thought better of it, muttering she might as well put it in the freezer. Margo smiled, hoping somebody had the foresight to take it from Ida Roper

Leabharlanna Poiblí Chathair Baile Átha Cliath
Dublin City Public Libraries

before she saw the stacks of casseroles and lasagnes, along with a rich chocolate cream cake, which had been handed over in the last two days.

Conor would have loved this. When they had moved to Ireland and to Rathmoney House twelve years ago after Elsa was born, he'd fretted he never would be accepted in the small community. He tried too hard, making the locals suspicious. It was Jack who had set him straight. Ida was more hesitant but was won over eventually by Margo's ample praise for her culinary skills, in particular her rhubarb and apple tarts.

Margo's head buzzed with all the expressions of sympathy; the overheard conversations, along with the whispers she wasn't supposed to hear; whispers that she surely would sell up and leave Rathmoney House. What was it about those who attended a funeral, that they thought they had permission to speculate on the future?

Margo sighed to think of the days when living at Rathmoney House was easy; the three of them on a big adventure together. Now they were a man down, and they would never savour that carefree time again, not now, especially after the arrival of the letter. She had sat here too long: night had turned into day, a new day when Conor was no more and others would quickly forget him. Worrying, she scanned the floor for the crumpled ball, scooping it up when she spotted it wedged between the front of the leather couch and the worn Persian rug. Elsa must not see it.

Steeling herself and pulling back the curtains so the early morning light crept across the typed words, she flattened out the page. Pain flared across her chest again. It was bad enough a twelve-year-old girl had to sit and see the life ebb from her father, but to think that she would some day have to know the contents of this letter was unbearable. That the letter had come as they had sat waiting for Conor to die, she resented deeply.

5

Shutting her eyes, she was back in his final hour; his laboured breathing, the tap on the bedroom door, Ida beckoning her furiously.

'What?' Margo had swung around, her eyes flinting with anger.

'There's a courier here with something official, he says you have to sign for it.'

'Tell him go away.'

'I did, but he's insisting.'

'Tell him to fuck off. For God's sake, does he not know what is going on here?'

'Margo, it will only take a few moments.'

Her face was wet with tears, her voice low and raw. Casting anxious glances at the bed in case Conor heard her pain, she waved Ida away.

'Mum, just go down. I can stay with Dad.' Elsa's small voice was nervous, shaking.

Margo took in the determination in her daughter's strained face. Placing her hand on Elsa's shoulder, she let her anger subside. 'Daddy likes it when you rub your hand across his forehead.'

'Like when I was younger?'

Margo, tears bulging under her eyelids, kissed her daughter on the head and whispered, 'Yes.'

Quietly, she'd let herself out of the room, her pace quickening once she had shut the door. Tearing down the stairs, she had seen a man standing, watching the dog working up a serious scratch on the top step.

'Does the fact that my husband is trying to eke out his last hours on earth mean anything to you? What is so important that I have to sign for it?'

'This is the residence of Conor and Margo Clifford?'

'Yes.' Margo clicked her tongue impatiently.

He reached into a satchel and handed her a white envelope. 'I was told to tell you not to ignore this letter.'

An electronic pen was pushed into her hands. She signed her name.

Ida shoved closer. 'What is it?'

'It doesn't matter. I have to get back to Conor.'

Margo had thrown the envelope on the hall table.

She had not thought of the delivery again until she'd been standing in black, Elsa at her side, waiting for the coffin to be carried downstairs. Placing her hand on the hall table for support, she'd felt the envelope tucked in behind a vase of roses sent by one of Conor's more generous clients. After the last of the hangers-on had been pushed out and she'd closed the door on the funeral party in the early hours, she casually picked up the letter.

Ripping it open, she scanned it absentmindedly as she walked across the hall.

Then, stopping suddenly, she read and re-read the words furiously.

Her breath choking in her mouth, she stumbled to the kitchen. Feeling for a chair at the table, she managed to sit down. Elsa's coat had fallen off the hook at the back door and lay crumpled on the floor, a mountain of napkins was balanced on a small table beside the stove; half-empty bottles of beer, cups and glasses were scattered across the table; a plate of fruit cake pushed into the middle. Beside it, the green glass bowl with apples, forgotten, shrunken and shrivelled. The dog, flopped on the armchair in the far corner, lazily wagged his tail. Cards handed in at the door were in a stack, a list of those who had been thoughtful compiled by Ida on top, so that when they came to them, the thank-you cards would go to the right people.

Shaking her head, Margo forced herself to read the letter again, word by word. Prickles of fear burned through her; her

7

mouth dried up, the words on the page swam in front of her and she thought she was hallucinating, that exhaustion had finally taken over. Placing the sheet of paper on the table, she rubbed her eyes, rolled her shoulders. Outside, a bird gave out a throaty call as the first glimmer of daylight showed itself.

Suddenly snapping up the letter, Margo moved to the drawing room, to her velvet chair by the window. This was her thinking chair, where she liked to ruminate on a problem, the drawing room a quiet oasis for her thoughts. It was here she had sat for hours, before she'd told Conor there was no hope. It was here she had sat begging for strength to break the same news to Elsa. Now she sat here for two or three hours, frantically wondering what to do with the letter, her desperation numbing her brain, so all she could do was clutch the piece of paper and sit.

Forcing herself, she scanned the letter again. Each word compounded the first flush of distress and heartache.

Who were these people to seek anything from her at this time? What they were asking, she could not do, would not do, ever. How dare they intrude on her now? How dare they impose with a request so ludicrous, it insulted her deeply. She ripped the letter in two, into four and then into tiny pieces, gathering every last speck from her lap into her fist.

Margo blistered with pain, loss seared through her, a chasm of loneliness and emptiness opening up, swallowing her whole.

Crows cawed a racket in the trees, the dog mooched in and collapsed at her feet.

'Mum, why are you still wearing that suit?' Elsa, in her pyjamas, was standing at the door, rubbing her eyes.

'I must have fallen asleep. I never got around to changing.'

Pushing her fist into her pocket, she released the bits of paper deep inside it, before opening her arms wide, smiling as Elsa ran into her embrace.

Chapter Two

Bowling Green, Ohio. Two weeks earlier.

Cassandra Richards was so anxious she had smoked two cigarettes in quick succession and now she was fussing about stupid details. That explained why she had pulled out a chair and stood on it to reach the top shelf of the closet to take down her big red purse.

She didn't even like that purse; Charles had bought it for her last fall. It was big and brash, with a round, gold buckle: she was feeling foolish holding it now, her nails piercing into the fake leather, the buckle digging in to her stomach.

After all these years together, it had come to this. Charles had never even said a proper goodbye.

It was clammy and warm in attorney Dale Winters's office; the fan droning ineffectively in the corner, whipping at the blind so it clanked against the window sill; the backs of her legs sticking to the plastic of the seat. She felt weary as she sat here waiting, her throat uncomfortably dry, her head aching.

Tilly texted; for a moment everything was normal. 'Karen says I can have waffles as a snack. Don't forget tonight is movie night.'

Dale Winters, a short, broad man, stood in the doorway and

called her name softly. 'Cassie, come through to the office. How are you this afternoon?' He tried to sound upbeat, but there was something about his voice which made her nervous. 'How is Tilly?'

Cassie looked at him. 'Good. Karen is sitting with her after school. I told Tilly I had to go get some supplies; I don't want her worrying too much.'

Dale did not answer. 'Cassie, I'm going to tell you straight, Charles has decided to play hardball.'

She pretended to look at the framed pictures on the wall behind him, trying to buy some time. It distracted her enough, so that when she spoke, her voice was peculiarly flat.

'Doesn't he have to pay child support for his own daughter?'

'I wish it was that simple, Cas. He's got himself an attorney.'

'But what about Tilly?'

Dale Winters cleared his throat. 'Charles claims Tilly is not his; he won't pay any child support.'

The handbag must have slipped from her grip, because she heard it crumple to the ground, the buckle pinging against the aluminium leg of the chair. Words caught in Cassie's mouth, sentences strangled in her throat before she could get them out. Her stomach churned, she thought she would throw up.

Dale got up and walked across the room to the water cooler. 'Are you OK, Cassie?'

What a stupid question, she thought; how could she be OK?

His voice was far away. He tried to push a paper cup of water into her hand, but she wouldn't take it.

'Charles wants a paternity test, but that's in our favour; he won't wriggle free from the result.'

'How could he even question it? We were childhood sweethearts.'

'It's only a tactic, darling. His attorney, Harry Mitchell, has a reputation for this sort of thing; it's a low, mean, no-good

Mitchell tactic. The only way to beat it is by taking the test and proving him wrong. After that, we'll go after Charles for every cent he has.'

'What is wrong with him, Dale? We're his family.'

'Don't torture yourself like this, Cas. Mitchell excels at shock tactics to try and force a low settlement. Time to call his bluff.'

Cassie jumped up, pacing the room like a panther in a cage. Snatching her handbag, she made for the door, tearing through the reception to the street.

Dale was behind her. 'What about this test, Cassie?'

'What about it?'

'It means Tilly needs to do it too.'

'How can he do this? What am I going to tell her: your daddy is so mean with his money that he's willing to deny you any support?'

'He's within his rights; it's best to comply. It's just a swab in her mouth, she needn't know why.'

Cassie thought for a moment. 'No, she *mustn't* know; she loves him, she misses him so much.'

Dale sighed, mopping his brow with his handkerchief.

'Funny how the whole world is going about its business, but my child's father wants to turn his back on her.'

Dale gripped her arm tight. 'We will win the war, wait and see.'

Cassie did not answer, but pulled away, setting off down the street, pounding the pavement so hard the soles of her feet stung.

She pretended she was hurrying, yet she had nowhere to go.

Then, as she reached City Car Sales, she stopped.

Anger surfed through her; she marched across the street, slipping past a pickup blocking the entrance.

Whipping her hair back from her eyes, she walked over to the biggest car on the lot. Reaching into her handbag, she pulled at her cosmetic bag, unzipping it. Scrabbling with her fingers, she pinched a tight grip on her tweezers. Moving closer to the car she kept her back to the building. She knew Charles always stood inside the top window, watching, waiting for the right moment to strike for a sale.

The paintwork was smooth, glossy; sunshine dazzling on the bonnet. Digging in with the tweezers, she scraped curl after curl of paint off, flicking off the specks as a snaky, shaky line formed. Triumph surged through her as the tweezers squeaked across the metal.

'Cassie, what the hell are you doing here?'

Charles Richards winced as he heard the screech of metal on metal, Cassie pushing the tweezers in for the deepest scratch, dots of silver and blue raining onto the ground.

'Stop, that car is worth tens of thousands of dollars.'

'What about our daughter?'

'Get away from the car, Cassandra. This is crazy.'

He moved to push her away, but she sidestepped him quickly. 'Answer me, Charles.'

'I'm not going to discuss this here. Go home, Cassie.'

Her voice was loud, hysterical, shaking. She no longer cared that people were gathering at the windows, observing, judging.

'Go to hell, Charles.' She shouted so loud her throat hurt; pain hurled through her.

She could see anger flash through him; red waved up his neck.

'Stop with your accusations. I have a right to fight this whatever way I want.' He spat the words out so hard, spittle puffed in a bubble from his mouth.

'What about Tilly? You don't have a right to hurt her.'

'This is not about Tilly. I love Tilly.'

His lips formed a sleazy smile, as though he pitied her. Looking around, she grabbed the nearby podium, still in place from the ribbon-cutting ceremony on the lot extension the week before. It was made of light wood, and she lifted it easily and launched it forwards. It sailed through the air, crashing into the showroom window, shattering the glass.

Shocked silence.

A woman on the sidewalk clapped loudly. Cassie flung the tweezers at Charles, before skirting around him and walking away, not sure which direction to take.

'You go, honey, the cops are on their way,' a man shouted after her. A couple in a car waved and sounded the horn. Cassie broke into a run, taking a quick left and then a right, her chest beginning to hurt. Sweat oozed out of her, but she pressed on. When she reached her car, she wanted to dip her head to the steering wheel and weep. Instead, she started up the engine, the car jerking forward in her haste. Shaking and unable to turn up at home so upset, instead she drove in the opposite direction, stopping at the railway crossing on the far side of town. She liked this quiet spot: the warehouses locked, the platforms deserted; the only trains that came through were freight, which never stopped. Sitting on the empty platform, she remembered when she and Charles used to come here, lounging about, kicking and hurling stones.

It was their go-to place. When they were in Europe, they had longed for the simple life here. That was why, a few months after Tilly was born, they came back. Charles joined his father in the family car dealership and life had trundled on until a month ago, when Charles had announced he was leaving her.

Picking up a stone now, Cassie fired it so hard that it hit one of the track's steel girders, pinging loudly. Taking out her battered packet of cigarettes, she pulled one out and put it in her mouth. Patting her pockets, she searched for her lighter. Realising she had left it in her handbag in the car, she cursed, throwing the unused cigarette onto the tracks.

She had let Charles go, hoping he would scratch whatever

itch he had, then come back to her. When, after five days, she called at the car lot, she was told Charles was in New York; she knew then he was never going to return home.

He was unapologetic when she rang him. 'I'm calling it a day, Cas. You know it hasn't been right between us for a long time. I want out.'

'If you stopped drinking…'

'Cas, we are done, let's not start throwing blame around.'

What about Tilly? What are you going to tell her?'

'Tell her I love her, but I need space.'

'Don't you think you should talk to her yourself?'

'I can't, Cas; the words will come out wrong.'

She had not spoken to him from that day to this, their communication since then had been purely through their attorneys.

Initially, when Tilly asked about her daddy, Cassie fudged, until one day the young girl spoke the words her mother was afraid to articulate.

'Daddy's left us, hasn't he?'

'Yes.'

'He never said goodbye.'

'It's complicated, honey.'

'Did he leave because of me?'

Cassie had rushed to her daughter, gathering her into a hug to reassure her, but she knew her words and caresses did little to calm the upset and uncertainty in Tilly's heart.

Tossing a last stone, she turned back to the car.

When she got home, the neighbour's cat was sitting on the veranda; toys she had forgotten to tidy up the night before were strewn in the far corner. Taking a deep breath, Cassie pulled back the screen door.

'Mommy, where were you? You've been so long.'

Chapter Three

Rathmoney, County Wicklow.

It was a grey day in Rathmoney. The mist wrapped around the tree tops and curled across the fields, encasing the land in cloying wet sheets of silvery mist. Margo, who slept with the curtains open, watched as the drizzle shrouded the house.

It was fitting that only a short time after Conor died, the colour of loneliness should visit; the grey was an exact match for her heart.

Getting out of bed, she pulled up the sash so the mist could encase her, too. The window gave way noisily as she shunted it open, the cold air swirling to all four corners of the room. Her mind was racing, going back over the letter, worrying over every word. She might have shredded the page, but the contents were embedded in her brain, the request as absurd now as when she first encountered it. All night she had stared into the darkness, willing Conor to help her share the burden: she was not sure she could carry it alone.

When she was young, she wanted to jump from an aeroplane into the snowy softness of the clouds; now she wished for this mist to envelop her, insulate her from what was to come. She stood, letting the fresh air nip around her, making her shiver and shake even more.

'Mummy.'

Elsa's call was long and loud, forcing her to return to reality, shut the window and hurry to her daughter's room.

'What was that noise?'

'I was airing the room.'

'I don't want to go to summer camp.'

'We have to get back to normal, sweetie.'

'Why?'

Margo, who was tidying up clothes from the floor, stopped to sit on Elsa's bed.

'It's what Daddy would have wanted.'

'How do you know? Isn't that what grown-ups say when they don't have an answer? Daddy didn't want to leave us.'

Margo pulled Elsa to her, wrapping her in a tight hug.

'I know,' she whispered into Elsa's hair.

Elsa burrowed into her. They stayed like that until Margo pulled away gently.

'We'd better hurry or you'll be late.'

'Are you doing breakfast?'

'I'll try.'

She knew what Elsa meant. Conor had got up every morning and made pancakes before school, shouting up the stairs when they were ready, like a chef in a restaurant kitchen.

She trudged downstairs; the hall tiles were cold, the kitchen damp. The room smelled of tar, the leftover trace of the dog's fart permeating the air. Max the Labrador pawed at the back door; she let him out to piss in the flower bed under the window.

As she cracked two eggs in a bowl, she thought she saw Jack walk into the yard. Lacing the fork through the eggs, she tapped the back door shut with her foot, anxious to avoid conversation. How could she pretend everything was normal when her very reason to get up every morning could be whipped out from under her any day now? What if what was in the letter was true? The very thought of it was torture. The dog nudged the door open again, before flopping behind her as she whisked the eggs fiercely into a yellow froth. Conor liked to lash vanilla into the mix, but she had none.

He did mornings so well; his dressing gown hanging loosely around him, the coffee machine switched on, heat blasting from the stoked-up stove.

Letting a knob of butter sizzle on the frying pan, she wandered out to the bottom of the stairs.

Elsa scuttled across the landing to the bathroom.

'Darling, hurry up, your pancakes are nearly ready.'

'I don't want pancakes.'

'What do you mean?'

Elsa leaned over the bannisters.

'I don't want pancakes. Ever.'

Her face was streaked with tears, her cheeks red.

'I don't want pancakes, all right,' she whispered, before disappearing from view. Margo stood in the hall trying to hold back the tears. Lovely, gentle Elsa driven cross and cranky by grief. Elsa denying herself her favourite pancakes as her mind attempted to process a loss too deep. What would happen if she ever found out about the letter? Would she ever forgive? Would she ever recover?

A piercing sound made Margo jump. Rushing to the kitchen, she waved a tea towel frantically to clear the smoke billowing from the frying pan, where the butter had browned and burned. Catching the pan, she threw it in the sink and turned on the tap, creating an angry, hissing, smoking mess. The dog pawed the outside door again, so she flung it open, all the time flapping the tea towel to clear the air.

When the alarm stopped, she slumped exhausted against the

door. She was still there when Jack rushed over from the nearby sheds.

'Are you OK?'

'I forgot the stupid pan.'

He stood awkwardly, taking her in; she was in her bare feet and wearing Conor's pyjamas.

'I'm off out to the far fields to check the fencing is in order,' he said.

She nodded and he left, waving to Elsa who arrived in the kitchen, throwing her bag on the table.

'What happened?'

'Nothing.'

Elsa made a face.

'I don't want anybody talking about it.'

'They won't. I had a word with the camp leader.'

'Everybody will be looking at me.'

Margo reached over, gripping her daughter tight around the shoulders.

'I think you'll find everybody will be very understanding. Ava's mum is giving you a lift and I'll walk down to collect you after camp.'

'I don't like Ava's mum, she asks too many questions.'

'She's the only school mum who lives close by. We will have to make do.'

Elsa shrugged her shoulders, jumping when they heard the beep of a car horn outside.

Margo wrapped her dressing gown tightly around her before opening the front door.

Rita Mangan jumped from the driver's seat and up the steps, her arms out to embrace Margo.

'You know I'm here for you night and day, you poor thing. Don't you worry about Elsa. Does she want to come back to ours for dinner afterwards?'

'No, but thanks.'

'I thought you might need a little time to yourself.'

'That's the last thing I need, Rita.'

'I just think if I lost my Roger, I wouldn't be able to get out of bed again, never mind get back to normal.' She stopped. 'Sorry, I'm prattling on.'

Margo shook her head. 'There's nothing that can make things any worse or better.'

Rita Mangan smiled, backing down the steps to the car.

Margo nudged Elsa in the ribs and the girl followed reluctantly.

Watching the car move down the driveway, swerving to avoid the potholes near the gate, Margo felt the tears rise. Life for them had changed so drastically and yet in other ways, not at all. Whining, Max the Labrador jumped up, dislodging the black wreath on the door.

Death was peculiar, she thought. It visited with such drama, but exited quietly, leaving nothing behind, only the garlands of loss. Reaching down, she pulled Conor's name card from the wreath, leaving the rest to the dog.

Shutting the door, she stood in the hall, the grandfather clock slowly ticking out time, carrying her further and further away from when Conor was alive. She had never felt so alone. She needed Conor more than ever now. Who else would understand? Who else would be able to fight off these strangers who wanted to steal her life?

Turning into his study, she imagined he might be there, his head bent over his desk or concentrating on precisely fixing his model trains on their tracks, taking a break after doing the morning jobs on the farm.

The room still smelled of him, the faint whiff of his aftershave and an outdoor smell she liked.

Sitting at his desk, guilt bubbled up inside her that she had shredded the letter. What if Elsa found out years later? She might be angry and aggrieved. Conor, if he had known of the letter, would have roared and shouted, created a fuss, but she only wanted it to go away. Maybe she could sell up, move somewhere else so they could not find them; but how could she take Elsa away from the home she loved?

When there was a gentle tap on the window, Margo jumped.

Ida waved cheerily, holding a warm apple tart in one hand and pointing to the front door with the other.

Annoyed, Margo went to the hall and pulled back the door.

'Margo, how are you? Jack was a bit worried about you, so I decided to call over. God knows I have time on my hands. Jack does everything on the farm and there's little for me to be doing in the house anymore. Jack says I should find something to do, maybe a job, but who gives a toss about a woman in her sixties?' She stopped to catch her breath. When she spoke again, it was softly. 'I'm sorry for prattling on, I am nervous but the more people you have around you at this time the better.' Ida stopped on her first step into the hallway. 'I don't mean to intrude. Jack said...'

Margo threw her hands in the air, marching off to the kitchen.

Not sure whether to follow, Ida fumbled with the tea towel swaddling the warm apple tart. 'I'll just leave this here for you.' When there was no sound from the kitchen, she slipped the dish onto the hall table and folded her teacloth back into her handbag. 'I'll go. Call over when you're ready,' she said, waiting for a few moments in case there was an answer.

The swish of the front door before it banged shut made Margo spring up.

She should not treat Ida like that.

Skidding down the hall, she yanked the door open. Ida had only got as far as the end of the house, where she was stooped petting the dog.

'Ida, I'm sorry, I should not have been so rude.'

Ida stayed still. 'I understand, Margo, it's not easy; I'm not taking it personally.'

Margo wanted to giggle; she knew Ida was taking it very personally. 'Come in, we'll have some tart.'

Ida straightened up and walked stiffly to the steps. When she got as far as Margo, she reached over, squeezing her arm tight. 'If you're sure I'm not intruding.'

'I'm sure, Ida.'

'We are here, me and Jack, for you night and day; I want you to know that.'

'Jack told you about my feeble attempt at pancakes, then.'

Ida chuckled. 'I might have to start giving you lessons. That's the problem when one person in the house cooks so well, the others are left hungry, when ...' Her face reddening, she slapped her hand up to her mouth. 'Me and my big mouth, but I don't mean any harm.'

Margo shook her head, leading the way to the kitchen.

Swiping clean a space at the table, she invited Ida to sit.

Ida, casting her eye around the room, took in the dirty dishes stacked five high and three deep on the draining board; the cereal boxes tipped over, the empty bottles and cans strewn across the table; the floor littered with the remains of a milk carton the dog had chewed and discarded.

Pointing to the stack of cards on the dresser, Ida sighed. 'I can help you with that lot if you like; you need to get the words of thanks out. It's expected.'

Margo shrugged her shoulders. 'Later, there are more important things for now.'

Ida got up from the table, opened the dishwasher and began to stack it.

'You don't have to do that.'

'I don't have to, but I want to. When Elsa gets back, you want her to come in to a home, not what is beginning to look like a student's doss-house. There are some things here from the time of the funeral,' she said, taking the plate of cake off the table and walking to the dustbin, where she let the slices slip away.

Margo did not answer, but sat in the armchair, her feet tucked under her, watching Ida as she clucked around the kitchen.

Arranging the empty cans and bottles in rows beside the bin, Ida muttered under her breath. 'I'll tell Jack to call later, to get all those off to recycling.' Turning her attention to the counter next, she picked up the bowl of shrunken apples. 'This fruit has seen better days,' she muttered, tipping it into the bin.

When Margo didn't comment, she swiftly turned around.

'Jesus, what have I said now?'

Margo went to the sink. Letting the cold tap run, she splashed water on her face. After about forty seconds, she turned off the tap and patted her face dry with a paper towel. She dithered at first, but the words bubbled up and she could not contain it any longer.

'Oh, Ida. What am I going to do? I'm in big trouble.'

'What do you mean?'

Margo, clenching her fists, moved between the table and the stove, attempting to take deep breaths to calm down.

'If it's money, you know we won't see you stuck?'

Margo let out a peculiar laugh. 'I wish it was, Ida.' She slumped back into the armchair by the stove. Ida pulled up a chair beside her and sat down, but Margo felt the need to disclose abating.

'We're here to help, you don't have to hold back with Jack and Ida Roper.'

'I know. I'm sorry. It's not that I don't trust you guys, I don't know how I would get up every day without you two, but...'

'You aren't ready.'

Margo nodded.

'When you feel able to tell us, that will be time enough.'

Ida moved to sort through a bundle of laundry at the table while Margo slashed away her tears and concentrated on her breathing. After a little while she got up, walking to the drawing room as she dialled Kiely Kileen Solicitors. Her head was thumping, her stomach in a knot as she asked to speak to her solicitor, Samantha Kiely.

'She's in court all day. I can give you an appointment for next Friday,' the secretary said.

'That's days away.'

She didn't hear the answer but mumbled that she would take the appointment, quickly getting off the phone before her distress was detected. She tried to escape into Conor's study, but Ida was waiting for her in the hall. Margo knew by Ida's face she was bursting to talk.

'You need a project to help you through the next few months.'

When Margo protested she didn't want or need any such thing, Ida held up her hand to stop her talking.

'Hear me out, that's all I ask.'

Unable to resist, her energy sapped, Margo stood with her arms folded across her chest.

'Conor always wanted Rathmoney House to be a high-end bed and breakfast, so why don't we fulfil that dream now?' Ida stopped for a moment, but when there wasn't a reaction from Margo, she continued. 'The extension is built, all you need is the furniture and a good spring clean of the main house.' She trailed her hand along the wood panelling. 'Treat every customer as if he or she is an inspector and you will have a good establishment,' she said, holding up her fingers, stained black with dirt.

'I don't think I'm ready to look after guests, I can barely look after myself and Elsa.'

'That's where I come in. Let me help you; I will set up and run everything behind the scenes.'

Agitated, Margo pulled on Ida's arm. 'What will we do about food? I can just about manage breakfast, but I will never be able to do an evening meal.'

Ida smiled brightly. 'I thought you would never ask. Jack made me promise not to say anything, in case you had plans of your own.' Reaching into her pocket, she pulled out a sheet of typed paper. 'I worked on a simple menu last night, in case you were stuck. One of my tarts for desserts and maybe a nice homemade soup to start. They will like the fact that the ingredients come from your own garden. For the main course, we can offer three options: roast beef, a creamy chicken dish, but I am stuck on the vegetarian option. How about I make a lasagne? Sure we can all tuck in if they don't want it.'

Ida hesitated. She was about to hand the sheet to Margo, when she faltered again. 'I hope I haven't been too presumptuous, you might have other plans.'

Margo guffawed loudly. 'The only plan I had was to try and get away with a few ready-made meals and hope they wouldn't notice.'

'Hello disaster, I won't let you go down that road.'

'I can't ask you to do all this Ida, you have enough to be doing on your own farm.'

Ida, walking around as though she was the presenter of one of those TV shows, smiled broadly. 'You'll have to get a nice sign as well. Visibility from the road is so important for passing traffic.'

Margo burst out laughing. 'I doubt there's much passing traffic looking to stay anywhere overnight on the back road from Greystones to Rathmoney.'

Ida, who was fingering the gold drapes in the drawing room, looked crestfallen. 'You'll have to make them want to come out this road. Conor obviously saw the potential by investing in the building.'

'He had huge plans, but I'm not Conor.'

24

Ida walked across the Persian rug. 'Margo, maybe a challenge is what you need right now.'

'I suppose.'

Ida rubbed her hands together with excitement.

Distracted, Margo said, 'There's so much to do, what will I do about furniture?'

'McCarthys on Main Street. Dan should be able to help.'

'Ida, I can't afford anything from that place.'

'His good furniture is perfect for Rathmoney.'

'Not if I can't afford it.'

'Leave it with me, I'm sure Dan will be prepared to come to some arrangement, it's not as if they are queueing outside the shop.'

Clearly not wanting to push Margo too far, Ida said she had better go home, letting herself out as Margo went upstairs, stopping at the landing window to watch her neighbour scurry down the driveway. She was not sure of what they were about to do, but Ida was right, it would be a diversion when she needed it most. A diversion not only from the unbearable loss of Conor, but a break from the distress that letter had brought into her home.

Chapter Four

Bowling Green, Ohio.

'Cas, are you OK?'

'Do I look OK, Bonnie?'

'You look like shit.'

Cassie had flinched when the doorbell rang, unsure whether to answer until she heard Bonnie's voice.

'What's up? It's not like you to ring in sick, not when you know we're so busy at work,' Bonnie said as she stepped in to the hall. 'What are you doing sitting in the dark? It's frying in here.' Bonnie marched over and opened the front window blind.

Cassie blinked in the harsh light. 'Charles has left us.'

'I thought as much.'

'He's refusing to pay child support.'

'That no-good moron, you better fight him hard.'

Cassie, her arms folded stood in the centre of the room. Bonnie turned on the fan, but it only shunted the hot air around, firing squalls of warm air in their faces.

'I want to fight, but...'

'Some ass put the CCTV footage from the car lot up on YouTube,' Bonnie said, waving her phone.

'Oh shit. No.'

'They are calling you Ninja Mom.'

'Has Tilly seen it?'

'Even if she hasn't, I'm sure someone at school will be delighted to tell her.'

'Play it for me.' Cassie stood watching the small screen. 'Thank God, there's no sound. I was over the top, but I don't regret it.'

'You're hurt and wallowing, nothing wrong with that, but now it's time to fight back.'

Cassie stared at Bonnie. 'It's a lot more complicated than you think.' Spying Charles's stack of car magazines, Cassie deliberately kicked them over. They spilled across the floor, the sight of them scattered a small thing that gave her satisfaction. 'Apparently he's in love with a woman he met at some conference in Baltimore.'

When Bonnie made to speak, Cassie flicked the palm of her hand up to stop her. 'He says he can't be sure Tilly is his, he won't pay child support.'

'What the hell is going on?'

When Cassie spoke again, her voice was so low, Bonnie had to lean forward to hear her.

'The situation is so bad, he's insisting on a paternity test.'

'Asshole. When is this test?'

'Tomorrow. The results will be back within two or three days.'

'Surely you're not worried?'

'I know Tilly is our daughter. What I can't forgive is that he would seek to deny his own flesh and blood.'

Bonnie looked her friend straight in the eye. 'Darling, you have to make him pay for his stupidity.'

'I'm not sure I know how to explain all this to Tilly. It's just a swab in the mouth, so we're both getting it done.'

'Do you want me to go along with you?'

'No need. Dale will be with us.'

Bonnie took in the room. 'When was the last time you cleaned up around here?'

'Quit it, Bonnie.'

'You go rest. I'll get started on this place,' Bonnie insisted, ushering Cassie from the room.

Cassie lit a cigarette and quietly tried to gather her thoughts in the gloom of her bedroom. It must be the stress of the situation, but she felt sick. She had been up in the middle of the night too, coughing. Curse Charles and all the trouble he had caused. She heard Bonnie tidying up in the kitchen. The sound of cutlery being gathered, the plates being washed, glasses placed on the top shelf, cupboard doors closing as cartons and packets were put away. There was a certain comfort in the familiar noises. She heard the clink of a bag of empty bottles. Empty bottles from Charles's last binge before he finally left them. She tried to remember back to when he wasn't drinking, when times were good, but she had to rewind too far. A rush of warm air slid through the house, Bonnie must have opened the windows to air out the rooms. The breeze nuzzled gently at the door when it reached the bedroom. But Cassie wanted a raging destructive wind, a storm to reflect her life, the pain in her heart; a tornado sweeping away whatever swirled into its path.

She had been chased by wind before, a story from a different time. Driving on the Ohio backroads in a black Ford Galaxy, the car radio too loud, Charles had swung into the side of a field, where row upon row of corn was ripening under a hot sun. She smiled even now to think how they lounged on the bonnet, losing their grip, slipping off with the intensity of their kisses.

'Catch me if you can, Charles Richards.'

He had laughed, hollering out her name, letting the sound sweep over the corn to the sky.

After a few minutes they were lost, panting and covered in dust.

They giggled at their stupidity, running hand in hand, trying to get back to the sound of the music, still blaring from the car at the side of the field.

Carefree years consigned to memories.

Bonnie knocked on the bedroom door and came in.

'I've made the place look nice. Why don't we go out, banish the cabin fever and buy you a new dress for tomorrow?'

'Going around shops is the last thing I want to do.'

'Just a rummage and browse.'

Cassie rolled her eyes. 'I'm not going anywhere. Anyway, I have plenty of good clothes. I can decide what to wear later.'

Bonnie walked across to the wardrobe, sliding back one of the doors. 'Girl, why are you keeping the creep's clothes?'

'I don't know, should I just throw them?'

'Why don't we do that now?'

Before Cassie had time to respond, Bonnie began dragging the clothes from the wardrobe. Gathering up a bunch of suits and golfing trousers, she stumbled to the door. 'I'll just chuck them in the trunk. Come on, grab a bundle. I'll take them to the clothes bank on the way home.'

It took two more trips to Bonnie's car before Charles's clothes were cleared out.

'The man must be walking around naked, the amount of gear he left here.'

'I imagine the new woman in his life has very different ideas on how to dress him, anyway.'

'Silly woman, if she thinks she can change him. Once a cheat, always a cheat.'

'You really don't like him, do you?'

'After what he's done to you, there's no going back,' Bonnie said as she opened the wardrobe's other sliding door.

'Lots of lovely clothes here.'

'I know you mean well, but what I wear is not going to magically heal me or make this situation disappear.'

'But it might give you a teeny bit of confidence. Do you really think it would be better to go along looking lousy? It could give licence to Charles and his attorney to bully you even more.'

Bonnie pulled out a long-sleeved blue dress, a shimmer of silver at the hem.

'You can at least try it on.'

'I bought it last summer for our staff garden party. Charles was in Baltimore, said he couldn't make it back in time.'

Bonnie handed her the dress.

'Wear it, it'll look sensational, and put your hair up.'

Bonnie left just as Tilly was getting off the school bus.

'And I will talk to Zack, tell him you need time, persuade him we can limp on at Zack's Realty without you for another day or so,' Bonnie said, before she drove off.

Tilly ran straight upstairs to her room, slamming her bedroom door hard.

Cassie threw a bag of popcorn in the microwave, listening to it pop before emptying it into a bowl. Slowly, she made her way to Tilly's room.

At first, Tilly ignored her mother's polite knocks.

'Tilly Richards, I'm not going away.'

Tilly opened the door halfway, pushing her hand out to cup a fistful of popcorn.

'Let me in, sweetheart; we need to talk.'

Tilly stood back. Cassie saw her eyes were puce from crying.

'A bad day, honey?'

Tilly nodded her head and Cassie reached over, pulling her gently to sit on the bed. 'Are you getting a lot of trouble over the YouTube video?'

'Why did you do it?'

'I was mad as hell. It's a one-day wonder, everybody will have forgotten about it in a few days.'

'I don't think so, it's got three hundred thousand views in a few days. Everyone at school says you and Daddy are getting a divorce.'

Cassie's heart broke. 'I didn't mean you to find out like this.'

Tilly's face puckered red, tears flowing. Cassie felt anger surge through her that Charles had caused this pain.

'Sweetheart, I'm sorry. Daddy should have told you.'

'Why does he hate us all of a sudden?'

'He doesn't hate you, sweetie.'

'Did you tell him we love him?'

Cassie caught Tilly into a hug, but she resisted, pulling away.

'You didn't fight for him, did you? You're always nagging him, saying he's lazy and he never does any chores.'

Cassie bunched Tilly's hair into a ponytail and let it fall loose again around her shoulders.

'It's a little more complicated than that.'

'Nancy in my class said I'll have to decide which parent I live with. She said she picked her dad, but he's so fussy she can't even have friends over; he says his place is too small.'

'Tilly, this is your home, that's not going to change.'

'He doesn't want me anymore, does he?'

A mix of sorrow and rage swept through Cassie. Charles should have to sit and listen to the pain in their daughter's voice; maybe then he would realise the damage he was causing.

'Where did you get that idea?'

'Nancy says if my dad has another woman, he'll want a new family.'

'You're jumping too far ahead, sweetie.'

'Why do I have to go for this test?'

'It's nothing to worry about.' Cassie was annoyed at herself that she didn't sound stronger.

'Nancy said she never heard of it.'

'Fancy, there's something that kid doesn't know,' Cassie muttered.

Tilly curled up on her bed and turned to the wall.

'I love you, Tills, that will never change.'

Cassie was halfway out the door, when Tilly called after her.

'I love you too, Mom.'

Cassie was nervous about the DNA test, even though she knew she had no reason to worry about the stupid results. Maybe after this expensive and dumb show of bravado, Charles would see sense and agree to a weekly support payment.

She wore her blue dress, her hair up as Bonnie suggested. Tilly walked close to her, slipping her hand in hers when she saw her father. Charles was all smiles, chatting up the receptionist. He was so sure in his own swagger, beaming at Tilly.

'Hey, kiddo. Come and give your daddy a hug.'

Tilly shrank back; Cassie glared at him.

When she later looked back on that day, she pinpointed that as the moment she started to hate Charles. Dale clearly got the vibe, because he squeezed her arm tightly.

'Ignore him, this is only the first round of many,' he whispered.

When Cassie's phone rang days later, she knew the results were back, but the secretary was telling her nothing.

'I can't discuss it; can you come in straight away and talk to Mr Winters?'

It was unusual that Dale didn't call her himself, but she tried not to read anything into the sudden formality attached to the meeting.

At Dale's building, the secretary directed her to his office, where he was waiting for her.

'Close the door, Cas.'

'Is there something wrong?' she asked as she sat on the chair in front of his desk.

'You could say that. The results are back.'

She perched on the edge of the seat. 'Is there a problem?'

The attorney cleared his throat. 'We have a very complex situation.'

'What's wrong?'

'The test shows that Charles is not Tilly's daddy.'

'What?'

Dale Winters's voice was flat. 'He is not the father.'

Her nervousness made her laugh. 'You're kidding, right?'

He shook his head. 'I would never joke about this.'

The words stabbed her; her knees buckled. 'What exactly are you saying?'

'There is more. Your swab was also tested.'

'And?'

'You are not a match either, Cas. There is no genetic link to either of you.'

His head bowed down, as if he suddenly had something important to read in the file in front of him. The temperature in the room rose. The walls sweated; the clock behind Dale clanged the hour. Beads of sweat dotted Cassie's back, blotching through her top. None of this was true, how could it be? Why would Charles do this to her?

It had to be a dumb mistake, a cruel joke. Her stomach heaved, she could hear her heart throbbing. She tried to speak, but no words came out. The situation, she felt, was hopeless. She wanted to bolt from the room, go home and be with Tilly, to feel safe again, yet she dreaded she might never be able to return to that time when everything was easygoing.

'This can't be.'

'That is what the results show, Cas.'

'But we are her parents.'

'You aren't. She is somebody else's child.'

'They mixed up the results. This can't be right.'

'It is a lot to take in Cas, but it's here in black and white. Tilly is not your child.'

Her tongue was caked dry; her head thumping. Dale's mouth was moving, his face dark, his eyes downcast. Words of denial stinging the air.

'Is it some sick joke? There has been a mistake, schedule another test.'

'DNA is not wrong; we can ask for a retest, but first we have to find out what could have happened.'

What was he talking about? What did any of them know?

'She puckers her nose like Charles. When she was slow to walk, my mom said I had been the very same. Or the time when she was only five, she packed her bags and announced she was moving to New York, just like her auntie did at the same age. What about the way she walks, leaning a bit too much to the left, like Charles? There are so many examples. Don't they count for anything? She talks just like me.'

Dale shook his head and mopped his forehead. Reaching over, he switched on a fan in the corner close to his desk.

'Charles has opened up a hornet's nest.'

'Dale, what am I going to do?'

When she jumped up, she saw him lean back in his chair, like she was some sort of mad woman threatening him. Suddenly feeling exhausted, she slipped back onto her chair.

She looked Dale straight in the eye.

'I don't understand any of this. Where is the baby girl I carried for nine months? Where is the baby girl I held after she was born?'

He fidgeted with the corner of a file, desperately trying to think of words of reassurance, but there were none.

'We will have to contact the hospital, see if it can throw any light on this.'

'What do you mean?'

'It's not beyond the bounds of possibility something went wrong there.'

'No.'

'We don't know; we have to find an answer and the hospital seems a good place to start.'

'Tilly was born in France. We came back home when she was three months old. Oh my God, what am I going to tell Tilly? Does this mean that my birth child is in France?'

He coughed to clear his throat. 'I'm saying we have to look at all possibilities and that's number one on the list.'

'Why can't we work from the possibility that the DNA test is wrong? Maybe the samples got mixed up or something.'

Dale drummed his fingers on the desk.

'Honestly, Cas, we can waste a lot of valuable time challenging this test, when the results are there in black and white. Naturally, the first thing I did when they told me the news was to ask if there could be any mistake, any chance of contamination or error. But their procedures are rigorous. The possibility of an error is next to none. If you really want another test, I will arrange it, but we are going to have to face the facts, and sooner is better than later.'

'The fact that Tilly is not our daughter?'

'We know she can't be.'

Waves of anguish and guilt churned her stomach. She thought she would throw up. Somewhere outside the room, a door banged; the tinkle of laughter in the distance. Tears gushed, she felt them pooling, soaking into her blouse collar, cold now around her neck.

Dale bowed his head.

Her stomach heaved again. She ran for the door, but did not make it, vomiting, most of it landing in the bin, the rest spotting the wall.

Dale ran to her, gently guiding her to a small sofa by the window.

'I can't lose Tilly. I won't let anyone take her away.'

He took out a handkerchief, holding it out to her, so she could wipe her mouth. 'We are a long way from that.'

'What happens next?'

'I will write the hospital seeking an investigation. The babies born the same day as Tilly and maybe within a few days of her will have to be tested.'

'But what about Tilly?'

'We are going to take this slowly, Cas; no need to say anything to anybody right now. Let me contact the hospital and get the ball rolling.'

'Tilly will have to know.'

'There will be time for that later.'

'Who are these other parents who have my daughter? Who are they?'

Dale shook his head. 'I don't have any answers right now.'

'What will I do, if they want her back? They won't do that, will they?'

'Let's not get ahead of ourselves, Cas.'

'Don't get on to the hospital, just leave it. I won't go after Charles for child support.'

'I'm sorry, Cas, but we have to see this through. We can't ignore it. First, we have to find out what happened. When we know that, we'll take it from there. It's gone too far; it's not possible to walk away from it now.'

She sat, her shoulders slumped, tears running down her face.

'Curse Charles and what he has done to us.'

'I gather he is as cut up as you are.'

'Is that supposed to comfort me?'

Dale knew better than to reply.

'Tilly will never forgive me, either, whatever way I do this.'

'You don't know that, Cas.'

'I know the world is round. I know I love Tilly to the stars and back; that is the only certainty now.'

Dale shifted in his seat and pulled on his tie as if to straighten it. 'There is one more thing.'

'What?'

'Mitchell says Charles is backing off; he will pay the child support, whatever you want, but he will have nothing to do with any legal battle over Tilly.'

'He started all this; now he wants to walk away and leave us in this mess. He is nothing but a damn coward. How am I going to fight this on my own?'

'Don't jump the gun, Cas. There's nothing to fight, as yet. Wait until we gather all the facts. You're not on your own; I am with you every step of the way.'

'This is all going to cost big bucks, money I don't have.'

'All that is for another time. Maybe there is family you can turn to to get a few thousand dollars together, just as a small fighting fund in case...'

'My mom died a few years ago and Dad is the only one left. It will kill him when he finds out what is happening.'

'Go home, try and pull yourself together and I will write the hospital authorities in France.'

Her head reeling, Cassie walked out of the office, not sure where she was going. There was no soothing her bruised heart, but she had to find a way to appear normal when she walked into their home, for Tilly's sake.

She drove to the park, pulling in near the playground. Children played and called out to each other. How many times had she sat here, marvelling how her daughter was so athletic like her father, remembering the time she ran into the woods and came back crying, holding an injured bird. They took the bird to the vet and a big deal was made about how Tilly was such a kind girl. The pride she felt that day, that she and Charles had brought such a beautiful person in to the world.

Cassie got out to walk in the fresh air. A little girl ran across her path, calling out to her mother. Cassie lingered to watch them.

'Excuse me, can I help you?' asked a woman standing with her own child held firmly by the hand.

Cassie didn't answer but turned away to the woods.

She loved this daughter of hers more than anything. They laughed and giggled together like best friends. Surely, she would have known if she was an imposter. But if it was true … what would happen now that she loved the imposter more than anyone else in the world?

Where was her birth daughter? Why did she feel so guilty to be even wondering what she looked like? Did she wrinkle up her nose like Charles or did she have his thick mop of hair? Was she a whizz at maths and did she dance at all?

Tilly had her shy smile, everybody said so; she was a girl with an endearing quiet way about her. When she laughed though, it was heartily and more like Charles, but how could that be? Were any of these similarities deep-seated or real or were they just mannerisms picked up along the way?

She took out her phone and rang Dale. 'I don't care. I want another DNA test or a re-test, whatever way they want to do it.'

'Cas, we talked about this.'

'She's my daughter, I'll never forgive myself if I don't fight for her. I have to have it.'

'I've already sent an email to the hospital.'

'I still want another test.'

Dale Winters sighed heavily. 'All right, Cas, if it means that much.'

'It does.'

She walked back to the car and took a few minutes to retouch her make-up before driving home. Opening the screen door, she saw her sitter Karen get up and snatch her bag from the stand.

'Tilly didn't want anything to eat; she said she wasn't feeling well.'

'Is she running a fever?'

'No, but she said she was tired, so I thought she should get her homework out of the way.' Karen stepped out onto the veranda, before calling Cassie to follow. 'I think she's getting a bit of trouble from some girls at school.'

'The YouTube video still?' She knew Karen had seen it, but out of politeness did not want to mention it.

'Kids can be so cruel,' Karen said as she left. 'Tell Tilly I said goodbye.'

Cassie took a deep breath and went to Tilly. 'Why don't we order in pizza?'

'I don't want pizza.'

'You pick, what do you fancy?'

'Karen told you.'

'Are kids at school mean to you?'

'They're always mean to me.'

'I know I haven't made it easy with my stupid row in public with your dad.'

Tilly didn't answer.

Cassie sat down beside her daughter. 'I'm not going to tell you a lie, Tilly, this is a messy business, but I promise to behave much better from now on.'

Tilly nodded, but kept looking at the journal in front of her. 'I just want things back the way they were.'

'That's not going to happen, sweetheart; I would be telling you a lie if I promised that.'

Tilly looked directly at Cassie. 'Go to Daddy, tell him we love him, we want him back.'

Cassie grabbed Tilly, wrapping her so tight she could not wriggle free.

'We can get through this together.'

'Nancy Montgomery says you are going to be arrested.'

'Tell Nancy if she says one more thing, I will talk to her parents.'

'That's not going to frighten her, she said her mother said you should be put behind bars.'

'I think it's time to strike the Montgomeries off our Happy Holidays list.'

She was relieved to see her daughter smile.

'Now what about that pizza?'

'Can we have pancakes?'

'Only if you help.'

Tilly got up and rushed to the drawer to get out her apron.

'Can I measure out the flour?'

'You can follow the recipe. I will be the *MasterChef* judge. You have twenty minutes, starting now.'

Cassie stood by her daughter, watching how she mixed the eggs and milk, before adding it to the sieved flour, baking powder, salt and caster sugar.

'These pancakes are going to be the fluffiest ever,' Tilly said. Cassie was relieved to hear the happy tone back in her voice.

'Melt in the mouth for sure, you are halfway through. Have you decided how you are going to serve them?'

Tilly smiled, ran to the refrigerator and took out a carton of raspberries.

'With a choice of homemade raspberry coulis or Canadian maple syrup.'

'I'm in the mood for both,' Cassie said, raising her nose in the air, so she came across as just a bit snooty.

'Certainly, madam,' Tilly said, making them both laugh out loud.

Chapter Five

Rathmoney, County Wicklow.

Ida was at Rathmoney House early.

'I had a chat with Dan McCarthy. He says if we drop down this morning, he will see what he can do about a deal on the furniture for the rooms.

'Ida, it will still be a lot of money, I don't know if I can find that much right now.'

Ida looked sheepish.

'It might be a bit late for that. Jack made up a lovely sign: gold and black lettering on a sky blue background. He is putting it up as we speak.'

'You should have consulted me,' Margo said crossly as she turned away to the kitchen.

'I didn't think I had to; we agreed I would organise everything.'

Margo was about to reply when Ida whooped with excitement.

'Oh my, it's all happening now. Look, a car is coming up the avenue. I told you Jack's sign would bring them in.'

Margo ignored Ida until she called out again.

'False alarm, it looks like some sort of courier delivery.'

Margo stopped in her tracks. When the doorbell sounded, she jumped.

Ida stepped further down the hall.

'Are you going to answer it?'

Gulping a deep breath, Margo pulled back the front door.

'Is this the home of Conor and Margo Clifford?'

'Yes.'

The man handed over a white envelope. 'Please sign here.'

Margo signed for the letter, her heart pounding. She was tempted to refuse it, send the courier away, but she knew she couldn't hide forever.

The man was already in his van by the time she shut the door.

Ida waited a few moments as Margo held the envelope, staring at it. Gently, she approached. Reaching out to touch Margo on the shoulder she spoke softly.

'You have been thrown, haven't you? Not got something addressed to Conor before, have you?'

Margo didn't answer.

'Come on and sit down, you can open that later.'

Margo turned to Ida. 'I'm sorry, Ida, I don't mean to be rude, but I think I need to be on my own.'

'All you have to do is say it, dear, I never like to intrude. I can ring Dan, say we will pop down later.'

'I'm sorry.'

'No need to apologise, Ida Roper knows very well when to leave somebody be. If you need me, you know where to find me.'

Margo walked to the kitchen, waiting until she was sitting at the table to open the envelope.

Sentences ran together; she could hardly focus. The hospital in France was conducting an inquiry into the birth of the babies there on 30 November, 2000. As part of that inquiry, they wanted the Clifford family to submit to DNA testing. Here they were asking the impossible of her again.

Why were they so persistent? Why couldn't they take her previous refusal to engage as confirmation that she did not want to know any further?

She remembered how much she had liked that little hospital, how welcoming the staff were; how they treated her as a celebrity because little Elsa was born in the chateau in the village, before being transferred to the hospital in the large town twenty kilometres away. When Elsa developed jaundice, they had acted swiftly, taking her away for phototherapy with fluorescent light.

Thinking back to Elsa's birth, Margo thought she might faint with fright, but the memory also galvanised her: she knew she had to do something, find a way to tell these people to go away, stop sending these letters. Racing up the stairs, she pulled on her jeans and jumper and grabbing her coat from the wardrobe, she hurried so she could make the DART train from Greystones to Dublin.

Margo sat in the reception of the offices of Kiely Kileen Solicitors fiddling with the strap of her handbag, checking and rechecking that she had the letter.

She heard the receptionist on the phone. 'I told her she has to have an appointment and you are busy all day.'

The woman at the other end of the line must have said something, because the girl's voice squeaked louder.

'She's insisting it's urgent.'

Margo listened intently.

'OK, I'll tell her.'

The receptionist stood up, calling her name. 'Samantha says if you can wait until she has seen her next client, she will try and fit you in.' Her voice lowered. 'Mrs Clifford, if this is about your late husband's estate, she has everything in hand, but it will take several weeks; we will be in touch after that.'

43

'It's another matter.'

The receptionist wrote something on a folder and nodded. 'You'll have to wait and take your chances, so.'

Margo joined a small group of people in the waiting area, sinking into a cold leather armchair. A young man in a tracksuit, his hood low over his head, sat beside her and lit up a cigarette. When the receptionist asked him to put it out, he laughed, letting the cigarette drop to the floor where he ground it in to the lino with his heel.

'I'm due in court if anybody cares. Wouldn't she fucking hurry up,' he said, looking all around him, as if to garner support.

When Margo's name was called out, she did not hear at first.

'I ain't no Mrs Clifford. Is that you, missus?' the youth said, and Margo got up to follow the receptionist.

Samantha Kiely was standing beside the window, looking out over the River Liffey when Margo was shown in to the room.

'Margo, I didn't expect to see you so soon. Rest assured, we are on top of everything.'

She reached out giving a short hug to Margo, before leading her to the couch. 'How are you holding up?'

'Not too good.'

'Give yourself time to grieve. You know we are working towards probate here.'

Margo felt tears push against her eyelids as she slipped her hand in to her handbag, pulling out the letter. 'You need to read this and tell me how I make it go away.'

Samantha reached over and took the letter, slowly opening it. As she scanned it, Margo saw the solicitor's eyes narrow.

Samantha Kiely said nothing, until she had read the letter a second time. 'They wrote before this, Margo?'

'The day Conor died.'

'And you have done nothing about it?'

44

Margo did not answer at first. When she did, her eyes were defiant. 'I tore it up, maybe that's what I should have done with this one too. Elsa is all I have; nobody is going to snatch her away from me.'

Samantha Kiely stood up and walked around to the desk. Placing the letter in front of her, she got out a pen and began to underline parts. 'This is a very serious matter. We need to respond today.'

'We are not having DNA tests.'

'Let's not be hasty. Why don't I reply to the letter, inform them of your personal circumstances and we will regroup, say in two days' time, when I have had time to research the matter.'

Margo jumped up. 'Nobody is taking my child away from me.'

'Margo, it's too early to be even thinking along those lines, let's try to calm down and assess the situation.'

Margo went to the window. 'It's easy for you to say, but I'm on my own now, I can't fight these people.'

Outside a bus whizzed past a bus stop without stopping, making those waiting shout and wave with clenched fists. A youth threw a half-full can of Coke after the bus, the liquid drenching a pavement display outside a hardware shop.

Margo spun around. 'I am not going to lose Elsa as well as Conor. I won't let it happen.'

Samantha Kiely, stealing a glance at her watch, clicked her tongue – but Margo was not sure if she was annoyed at her or over something else.

'You're being too hasty, give me time on this, Margo. We will meet in two days. Meanwhile, I will get a letter off to France asking for more details.'

'I shouted at you, I'm sorry.'

'Totally understandable. I won't say not to worry, but Margo, I assure you, we will get through this.' She gripped Margo's shoulders hard, before leading her to the door. 'See you on Friday.'

Margo did not respond when the receptionist smiled at her, nor when the young man in the hoodie came too close as he pushed past her down the corridor to a consultation room.

Out on the street, she walked across Parliament Bridge, stopping halfway to sit on the concrete seats. She should not be going through this on her own, but how could she tell anyone? Maybe at a later stage; but for now she wanted to avoid the outrage of others. If she didn't think about it too much, it might resolve itself before it blew up further. But somehow she knew this was only the beginning. The sick feeling in her stomach was testament to that.

Wrapping her wool coat around her, she turned up the boardwalk, passing a homeless man huddled in a sleeping bag, a handwritten sign at his feet asking for money for a hostel. There were groups swigging beer from cans and pale-faced junkies shivering, even though the sun was shining. At O'Connell Street, she crossed over, walking down Talbot Street, a straight line to Connolly Station. At the Tea Time Express she stopped to buy a chocolate cake – Elsa's favourite – smiling when the assistant recognised her.

'All on your own today?'

'Yes.'

Loss tinged through her, but Margo smiled, knowing strangers never want to hear your troubles.

Sensing she may have unintentionally said something wrong, the woman behind the counter picked up an eclair. 'Doesn't your fellah love the chocolate eclairs; we made too many of them today. I will throw one in for himself.'

She saw Margo's eyes cloud over, so she did not say anything else, slipping the eclair into a paper bag and putting it on top of the cake box.

Margo carried the box and bag from the shop, continuing on

her way to the station. She crossed at the traffic lights and made to go in the station main entrance.

A man sitting on the ground, a piece of cardboard tucked in around him to keep out the concrete cold, rattled a takeaway cup and asked for a donation towards some food.

Margo slipped the bag containing the eclair to him. 'I thought you might like this.'

He opened the bag shyly. 'How did you know I have a sweet tooth?' he laughed, taking out the eclair and biting into it, letting the cream squelch onto his beard.

She didn't answer, but scurried to catch the DART home, so she could get to Rathmoney in time to pick up Elsa.

Elsa scampered to the car, smiling brightly. 'I have to pick daisies and make a daisy chain, can we do it together?'

'I suppose so, let's get home first,' Margo said, realising this was the first time she had heard Elsa happy since Conor died.

Max ran out to greet the car, tail wagging.

'I saw a really good patch of daisies at the side near the gate, can we walk back?' said Elsa.

Margo nodded and when she parked, Elsa bolted from the car, skipping along the avenue with the dog.

She followed at a slower pace, happy her daughter was so carefree again, but a slab of worry was permanently pressed on her heart, fearing these types of days were numbered.

At the gate Elsa had already picked a bunch of daisies, the stems long. 'I want the longest chain, pick some more,' she instructed her mother and they bent down scrabbling at the roots, nails scraping the ground to get the longest stalks. When they had picked two full bunches each, they strolled back to the house, Elsa and Max bounding ahead. If anyone saw them, they might remark on the happy scene, but for Margo this was a reminder of the way things used to be, and might never be again. In such a short time, things had changed utterly at Rathmoney House. Conor's dream of a guesthouse was still alive, but Conor was no more.

Margo drifted up the avenue past the grove of apple trees, the polytunnels where Conor had worked so hard, now empty, dirty and damp after months of neglect while Conor had battled cancer and lost; the path to the walled kitchen garden now overgrown, the wide flower beds weed-filled as she neared the house. The front door had been left slightly ajar because Ida was there, but the shutters were across the top windows still, the heavy drapes pulled together at the front bay window.

She remembered the first day they had viewed this house. On a four-day property viewing trip, when they had come across Rathmoney House and estate, they'd known it was going to be their new home. Conor had called it a magical place beside a river; the aspect beautiful. She'd loved the clematis, the pink flowers creeping across the front in spring; the large windows with their little rectangles of bevelled glass, the big wooden door with the huge jailer's key to open it, the sweep of the granite steps at the front. They'd known even before they stepped inside that this was going to be the place they called home, the reason they would not return to the States when their time in France came to an end.

Inside, the house was so cold they had stomped their feet as though they were on ice. The stairs creaked, the floors were dull with dust, the chandeliers yellowed with age, the shutters pulled across the windows, dowdy and dirty. Bits of furniture were still in some rooms, the attic full of possessions once stored away carefully, now forgotten.

The auctioneer had said they could clear the house for them, but they declined, happy to buy not just the building, but the history of Rathmoney House, too.

Conor immediately installed a heating system and had solar

panels hoisted onto the roof. He had a bridge built across the river at its widest point and put in a path along the river bank.

The injustice was that now, after twelve years, the house was exactly the way they had wanted it to be, but for Elsa and herself, it threatened to overpower them and make too many demands.

A new chapter was beginning for Rathmoney House. Silently, she vowed to stay in this place, no matter what – the home they had made with Conor. Only in this place could she fight the good fight, garner her strength to protect her daughter.

Margo was standing watching the evening light tint the roof tiles when she heard Elsa call out. The Labrador at her heels, Elsa came rushing back to her.

'Hurry up, Mummy, you have to help me with the daisy chain.'

Margo allowed Elsa to pull her along, Max barking excitedly at the two of them.

Before they reached the front steps, Elsa stopped. 'How are you going to make this into a guesthouse without Daddy?'

'Ida is going to help me.'

'Mum, just let Ida be the boss.'

'I think I will.'

Elsa ran up to the front door.

'Do you think Daddy would be happy about the guesthouse?'

'I hope so, he really wanted to invite people to visit Rath-money.'

'It would be nice if a few kids came, we could have some fun down by the river.'

Margo smiled, pushing back the front door.

Elsa ran to the kitchen. Gently placing the flowers on the table, she called her mother to come sit and help make the daisy chain.

Chapter Six

Bowling Green, Ohio.

Cassie did not tell anybody what was happening. If her father sensed something was amiss, he tried to ignore it at first. When he tentatively asked after Charles, she answered a bit too sharply that he was busy, business was booming. Her father, who as editor of the local newspaper once knew the business of every bigwig in town, looked at her oddly, but did not labour the point. Instead, he filled the void created by the unspoken with chat about his new neighbours.

'It brings back joyful memories, seeing kids playing in the back yard.'

'Did they introduce themselves? If Mom was here she would know every last thing about them.'

'They're busy, like everybody these days. I wouldn't know what to say.'

'"Welcome to the neighbourhood" might be a start.'

'I hear them opening and closing the car doors early in the morning. They live out their lives beside me, but we don't get to interact in any meaningful way. Their schedule is very different to mine, they don't exactly take time out to sit and look at the night sky.'

'Who does that anymore, Daddy?'

'Nobody around here, anyway.'

Vince Kading reached over and squeezed his daughter's hand. 'You can't hide things from me. I know by the set of your mouth. What's up, doll?'

Surprised after all these years that he should call her by that name, she desperately tried to find an answer.

'I'm a big boy, you can tell me all about it.'

'What do you mean?'

Vince gestured at his daughter to sit down beside him. 'My friend Mickey is very well up on the internet and what I think you call social media. He rang the other night, said look up City Car Sales on YouTube. I guess you know what I saw.'

'I didn't think you could do any of this stuff.'

'When you are on your own, you will do anything to fight the loneliness. You were stir crazy in that video, but I figure Charles must have done something to deserve it.'

'I don't really want to talk about it.'

'I'm on your side, no matter what.'

She picked at the edging on the floral couch.

'Are you getting a divorce?'

'Yes.'

Cas felt like a child again, sitting beside her father, fumbling with her fingers.

'How are you going to fight him?'

'I have an attorney.'

'I mean funding. I can help.' Vince stood up and walked to his bureau, where he unlocked a drawer and took out a white envelope. 'Three thousand dollars for you.'

'I can't take your money, Dad.'

'All that I ask is that you fight like hell for Tilly, and that no-good asshole does not win that battle.'

He placed the envelope on Cassie's lap.

She said nothing, looking out the window past the veranda and the flagpole where every holiday her father raised the flag.

'Cas, what's wrong?'

'I can't take your money, I can't keep that promise.'

'What do you mean?'

The words came out slowly, the sentences in tones so low, Vince had to lean in to catch every word.

When she had finished, he held his head in his hands for a moment, shaking it from side to side.

'Charles has landed us in a right mess.'

She picked up a picture from the side table: Tilly and her grandad on their first camping trip away. She desperately wanted a cigarette, but she knew Vince would not approve.

'How long have you known this, Cassie?'

'Since yesterday. Dale Winters is my attorney, I've told him I want another DNA test. Charles has agreed, but after that he says he is walking away.'

Vince clenched his fists tight. 'I always thought Charles Richards was a yellow-livered son of a bitch; now I have the proof. Wait until—'

'Daddy, let it go, we have to conserve energy, put everything into fighting for Tilly.'

'I will fund it all, I know your mother would want this.'

'I'm not sure money is going to win us this battle. What if they come to take her away to France?'

Vince pulled Cassie to him, gripping her tight.

'This is the United States of America. Nobody is going to take Tilly from us. She is my granddaughter, no test is going to change that.'

'I haven't explained it to her yet.'

'Best not, until we have an idea what's happening, not a word to anybody. We don't want the press getting a hold of this.'

'Dale says DNA doesn't lie.'

'Wait until we get the results of the second test.'

'They are putting a rush on it. I have to drop in on Dale; he has an email from the hospital in France. He won't tell me what it says until we're face to face.'

'I knew you should have come home to have the baby. Your mother was so worried. Turns out she was right.'

'There's no point thinking like that now; it was a really good modern hospital.'

'Not so good, if it allows a mix-up to happen.'

'We don't know for sure yet.'

'I know one thing: down the line somebody is going to have to pay for the awful upset this has caused.'

Cassie kissed her father on the cheek. 'I'll ring later, let you know what Dale said.'

'Give him the three thousand dollars, tell him to put everything into this fight; there is more where that came from.'

'Daddy, I don't know what I would do without you,' she said, patting her father's back, before letting herself out the side door.

Stopping for a moment to take in the flower display, she marvelled that her father tended to those flowers, even though every day her mother was alive, he'd complained they were a cursed nuisance.

Dale was in reception when she arrived. 'Come in, Cas, we have news.' He waited until they had stepped inside his office and closed the door before he spoke again. 'They are taking the matter very seriously, have ordered an inquiry and also asked all parents to attend for DNA tests. There were twenty children born over that weekend. All but two children were from that locality and may still be living there or traceable. Another couple were foreign like yourselves and are thought to have moved from the area soon afterwards. They are tracking these people down. They hope to have most DNA tests completed and results back within days, depending on the co-operation offered by the parents.'

'What am I supposed to do in the meantime? Twiddle my thumbs, try to figure out how I am going to tell my daughter that the last twelve years have been a sham?'

Dale shuffled the pages of the file in front of him.

'Cassie, they have to follow procedures; who knows where this is going to lead. You are not the only parents facing this conundrum and for all anyone knows, there are more. I know it's hard, but you need to be patient.'

'I want to run away, Dale. Charles is running away. Why can't Tilly and I?'

Dale tidied up the file, straightening the pages before closing it.

'Thinking this way is not going to help, Cas. This is all about doing the right thing. What would Tilly say if, in later life, she realised you didn't fight for her? I wouldn't like to be there for that conversation.'

'But she needn't find out.'

Dale did not reply.

Cassie threw her arms in the air. 'I won't give up Tilly for anybody. I won't have her sent across the world away from us, her family. Tell me you'll fight for her to stay here, where she is loved.'

'I'll do my best, you have my word.'

She reached into her jeans pocket and pulled out the envelope filled with dollars. 'Vince wants you to have this.' She plonked the envelope on the desk, and the dollars spilled out.

Dale picked up the phone and asked his secretary to come in to the room. When the young woman entered, he asked her to gather up the dollar bills, count them and make out a receipt.

The girl said nothing, but quietly did as she was asked.

When she left the room, Cassie spoke. 'I don't want to be called Mrs Richards anymore, Dale. Cassie Kading will do.'

'I don't blame you, Cas. I will never understand what possessed Charles to turn his back on his family, especially now.'

'I apologise if I was rude earlier.'

'Cas, no need. You're going to need all those qualities and more for the battle ahead. I will make contact as soon as the hospital updates me again. It should only be a few days.'

As she got up to leave, he called after her.

'Stay brave, Cassie.'

Feeling nauseous and her head spinning, she took the road south to the quarry. It was still too early for the bathers to have taken over the place, so she parked, getting out and walking to a quiet spot near the trees. Flinging a rock into the water, she watched it plop, the circles nudging across the surface, expanding wider and wider.

Charles was the rock, his selfish insane idea to resist or reduce child support payments had started all this. Now it was about to spiral out of control, gather others in its wash and could well cost her a daughter. It had already cost both herself and Tilly their extended family. Charles's relations would step in behind him. His sister Crystal had already made a point of insisting that Cassie not be the realtor sent to show her around any property. Crystal had always doted on Tilly, but had never warmed to Cassie. No doubt she would be Charles's willing assistant now as he broke up their family.

Cassie knew she was going to have to be strong, but she didn't know how. She did not even have a measure of the enemy and yet she was supposed to prepare for battle.

A man parked his jalopy of a station wagon, jumping out of the driver's seat, rushing past in his swimming trunks.

He waded out before shallow-diving, swimming strongly

across the water, forcing it to push aside in the face of his determination.

That was how strong she had to be now, except she had no idea what to do.

When her phone rang, she wasn't going to answer it until she saw Bonnie's name flash on the screen.

'Just checking in on you, girl. How are you today?'

'I'm at the quarry.'

'Cas, what are you doing there?'

Cassie sighed. 'I needed somewhere quiet to recharge for the legal fight ahead.'

'What are you talking about? Is it the test results? I thought that was a shoo-in.'

Cassie did not answer.

Bonnie spoke quietly in to the phone. 'You stay there, I'm on a break. I can be with you in ten.'

Cassie knew Bonnie would keep her word, so she sat on the sand under the shade of a tree. A few more bathers gathered, but she ignored them, slipping off her sandals, letting the sand run between her toes.

Charles never liked to come here with Tilly, complaining they could never take their eyes off her, because it was so deep.

Cassie loved it, particularly when the weather was not too hot and only the divers braved the water, disappearing into the depths, coming back with stories of what they saw down deep when visibility was good.

When she saw Bonnie kick off her high heels and run across the sandy shore, she laughed.

'It's not what you think, Bonnie.'

'This is a funny place to come to recharge.'

'It might as well be here as anywhere else.'

'Surely Charles has to pay maintenance now you have the DNA results?'

'Except, I don't have the results I expected.'

Bonnie dropped her handbag on the sand.

'What are you talking about?'

Cassie bowed her head. 'Not only have I lost my husband, but now there is a real possibility I could lose my daughter.'

'No.'

'The last twelve years count for zero.'

'Demand another test.'

'I have, but I'd better get ready to fight for Tilly.'

'Will it come to that?'

'I have no doubt, Bonnie. I need you with me on this.'

'What does Charles say?'

'He's taking a step back. I'm on my own.'

Bonnie dragged Cassie to her feet, smothering her in a hug. 'You are not alone. I'm with you all the way.'

Cassie pulled free. 'I've only told my dad. Tilly must suspect nothing, not until we know for sure what is happening.'

A group of bathers came, spreading out over a large area under the trees. One young man set up a boom box for his music.

'Let's get out of here,' Bonnie said.

'I have to pick up Tilly from the school bus.'

'Maybe we can meet tomorrow night?'

'I won't be able to get a sitter at such short notice.'

'In that case, I'll come over to yours around nine.'

'I'm not sure, Bonnie. I'm just so exhausted these days, I fall asleep so early.'

Bonnie shook her head.

'I'm not going to even hint at this dreadful situation, but we girls could have a glass of wine, maybe talk about every other woman we know. A gossip can often nicely distract from the deadly serious.'

Cassie smiled at her friend as she got in her car to drive across town and home.

She did her best to compose herself. Tilly was observant; she would pick up on any agitation in her mother and Cassie knew this. The night before, she had stolen into her daughter's bedroom as Tilly slept. Pulling over the stool from the dressing table, she sat close to her daughter's bed, watching her sleeping. Tilly slept deeply and twice Cassie blew gently on her face to see her twitch, just to make sure she was alive. Somewhere off in the distance, the night freight train had rumbled through on the way to Chicago. For a brief moment, she'd wondered if she should have escaped to the big city too, but a young child was not the right companion to take on a road trip.

When she saw Tilly bunch her hand under her chin, she'd smiled because she knew she did the same thing herself. Could she ever find a similarity that would beat a DNA test? Nothing could, but still she searched for something, anything she could throw at the science.

It was while she was debating in her head that Tilly woke up. Cassie had noticed that when she sat up, she looked very pale.

'Mom, you scared me, what are you doing?'

'I just sat down for a bit, I must have nodded off.'

'I'm fine, Mom, go to bed.'

'Are you feeling OK, sweetie?'

'Just very tired, Mom.'

Cassie thought they were so alike, both aching with tiredness after a stressful day. How she longed for an ordinary day in an ordinary life. Somehow, that seemed unattainable right now. Later, she had sat out on the porch and lit up her last cigarette, puffing wispy rings into the night air.

Chapter Seven

Rathmoney, County Wicklow.

Margo ran her finger along the bed, pressing the last crease from the eiderdown. 'Do you think they will ever know all the hassle we've been through to get the rooms looking so good, the dawn-to-midnight work over several days?'

Ida, who was checking under the bed, popped her head up. 'You will never hear from guests, only when they want to complain. I've never had the paying kind, but I have had people to stay. They are nothing but a ball of nuisance.' She hopped up triumphantly, a screw in her hand. 'There, nobody can say you don't clean under the beds.'

'Who in their right mind would get down on their hands and knees, looking under the beds?'

'You don't know your onions, my dear. Remember the reviewer from the national newspapers who commented on the presence of a lipstick stain on the underside of the bed in a certain establishment.'

'That's ridiculous.'

'She never did answer the speculation as to what she was up to, when she happened on the stain.'

Margo shivered and made a face.

Ida moved to the window next, spraying the panes and crumpling a sheet of newspaper. Streaking the paper across the glass, she stopped to wave when she saw Jack clearing the path beside the river. 'He's going to tidy up the flower beds. We won't give them any chance to find fault.'

Margo thought Ida should be the one running a guesthouse, she enjoyed it so much. When they got their first booking over the phone, she had danced a jig in the kitchen. She was so grateful to Ida, but she worried she was taking on too much.

'It will push us to our limit, but we can do it,' Ida said.

When they had gone to McCarthy's in Rathmoney, looking for furniture, Ida had taken over, striking a deal that Margo could only dream of.

Walking in the door, she had elbowed Margo in the ribs. 'Leave the talking to me.'

Sweet as syrup, she'd chatted to Dan McCarthy until she'd inveigled out of him that business was not so good and the recession had left his company on its last legs.

'You see that dark furniture over there? Lovely mahogany, but nobody wants the dark stuff anymore; they all want white flat pack from Ikea.'

'The days when people bought good furniture expecting it to last are long since gone,' Ida said.

Margo wandered about, looking at prices, until Ida called her over.

'You know Margo, she owns Rathmoney House.'

Dan McCarthy slicked his hair back and straightened his jumper. Extending his hand, he took Margo's gently. 'I didn't know your husband, but you have my sincere sympathy.'

Before she had time to thank him, Ida started to blather on. 'Margo here is in a bit of a bind; she needs to open the house for paying guests by Friday and to furnish two rooms.'

Dan McCarthy walked around the counter. 'What's your budget?'

Ida dithered as if trying to find the right words. 'That's the problem, Dan. Until everything is finalised in relation to Conor's death, Margo has cash-flow difficulties.'

Dan McCarthy, who was fiddling with a tag on a bunk bed, looked at Ida. 'It sounds to me, Ida, you may have a proposal for me.'

'I was hoping you could help Margo out. Maybe we could put in place a little plan to help you both.'

'I'm listening.'

'She needs two singles and one large double or king-size bed, bedside tables and wardrobes for two rooms. And if you had rugs to go with the cream walls, that would be super.'

'What sort of quality are you looking for?'

'It has to be good, stand up to a bit of wear and tear. What about that nice mahogany furniture? Couldn't we do a deal; you get rid of the stuff nobody wants and Margo gets good furniture, befitting luxury guest accommodation?'

'There is a hefty price tag on that lot.'

'Which nobody is paying.'

'You're a hard woman when you want to be, Ida Roper.'

'I'm not saying anything that isn't the truth.'

'I will need some form of payment.'

'Dan, putting it to you straight, could Margo here pay you off month by month at say two hundred euros? If business starts to boom, she can increase the payments.'

'You wouldn't be asking Ikea to accept those terms, Ida.'

'I won't be going to Ikea either, to re-do the sitting room and upgrade my suite for Christmas.'

Dan McCarthy smiled. 'You win, but I will need a decent deposit, there is thousands of euros' worth of furniture here.'

Ida reached into her handbag and took out a wad of cash. 'Will five hundred euros do?'

Margo made to pull Ida's arm to stop her, but she was slapped gently away. 'Later,' Ida said, her tone firm.

Dan beckoned them to follow him to the storeroom behind the shop. 'I have sleigh beds here, beautiful mahogany, king size and two big singles. Ex-display. I am willing to let them go at half price.'

'I knew we were right to be straight with you, Dan.'

'The mattresses are hotel quality, so you are getting a bargain,' he said to Margo, inviting her to try one out.

'You are very kind, Mr McCarthy,' Margo said.

'There might be something you can do for me. Our daughter is getting married soon. We have family coming over from the UK; maybe you could give a good rate, if we sent a few people your way?'

Ida clapped. 'Well, isn't that a lovely way to do business. Margo says yes.'

Margo was slightly annoyed at how much Ida had taken over, but in truth she knew that without her, she'd never have got this far. She'd still have been standing in the empty rooms at Rathmoney, not caring or knowing how to do anything without Conor by her side. She followed Dan back to the shop floor to pick out the wardrobes and lockers.

'I suppose I'm going to have to deliver later today as well,' he said, a smile on his face.

'Would you, Dan?'

'Of course I will. And I'll bring out a little contract for Mrs Clifford to sign. Best get it on some legal footing.'

Ida made to say something, but Margo piped up before her.

'I would like that very much, and please give me a date when I need to give you the first instalment.'

*

That evening after he closed the shop, Dan McCarthy pulled up outside Rathmoney House, his two sons with him in his white van. They hauled the furniture upstairs, stopping to catch their breath as they pushed and pulled the mattresses.

'This is good furniture, Mrs Clifford. If you are painting, throw over dust sheets, you don't want any paint speckles.'

When they had all the pieces in place, Dan returned to the van.

'I have two old rugs from the Far East. You don't have to buy them. We had these in the house for years, but the missus won't have them in the place anymore. Are you interested?'

Rectangular, they were a perfect size for the bedrooms.

'I can't imagine throwing out anything as good as this. Are you sure?'

Dan McCarthy instructed his sons to carry the rugs upstairs. 'It's a sad state of affairs when not even the wife of the furniture salesman wants the pieces he sells anymore. She spends her weekends traipsing around Ikea. The only room I've stopped her infecting with the flat-pack look is my own little study in the box room.'

Margo chuckled, but she detected a sadness in Dan McCarthy.

He got into his van, leaning his head out the window.

'Here's the contract. Pay me on the last Monday of every month. If the business goes under in the meantime, we can call it quits.'

She smiled at him, standing on the driveway to wave him off.

'You're daydreaming, missus.' Ida playfully elbowed Margo in the ribs, breaking in on her thoughts and bringing her back to the job at hand.

Margo did not answer, but ran a duster over the dark wood of the bedside locker before arranging a small tulle bag containing two Baileys chocolates to the side.

'You're worried,' Ida said gently.

'What do you mean?'

Ida leaned against the window sill. 'Jack has noticed it too. You're just not yourself, your heart isn't in it, Margo.'

Margo sighed. 'I have a lot on my mind, Ida.'

'Maybe I should not have pushed so hard.'

'It's not anything to do with this, Ida; this guesthouse thing is helping to keep me half sane and for that I am hugely grateful.'

Ida noticed Margo was close to breaking down, so she pretended to fuss, plumping up the cushions on the bed. Margo, glad of the diversion, shook her shoulders and busied herself rearranging the ornaments on the window sill.

'Ida, I will pay you back, you know that?'

'Course I do, silly.'

The first guests were due at two, but Ida had been at Rathmoney since nine o'clock, almost as soon as Elsa had left for camp.

'I thought I would bake the scones here. Nothing like the smell of home baking when you walk in the door. That's the sort of welcome we want to give our guests. Have you checked the rooms?'

'But we did it before you left last night.'

'Condensation, mice, anything could happen, so best give them the once over.'

Margo said she would do it once she was dressed.

'I hardly slept a wink last night with the excitement. This is such a big day for Rathmoney House.' Ida couldn't hide her enthusiasm.

Margo said nothing, but escaped to her bedroom, leaving Ida in charge.

Ida's last words as she left the kitchen were instructions to 'doll herself up', advice that Margo intended to ignore. She checked in on the guest suites, standing at one of the new bedroom windows looking out over the estate. From here you could see the length of the flower beds running parallel to the river, the wooden bridge Conor had specially designed, spanning the widest stretch of water. He loved that bridge, regularly walking Elsa across it when she was small. Once, as they stood in the centre, a heron had swooped under, flying gracefully down the river, in the hope of diverting attention away from its nest of chicks. The fact that such a large bird had negotiated the bridge made Conor proud: it had been accepted as part of the landscape.

He had intended reseeding the paddock at the other side of the bridge with a special mix of wild flowers, but somehow, in all the years, he had never got around to it. Now, the field would remain as it always had been, a summer paddock for the horses. Margo had enough on her plate, without worrying about a field.

In her heart, she knew when she met with her solicitor again, her worry would be compounded, her troubles quadrupled. The guesthouse would not matter if she stood to lose her one living link to Conor, the daughter she cherished more than anyone, more than anything and more than Rathmoney. The guesthouse was the realisation of Conor's dream and she was very grateful to Ida for that, but her stomach was in a knot of worry over what could happen over the next weeks and months which could change all their lives forever.

She was still standing at the window when she heard a commotion from downstairs: Ida giving instructions in a loud voice to her husband. Shortly after, she saw Jack approach the flower beds with a knife in his hand and randomly choose a selection of bronze and green fennel. He did not see her watching him, squatting low to get the tallest stalks. When he went back into the house, she heard Ida's voice again and somebody tramping up the stairs.

When Margo opened the bedroom door, Jack was standing with two glass vases of flowers hiding his face.

'I didn't know I owned such a thing as a vase,' she said, admiring the grand bouquet of flowers in each, the fennel circling pink and white roses. 'Those roses are not from the garden either.'

Jack shrugged his shoulders. 'You know Ida and her fancy ideas, she had me nip down to Aldi and buy two bouquets, she wasn't happy with the quality of your own and who would cop the supermarket roses, if we bunched the fennel from the far beds around them. She might be right.'

He stood, a vase in either hand, waiting for instructions.

'Maybe put a vase on the little table in the corner in each room.'

Jack placed one of the vases gently on the table. 'You'll have to excuse my wife, she is living her dream here at Rathmoney. I hope you can put up with her.'

'I couldn't have got this far without her.'

'She can be a huge pain in the arse, but she just wants the best for you. I always resisted the idea of a guesthouse at our place. I'm only beginning to realise I have totally denied Ida all these years; for her it's not work at all, but a pleasure.'

'She's a natural.'

'And finally all those tips she picked up in those TV programmes can be put to the test.'

He guffawed out loud and she found herself laughing too, for the first time in a long time. The laughter rippled through her, but afterwards, she somehow felt hollow. Guilt traced across her heart, chasing away the warm feeling still lingering from that moment of companionship.

Chapter Eight

Bowling Green, Ohio.

'Are you sure you're OK, Cassie? If you want another few days, you only have to ask.'

Cassie looked at her boss.

'I'm good, Zack.'

'You look far from good, Cassie.'

'I'm just tired, I haven't been sleeping well.'

'Word is your visit has cost City Car Sales thousands of dollars in repairing the damage to property and vehicles.'

Zack Slocum, a rotund man who liked to wear a striped shirt with braces and a bow tie, ran a tight ship at Zack's Realty.

He demanded his realtors be on time for appointments and display a level of courtesy which put his business at the top of every popularity poll in the town.

'I need to return to work, things are difficult right now.'

'No kidding. I'm an understanding employer, Cassie, but I haven't had any reassurance from you that there won't be any repeat episodes.'

'I didn't know anybody was going to upload it, I sure as hell didn't know it was going to make me an internet star, Zack.'

He sighed, leaning back in his chair.

'Cassie, I'm a simple man; I like things to run like clockwork and when they don't, I see red. If there's a repeat of that type of behaviour and your personal life starts to interfere with the business we do here, then I'll be left with no choice…'

'Zack, it won't happen again.'

'Mrs Slocum drew it to my attention, Cassie. How can we have somebody who can become unhinged looking after clients and their property?'

'It's not going to affect my job, Zack.'

'For both our sakes, I hope it doesn't, Cassie.'

He clapped his hands, signalling the end of their meeting.

As she sat down at her desk, she was overwhelmed by a desire to kick it over, tell Zack go to hell, but she knew right now this job was precious to her.

Zack called out an address and told her to go call on Mrs Barton.

'She has a beautiful old place over on East Court. It'll sell for big bucks, but the old lady is fussy. Every realtor in town has tried to get that house on the books; you just make sure you bag it exclusively for Zack's Realty.'

Glad to get out from under Zack's gaze, Cassie drove to East Court Street.

Rebecca Barton was sitting out on her veranda.

'Good morning, Mrs Barton.'

The old lady smiled, waiting for Cassie to climb the steps. 'Come sit, dear.'

Her eyes were kind, but Cassie felt them challenge her as if this was some sort of test. Her usual routine of pulling out the clipboard and starting to ask questions could mean getting nowhere with Mrs Barton.

'I have some chilled lemonade here, would you care for a glass?'

'Yes, thank you, ma'am.'

'You are Vince Kading's girl, aren't you?'

'You know my father?'

'In a previous life, when my Ed had a general store in town, he used to advertise in the newspaper and Vince used to call to the house, while they sorted out the seasonal advertising. Your father liked to have a hot chocolate in the sitting room in winter and a cool lemonade on the veranda in the summer. How is your daddy keeping?'

'Well, thank you. My mom passed away two years ago, but he is doing OK.'

'When Ed died, Vince brought the nicest bouquet of flowers from his own garden.'

Cassie relaxed in to the wicker chair and sipped her mint lemonade.

'You have a fine old house, Mrs Barton.'

'Please call me Becca.'

Rebecca Barton got up to stand leaning against the veranda balustrade.

'What should I call you?'

'I am Cassandra, but everybody calls me Cassie.'

'Cassie, I don't want to leave here. This house has been in my family since it was first built in 1900. The memories keep me company these days, but my son – who lives in New York – doesn't understand.'

She swung around when Cassie remained quiet. 'Already I like you; the realtors who were here before made excuses for that silly son of mine, but you have not jumped to his defence. Why?'

'It's not my place. I think you should be able to decide for yourself what you want to do with your own home.'

'Why, thank you, Cassie.'

She sat down in the wicker chair opposite.

'You're wondering how you are going to persuade me to sell

up, so you can get back to Zack and say you have this pretty house on the books?'

'Ma'am, you should only put your house up for sale if you want to. It's a big step to take, you should only do it if you have clear plans for what comes next.'

'My son wants me to come and live with his family. He lives in the Upper East Side in Manhattan in a beautiful penthouse apartment.'

'You are very lucky.'

'Yes, he is a wonderful son, but what Todd doesn't realise is I like my life here. What would I do all day, stuck up in the New York sky with nobody to talk to? That boy could never understand the benefits of sitting out, just talking to folks.'

'I'm sure he would if you explain it to him. He was brought up here, wasn't he?'

'He was, but unfortunately his wife wasn't.'

'Becca, my own life is a mess, I don't know if you should listen to me, but follow your gut. If your gut is telling you to stay put, maybe that's what you should do.'

'You are going to get into trouble, if you don't go back with my house on your account.'

Cassie smiled. 'I'm in trouble with Zack already, another bit won't matter.'

Becca Barton laughed out loud. 'You really are a sweet one. You tell your dad to stop by, we can chat about the old times.'

Cassie was halfway down the steps when Becca called her back.

'Maybe we could do something that will suit us both, if you are willing to hear me out.'

'As long as it's legal, I suppose so.'

'Come back and sit yourself down.'

Becca waited until Cassie was comfortable. 'I know what is happening. I had a young realtor here last week, who went to so much bother to try and persuade me to put the house on the market. I sent him off with a flea in his ear. Todd went crazy, he rang Zack's Realty yesterday. Sounds to me like good old Zack Slocum gave you the toughest job in town to see if you could bring home the bacon. Zack always was a stinker like that. Well, why don't we get both these men off our backs?'

'I'm not sure we can do that.'

'You can take on the marketing of my house, Todd and that wife of his will back off if I put it on the market, and we will make old Zack fall at the first hurdle of making your life a misery.'

Cassie moved to the edge of her chair and placed her hand gently on Becca's lap. 'But, Mrs Barton, aren't you forgetting you don't want to sell up?'

'Now, now, Cassie, I expect more from you. I expect you to understand, I never want to leave here and when I do, it will be in a box.'

'So why put it on the market?'

'Because I like you and it means Zack, who I hear is quite exercised by your behaviour at City Car Sales, won't be able to fire you.'

'You don't have to help me like this, Becca. And by the way, has everybody seen that clip?'

'Most of us applaud you for it, but there are always men like Zack, who take it personally when a woman speaks their mind. You go back with my house on your books, his hands are tied.'

'I don't understand.'

'When you leave here, I intend to ring Zack to tell him I will leave the property with his company, as long as you are my realtor. He is not to even think of sending anybody else out here. Zack wants the house on his books; he knows I have run every other realtor in town off the property. He wants to brag that he got the old lady to sell up.'

'Why are you doing this for me?'

'I am doing it for Becca Barton. I will have the pleasure of your company and as a bonus, Todd and his annoying wife, Melanie, will be off my back. More lemonade?'

Cassie held out her glass, so Becca could fill it from the jug.

'Don't you think Zack will get a bit suspicious when you won't accept any offer? With a property this grand, there will be a lot of interest. This is such a fine historic house and near the elementary and high schools, a prime location.'

'You are beginning to sound like an eager realtor.'

'That's my job.'

'This plan of mine will give us both a bit of breathing space. Maybe it will give you time to close off your divorce; I hope to heavens you are divorcing the cad.'

Cassie didn't say anything.

'Go for a complete change and please look for a job where your contribution is cherished.'

'I suppose you wouldn't like to make a suggestion on that front too?' Cassie laughed and Becca wagged her finger in mock admonishment.

'Darling, when Billie Jean King beat Bobbie Riggs, she showed us women can do anything. You can do it, Cassie, you just have to decide what "it" is. I'm sure we will become friends along the way.'

'I think we might be already. Now, show me around your lovely home and let me take the measurements. I will drop around tomorrow to take the photographs.'

'Good, I look forward to seeing more of you.'

Becca led the way into a spacious hallway, a wooden staircase leading up to the top floor.

'This house is too big for me. I live in the front sitting room, the kitchen and the front bedroom upstairs. The rest of the rooms I air out every day, they are in good condition. Let me show you my kitchen. Years ago, Ed built in a little desk, so I could sit doing the household accounts, while looking out on my garden. I don't have much totting up to do these days, but I still like to sit there.'

She led Cassie into a bright kitchen with cupboards painted white.

'It's not going to be the fancy of many people these days, but I still love it. This was a great house to bring up my little family in…'

Her voice trailed off and Cassie noticed a shadow creep across her face.

'We had a tragedy; I lost my daughter when she was only eleven. A car accident. She fell off her bicycle on Wooster. The driver was too close and couldn't swerve.'

'I'm very sorry for your loss.'

'I know. Todd was younger, only five at the time; he doesn't understand I can never leave the house where Amelie grew up.'

'Maybe we should look at the front rooms,' Cassie said gently and they walked together to the sitting room.

'This is where I like to be, surrounded by pictures of my family. No view of the Manhattan skyline is going to be better than that.'

Cassie used her machine to take the measurements, walking into the dining room next. 'I can go upstairs and then down to the basement on my own if you like.'

'You do that. And I will make some coffee.'

When Cassie had finished, she came back into the kitchen. The table was laid out with china cups and saucers, a plate of biscuits set to one side.

'You went to a lot of bother, Becca.'

'It's nice to have somebody visit,' she said, pouring the coffee from her white pot. She let Cassie take a sip before she asked her next question.

'So: Charles Richards, are you definitely divorcing him?'

'Yes, I am.'

'You are best rid of him. Even a little old lady like myself knows he and his drinking are bad news. He is a stupid man, you deserve a lot better.' Becca bit her lip, lest she say anything else.

'I really should be getting back or Zack will come looking for me.'

'Tell the old goat I will ring him this afternoon.' Becca caught Cassie by the arm. 'Don't you worry, I won't let the cat out of the bag if you don't. It will be interesting to see what people are going to offer for an old place like this.'

'Won't Todd be disappointed when you don't accept any offer?'

'So what if he is? I am the rightful owner of this property and it is within my grant to accept or decline any offer. There is not a damn thing my son can do about it, either.'

Cassie giggled.

'I hope when I am your age, Becca, I have as much energy and pizazz.'

'Pizazz, I like that word.'

She stood on the veranda, watching until Cassie had disappeared out of sight.

Once Cassie had left Becca's street, she rolled down the car windows and lit up a cigarette. Charles's drinking must be worse if Becca had mentioned it. When she pulled into the office parking lot, she quickly stubbed out her cigarette, pushing the butt deep into the bin, and sprayed perfume around the car as Zack ran out to to greet her, a wide grin on his face.

'You did well, girl, the old hag has been on to confirm she wants us to handle the sale. She likes you.'

He rubbed his hands together in anticipation of the commission.

'I don't know how you persuaded the old bag. I even had a bet on with Cal; he insisted you would never do it. Honey, I am off to collect my winnings. I won't be back,' he shouted.

Cassie went in and sat at her desk. She realised she had not considered what was happening in France nor felt a raging fear over Tilly. At least focusing on Becca Barton's problems had given her a break from her own.

Chapter Nine

Rathmoney, County Wicklow.

Margo had allowed Elsa to go on a sleepover so she could have time to prepare for her meeting with her solicitor, but what did she do? She sat in Conor's study with a bottle of whiskey until the morning light started to spill across the sky and the birds began to shuffle and sing. She did not even bother to shower, but threw on her orange wool coat over her jeans and blouse and got the first train to Dublin.

A woman who had also got on at Rathmoney shook her awake at Connolly station. 'I usually mind my own business, but just in case you intend getting out in the city, otherwise you are headed Northside.'

Margo jumped up, thanked the woman, and wiping the spit dribbling from the side of her mouth, stepped out of the carriage onto the platform.

Pulling her coat around her, she moved with the crowd, not sure what she was going to do until her 10 a.m. appointment with the solicitor. She dithered outside the coffee shop across the street from the station. It had been Conor's favourite. She ordered a hot chocolate, waiting at the counter until it was ready. Sitting down, she wrapped her hands around the cup, the warmth seeping up her arm. Conor had liked the takeaway coffee here, too; any time he'd come to Dublin he insisted on getting off at Connolly so he could order a caramel latte.

Did they know him? Did they know he was dead? What would they say if she told them? Same as everyone, she supposed: be embarrassed, mumble words of sympathy before moving away.

It was the hardest part; life for everybody else went on yet hers was stalled, the life pushed out of her, as sure as it was stolen from Conor.

Dipping her head into the high collar of the coat, she wondered would anybody notice if she fell asleep. She was snoozing when a woman knocked against her shoulder, jolting her awake.

Still too early to go to the solicitor's office, she sat in the café window sipping her hot chocolate. Commuters just off the train were beetling along, their heads down, deadlines to meet. Her husband was dead, but his dream of a guesthouse had not only become a reality, it was a success in its first week. She felt like shouting out loud for all to hear that with the help of her very good friend Ida, she was coping and together they were putting Rathmoney on the map.

A father and his toddler daughter ambling along the street caught her eye. Conor had loved to take Elsa for walks around the grounds of Rathmoney House. Often, they had sauntered down by the river, lingering on the bridge to toss stones into the water. Sometimes he held her up to pluck the large leaves of the sycamore tree, so they could drop them over one side of the bridge and watch as they bobbed along the top of the water, father and daughter in competition against each other, shouting, wishing their leaves to be whipped faster by the current.

As Elsa grew taller and began to play outside alone, Conor had fenced off the river with simple chicken wire. There was little of it left now; the last bad storm had torn it from the posts and she didn't think they had bothered to tidy it up, so the grass and ferns grew up through the wire mesh covering the river bank.

She watched as the little girl ran ahead of her father on the street, making him quicken his pace and grab her hand. She waited until they had crossed the road and were out of sight before she left the café.

Wandering towards O'Connell Street, she stepped over the cardboard cartons scattered outside a group of shops. Heading on down to the quays, she pushed her head deep into her collar again to ward off the biting cold wind whipping in over the River Liffey.

At Kiely Kileen Solicitors, the receptionist was setting up her desk for the day. 'Mrs Clifford, Miss Kiely is not in yet. I'll show you to her office; she won't be long.'

It was a small, tidy office; the mocha colour on the walls – no doubt picked to hide the dirt – now flaked away in a wave of rising damp under the window ledge. The window looked out over the double-decker buses on the quays and the river loaded with brown cold water, the wind making it spew up a yellow-white foam. A woman called out in the corridor. Margo, tramping across the room with heavy, deliberate steps, fidgeted with the toggle of her coat. How she wanted to wake up Conor and tell him they were in trouble and he had to help.

She had sat with him for thirty minutes after he died, cupping his hands linked across his chest. There was nothing left of him, the man she knew, the soft hazel eyes, the smile that dipped in one corner; even his thickness of hair had been decimated by the chemicals of chemotherapy. That he was gone was devastating enough, but that she was left with a tsunami of trouble ahead was unbearable.

When she heard a rush in the corridor outside the room, she

knew it was the solicitor, so she sat down again in front of the desk.

Samantha Kiely swept in, her rain-speckled coat spreading out in a fan behind her, her glasses fogged up. 'Margo, I hope I'm not late.'

'Some would say I have all the time in the world.'

Samantha ignored the barbed tone of her client's comment as she took out a handkerchief and cleaned her glasses, before lifting her desk phone and asking for the Clifford file.

'Can you tell me what is happening?'

The solicitor cleared her throat to answer, but stopped when there was a knock at the door and a girl placed a file on the desk.

Samantha waited until the door was fully closed. 'Margo, I have heard back from France and also from the United States.'

'I'm not sure I want to hear this.'

The solicitor tapped the desk firmly with her pen. 'Margo, please.' She did not wait for a response but opened the file and took out two letters. 'We wrote to the attorney of the parents of one Tilly Richards, resident in Ohio in the States. DNA tests there – as a result of a dispute over maintenance – have shown that neither of the presumed parents, Charles or Cassandra Richards, can be the true biological parents of the child. The girl was born in the same hospital in the south of France where Elsa was born. All babies born there that weekend have been DNA tested.'

'So it's a wide net. I have nothing to worry about.'

The solicitor shook her head. 'I wish it were that simple. The results are in on the eighteen other babies. They are all genetically connected to their parents. That leaves the couple in Ohio and yourselves.'

Genetically connected. There was such a musical ring to those words and yet she couldn't sway to the notes, she was excluded,

Elsa was excluded. A simple test result and they were as good as telling her that she and her precious daughter did not deserve to be connected. Where were they when Elsa had cried every tooth through into the early hours; when she'd been called nasty names and bullied because Margo had cut her hair too short; when she was so consumed with worry about her father's diagnosis she wet the bed twice every night, or when in grief at the death of her father, she could barely talk for three days?

'Margo ... Margo can you hear me?' The solicitor got up from her desk and came around to her. 'Are you all right?'

She wanted to answer, but the words would not come out. She thought she was shouting 'No' over and over, but she knew by the solicitor's anxious face she was not making any sense. She only realised she was bent over, curled up with rage and grief, when she let Samantha help her sit back properly. She heard herself say thank you as the solicitor returned to her side of the desk.

'Margo, can you continue on or do you need a break?'

'Let's get this done. Delaying it won't make it any easier.'

'You will have to have a DNA test. There is no other way.'

'Every other couple has the right child?'

'Yes, except the couple in Ohio.'

'So the answer is clear already. By law, Elsa and this Tilly are with the wrong parents.' Margo shook her head. 'But what about love? What about all the years, our history, our future? What have I done to these people that they want to ruin our lives?'

'You haven't done anything, but now that the issue has arisen, they are obliged to see it through to the end.'

Margo pushed against a tower of files at the side of the desk. 'Oh God, no, they are going to take Elsa from me, aren't they?'

The solicitor told Margo to sit back down. 'I realise it is a lot to take in, but the priority now is a DNA test.'

'Can they force me?'

'Surely you want to know yourself?'

'I don't know.'

'I think what they are trying to do is find out if this girl in Ohio is your child and if Elsa is theirs. We will deal with whatever comes after that. Everybody is sympathetic to your personal situation. The most important thing now is the test. Mediation could follow. There have been cases where very young children have been swapped back and cases where the status quo remains, but it is too early for us to go down that road.'

Margo leaned forward. 'We need it to happen. It is the only suggestion I will consider. I don't need a DNA test. I just want everything to stay the same.'

'With respect Margo, I don't think you should be so hasty.'

Margo bolted for the door.

Samantha Kiely ran ahead of her and gripped the door handle. 'Stop, Margo, we have to discuss this; you don't want a situation where they go to court and force you to have the DNA test.'

Tears streaming down her face, Margo returned to her seat. The solicitor picked up the phone and ordered a pot of tea.

'We have a little time. I have told them you are grieving the loss of your husband. I have asked and they have given us one week.'

'What makes you think I will allow this?'

'I'm not sure we have any choice, Margo. Elsa has a right to know. The other couple have a right to know. And remember, if she is their daughter then you possibly have a daughter you have never met.'

Pulling her coat tight around her, Margo looked at the solicitor. 'Tell me how come my little girl is so like her father she even says some things just like he did; mispronounces her words all the time.'

'I can't answer any of that, Margo, but I know the first step is the DNA test.'

'You think we got the wrong babies?'

Margo got up again, moving to the window. The River Liffey was spitting foam still, but she wanted it to be raging, mirroring what she felt inside. With her finger, she traced a stick figure through the condensation on the window pane, drawing a sad face, before she quickly blotted it out with her sleeve.

'So let me get this straight. You are saying I can delay it, fight it, but eventually we will have to take this test and confront the result it throws at us.'

Samantha Kiely straightened up at her desk. 'That's exactly what I'm saying. Margo, on a moral level we can't fight this. What happens after we know the result is a different thing altogether.'

'What about Conor; wouldn't they normally need a sample from him?' Margo swallowed hard, steeling herself for the answer.

'I'll have to consult with an expert in this area, I don't know what is required.'

Leaning forward, Margo thought she was going to pass out but managed to fight it off. There was a knock at the door and a girl handed in a tray of tea. The solicitor busied herself pouring out two mugs.

'My mother always swore on the powers of a hot, sweet tea.'

Margo felt the mug being pushed into her hands.

'I know it's a lot to take in, Margo.'

'These people in America. What are they like?'

'The mother, Cassandra Richards, is on her own and in as bad a place as you, I understand. Her husband wants nothing to do with this battle. He walked out on their marriage a while ago.'

'So why can't we leave it as it is? We both love our daughters. Can't we both back off?'

The solicitor looked out over her glasses at Margo. 'I think it's a case of the can of worms has been cracked open and we all have to deal with it.'

'I will take your advice, but I honestly don't know what I will tell Elsa.'

'Let's take it one step at a time.'

'This other mother, is she a good person?'

'I only know what her attorney said; I talked to him on the phone yesterday evening. She is beside herself, loves her daughter deeply. She never wanted to be in this situation either.'

Margo banged down her mug of tea so fiercely, some slopped out. 'Why is she persisting then? Why can't she leave me alone; leave us to grieve in peace?'

'You know it's not as simple as that. There is only one way now, and that's forward, wherever it takes us.'

Easy for anyone else to say. There was only one outcome possible and what would they do then? Did they expect her to turn her back on the only daughter she knew? What sort of mother did they think she was? Every part of her wanted to scream, to tell them to go to hell. She wanted to rush home, grab her daughter and run. But where would she go? Where was Conor when she needed help so badly? Tired and feeling defeated, she swallowed hard and looked her solicitor straight in the eye.

'When do I have to have this test?'

'I will arrange it. Elsa will have to be tested as well.'

'What should I say to her?'

'For now, just say it's a simple procedure you both have to endure: explanations can follow later.'

When Margo thought back to the meeting, she could not remember saying goodbye to Samantha, only the walk down Dame Street, the buses whizzing past her, school kids messing at the bus stops. At Trinity College she crossed over and strolled in the gate, hoping to find some peace and quiet as she took the shortcut to Pearse Station.

A woman with a buggy cursed loudly as she negotiated it across the cobbled courtyard; a photographer tried to cajole a group standing on the chapel steps to stay still for a group shot. Rushing along, she wanted to dance around the grassed area to draw attention to herself, to tell them she did not care, nothing mattered but Elsa. Was Elsa Clifford supposed to be Tilly Richards? The very thought made her stop, empty retching taking her over, so that a man asked if she was all right.

She smiled at him to reassure him, so that he would go away. When her stomach settled, she scurried along to the little gate in the wall across from the station. She ran for the DART, sinking into the seat and closing her eyes, the sway of the train strangely comforting. There was a very small glimmer of hope that things may remain the same and she needed to hang on to that now.

Chapter Ten

Bowling Green, Ohio.

Cassie was at her desk early, but Zack still managed to be in before her.

'What's going on with the old lady's place in East Court?'

'We have plenty of interest, two more showings this morning.'

'But she's turned down a good offer?'

'Mrs Barton is pretty fussy.'

'Todd wants a quick sale. He says they need her in New York, his wife is due their second baby any day. This problem in Ohio needs to be tidied away. The old lady is being awkward; you have to get beyond that.'

'I'll visit her today.'

'You see that you do.'

Cassie's phone rang.

'Can you talk, Cas? The DNA results are back. Also, I have word back from France.'

She went cold. She stepped out into the yard. 'Go ahead, Dale.'

'The second DNA result confirms the first result.'

She did not answer. Inside the building, she could hear Zack spouting on, the new assistant lapping up every word. A cat ran across the top of the back wall, its tail up. Cassie paced up and down the yard as Dale continued to brief her.

'The hospital lawyers have come back to me with the results of the inquiry so far. They say eighteen children and their parents were tested and all came back as genetic matches to each other. However there is one baby who was born within an hour of Tilly, also a girl. This couple were foreigners, too, the father worked for a multinational in the Paris office as far as they know. They were in the village for the weekend when the mother went into labour. It's a waiting game, until they test these people.'

'How do they know so much?'

'Bizarre, but the local gazette ran a story because the woman was in the local chateau when she went in to labour, but there was no ambulance to attend her for two hours because of a major incident in the nearest town. Turns out the chateau owner, an elderly man, delivered the baby.'

'Nice story, if only we knew what happened next.'

'They live in Ireland now. There is just a mother and the daughter, I have managed to talk to the attorney on the case. The father passed away recently. I gather the mother is as shocked as you are.'

Cassie felt her stomach tighten.

When she did not answer, Dale filled the silence with words.

'Cas, this is new for all of us. I can email France now, say we want this matter resolved at the earliest opportunity.'

'I just want to keep Tilly. I want things to stay the way they are.'

'That can't happen, you know that. The hospital knows it has to get to the bottom of this. One way or another, it is going to face a hell of a lawsuit. I am working on the papers already.'

'All the money in the world is not going to be much good to me, if I lose Tilly.'

She looked up to see Zack standing in the doorway, clearing his throat and pointing at his watch. She made her excuses to Dale and rushed off the phone.

'You must take personal calls in your own time. How many times do I have to say it?' he snapped, before turning back to his office.

Becca Barton was in a quiet mood when Cassie arrived.

Sitting on her wicker chair, she picked idly at the arm, flaking off tiny bits of paint.

'I'm getting tired of people traipsing through my home, Cassie. I never knew it would be so exhausting.'

'I could secure the appointments for a time you are out.'

'Somehow, I think that would be worse, more of an intrusion on my privacy. Are you OK? You look very pale.'

'Just feeling a little nauseous.'

'Has something happened?'

'I heard from my attorney before I came out.'

'You take that Charles Richards for all he has, it's not as if that family can't afford it.'

'Zack has ants in his pants about this house,' Cassie said, in a feeble attempt to divert the conversation.

'I suppose he told you Todd wants me to accept the latest offer. You know he only wants me as a babysitter. They haven't even asked me what I think of the idea.'

'Don't you want to do that?'

'Here in Bowling Green, where I could continue my life, it would be my absolute privilege to help take care of my grandchildren. Locked away in a tower in Manhattan, with Cruella De Vil watching every move I make, torture.'

When a car pulled up outside the house, Becca made to scurry off. 'I will be in the garden, stay for a coffee when you get rid of them.'

Cassie showed around two couples with young children. Before they went out into the back garden, one of the women pulled her aside.

'The old lady, can you give any advice on how to handle her? What should I say?'

'I don't know Mrs Barton very well,' Cassie fudged.

The woman, annoyed, pushed past Cassie and the other viewers chatting at the sink and marched across the small patch of grass where Becca was bent over, examining her raspberry canes.

'Mrs Barton, you have a lovely home here. My husband and I are happy to offer several thousand dollars above the asking price. Would that be acceptable to you?'

'I think you need to talk to the realtor, dear.'

'I know you are reluctant and have refused previous generous offers. We are looking for a forever home for our family, so name your price.'

'I don't know anything about house prices, talk to the realtor please,' Becca repeated.

'We thought if we appealed to you directly...'

'It's not just me; you see, Marvin and Mel have to be happy too, before I can accept.'

'Are they family, may I talk to them?' The woman's determination was undimmed.

'I'm not sure they will talk to you, dear, sometimes they won't even talk to me.'

'Where can I locate them?'

'They like to be in the front sitting room mainly, but sometimes they are cheeky and hang around the bedroom. Last week they were so upset after a viewing, they threw pots and pans all over the kitchen.'

'Pardon me, I don't understand.'

'Ghosts, dearie; they have their moments, but they are great company.'

The other couple viewing the garden stopped and stared at Becca. 'You mean the house is haunted?'

'Such a loaded word, don't you think? Marvin and Mel, those are my names for them, they are a friendly presence, which at my age is really rather sweet. I am never completely on my own.'

The couple moved away, hastily saying their goodbyes to Cassie.

The woman who started the conversation also rushed across the yard.

'You never told us this place was haunted; it really has been a total waste of a viewing,' she said, pushing past to the front door.

Becca was standing in the middle of the grass, laughing.

Cassie shook her head. 'Zack is going to be fuming about this.'

'Who cares? That dreadful pushy woman wouldn't have been right for this house anyway. Come sit, have coffee. Tell Zack you had to calm me down, persuade me to keep the house on the market.'

She walked ahead to open the windows in the sitting room, pressing the coffee machine on as she passed through the kitchen on her way.

'Open the windows in the kitchen as you come through, will you? I want to drive the memory of those awful people away.'

'I swear when you are gone, you will come back and haunt any new owners,' Cassie laughed.

'What a good idea,' Becca said as she poured the coffee into the white coffee pot.

'Now we have a bit of time on our own, I hope you are going to tell me what is really eating you.'

Cassie reached into the refrigerator for the milk. 'I can't talk about it.'

'I won't blab, if that's what's worrying you.'

'If I could tell you, I would, but for the moment, I need to keep it to myself.'

'It's not for me to tell you how to do things, but I'm here if you need me. Let's sit on the veranda.'

Cassie followed her out and they sat quietly sipping their coffee. A teenage boy approached and asked if he could mow the grass. Becca said he could in a few days, provided he was neat and tidy.

'This time make sure the box is on correctly at the back; I am selling this house, so everything has to look tip top.' She turned to Cassie. 'Todd is coming down at the weekend. He says he is flying in specially to try and talk sense into me.'

'What will you do?'

'I'm going to bake his favourite pie and ignore everything he says. He always was like a dog with a bone when he got an idea in to his head. I'm sure it serves him very well in New York, but here, it's tiresome.'

'Zack is beginning to get annoyed at the rejection of so many good offers, too. He says he doesn't know why you put it on the market, if you weren't going to complete the sale.'

'I'm sure Mel and Marvin will cut down the interest; word will spread.'

'Except, Becca, if you ever do want to sell it, you might be stuck with a haunted house on your hands.'

'That will be Todd's problem, not mine.' She looked directly at the woman she had come to see as her friend. 'But enough about me. You have a lot on your mind.'

'Does it show so much?'

'There's a well of worry in your eyes. I hope you have somebody helping you fight Charles Richards.'

Cassie shook her head. 'He's the least of my worries right now.'

'You know the saying: a problem shared is a problem halved,' Becca said, gently touching Cassie's arm.

'Thanks, Becca, but I wouldn't know where to start.' Jumping up, she made to gather up the coffee cups.

'You leave that, I have all day.'

'I don't have any more appointments here scheduled this weekend, so I hope to see you next week.'

'Todd will have been here and gone, I don't know what mood I will be in.'

'He might want to talk about taking the house off the market.'

'I don't think so, Todd is a stubborn man; but I'd say we are good to carry on our plan for a while longer.'

As she expected, Zack was waiting for Cassie when she got back to the office.

'Todd Barton has been on; that man is not happy.'

'We just haven't found the right buyer yet.'

'No kidding, how many people with deep pockets have walked through that house?'

He was about to shout further, when his assistant told him there was an urgent call.

Cassie sat at her desk, sifting through her messages, hoping to find an appointment which would get her out of the office for the rest of the afternoon.

When Zack shouted her name, the glass partition shook, making a creaking noise.

'Get in here, Cassie,' he shouted one more time.

Straightening her clothes, she walked into the small office.

'I have come off the phone to Dan Thawley. Apparently his daughter was mad keen to buy the Barton home, but she says it's haunted.'

'Mrs Barton said it today, I'm not sure it's entirely true.'

'If word gets around, and it will, we'll never sell it. Why did the old lady say such a thing?'

'I don't know.'

'I'm going to have to talk to her son, get him to sit that woman down and tell her to shut her mouth. She's going to have to stay away from the house when you are showing it.'

'She likes to be there to keep an eye on things.'

'Todd will make her see sense.'

Zack waved his hand in the air, as if to dismiss her. Cassie saw him a little while later, his feet up on the desk, chatting on the phone. When he was finished he came out to her.

'Todd says his mother is just being awkward; we're to continue showing the house, the more viewings the better, to wear her down.'

Cassie smiled, wondering who was going to wear down faster, mother or son.

When she got home, Tilly called out from the kitchen.

'Mommy, change your clothes, get into your pyjamas, a bite to eat is ready in ten.'

Cassie wondered when her little girl had grown up into such a thoughtful young teen. She resisted the temptation to peek past the swing door to the kitchen, but did as she was told. When she came downstairs, a movie was ready to go on Netflix, to the side a huge bowl of popcorn, steam rising from it; pizza was set out on a big plate on the coffee table, plates and napkins stacked nearby.

'I used the pizza from the freezer, is that OK?'

'More than OK, this looks really good.'

'Wait, there's garlic bread as well.'

Tilly tore into the kitchen.

'Do you need help?'

She heard the oven door being banged shut and Tilly

muttering, before she emerged with a smile on her face, like a diner waitress.

'This is so lovely. Tilly Richards, you are such a sweet girl.'

Tilly hugged her mom tight.

They were on their second slice of pizza when Tilly spoke again.

'Mom, I don't want to go and live with Daddy ever, not even on weekends; not after what he's done.'

'Tilly, I know you are hurting right now, but you won't always feel like this.'

'I want to be with you forever, Mom.'

'I know, darling. I love you to—'

'To the stars and back, I know.'

They both giggled and Cassie held her daughter close as they snuggled together, watching a movie they had seen many times before.

Chapter Eleven

Rathmoney, County Wicklow.

Jack Roper tapped gently on the back door and waited. He knew Margo was up, because he had seen her standing at the top bedroom window shortly before Elsa went out onto the front steps to wait for her lift to camp.

Elsa waved to him in the field, where he was giving a bucket of feed to the horses, but Margo didn't seem to notice him at all. Ida had told him to call in on the house, but he wasn't sure if he was going to be welcome.

He knocked a little louder, making the dog rush around from the front of the house, wagging its tail, snuffling about his boots.

Relieved there was no answer, he made to turn away, just as he heard Margo call out his name and lift the latch on the door.

'Jack, I'm sorry. I was upstairs.'

He dithered, not sure how to start the conversation. 'Would you like to come in?' Margo asked.

He took off his cap and pulled out a chair at the kitchen table.

She switched on the kettle before joining him to sit.

'I suppose you want to put things on an official footing.' He didn't answer straight away, so she continued. 'Jack, it has been on my mind; I desperately want to keep the farm on, but I can't continue to impose on your kindness.'

'I said I would do it for as long as it takes.'

'I really appreciate that, but I am being unfair on you. Probate should be through in the next few weeks and when it is, I'm hoping we could come to some sort of arrangement.'

Her voice trembled and he thought she was going to cry, so he looked away, throwing his eye over the dresser, where stacks of sympathy cards were still shoved among the china display plates.

She got up and threw teabags in the white mugs, making sure to put three sugars and milk in Jack's. 'Would you like to take over the land and use it as you want, as long as you look after my own animals as well?'

Jack spluttered into his tea. 'That is a lot of good land, don't be too hasty.'

'I can't let the farm go, Conor put too much into it; but this arrangement, I think he would be happy with.'

'Will you give me a bit of time to think on it?'

'I'm not going anywhere.'

'Ida wanted me to drop by, she thought there was something else up with you. We are worried about you.'

Margo sagged into the big armchair beside the fireplace. 'I'm not coping, Jack; I have to hold it together for Elsa, but I don't know if I can.'

Her face crumpled. He concentrated on tracing the pattern on the table cloth.

'I'm lonely. I miss Conor so much.'

'Tell me if I am speaking out of turn, Margo, but Conor would have hated to see you like this. He depended on you being strong for Elsa.'

'It's all right telling or wishing a person to be strong, it's another thing trying to live it every day.'

'Margo, is there something else bothering you?'

For a moment Jack thought she wanted to tell him, but the words wouldn't come; where she was heading required a new language and she had yet to master it. Dipping her head, she tried to hide her distress, but she could not stop the tears.

Jack got up, but not sure what to do, reached into his pocket and took out his mobile phone. Ida answered straight away.

'You'd better come over, there's a bit of a situation here,' he said.

Margo attempted to dry her tears as Jack patted her on the shoulders, muttering that it would all work out fine.

Agitated, and to fill the time until Ida arrived, he attempted to tidy up and stack the dishes in the dishwasher. Conscious of the noise he was creating, he tried to slow his movements, all the time keeping an ear out to hear his wife's footfall on the front steps. When he heard Max rush to the hall, his tail wagging, he knew Ida was hurrying up the driveway.

This time she did not get a chance to knock before Jack pulled the door open. 'She's in a bad way, you need to handle this.'

Ida, who had rushed across in her gardening jeans, stopped at the mirror to fix her hair before entering the kitchen.

'Margo, sweetheart, we are here to help,' she said. Jack suspected she was using the royal we, because he knew his wife was not going to let him stay. Almost on cue, she swung around to her husband.

'Jack, you can leave it to me, we women need a bit of space.'

Feeling cross to be dismissed in such a perfunctory manner, he nodded and without saying anything, stepped out into the back yard, waiting for the Labrador to fall in beside him.

Ida closed the door firmly behind Jack and switched on the kettle. 'You cry your eyes out, my dear, then when you are ready, we can talk.'

Margo barely heard her, the pain in her heart threatening to swallow her whole.

Ida pottered, getting down the china cups and saucers because she never liked to drink from a mug. She was searching for a teapot, when Margo got up and picked one off the top shelf of the dresser.

'You'll need to wash it. Conor was the last to use it.'

'Are you sure? I could search for another.'

'It's OK.'

'I know you have the mugs, but a good chat requires a pot of tea and china cups.'

Ida squirted washing-up liquid in to the teapot and let the warm water fill it. Her back to Margo, she scrubbed the brown scum from the inside, holding it up to the light to make sure it was clean when she was finished.

'No one is going to judge you, Margo, because you are finding it hard.' She did not turn around, but sensed Margo was listening. 'You have to give yourself time to grieve; maybe you are rushing things.'

She placed the teapot on the worktop beside the kettle and began to rummage in the overhead press. Taking out the packet of Earl Grey tea, she swung around to Margo.

'I can only drink Earl Grey now. I used to think Conor was an old fogey for insisting on it.'

She started to giggle, but suppressed it when she saw Margo's face. 'I'm rabbiting on, you should have stopped me. Jack and I will help whatever way we can, you just say the word. Is it the guesthouse? Because that will take time to build up a reputation and we are off to a flying start.'

'It's not that. There isn't a person on earth who can help me.'

Ida switched on the kettle to reboil the water.

'That's ludicrous talk, what makes you say that?'

She was pouring hot water into the pot when Margo blurted out the words.

'They're going to try to take Elsa away from me.'

Ida put down the kettle. 'No, who would do such a thing? No. No. No.'

Margo, who was fiddling with the edging of a velvet cushion, threw it in exasperation across the room.

Ida sat down at the table. 'I know you're a great mother, so how could anybody even think anything else. Has someone made a complaint?'

Margo shook her head. 'Leave it, Ida, I shouldn't have said anything.'

Ida got up from the table, moving across to where Margo was sitting. Grabbing both her hands, she knelt down beside her. 'Margo, we have known each other for long enough since you took over Rathmoney House. If you are in trouble, I want to know.'

She stopped to take her breath, her face reddening with the exertion of the kneeling. 'Spit it out, girl; the sooner you let us in, the sooner we can put three heads to solving it.'

Margo's mouth was dry, her head thumping, but she leaned towards Ida and let the older woman stroke her head. 'You don't understand.'

'I sure as hell don't, until you tell me what's going on.'

Ida, frowning because her knees hurt, stood up and pulled over a chair beside the stove. 'I'm not going anywhere, Margo Clifford, just so you know.'

'A crowd in America are making us have a DNA test; they think Elsa might be their daughter.'

Margo said it so fast, it took a few seconds for the gravity of the content to strike Ida.

'What, how can that be?'

Margo set off talking fast again, but Ida put up her hand to stop her.

'Whoa, slow down and start at the beginning.'

Margo started with the letter. As she continued her story, she saw Ida's expression darken, her face crumple, her lips tremble.

'How on earth could this have happened?'

'They don't know; there might have been a mix up in the French hospital.'

'Holy divine Jesus, there must be some mistake. Why now?'

'My bad luck to have lost my husband and now this.'

Tears tumbled down Margo's cheeks, she could not get the words out anymore. Ida reached out and drew her into a hug.

'Anyone who dares to walk up that driveway with the intention of taking that little girl will have to step over the bodies of Ida and Jack Roper. That girl belongs here and here she is going to stay.'

Jack made to come in the back door, but Ida gestured to him to leave and he did, no doubt wandering home to make a sandwich for lunch.

'You need to get someone top notch to fight this for you. I'm sure Samantha Kiely is fine for the more routine work, but...'

'She's good; talks like she knows what she's doing.'

'What are you going to tell Elsa?'

Margo shook her head. 'Oh God; I don't know.'

'Maybe it will work out and you are worrying for nothing.'

'I think the DNA test is purely to confirm what they already suspect.'

Ida could feel tears bloating inside her, so she concentrated instead on the family picture on the wall – Conor, Margo and little Elsa on Conor's shoulders – all three of them grinning.

The last time Ida had been so lost for words was when the obstetrician told her she would never be able to have children. An emptiness nested in her heart and if the truth be told, it was

99

still there. When Margo had moved in to the old house, at first she had envied the tight-knit little family. It was only over time that she learned to enjoy their friendship.

Slowly but surely, the closeness between the neighbours deepened and now she felt the same pain at this latest news as if Margo was her daughter and Elsa her cherished grandchild.

The two women sat, neither of them talking, the hens outside scraping the ground and cackling among themselves. In a far-off field a cow called out to its calf and a gaggle of geese near the river advanced across the field, waiting for Jack to finish his lunch and throw them a bucket of scraps.

When the stress of the silence settling over the kitchen got too much for Ida, she got up and, gripping the teapot tightly, she poured the tea, spooning two sugars into Margo's before handing her the cup and saucer.

'We will wait for the results and when we can see them with our own two eyes, we will devise a strategy. We are with you every step of the way. This is Operation Elsa and this team will win,' she said, before picking up her cup and sipping her tea. Hearing Jack in the yard a few minutes later, she excused herself and Margo heard her briefing him outside.

When they came back into the kitchen, Ida Roper had a determined look about her. 'Jack agrees, we will stop at nothing to keep Elsa here where she belongs.'

'How will I ever repay you?'

'Nonsense, we are friends, friends help each other, full stop.'

Chapter Twelve

Bowling Green, Ohio.

Rebecca Barton stepped down the basement stairs, making sure to tread carefully. She was looking for something in particular and she wanted to find it before Cassie came to visit. Becca knew today would possibly be the last time the two of them lingered on the porch. When Cassie had rung yesterday afternoon to say Zack was worried about selling the house, Becca thought she had sounded a little jaded.

'He's a man in too much of a hurry to make his commission,' Becca had huffed.

Cassie had not replied, but said she would swing by after lunch today.

Becca felt for the switch and turned on the light. Nobody, not even prospective buyers, had bothered to come down here for a very long time. It was chilly and smelled stale. A layer of dust was ingrained, so her footsteps were muffled. Cobwebs woven thick snatched at her head. On one side stood Todd's first bicycle; in all the years she hadn't had the heart to throw it out. Once it had been shiny, wrapped in a bow, but these days it was dull and dejected, a mirror to her life then and now.

The boxes stacked against one wall were all clearly labelled:

Becca always had been efficient, though now she knew it would make it much easier for Todd and his wife to dispose of her possessions. She turned away from those marked 'Amelie', instead pulling the 'bits and bobs' box into the centre of the floor and lifting the flaps, a cloud of dust puffing into the air.

Pushing past the diaries and notebooks she had once used to record precious memories and thoughts, her hand stopped when she came across the packet of paper airplanes. Todd liked to fold them into shape and slip a 'Love You, Mommy' message between the wings before flinging the aircraft across the kitchen to land on her desk. She could show them to him when he next came, but maybe he would be too cross to meander through the past.

Shoving the packet out of the way, her hand touched a slim, navy case. Tugging it from under another pile of notebooks marked 'Family Recipes' in block letters, she ran her finger along the length of it, releasing the lock in the middle to open it.

Becca gasped, remembering when Ed first handed it to her across the breakfast table. Quickly snapping the box shut again, she pushed it into the pocket of her sweater as she made her way carefully up the steps, making sure to turn off the basement light on the way.

Becca waited until she settled herself on the veranda before she slipped the box from her pocket. She remembered the morning Ed gave it to her. There was no particular reason for the gift, he said, and insisted she should leave it at that. That after all their years together, her husband had finally and spontaneously decided to be romantic should have been enough. But it was a surprise to her that he had picked a necklace so beautiful and so fine, and something she could not let go, grilling him on how he had picked it and goodness, how much he must have paid for it. At first, he brushed off the enquiries, but as the days went by and she did not relent in her cross-examination, Ed Barton snapped.

'Darling, do you really think I have time to be mulling over necklaces? Just be glad of it.'

'It's so beautiful, I know it was expensive; I just want to know where you got it.'

'It's not stolen, honey, if that's what you're thinking.'

'You don't usually choose such expensive presents or jewellery, not even on my birthday.'

'Darling, accept it as a romantic gesture from a husband to his wife. Leave it at that.'

'But...'

Her insistence, perseverance and her dogged determination not to accept the necklace without a full analysis of his intentions hurt Ed Barton deeply. Like a wounded animal, he lashed back, this time in an explosion of angry words.

'For pity's sake, woman, do you really think I would spend over a thousand dollars on a gaudy necklace? I won it in a game of poker. If I had known it would cause so much earache, I would have accepted a monthly cash pay-off of the debt instead.'

Becca opened the box, running her fingers over the gold chain with the pattern of green and red stones, delicate pearls leading to a pendant holding a larger drop pearl. From the Chanel collection; it was a good eye who had spotted it in the Cleveland jewellers, more used to selling plain silver and gold. This necklace needed an elaborate outfit or a great confidence on the part of the wearer. In the intervening years Ed had enquired several times if she was going to wear it and each time she had an excuse. The truth was, once she knew the full story of how her husband came to be in possession of the necklace, she felt she had no right to wear it.

Ed had taken it in payment from Cassie's father when he had gambled 1,500 dollars' worth of chips on a bad hand of cards.

Stuck with a huge debt and Ed's insistence he would not accept payment by instalments, Vince Kading had little choice. He had handed over the jewellery, bought for his wife Mary's birthday, along with the sales receipt, to settle his shameful debt.

When Ed finally gave in, admitting how he came by the necklace, Becca had wanted him to give it back.

'What do you want me to do, ruin my reputation?'

'How?'

Her husband had shaken his head as if he was dealing with a first grader. 'If I hand it back to Vince Kading, I might as well be telling the world Ed Barton has gone all soft.' He stormed out the front door but stopped to shout back through the screen. 'Vince knows the rules and he knew them when he sat down for that game of poker.'

There were times in the years that followed when she had wanted to thrust the box into Vince's hands, but she did not want to embarrass the man who had been left with nothing to give his wife but an explanation.

Snapping the box shut again, Becca sat and waited for Cassie to arrive. Old man Langley across the way waved from his swing seat, a child rollerbladed past and the neighbours called out to her as they got in their car before driving off.

Cassie brewed a strong coffee and drank it in the yard before making her way to Becca Barton's. The appointments to view had dried up and three excellent offers had been turned down. Zack was furious. He had phoned Cassie repeatedly to make sure she knew her instructions, to do everything to make the old lady see sense. Cassie had no idea how she could do that and no idea how it would affect her job when she brought the inevitable bad news back to her boss.

She was parking at East Court when her phone rang again.

'Mrs Richards, this is the principal at Tilly's school. Can we talk?

'Is Tilly OK?'

'I know there has been a lot of upheaval in her life recently, but several teachers have come to me voicing their concerns about Tilly. She is tired all the time, doesn't seem herself and never wants to take part in anything anymore. Very unusual for a child just returned from summer vacation.'

'There has been a lot going on.'

'Maybe a visit to her doctor is in order; a check-up would answer some questions.'

'Thank you, I certainly will look into that.'

Cassie, sure that it was the upheaval and uncertainty which were causing all Tilly's problems, felt a surge of anger against Charles and his selfish pursuit of a new life. She also knew Tilly must not find out about the DNA tests.

Becca was waiting on the veranda. 'You look agitated. Has that son of mine been causing trouble again?'

'No, I just took a call from Tilly's school.'

'Nothing wrong, I hope?'

'The principal confirmed some of my worries: Tilly appears to be a little off, health-wise, these days. Her advice is to get it checked out.'

'You do that, get a good tonic for her. Young people lead such busy lives. Get something for yourself too, you look all washed out,' Becca said, motioning Cassie to sit.

Cassie settled herself on the wicker chair and took out her file. 'I'm just waiting for everything in my life to calm down.' She wanted more than anything to discuss her situation with Becca, but somehow she could not find the words. 'Zack is mad as hell. You need to talk it out with Todd.'

'The boy is so like his father, he'll just blow his top.'

'Surely he wants you to be happy?'

'Happiness has not entered this equation and it never will. Todd wants to realise assets as well as getting a free babysitter. Let's face it, if I am under his nose in New York, he is guilt-free; the minute I show my age, I'll be in the first cab to an old folks' home. He won't care. I'll have nobody to talk to; they'll come and visit, maybe every other weekend at the start and as time goes by, it'll just be at the holidays.'

Becca's words tumbled out so fast that when she stopped, she felt out of breath.

Reaching over, she tapped Cassie on the knee. 'Forgive me. The truth is I'm angry at life, that it has come to this, that even when I voice my own vehement opposition, my own flesh and blood chooses to ignore me.'

'Do you want me to call him?'

'For what? He'll say I am a silly old woman.'

Cassie let out a long slow sigh.

'I'm even boring you.'

'Not true, I just don't know how to help you.'

'You helped me enough already, by not forcing me to sell my home.'

Cassie smiled. 'Zack is mad keen for a sale, he wants to reduce the price for a last push.'

Becca got up and leaned on the veranda balustrade. 'I'm sure tired of everybody deciding what they want to do with my house. Cassie, I thank you for giving me time. It has shown me the way out.'

'Go on.'

'Why should I sit still and spend my last years trapped in Todd's apartment or an old folks' home? No. I have decided to see this great country of ours. I leave for Chicago next week. I'm changing trains in New York, but I won't stop over for a visit with Todd until near the end of my trip this time next year.'

'A whole twelve months?'

'I have picked my favourite cities and booked elongated stays in some places. First Chicago, then Boston; I have family in San Francisco too and will stay a few months with a cousin I have not seen in a long time. Be happy for me, I will finally get to fulfill a long-held dream to stand by the Pacific Ocean.'

'What does Todd think?'

'I haven't told him; he would make a terrible fuss.'

'Will you leave the house on the market?'

'I'm afraid not and I don't want to get you in to trouble with Zack, but I have rented out the house to one of the Langley children across the street. He and his family have taken a twelve-month lease. It is all going to work out very well.'

'I thought you would never leave the house.'

'So did I, but now I am thinking and doing for myself. I am off to follow my dreams.'

'I'm so happy for you, even if I have to tell Zack.' Cassie smiled, realising how rarely she had done so since getting the DNA test result. But something about Becca's newfound vigour gave her a feeling of hope.

'The longer this went on with Todd, the more I realised I have spent my whole life doing things for my husband and family. What am I holding on to? Those I loved who have passed away are secure in my heart. I'm being strangled by the past here. It's time, even at my age, to embrace the new, strike some things off the bucket list of dreams.'

'Good for you, Becca!'

'All the times I asked Ed if we could train across the country, stopping off where we liked. All the times he promised, it's not as if we couldn't afford it. But it never happened. So I have decided now is my time.'

'Zack will go crazy.'

'That's my one regret, I may have landed you in somewhat of

a pickle, but I have written a letter to Zack explaining everything and including a generous fee.'

'We didn't sell the house, Becca, you don't have to do that.'

'Nonsense.'

She reached into her pocket and took out the neat slim jewellers' box. 'There is something else I have to sort out.' She slipped
the box across the table to Cassie. 'Open it, see what you think.'

Cassie snapped the box open. The smile on her face faded,
her eyes clouded. Becca noticed the tremble of her hands as she
lightly touched the chain.

'Chanel. Where did you get this?'

'My husband gave it to me a long time ago.'

'I know this necklace.'

'Try it on.'

'I can't do that. It's so beautiful. My mother would have loved
it so much. She had a picture of it; she said she told my father
she wanted something beautiful, something expensive, over the
top and designer. She saw it in the jewellers' in Cleveland and
she persuaded my father to go and find a way he could pay for
it by instalment. She wanted it for their wedding anniversary.'

'He didn't give it to her for that anniversary, did he?'

Cassie shook her head. 'He presented her with this.' She
held out her hand to show a simple gold dress ring with a blue
stone on her right hand. 'This ring. My mother laughed. She
was surprised and asked after the necklace. I was sent out of the
room, but there was the most terrible row.'

Cassie picked out the necklace and let it fall through her
fingers. 'Years later, my father told me he lost it in a game of
poker, the night he collected it from the jewellers'. He wasn't
a gambling man usually. He went into the game hoping to get
enough money so he could buy a matching pair of earrings, but
instead he lost the necklace to another player.'

'To my husband.' Becca sat back on the chair watching Cassie.

'No way, Daddy said it was a person out of town and he was lucky not to be dead.'

'The poor man, he was trying to hide his embarrassment. If he were a gambler, he would not have gone up against my shark of a husband.'

'My mother was fiercely disappointed; the necklace was never mentioned in the house again. I think she wanted to be able to leave something nice for me to remember her by.'

A sea of tears swept up inside Cassie. Putting the necklace back in the box, she shook herself and gathered up her folder.

'Becca, I had better get back.'

'Take the necklace, it's my gift to you.'

'I can't do that. It must be worth... well, a good few bucks.' Cassie couldn't even bring herself to imagine its value.

'I hope it is; take it, in memory of your mother.'

'I can't.'

'Time for her daughter to get what is rightfully hers. If you don't take it, Cassie, I will send it over to the house myself.'

Cassie picked up the box.

'And tell your daddy I'm sorry. If it's any consolation, when I heard how my husband came by it, I never wore the necklace.'

'You are a kind woman, Becca.'

'I am a sentimental old lady. Wish me luck on my travels.' She pulled Cassie into a brief but tight hug, then stayed on the veranda to wave her off.

Chapter Thirteen

Dublin, Ireland.

Ida accompanied Margo to Dublin on the day of the DNA swab and test, picking her up at the front door after Elsa left to go to a friend's house. Up since the first fingers of light crept across the sea, Ida was rattling on about the setting up of a new shop in the town.

'Mary Foster who owns the shoe shop has decided Rathmoney needs a thrift shop. I'm not sure I like the idea at all, vintage shops are fine, but this will only attract the wrong sort, looking for somebody else's leftovers.'

'You're running the risk of being branded a snob,' Margo said quietly, hoping her disapproval might stop Ida gushing on. Ida parked the car at Greystones and did not say anything more on the subject until they were on the train to the city.

'Why would anyone call me a snob for voicing my concerns?'

Margo smiled, but did not reply. Ida straightened in her seat, staring at the Irish Sea, throwing itself at the rocks below, eroding and corroding.

'I for one don't want to see the likes of Mary Foster walking about in my old twinsets. I don't want them to go to waste, you understand, and they can be worn by somebody else—'

'Except Mary Foster.'

'It's what I feel. I just know that woman will be there under the guise of supervising, tearing through the clothes and waiting to snap up my best twinsets.'

Margo laughed out loud. 'Ida, that's ridiculous.'

'It isn't. Would you like anybody else swanning around in those fancy designer clothes of yours?'

'I inherited those dresses with the house. I could never have afforded them. And I won't be giving them to the thrift shop any time soon, Ida.'

'Or Conor's clothes; he was always well turned out.' Ida had intended to say more, but she stopped suddenly, anxiously looking about the train carriage in case others had detected her embarrassment. 'I've opened my big mouth again, haven't I?'

Margo took in the sweep of Killiney Bay. Once she and Conor had taken a boat far out in the bay, lain on the roof of the wheelhouse, their faces to the sunshine. Every now and again they had sat up on their elbows, watching the shore, the trains like toy models going in and out of the tunnels. Margo had dived off and swum in the sea but Conor refused, making the excuse that somebody had to stay with the boat.

Ida tapped her on the knee. 'I'm sorry, Margo.'

'I haven't gone through Conor's clothes yet.'

'When the time is right, you'll do it.'

'Hard to know when that will be.'

They remained quiet for the rest of the journey, walking side by side to the centre where the mouth swab was to be taken and the DNA test carried out. Margo was so grateful she did not have to bring Elsa here. Samantha Kiely had gone to a lot of bother to arrange a private swab-taking from Elsa, so she did not realise the significance of what was happening. Samantha had come to Rathmoney House early one morning to be present as a doctor took the swab and placed it in the safe custody of the solicitor. Margo wished she could have done the same, but Samantha insisted it was better she travel to Dublin. Before they approached reception, Ida pulled on Margo's arm.

'Are you sure about this?'

Margo nodded, though inside she wondered whether Conor would have approved, if he were still alive. Just then, her name was called. She took a deep breath and followed the woman who stood there. Too late to change her mind.

When she came back, Ida was perched on the edge of her seat, waiting.

'Ida, I just want to get out of here.'

'Why don't we go for a cup of tea? No point in rushing to the station, when we can get the later train.'

'But what about Elsa?'

'All taken care of, Jack will pick her up.'

They walked down Parliament Street to a little restaurant at the gates of Dublin Castle.

'I fancy this spot whenever I'm in town, it's far away from the crowds,' Ida said as she ordered a pot of Earl Grey tea for two. 'We can forget about our troubles for a while.'

Margo smiled. 'Do you think this will work out Ida, this mess I'm in?'

Ida sighed loudly. 'We have to make sure it does, for all our sakes and particularly for our Elsa.'

'She's lucky to have you, Ida, especially since she never knew her grandmothers; both sets of grandparents died before she was born.'

Ida grinned. 'Believe it, I'm the lucky one, she's a light in my life.'

Behind the smile, Margo saw tears spring to Ida's eyes. 'I've never seen you so nervous,' she said. 'We will fight hard.'

'I know, but at what price for you and Elsa? I am so worried for the two of you.' Ida dabbed her eyes with a tissue. 'Don't get me wrong, I have every confidence we will fight this. I've never told you but I had a small girl once and I lost her. I don't want anything like that befalling either of you.'

Margo, who was fiddling with the sugar bowl, stopped what she was doing. She was not even sure she had heard Ida right.

'You had a daughter?'

'For all of seventy-two minutes; but I treasure that time together forever. Elizabeth would be an adult now, maybe married...'

Ida's voice trailed off. The waiter came with tea, but neither woman seemed to notice the pot placed between them. Ida leaned a little closer.

'She was so beautiful, so fragile, but she was never meant to live. I told them *I don't care about the tubes, she will take her last breath in my arms.*'

Margo gripped Ida's hands.

'I'm so sorry for you, Ida, and for Jack too, the terrible pain you must both still feel.'

'Jack took it badly.' Ida stopped as if trawling her mind to find the words for what she was to say next.

Margo, detecting a flint of anxiety in her eyes, squeezed her hands in a gesture of reassurance. 'You don't have to tell me, if you don't want to; I understand.'

Ida, tears splashing onto the wide collar of her coat, shook her head. 'Jack wasn't even the father, but he grieved hard.'

Margo poured the tea, pushing the cup and saucer towards Ida, not questioning but knowing she must let her friend tell the story in her own way.

'I love Elsa partly because I see in her the little girl called Elizabeth, the girl who was never given a chance to grow up. You don't mind, do you?'

Margo smiled, shaking her head. 'Elsa is blessed to have you and Jack. We both are.'

'Jack grieved like a man who was more than a father.'

Ida started to tell her story and Margo let her, realising this big-hearted woman, who had stood beside her so strongly, now needed to unburden herself.

'When I was in my early twenties I fell madly in love with a man. Michael was married, but we ran away together. We stayed in a lovely old house in the Wicklow mountains. It was the most special time of my life. For three weeks it was the two of us, dawn to dusk in the mountains.

There was no divorce in those days, only shame and those ready to throw it at us. I was young, I didn't much care what anybody thought.'

'It's hard to think of you ever going against the grain.'

Ida snorted out loud. 'When I did it, I did it in style. I paid a price though; those were the days when there was little forgiveness for following your heart. I was carefree and happy until I fell pregnant. I was a silly young girl in love. It was only when Michael bundled me into the car and dumped me at the gate of my mum's on Parnell Street, I copped what was really happening.'

Ida stopped to mop up some tears. 'There was no question but I was going to keep the baby. Michael disappeared from the scene and I heard a long time later he got back with his wife and they went to the States. He is some bigwig there still, I suppose.'

Ida's face reddened. 'I was on my own and my mother led the charge of the outraged, who regularly told me I would rot in hell for what I had done. I think when Elizabeth died, the fury was replaced by a misguided and false sympathy.'

Margo reached over and put her arm around Ida. 'I'm so sorry, I had no idea.'

'How would you? It's not something you tell a person immediately. When I was pregnant, I met Jack, he was such a kind man. When he offered to marry me, I was so happy. I always felt he loved me and I knew I could learn to love him. He lived in what is our house now. There was just himself and his mother. That woman was a nasty piece of work, but he was not backward at coming forward to defend me.'

Ida stopped to stare around the room as if she was seriously examining the artwork on the walls. When she spoke again, her voice was shaky and low. 'The little mite came in to the world at 1 a.m, and left it at 2.12 a.m. With Elizabeth gone, I thought it was the end of us. Jack was as cut up as myself, but he was a rock, never leaving my side.'

She looked at Margo and smiled. 'God did look down on me though, when he decided to take Jack's mother four weeks later and we were left in the big old house on our own.'

'You didn't have any children afterwards?'

Ida shook her head. 'Jack never said, but I know he was disappointed; he would have been a lovely father. My own mother said it was God's punishment for my terrible sin. When I asked her why then did Michael go on to have two more kids, she had an answer for that; those children were with his wife and that made the world of difference.'

'But you are happy with Jack?'

Ida's face flushed. 'I worship the ground he walks on, he took me in when nobody else would and he stood by me. We have made a life together. I know I annoy him with my fussiness, but I love him and he loves me.'

'Anyone can see that.'

Margo thought back to a different time in New York City. She was a dress design student, Conor was studying engineering. She was sitting in a diner in Times Square, a milky coffee and a blueberry muffin in front of her. Slicing open the muffin, she had been outraged when there were no blueberries to be seen.

Cross, she had called the waitress, politely pointing out a blueberry muffin should at least contain one blueberry. Shrugging her shoulders, the waitress offered to call the chef in on the conversation.

Conor sat at the table opposite. Afterwards, he told her he was ready to intervene if things turned nasty. The chef, a broad man with a dirty apron tied around his waist, had marched to Margo's table. Trying to stop her voice from shaking, Margo held up her muffin.

'I would have liked to find some blueberries in the blueberry muffin,' she said. The chef said nothing, but had reached into his pocket, taking out a handful of blueberries. Slowly, he squished them slightly between his fingers, before squashing them on top of the muffin.

'Ma'am, your blueberries,' he said, before stomping off. Margo, too shocked to reply, had gathered up her things and made for the door. Conor had thrown ten dollars on the counter and walked out after her. 'You were brave in there,' he said.

'Stupid, not brave.'

'Maybe,' he said, and they'd laughed as they walked down the sidewalk together.

The memory overwhelmed her: suddenly, she felt nauseous.

'Can we go, Ida? I need to get home.'

'We can. It was good to get away from Rathmoney, but maybe a bit too soon.'

'I feel like I'm drowning.'

'When my little girl died I felt that way too, but grief can be a beautiful thing, it makes you cherish what you have. That your situation is compounded by all this American stuff is unfortunate, but time will help.'

Margo stood up and snatched her bag. 'Come on. Rathmoney House is the only place for me. It's the only place I feel safe.'

Ida waved a five euro note at the waiter as Margo walked out quickly. Ida raced after her down the street while still trying to get her coat on. Margo turned around to Ida, who had one hand through her sleeve, the other clutching her handbag.

'I miss him so much it hurts every minute and every second of the day and this American business is draining away every piece of energy I have. I don't know if I can get through it alone.'

Ida slipped on her coat, before putting her arm around Margo. 'You are not on your own, never feel that.'

They walked to the station, Ida staying close to Margo until they got to the platform turnstile.

Chapter Fourteen

Bowling Green, Ohio.

Cassie got up extra early to make a stack of pancakes. When Tilly came to the kitchen, she had the plate warm, the first pancake in the pan, the jar of chocolate sauce open on the counter.

'Three or four, hon?'

'I'm not hungry.'

Cassie was worried – this wasn't like Tilly. 'Are you feeling OK, sweetie?'

Tilly hesitated. 'I'm tired, that's all. I feel weird, my legs are so heavy.'

'Maybe we need to get you to the doctor.'

'Do I have to?'

'I think it would be a good idea.'

'I miss Daddy.'

'I know, sweetheart.'

Cassie sat up to the counter beside her daughter. She noticed her fingers appeared a little swollen, but when she moved closer, Tilly hid her hands under the counter.

'There's nothing wrong with a check-up every now and again.'

'But I'm just a kid.'

'Maybe you're a little run down, there have been a lot of things going on.'

'Like Daddy leaving us.'

'That's something we can't change, honey.'

'What about the tests we did?'

'Why?'

'You said it was to check if we're healthy.'

'Oh those. It showed Daddy has a hole in his head, which is why he has been so stupid.'

Tilly slapped her mother on the knuckles. 'He's still my daddy.'

'I know, but let me kick him every now and again.'

'Rachel Rogers says her mom and dad stayed friends.'

'Good for her. Maybe a few years down the line.'

'I want us all to be friends.'

Cassie got Tilly's knapsack. 'Come on, we don't want to be late.'

In the car, she thought Tilly was quieter than usual. 'I'm going to make an appointment, maybe we can go visit the doctor later.'

'All right,' Tilly said, making a point of putting in her earphones, so she did not have to talk anymore.

Zack was sitting at Cassie's desk when she got in.

'I thought I would sit here and see what it's like to be in your shoes.'

'What do you mean?'

Zack turned around to make sure the others in the office were listening. 'Cas, you agree we're in the business of selling property, and from time to time we also rent out property for our valued clients, a part of the business that brings in a steady income?'

Cassie nodded, trying not to look rattled. She put her bag down and took off her jacket, hoping by doing something normal, it might take the wind out of Zack's sails. The office phone rang, but when his secretary went to answer it, Zack motioned her to stop.

'I want you all to know Cassie has surpassed all expectations.' The corners of Zack's mouth dipped in a sneer, his eyes were cold. 'Not only have we lost the sale of a fine historical home in East Court Street as the vendor has now taken it off the market, but to rub salt in, the very same householder has rented the property, through another real estate company. I think that fits the adding injury to insult category. Thank you, Cassie, for making Zack's Realty a laughing stock.'

The phone rang again; this time the secretary picked it up. Cassie was about to answer Zack, when the secretary called out. 'Cas, for you. It's urgent.'

Cassie gripped the phone receiver.

'Mrs Richards, this is the school superintendent, I'm afraid Tilly has collapsed, the paramedics are dealing with her now; she is on the way to hospital. Do you have somebody who can drive you there?'

'What happened? Was there an accident?'

'No accident, she collapsed during class.'

'How can that be?'

'I'm sure she will be fine, the paramedics were very good with her. They said you are to go directly to reception in the emergency department.'

Cassie turned to Zack.

'I have to go, Tilly has just been rushed to hospital.'

'Tilly? What's wrong?'

Cassie did not answer, but ran for the door, fumbling in her bag for her keys.

Zack streaked after her. 'Don't be an idiot, you are in no fit state to drive, hop in the pickup.'

She was surprised at Zack's offer of help, but did not say

anything as they sped along the streets, Zack driving up to the entrance of the hospital emergency department. Cassie pushed her fist in her mouth to stop the tears she knew were waiting to overflow.

At reception, she banged impatiently on the counter. 'My daughter is here, tell me where.'

'Maybe, if you give your name,' a harassed-looking receptionist replied.

Once she said Tilly's name, she was immediately directed to Intensive Care. Racing, she skidded down the corridor.

A nurse stopped her outside the double doors. 'Whoa there. Are you Tilly's mom? The doctors are with her. It could take a while. Do you have anyone to wait with you?'

Zack rushed up behind them, panting and out of breath. 'I'll stay with her.'

Cassie gripped the nurse's arm tight. 'Why can't I see my daughter? What's wrong with her?'

'A doctor will speak to you as soon as he can.'

Cassie pulled on the nurse's arm. 'You know something, tell me, please.'

'She was brought in with cardiac arrest.'

Cassie couldn't take in what the nurse was saying. There had to have been some mistake. 'She's twelve years old. How could she have a heart attack?'

'I'll tell the doctors you're here.'

Cassie slumped against the wall. Zack took her hand gently, guiding her to a chair. 'Should I ring Charles?' he said. 'Shouldn't he be here?'

Cassie was too numb to answer.

Tilly, the girl with the lopsided smile, the girl with the kind eyes; her daughter; the baby she breastfed; the little girl who laughed and smiled every day of her life. The girl who loved to run and jump. What was happening? How could she have a heart attack?

In the distance she heard Zack mumble into his phone.

'Charles is here, Cas, the school informed him. I've called your father.'

She nodded, too busy watching the doctor in his white coat approach. It was impossible to gauge the tone of his news from his face.

'Tilly's parents?'

'I'm Tilly's mom.'

She wanted to rush past him through the double doors and find her daughter. She was shaking as the doctor spoke slowly in a calm voice.

'Tilly is a very sick girl, but we have managed to stabilise her.'

A shout from the corridor and Charles ran to them.

The doctor put his hands out to stop him. 'I don't know who you are, but we must have calm. There are a lot of very ill people on this floor.'

'Charles Richards, Tilly's dad.'

'Maybe it would be best if you two sat down.'

'What do you mean?' Charles said.

'Your daughter was brought in with cardiac arrest.'

'Her heart, how come?'

'The heart attack was the body's response to an emergency situation. Tilly has a kidney problem.'

Cassie caught his hand. 'What are you going to do now?'

'Like I said, she has been stabilised. We will continue to monitor her over the next few hours, carry out tests and have a better picture very soon. She needs dialysis, and we will be referring her to a nephrologist, who will arrange for her to be assessed further.

'How could this have happened?'

'It's too early to say and probably no point going over that at this stage. We have to deal with the situation we have. We will see how she gets through this evening and tonight. I will brief you both again in the morning.'

Cassie turned to Charles. 'You leaving, that is what did it. She has been so stressed, not eating and generally down.'

Charles jumped up. 'You can't pin this on me. I won't let you.'

The doctor clapped loudly. 'I will have to call security if this continues. If you want to see your daughter, you are going to have to behave. Tilly needs both of you right now.'

Cassie and Charles both stopped.

'Do I have your word there won't be any more bickering?' The doctor stared hard at both of them. They nodded.

'You can see Tilly now. She's not awake, so please don't be alarmed when you see her.'

Zack tipped Cassie on the elbow. 'Don't worry about work, just sort things out here. Tell Tilly we are all rooting for her.'

Cassie held back her tears and sat by the bed, her hand cupping Tilly's. Charles stood by the window, his hands in his pockets, his eyes anywhere but on his daughter lying hooked up to machines. The nurse came and told them not to worry. They stayed in the room, both thankful to hear the rhythmic sound of their daughter breathing with the aid of an oxygen mask.

After a while, Charles shuffled away from the window. 'There's something I have to tell you.'

'Can't it wait?'

'It can't.'

Rolling her eyes, she sat back, waiting for him to speak.

'Can we step outside, Cas? I don't want Tilly to hear.'

She knew by his voice it was serious, so after kissing Tilly lightly on the forehead, she followed him to the door.

'Make it quick, I don't want her waking up and nobody to be in the room.'

'I'm moving to Baltimore.'

Cassie could hardly believe what she was hearing.

'You tell me that now?'

'I'm going tomorrow, but I can be back at the weekend.'

'You're going to Baltimore, even though your daughter is wired up to machines in hospital?'

She wanted to lash out and afterwards, she wondered if she should have let that feeling take over. 'You don't care as long as you get what you want, and what you want is in Baltimore. Your wife and daughter clearly mean nothing to you anymore.'

'That's not fair. How was I supposed to know this was going to happen? I'm in charge of the car lot there now; it's a huge step for the company.'

'For your daddy's company, we know. I note your family have to be kept away from storming the hospital, all offering their help. You go and work hard, dear; I will be at my daughter's bedside.'

'*Our* daughter, Cas. My family *have* offered to help, but I told them it's complicated and best stay away. Crystal wants to visit, she said she will drop by in a few days. Where is Vince?'

'He should be here any minute.'

She pushed past Charles back into the room, almost squeezing Tilly's hand too tight as she sat down again.

When Vince arrived and put his hand on her shoulder, she jumped.

'I saw him leave.'

'He's gone to Baltimore.'

'He's coming back, right?'

'At weekends.'

Vince pulled up a chair. 'Are you telling me he has walked out with his daughter like this?'

Tears flowed down Cassie's face. 'You know why, Daddy; I don't want to say it.'

'What a creep.'

Cassie looked startled as if she suddenly thought of something important. 'What if they can't do anything for Tilly, what are we going to do?'

'Don't torture yourself, Cassie, wait until the doctors brief you properly. We will cross every bridge when we come to it.'

She saw the pain in his eyes and she let it go, for the moment.

Cassie was still asleep, her head slumped on her arms on the mattress beside her daughter when Tilly opened her eyes at around 5 a.m. Slowly, Tilly lifted her hand and gently rubbed the top of her mother's head, before slipping back to sleep, her hand still resting lightly on Cassie's hair. When Cassie woke an hour later, she felt her daughter's gentle touch.

'Darling, Mom's here. I'm not going anywhere.'

Tilly stirred, opening her eyes and smiled for just a moment.

Cassie remained awake, her eyes locked on the heave of her daughter's small chest. When the nurse checked in, she barely noticed. A half an hour later, Tilly stirred again and asked for a drink. Cassie placed the straw from a cup of water in her mouth. When she had drunk a little, Tilly pushed the straw away and looked around the room.

'Am I going to die?'

The question was so direct, the look in her eyes challenging Cassie to answer.

'You're very ill, but you are not going to die.'

'Where are daddy and grandad?'

'Daddy was here earlier. Grandad is waiting outside.'

'Everything hurts, Mom.'

'I know, darling.' Cassie gently caressed her daughter's face.

'You look tired, Mom.'

'I am, sweetheart. Shall I bring in Grandad?'

Vince, a worn-looking stuffed toy dog under his arm, walked

slowly to Tilly's bedside. 'I swung by the house last night and picked up Snuggles. I thought you could do with him.'

Tilly's eyes lit up and she grabbed her favourite cuddly toy, pressing it under her chin. 'Thanks, Grandad.'

'You are more than welcome, my darling. I told Snuggles he has a very important job now to help you get better and there is to be no slacking.'

Chapter Fifteen

Rathmoney, County Wicklow.

'Mummy, were you thinking of Daddy?'

Margo swung around to see Elsa, her hair falling over her face, her hairbrush in her hand. She had been thinking of Conor, because today was the day they dug him up. Damn those DNA tests, that the man she loved had to be pulled from the ground by people wearing masks and gloves. She wanted to be there and yet she didn't.

'Daddy always wanted to plant daffodils the length of the driveway, but we never got around to it.'

Margo looked around the room; there were memories of him everywhere inside, and yet outside, there were not as many reminders of Conor, though he was the one who had tended to the kitchen garden and the grounds.

'We can plant daffodils this year for him. When the flowers come next spring, we can remember Daddy,' Elsa said.

'Maybe.'

'I can do it. Daddy taught me how.'

Margo hugged her daughter, taking the brush from her and sweeping her hair in to a high ponytail. Elsa, her head down looking at her phone, said nothing further and Margo was relieved. If they planted the daffodils, she wasn't sure what their blur of yellow would commemorate come spring.

Elsa pulled away from her, smoothing the stray strands of hair with her two hands. 'Ava invited me over to her house after camp.'

'Just be home by six.'

They saw Rita Mangan's car come up the driveway and Elsa pulled her mother's hand. 'Can I give you a kiss here instead of the steps?'

Margo bent down for Elsa to kiss her on the cheek.

Elsa bounded down the steps when the car pulled up. Within a minute they were halfway down the driveway. Margo stood at the front door, until she saw the car turn left on the Greystones Road and out of sight.

A French couple were due this morning, so she set to work in the guest room cleaning the inside of the window, polishing the dressing table and bedside tables, anything to keep busy. Checking the bed she had made up the night before, she placed small bags of lavender on each pillow. Giving the rooms a last once-over, she spied Ida lingering on the avenue. Not wanting another enquiry about the DNA test, when she heard her push up the latch on the back door, she stayed upstairs, waiting for Ida to start tidying away the breakfast things in the kitchen. She was only glad of one thing: the graveyard where Conor was buried was a mile outside the town in the opposite direction, so Ida may not have heard that a section had been screened off for a body to be exhumed. Samantha Kiely had said they were starting at sunrise and would be finished and have Conor reinterred by the afternoon.

She didn't want it to be this way, but it was the only way to have certainty. When Samantha had applied to the court for an order, that was the argument she had put forward for the unusual application to allow the exhumation of the remains. That his coffin should be disturbed, the letters and keepsakes

128

she and Elsa had left there were to be touched again by human hands was so painful, she could hardly breathe. She had offered his hairbrush, his toothbrush and anything she could think of in the absence of paternal grandparents or siblings, but for a definitive result, this is what had to be done.

The hospital had agreed to go halfway on the costs. Shaking away the thoughts of Conor, she made her way downstairs.

It was a shock to see Ida sitting at the table, wringing her hands, as if something was seriously wrong.

'Ida, what's up?'

'I thought you might have gone back to bed.'

Margo slumped onto a chair opposite.

'Is something the matter?'

Ida shuffling her shoulders attempted to smile. 'Compared to what you're facing, I feel silly sharing my troubles.'

'Like you said, we're friends; spit it out.'

Ida straightened up. 'Are you ready for today's guests?'

'You can't distract me that easily. The room is finished, even the lavender on the pillows. Now, spit it out.'

'You'll think me crazy.'

'Maybe, but spill the beans.'

The tips of Ida's ears had gone red and her nose tilted slightly up, showing she was trying hard to maintain her composure.

'It was when I was in the thrift shop this morning.'

'Stop right there: the thrift shop?'

'I decided I was being a bit snobbish about the whole thing, so I took a few items of clothing.'

'Twinsets, you mean.'

'I was there helping Mary Foster put some of the cardigans out on rails when a man walked in.'

'He had an American twang and was asking about accommodation in the area. Mary mentioned Rathmoney House. I had to have my say, didn't I?'

Ida stopped to flick some crumbs from the table.

'For God's sake, Ida, go on.'

'It was him.'

'Who?'

'Michael, who left for America with his wife all those years ago.'

'That Michael? Did he recognise you?'

'Of course he did, I'm not that much different, thicker around the waist but...'

'And?'

'And what? We talked.'

Margo trotted her fingers across the table to feign impatience. 'Is that it? I want details.'

'He recognised me straight off. I explained I was only helping out, dropping off a few cast-offs at the thrift shop. I'm afraid I told him I wasn't sure if there were vacancies at Rathmoney; it was a fine establishment and nearly always booked out.'

'Thanks a bunch, Ida.'

'Don't be too hasty; there's more.'

'Go on.'

Margo knew it was serious because Ida sat with her two elbows plonked on the table, something she would never dream of doing if she was not so distracted.

'He invited me for a coffee and we went to McLysaghts and sat by the window so May McLysaght couldn't throw her ear in.'

Ida jumped up from the table in a sudden rush of shame, the chair toppling back. Reaching for it she apologised, saying she should not burden Margo further.

Margo rapped on the table. 'Ida, don't be foolish It will burden me more, if you leave me hanging like this.'

Ida turned to the sink and the small window overlooking the yard. Jack, attaching a trailer to the tractor, waved when he saw her.

'All these years I cheated on Jack in my head, thinking about Michael and how it should have been, but I sat there at McLysaghts and I didn't even like the look of him.'

She swung around to Margo. 'He just went on and on about how well he had done, what a lot of money he had made and how unfortunately he lost his wife three months ago. He even said he came back to find me and maybe we could rekindle what had once been between us.'

'Cheeky.'

'Insulting. The bastard is lonely, now that he has lost a wife. What did he think I was going to do, fall into his arms?'

'Did he ask about the baby?'

'Did he hell, all he wants is a warm body to cuddle up to. He makes me sick.'

Ida picked at crumbs on the worktop. 'Margo, I made a holy show of myself in McLysaghts. I picked up my cup of cappuccino and very calmly poured it into his lap. I stood there, while he shouted he was scalded. Ever so calmly, I told him I was a happily married woman and the best thing he ever did was to ditch me.'

Margo guffawed loudly. Ripples of laughter flitted through her, making her whole body shudder. She tried to stop, but the more she attempted to put on a serious face, the more she laughed, until tears ran down her face.

'I am awfully glad my embarrassment in front of the whole town is such a laughing matter,' Ida said in her 'marbles in the mouth' voice. Striding across the room, she added loudly: 'There is nothing to laugh about. I have an awful lot more to cry about. I pined away for that man all my life. I wronged Jack, who took me in when I was pregnant and grieved hard, maybe harder and deeper than me when we lost the baby. Will he ever forgive me?'

Margo got up and bundled Ida into a hug. 'Jack loves you and you love him. Take the positive from this, not the other stuff.'

Ida pulled away. 'You don't understand. In my head I have always treated him as second best. Look at the way I boss him about.'

'I think the rest of us take that as a strong measure of your abiding affection.'

Ida began to cry streams of tears she did not bother brushing away. 'That bastard said he never gave up on me but he had to stay in the marriage or the American visa wouldn't be valid. What a load of codswallop. He thinks we are hicks not living in the modern world at all. He said he came back as soon as he was free. He never once asked about Elizabeth, not even if we had a boy or a girl.'

Ida gulped and stopped to catch her breath. 'How dare he treat me like I was an idiotic girl, who had spent my life waiting for him. I'm so angry at myself for letting the thoughts of what might have been colour my relationship with Jack.'

'I think Jack loves you for what you are, Ida.'

'I don't want to tell him about this, but after what I did in McLysaghts, the whole place will be full of it. It'll be worse if he hears it from someone else.'

Margo cupped Ida's face. 'Clean yourself up and go to Jack. Trust him.'

'He's such a good man, but I've made a fool of him; everybody will be speculating, digging up the past.'

As Margo led Ida to sit down, her phone vibrated in her pocket. 'What really matters is you and Jack.'

She walked to the drawing room to answer the call. Samantha Kiely sounded rushed.

'Margo, I'm on my way back to the office from the graveyard. Do you think I could swing by and we can talk?'

Brought sharply back to her world, Margo agreed and put the phone down. She sat in her chair by the drawing-room window, staring past the gardens and fields to the sea beyond, all the time screaming in her head.

Jack saluted as he drove past on the tractor. She hoped Ida would put her trust in him. The two of them belonged together, belonged here. But Margo wanted to run from this place with Elsa, go to some faraway place, be totally unreachable. Not knowing what to do, she sat and waited for Samantha. Conor had often stood here in the evenings, a tumbler of whiskey in his hand. From here you could see the whole driveway, which had only one small bend.

'If the bailiffs ever come, we will see them first,' he'd said, that first day they'd moved in. They had decided on a whim to move from France to Ireland to bring up their daughter on the outskirts of the small town of Rathmoney. It was a big move for two Irish Americans; but somehow, after Elsa was born and Conor's company recalled him to New York from France, they knew big city life was not for them. It was a simple life they enjoyed at Rathmoney. Conor had been determined to fit in and carry on the farm and kitchen garden business of the previous owner. He had even set up his own jam business, Rathmoney Preserves, which were stocked in the local tourist shops. She had no idea how she would continue that now, or if she wanted to take on all that work.

Fiddling with a hole in a seam on the armrest of the wing-back, she saw Max stand up and bark at the strange car turning into the driveway. Margo watched the solicitor park and get out, pushing the inquisitive Labrador away with her briefcase. Standing up and straightening her clothes, Margo made for the front door.

'What a beautiful place you have here,' Samantha said.

'Do you want to come into the office or will the drawing room or kitchen do?'

'The drawing room is fine.'

Laying her briefcase on the coffee table, the solicitor clicked it open and took out a file marked *Elsa Clifford*. 'They have got the DNA samples and now all the relevant tests can be done. They are putting a rush on it and I should have them back by Friday. It would be helpful at this stage if you gave permission for it to go to the next level, so they can confirm which child is genetically linked to which set of parents.'

Margo heard all the important words, but they meant nothing. What she wanted was one last touch, one last look, one last goodbye with this man she loved probably even more now that he was not here.

'Those second tests are crucial, whether Tilly is your biological match and Elsa—'

'Stop, please.' Margo perched on the edge of the velvet chair. 'I can't hear any more; not now, please.'

Samantha put the file back in the briefcase. 'Come into my office Friday. I'll have made contact with the US and France by then; we will have a clearer picture on what to do next.'

Margo did not answer, she could not summon up the words. She heard the solicitor leave and Ida call her husband into the kitchen, closing the door to the hall so they could not be heard.

Margo sat in her chair, thinking, watching Max as he chased a ball across the front flower beds, stopping to dig for a stone beside the untidy mound of spent dahlias. She wanted to rap on the window and order him to stop, but she could not muster up the energy.

The wind whipped up in a bluster, pushing the spent brown-stained petals of the dahlias across the gravel driveway, spots of colour on a grey, stone background.

The horses lolling in the paddock, the cows uninterested in the far fields, the river flowing by the oak trees, their branches swaying in the light breeze. Crows kicked up a racket in the far grove of hazel trees. How could it all remain so calm, so constant, when her world inside this house had changed and was about to change again, dramatically and drastically?

She heard Ida and Jack lift the latch on the back door and she waited for them to turn the corner of the house. They would not be happy when she told them Conor had been disturbed to satisfy a DNA test. She couldn't face their indignation today. Today, she had to take time to decide what next.

When she saw them walk down the path on the far side of the house, she caught Ida's happy face and smiled that a problem for them could be so quickly sorted. Her problem would never be solved enough, but instead would surely break up into a thousand different pieces, each as deadly as the first.

At this juncture, she could not contemplate how she would ever explain any of this to Elsa, so she sat quietly in her chair listening to the rising wind challenge the big stone walls of the house, which stood steadfast and firm. This gave her some consolation and maybe a little strength. Here at Rathmoney House, she must recharge for the battle ahead.

Chapter Sixteen

Bowling Green, Ohio.

Cassie woke up coughing, phlegm rising up through her. Rushing out of the room so she wouldn't wake or frighten Tilly, she stopped at the nurses' station.

'Are you OK, honey?' one of the nurses asked.

'Why do I always wake up coughing like this?'

The nurse took a paper cup, filled it at the water cooler and handed it to Cassie. 'Maybe when everything else settles, you should get that checked out.'

'From what I know, nothing ever settles down, you just move on from crisis to crisis.'

'Don't leave that cough until it becomes a crisis, promise me.'

Cassie smiled. 'I promise.'

'Believe things will get better, it will give you strength.'

'In that case, I believe one hundred times over.' Cassie laughed.

'The doctors will call by soon, give you the full picture.'

Cassie did not answer. A twinge of fear pierced through her. She scurried back to the room, where Tilly was now awake.

'Who were you talking to?'

'The nurse; the doctors will be here soon. How are you feeling?'

'Where is Daddy?'

'He is very busy, sweetheart, but he was here last night, when you were asleep. He had to go to Baltimore today.'

Tilly closed her eyes again and Cassie stopped talking.

She should call Vince and tell him the doctors would be here soon, but she needed time to think, to prepare herself. When she was asleep in this hospital bed, Tilly looked so young, so vulnerable. A part of Cassie wanted to run away, pretend none of this was happening, but instead she steeled herself, softly stroking her daughter's forehead.

When her phone beeped, Cassie moved away to the window.

'How is she? I hope you told her I was there last night.'

'She woke up a while ago and asked for you.'

'Did you tell her?'

'That you had to rush off to Baltimore? Yeah.'

'But she knows if I could, I would be there. Right?'

'She went back to sleep. There was no big discussion.'

'What have the doctors said?'

'We're waiting for them to do their rounds now.'

Cassie sat watching her daughter breathe lightly under the oxygen mask. How could this have happened? Were there signs she missed? Had she been so blind to what was happening to Tilly, because of the distraction caused by Charles?

Looking across to the next building, sleek grey walls punctuated with small square windows, she saw in one a woman standing with her arms folded tightly, her forehead a concertina of pain. Cassie wanted to step away, but she was drawn to this woman she did not know, a woman as anguished on the outside as she was on the inside. Somebody must have called or come in to the room, because she hastily wiped her face and turned away out of sight. Cassie leaned to the side to see more, but the woman had disappeared to deal with her own crisis. All these rooms, all these floors, each person grappling with news, good and bad.

She longed for home; a mundane day, Tilly racing about searching for matching socks, leaving the faucet in the bathroom dribbling because she could not tighten it enough. Tilly pestering for a puppy, moving from leaving sweet notes on her pillow to bombarding her phone with cute puppy pictures. A pang of longing seared through her for an ordinary day in an ordinary life.

When Vince walked in the room, Cassie got up and hugged him.

'Did she wake up?'

'She asked for her daddy.'

'Of course she did,' Vince said, his voice thick with contained anger.

'Leave it, Dad, the doctors will be here soon.'

'I just don't know why he's not fighting to be the one allowed to stay in the room all night.'

'He texted.'

Vince snorted, a sneer which bounced around the bed, making Tilly stir.

'He wanted to know what the doctors said.'

'Maybe if he was here, he wouldn't have to rely on second-hand information.'

'Daddy, leave it. Don't you think this is bad enough?'

Vince, hearing the pain in her voice, hushed his mouth, sitting down and clutching Tilly's hand. Cassie sat at the other side of the bed, leaning in to her daughter, scanning her face, looking for clues.

'She's breathing better, I think.'

The door swung open and the medical team stepped in.

They introduced themselves, but Cassie could not follow all the different names. She wanted to stop them waking Tilly up, but she was nervous and stood back as they appeared to talk and diagnose among themselves. She felt like a stranger listening to a foreign language, wondering when to interrupt. After a few minutes the head of the medical team turned to Cassie.

'Let's let her go back to sleep. Maybe we should talk outside.'

She followed the medics out of the door, and the consultant introduced himself as Dr Tim Rangan.

He smiled and she noticed an unusually large gap between his teeth.

'We can use the office down the hall. Do you want somebody to come in with you?'

'Tilly's father can't be here, but can her grandad sit in?'

She beckoned to Vince, who followed them along the corridor.

The doctor sat behind a large desk and opened Tilly's file.

'Mrs Richards, your daughter is a very sick young girl. It will take time, and I should tell you at the outset, possibly even a transplant, but she should get back to the happy child she was.'

The words pierced her brain, making her want to scream. 'A transplant?'

Cassie could barely say it. She looked at Vince, shock making his cheeks go red.

'Various tests have been ordered, but if she is deemed suitable for kidney transplant, that would be the best course of action.'

'She is so young, how can she need a transplant?'

'I know it is a lot to take in, but this is an urgent matter. We want to do it now, before her situation gets more precarious.'

'That is major surgery, can't you prescribe something instead?'

'Mrs Richards, Tilly needs to be on dialysis now, a transplant is the only way she will get a normal life.'

He looked from Cassie to Vince.

'As I said, a battery of blood tests and assessments will have to be carried out to see if Tilly is a candidate for a transplant. If that is the case, then she will go on the waiting list for a donor, or a living donation might be something to consider.'

He paused, letting his words sink in. Cassie thought she might throw up, she felt so sick. The doctor's words charged around her, so she couldn't properly make them out. Her mouth dried up and she felt her cough return. She swallowed hard, her head bursting, the word *donor* ringing in her ears. She saw the doctor looking at her, but she could not respond.

Vince patted her on the shoulder as if somehow, he was trying to pull her back into the room. 'This is all a huge shock to us, maybe you could outline in more detail what needs to be done.'

The doctor picked up a pen, holding it aloft for emphasis. 'Tilly's kidneys are in very bad shape.'

'But wasn't it her heart which gave out?'

'Tilly's failing kidneys are causing stress for the other organs of the body; the cardiac arrest was the result of that. The priority now is keeping her stabilised on dialysis and clearing her for transplant.'

Cassie leaned across the desk. 'Does this mean she might die?'

The doctor did not flinch. 'If a match cannot be found, the situation gets more unpredictable. Even with dialysis, she is not in good shape. The best course of action is a transplant as soon as possible.'

Cassie moved to the window.

The doctor continued to talk. 'During this time, maybe you should consider a living donation. What usually happens is family members come forward. Even if there is a good response, only a few go forward for further tests and assessments. Grandad, you will be out I'm afraid, because of your age.'

The doctor smiled gently, but continued quickly when he realised there was no response from the others in the room.

'If Tilly comes through on all her work up to transplant, we can start testing family members, yourself Ms Kading, and of course Tilly's father and as many relatives or friends as you can find. However, I would caution that this is major surgery and a huge decision for anybody to consider.'

Without turning from the window, Cassie spoke. 'Daddy, will you tell him, please.'

Vince swallowed hard. 'There is a complication you should know about. Tilly is not Cassie's biological child.'

'What we need is a blood and tissue match; there are a lot of factors to consider. I would still advise that we test you,' Dr Rangan said.

Cassie swung around. 'And what if I can't save my daughter, what am I to do then, watch her slowly die?' She felt she was screaming, wanting to pick a fight with the man who she knew was only trying to save her Tilly.

Dr Rangan stood up. 'Cassandra, your daughter needs you right now, in a lot of different ways. We will climb all the hills and mountains together.' He too went to the window where Cassie was leaning, her head bowed. 'Go for a little break. Grandad can keep Tilly company for a while.'

Cassie nodded politely.

'A positive attitude is very important for Tilly,' Dr Rangan said as he left the room.

Cassie slumped in the chair. Her phone rang. She started to cry when she heard Charles's voice.

'Cas, what is it, what did the doctor say?'

'She needs a kidney transplant. Things aren't good right now.'

'I've kept up the health insurance, so at least we don't need to worry about that.'

'You have to make yourself available, to see if you're a donor match,' she said as she gesticulated to Vince to go to sit with Tilly.

'But I'm not the birth parent.'

'That doesn't matter, apparently. It's all about blood and tissue matches.'

'I don't think I can do that, Cas, it's a bad time for me.'

Cassie sucked in air, because she was afraid of overreacting. 'Tilly needs a kidney transplant so she can have a normal life, she may even need it to survive. You do understand that, Charles, don't you?'

Walking down the corridor to the coffee shop, she listened as Charles rambled on about how sorry he was, but he was so busy and maybe he would make it up to the hospital in a few days. Kidney donation was a huge decision and he could not be away from the business for a single day right now, never mind undergo major surgery. She heard words like 'busy', 'important', 'sorry', always 'sorry'.

'I don't want to hear any more, Charles. Tilly is our daughter and we have to do everything to save her.'

'I know you don't want to hear this, Cas, but Tilly is not our daughter, that girl is somewhere else.'

Cassie stood still in the middle of the corridor. A nurse pushing a cart told her to watch where she was going. A patient told her to get to one side. She ignored them all.

'What did you say?'

'I'm only saying what you are too afraid to say, Cas.'

'So now you move from the fair-weather dad to the no-show dad. You asshole, I hope you rot in hell. Fuck off out of our lives, we are so fed up of you.'

She screamed the words as loud as she could; every bit of her body shaking. When she felt somebody take her by the elbow and career her down the corridor past the staring hospital staff, nurses and patients, she didn't care.

'Girl, you told him good. The whole county is in no doubt now about Charles Richards,' Bonnie said.

'Was I that loud?'

'Louder.' Bonnie led Cassie to a seat. 'I wish I could offer you alcohol, but coffee will have to do.'

When Bonnie came back with two paper cups of coffee, Cassie was hunched over, her head in her hands.

'I got a message from Vince, he told me. I came right away.'

'Charles doesn't care.'

'Forget loyalty to that asshole, Cas.'

'He said Tilly is not our daughter, I don't think he will even agree to be tested, to see if he can be a kidney donor.'

They sat, neither saying anything for several minutes, neither touching their coffee.

'I have to get back, I don't want to leave Tilly for too long.'

'I'll do it.'

'Do what?'

'Give a kidney, a bit of a kidney, get tested, whatever.'

Cassie sat down again. 'Bonnie, you are the best friend a girl could have.'

'I hope the doctor is nice-looking. Don't tell my Greg but there has to be something that makes this worthwhile, as well as saving Tills, of course.'

Cassie laughed out loud. 'Come with me next time I meet Dr Rangan and you can see for yourself.'

'Sounds like a date,' Bonnie said, linking Cassie's arm as they walked back to Tilly's room.

Chapter Seventeen

Dublin, Ireland.

'Can't I go with you?'

'Darling, it will be very boring for you, I'm only going to meet the solicitor and coming straight back.'

Elsa's face crumpled. 'Dublin is too far, I don't want you to leave me.'

Under ordinary circumstances, Margo would have laughed, told Elsa to stop being so silly, but the anxiety in her daughter's eyes showed these were not ordinary times.

'I have to meet the solicitor, get the paperwork right for the house and land.'

'I never want to leave this house. Ava said her mum bets we have to move very soon.'

'Does she?'

Elsa squirmed, realising she should not have said so much. 'I told her we were never moving, because we loved Rathmoney House and Daddy wanted us to stay here. If we moved, he wouldn't know where to look down on us.'

Margo gently stroked her daughter's face. 'Rathmoney is our home, why would we leave it?'

'Ava says her mum said we will have to sell it, because we

won't be able to afford to keep it. She says she gives us six months, tops.'

'Sounds like Ava's mum might want to buy Rathmoney House herself.'

Elsa, who had begun to play with the dog on the kitchen floor, looked up at her mother. 'Ava said her mum never stops talking about this house and what she would do with it.'

Margo plonked the bowl of cereal a little too hard on the table.

'I told her to tell her mum to stop thinking like that, because me and you were never leaving Rathmoney. Daddy would never let that happen.'

'You told her right.'

Elsa's face crumpled again, tears blotting her cheeks. She stood up and ran to Margo, burying her head against her shoulder.

'Darling, is there something else?'

'Ava said Daddy wouldn't be able to help us, because he's gone forever.' She hugged Margo tighter. 'I told Ava I hate her and she didn't know what she was talking about, but she said I was stupid.'

'What does she know, eh? You ignore Ava.'

Elsa pulled away enough, so she could see her mother's face. 'Mum, there's more.'

Margo knew by Elsa's voice, it was serious.

'I told her she knew nothing, and that Daddy sends us messages all the time. She laughed at me and I ...'

Margo looked at her sweet girl with the earnest face. Conor always said she was more like Margo, but what did he know?

'I slapped her across the face, it made an ugly red stripe on her cheek. Mummy, I miss Daddy, I want everything to be back to normal.'

Margo kissed the top of Elsa's head.

'We all want it to go back to normal, but sometimes life is not like that. You should not have hit Ava, no matter what she said.'

'I know. And now she says they won't give me a lift in the mornings.'

'We will soon know about that, it's nearly time.'

'I don't want to go today. I don't want to go in Ava's car.'

'Shush, shush, I am sure we can sort it.'

'Ava didn't tell her daddy when he collected us, but I know she will have told her mother later.'

'I'm sure everything will be fine. I will talk to Ava's mum, and you must apologise for the slap.'

'Even if I don't mean it?'

Margo hugged her daughter. 'Ava doesn't understand, does she?'

Elsa shook her head.

'Maybe she's afraid because you lost your dad...'

'Afraid of losing her dad?' Elsa sighed. 'I'm sorry for slapping Ava.'

'Of course you are, now let me ring Ava's mum straight away.'

Elsa nodded, sitting on the chair by the stove as Margo stepped out of the room to make the call. When Margo came back in a few minutes later, smiling, Elsa ran to her.

'Rita understood and we thought when she calls tomorrow you can apologise.'

'What about today?'

'I guess you can come to the city with me, but at the solicitors, I will have to go in on my own.'

'Can we have a slushy like when we...' Elsa stopped, floored by memories of family trips up to Dublin.

'That's a good idea, and maybe a 99 at Teddy's on the way home.'

Elsa perked up again. 'It's a deal.'

Hand in hand, they went upstairs to get ready.

'Do you think Ida would like to come with us?' Elsa asked.

'Ida will be busy meeting and greeting guests, that's when she is happiest,' Margo answered and they both giggled.

Margo thought of that carefree laughter now as she waited in Samantha Kiely's office, Elsa busy colouring at the receptionist's desk. Margo held on to the moment, the happy way Elsa had chatted as they sat on the train to Dublin. She didn't want to let go of that warm feeling, knowing that all too soon it could be a distant memory.

Samantha Kiely breezed into the room, a big smile on her face. 'I have just been talking to your beautiful daughter; what a smart young girl.'

'Like her daddy.'

Sitting at her desk, the solicitor opened the file in front of her. 'As you have probably guessed already, the latest DNA results from your husband confirm you and Conor cannot be Elsa's parents, there isn't a genetic match.'

Margo turned away to look out the window. The river flowed on; the buses whizzed past, puffing out black smoke; people dawdled outside an Italian café on the far quay. Here in this room, her life was irreversibly changed, but outside, life trundled on. She wanted to bolt from this office, grab her daughter and flee, but knew she could not.

The solicitor shuffled her file in an attempt to focus Margo's attention. 'All secondary tests are now completed, too. I have heard both from France and the US. The bottom line is you and Conor are a match to Tilly, the American couple are a match to Elsa.'

'You say it so easily, so lightly. What am I going to do?'

She didn't wait for an answer but got up and began circling the room. Pain rooted in her chest, her stomach churned. The solicitor continued to talk.

'There is another complication you should know about: the other girl, Tilly Richards, is in hospital; she needs a kidney transplant operation.'

'Sweet Jesus, will the bad news ever stop?'

'You need to focus, Margo. There could be tougher times ahead.'

'What could be tougher than this?'

'Let's not go down that road.'

Samantha asked her to sit down. 'Pull yourself together, Margo,' she said firmly, so Margo did as she was told, her arms tight across her chest because she was afraid she might have a heart attack. 'It is best if a compromise can be reached through mediation. The hospital has agreed to appoint a mediator. He or she will interview you and Elsa.'

'Can't Elsa be left out of this?'

'No, Margo, unfortunately she can't. I think the time has come to decide how you talk to Elsa about this. Mrs Richards and Tilly will also be interviewed, but with Tilly so ill, there will have to be some variance on the schedule.'

'I don't understand; I don't have anything to say to a mediator. Elsa is my daughter and no test is going to change that.'

'Margo, we have to deal with the situation at hand. The test results are the reality. The hospital appointing a mediator is a good thing. I had a conversation with the US attorney and we must now initiate proceedings against the hospital.'

'I don't care about any of that. What about these two young girls? Surely their best interest is to stay with the people who love them.'

'Margo, we all want the best outcome. We issue proceedings against the hospital in the next few days.'

'Will a court have to decide about the girls?'

'Only if we can't broker a deal through the mediator.'

Margo jumped up again. 'What bloody deal? I am never letting Elsa go; if I have to run away with her, I will.'

Samantha Kiely sighed loudly. 'Sit down, Margo. Listen, please.'

When she was sure she had Margo's attention, she went on.

'You are not the only one caught up in this mess. There is another young girl and her mother dealing with this situation, but also the devastating news about her health. Think of it, Margo, that girl is also your birth daughter.'

Margo turned away. This girl somewhere in a hospital bed in America was the girl she had tried so hard to keep in the womb, the baby she'd sung to each night, before they had even met. This was the girl she and Conor made, the girl who was the mirror for all their hopes and dreams. Elsa was the girl she had loved for twelve years, but she couldn't deny that for nine precious months, she had loved Tilly, promised her a happy future.

'What do I have to do?'

'You must tell Elsa, prepare her, reassure her. I will email France, suggest you will meet the mediator in my presence and I will also alert them to your preferred outcome.'

'What do the other people want?'

'It's only the mother and she is of the same opinion as you, she wants to keep her daughter, Tilly.'

It felt like a ray of hope to Margo. 'What's the problem, if we are in agreement?'

The solicitor looked directly at Margo. 'With respect, I don't think you are getting the point, Margo. Things cannot stay the same. The most we can hope for is an agreement to continue all living as you are, with a proviso that the girls – when they reach eighteen – can make their own decisions and that in the interim, a relationship is kept by both sides.'

Margo pulled a tissue from her handbag and dabbed her eyes. 'I can't cry or Elsa will know something is terribly wrong.'

'Elsa needs to know.'

'No, it will be too much for her.'

'She needs the truth, the sooner you do it the better. Do you want me to do it for you?'

'No, I have to do this myself.'

Samantha Kiely stood up. 'Go home, rest before thinking about any of this again. I have to go to a consultation in the Four Courts, but we will talk soon.'

Margo walked slowly to the door. She was leaning on the door handle, when she turned to the solicitor. 'Can you pass on my best wishes and prayers to Cassie and Tilly? I can only imagine what they are going through.'

'I will, and I will be in touch when there is a development.'

As Margo walked through to reception, Elsa saw her and held out the picture she had drawn. 'It's you and me with Max and Rathmoney behind us, and Jack and Ida at the gate.'

Margo looked at the drawing, wishing they could stay like that, without interference from the outside world.

'You see we are a family still, just different. I put a star in the sky to represent Daddy, even though it's the day.'

Margo put a smile on her face. 'It's lovely, I think we should go buy a nice frame for it.'

Shaking her shoulders, she shrugged off the despondent feeling. This day was going to be a mummy and daughter day, a day so casually taken in the past, but now so cherished. A precious day before she had to break the spell.

'What about a nice lunch and a stroll along St Stephen's Green?'

'Can we go to Smyths to look at the Sylvanian Families and then get a cake at Tea Time Express on the way to the station?'

'We can.'

Elsa did a little dance of delight and they set off, Elsa chattering happily, Margo doing her best to act normally.

They had such a perfect afternoon together, coming home happy and tired late in the evening. Ida had left a note on the kitchen table, saying she had served dinner to the guests and would return in time for breakfast.

'Mum, can I sleep with you?'

Margo agreed and they curled up together, the curtains drawn back in the front bedroom, watching the stars over the sea.

'I know Daddy's star.'

'Show me.'

'Daddy told me before he died, pick the brightest one and that's him. My brightest star can be different to yours.'

'I like that.'

Elsa fell asleep soon after, Margo lay gazing at the myriad balls of light in the sky.

The next morning when Rita came to collect her in the car, Elsa apologised and hugged Ava and they set off happily to camp.

Margo waited until the guests had been served breakfast and checked out, before she sat down in her thinking chair.

Ida, realising there was a weight of worry on Margo's shoulders, slipped off quietly to make up the guest rooms. Later, as she was leaving, she saw Margo standing by the drawing-room bay window.

Tentatively, Ida stepped in to the room. 'Have you got news?'

Margo concentrated on a magpie hopping over the gravel path to peck a bone discarded earlier by Max. 'One for sorrow, Ida.'

'Where there is one, there are two,' Ida said, crossing to the window to prove herself right.

'There isn't a second one in sight and why would there be? Two for joy would not sum up my life at the moment,' Margo said quietly.

'What news from the solicitor?'

'A lot, but it boils down to this: Elsa is theirs, Tilly is ours. And to top it all off, Tilly is very sick.'

'What are we going to do?'

Margo steadied herself by gripping the curtains tight, scrunching the gold silk of the drapes so hard, Ida was afraid she would pull the lot down. 'You mean what I am going to do, what do I have to do to make this right?'

Ida wanted to call Jack, but she was too scared to leave Margo on her own, even for the short time it would take to get her phone from her bag in the kitchen.

'I am going to sell Rathmoney, move away with Elsa.'

'What, are you mad? You can't do that.'

'You two can buy it, you can run the guesthouse, Ida. I know I said I couldn't leave the home we made here with Conor, but I've got to think of Elsa. I can't stay here anymore. I won't stay waiting for them to come up that road to take my daughter.'

Ida made to hush Margo, but she shrugged her off.

'You will buy it, won't you? I couldn't bear to think of anybody else in Rathmoney House.' Tears choked her, making her speech sound slurred. 'I need to pack, we can leave tonight, you will look after everything here, won't you?'

'You can't run away like this. See sense, Margo.'

'Ida, I need to run away, to hide Elsa.'

Ida stepped in front of Margo. 'Do you think I will let you go anywhere, the state you are in? And I know you're trying to do the best by Elsa, but you're not helping her by running away together.'

Ida marched to the drawing-room door, firmly closed it and turned the key in the lock, before taking the key and slipping it in her pocket. 'We are going to sit and calm down and when we think we are calm enough, we will discuss sensible options.'

Outside in the hall, the dog came to the closed door, snuffled about and whined. Margo sat on the couch. Looking down at her hands, she saw they were shaking. How could it have come to this? How could she have changed so much? Once she was an independent, busy woman and mother, designing dresses, taking commissions, an equal partner with Conor in all that was Rathmoney House. As Conor built up Rathmoney, she started a small but lucrative business designing one-off dresses for wealthy women from Dublin city. When Conor became ill, she pushed the dress designing and dressmaking to one side with the intention of picking it up in the future. She doubted that would ever happen now. Somehow she had morphed into this helpless woman, afraid for every day. Like a frightened rabbit caught in the headlights, she was no good to Elsa like this – and she knew it.

Ida walked to the bookcase containing Conor's favourite travel books. Reaching up to the top shelf, she stretched, removing two books and pulling down a bottle of brandy.

'Conor said he kept it for emergencies. I certainly classify this as an emergency.'

'How did you know about that bottle?'

'When you are as pernickety about dust as I am, you get to know every nook and cranny.'

'We don't have any glasses in here,' Margo said, wiping her eyes with a tissue from her jeans pocket.

'There are times to dispense with the niceties and this is such a time,' Ida said, unscrewing the cap and pushing the bottle towards Margo. 'Go on, take a swig.'

Margo tilted the bottle until she could splash the brandy in to her mouth. Coughing and smacking her lips, she thrust the bottle at Ida.

Ida carefully sloped the bottle, shivering as the brandy's warmth raced through her. Composing herself, she eyeballed

Margo. 'There is nothing you can't overcome with a bit of support and help. Bolting is not the answer.'

'I just want it all to go away. I want them to leave us alone.'

'What about the solicitor, what does she say?'

'Some sort of mediator is going to interview us all, write a report and recommend a course of action.'

'Well they can take a hike, our Elsa is not leaving Rathmoney.'

'I wish it was that easy, Ida. He's going to want to talk to Elsa as well, Samantha is insisting I prepare her, tell her everything.'

'When are you going to do that?'

'I should have told her yesterday in Dublin. But it was such a good day, I couldn't face it.'

'They can't force you into anything, you don't have to tell Elsa until you are good and ready.'

'I need time to mentally prepare. I have no answers and I need them.'

'When is this mediator due?'

'It is part of the hospital investigation, they will make contact through the solicitor.'

'Which means it could be weeks before they make it to Rathmoney.'

'I suppose.'

'And especially when there is legal action on the horizon, they will be going out of their way to cross all the 't's and dot all the 'i's.'

'What are you getting at?'

'You can tell Elsa when you want to. When you – and only you – decide it is the best time. This is not something you want to rush.'

'Are you saying I should take control?'

'I bloody well am.'

They saw Rita Mangan's car come up the driveway to drop Elsa off.

'Will you be all right, not do anything stupid?'

'I think so.'

'You stay where you are. I can let Elsa in on my way out the front door.'

Ida tiptoed out of the room, but Margo called out to her before she got down the hall. 'Thanks, Ida, for the clear thinking and buying me time I never knew I had.'

'Spend that time gearing up to fight, not run away.'

Thanks. I can see a little clearer through the tunnel now.'

Ida didn't answer, but concentrated instead on Elsa, who was out of the car and tearing up the steps. Margo quickly tidied her hair and plumped up her cheeks to give herself a little colour. She could hear Ida holding Elsa at the door, giving her further time to compose herself.

'Be a good girl, I think you tired your mum out yesterday, you two had so much fun in Dublin.'

'You'll have to come next time, Ida.'

'I might just do that,' Ida called out as she set off down the avenue.

Chapter Eighteen

Bowling Green, Ohio.

Cassie sat at the kitchen table. It was a rare visit home to rest and recharge while Vince stayed with Tilly.

On Facebook she was reading about a mum in Florida who drove around her city with a big sign. 'Please can you give a kidney to save my daughter.' Maybe that is what she had to do because nobody in Cassie's immediate family was a suitable match for Tilly. Cassie had taken it badly when she wasn't a match, insisting on more tests, but the doctor told her to move away from outrage and instead to concentrate her energies on trying to recruit potential donors.

Charles finally put himself forward after she rang and begged him. She felt sick to her stomach the way she pleaded with him, but a woman trying to help her sick daughter could not stop for anything. Bonnie put a request up on Facebook and Zack came forward, but on each occasion when Cassie felt renewed hope, news of some disqualifying detail came soon after.

She had only one last hope left now, but it was a gamble she knew could go badly wrong. Pouring a cup of coffee, she stepped out onto the little deck over the back yard. She thought of all the days she and Charles had sat here, watching Tilly play. They were happy in each other's company back then, relishing time spent together. If Tilly had got ill, they would have shouldered the strain together, Charles driving the search for a donor. Now, he was reluctantly on the sidelines of their lives and with the divorce nearly finalised, very soon he was likely to disappear altogether. A part of her envied him his happiness in a different house, with a different partner, far away from the stress she and Tilly lived with every day.

Next door, a man started up his lawnmower so she went back inside.

There was only one way of finding out if her plan for Tilly would work and that was to sit down and do it. Dale had told her the names of Margo and Conor Clifford, Tilly's biological parents. Googling both their names, a death notice for Conor Clifford, Rathmoney House came up along with the Rathmoney guesthouse. Dale had mentioned a big old house and she hadn't been able to resist looking.

Clicking through the gallery of pictures, she wondered what Tilly had missed out on; what had she offered in comparison to this beautiful home? Scouring every photo, she was disappointed there were no snaps of the Clifford family.

When she found the email for reservations, she sat down to write to Margo Clifford, the woman who had raised her daughter. Dale told her there should be no contact, it was all at too sensitive a stage, but maybe, just maybe, this woman might respond to a direct communication, mother to mother.

She drank two cups of coffee and was reading over the email one last time when Tilly texted her from the hospital. Hitting send, she reached for her cellphone.

'Nancy texted they need somebody on the soccer team for a match on Sunday. I'm fed up of hospital.'

Cassie texted back: 'It won't always be like this, darling.'

'Am so fed up, will I ever get back to the way I was?'

'You'll be even better once you get a new kidney, we just have to wait.'

'What if I don't get one, what happens then?'

'You will get one, I really believe that.'

'But when?'

'We have to be strong and patient. I'll be back in the hospital in 30 mins.'

Chapter Nineteen

Rathmoney, County Wicklow.

Margo was reading the email for the tenth time when Ida came in the back door.

'Have the guests arrived yet? I didn't see a car.'

'No sign yet.'

Ida stood, her hands on her hips. 'Are the rooms ready, aired out, fresh sheets?'

'Done, just the drawing room and the hall to be hoovered.'

'I'd better get cracking on that.'

Margo shook her head. 'Sit down, Ida, I could do with your help here.'

Ida fingered the buttons of her cardigan nervously. 'What's wrong?'

Margo shoved the laptop across the kitchen table as Ida pulled out a chair to sit down.

Ida opened her handbag and took out her reading glasses, fixing them on before scanning the screen. 'Jesus Christ, what is happening? Is this for real?'

Margo didn't answer.

'They can't ask this, can they?'

'Read what she says. It's a mother asking a mother, Ida.'

'You're not going to.'

Margo shrugged her shoulders. Ida reached for her phone.

'We will have to get Jack in on this, he is good in a crisis, always stays detached and keeps a cool head.'

Margo pulled the laptop near her, so she could read the letter again.

From: **cassierichards@gmail.com**
To: **rathmoneyhouse@gmail.com**

Dear Mrs Clifford,

This is a very difficult email to write and I know I am probably the last person you want to hear from. My attorney has also told me not to contact you, but I found your email through your guesthouse website.

Please hear me out.

We are both in a difficult predicament and I know we both love our daughters. I know Elsa is your daughter and you don't want to be separated from her. Tilly means the world to me, I love her so completely.

You should also know we are dealing with an ongoing situation here. Doctors tell us Tilly is in need of an urgent kidney transplant. Every day has become a struggle for her. She is on dialysis.

We have all been tested, even my estranged husband, and it's no surprise to us we are not a match. I have been praying for a miracle, but she is getting weaker; the doctors don't say it directly, but I know and feel her plight is precarious.

I woke up this morning and I realised I had to make a miracle happen. I am hoping you will help me on that road. Is there any chance you would consider taking a test, to see if you are a donor match?

It's an enormous ask, but I know as a mother you will understand; I am asking you, one mother to another.

Let's not talk about what happens next if you are a match, we will cross that bridge if we have the good fortune to reach that point.

Margo, I know you love your daughter and I so love mine. I know you would do anything to help your little girl, to save her life even, and I will do the same for mine.

In that spirit, I ask please will you take the direction of my doctors and schedule a test to see if you can be a donor to Tilly. I don't make this request lightly and I know it's a huge decision for you, but please, please at least consider the initial tests.

If you turn out to be a suitable match on all levels, I will be asking you to once more consider helping my Tilly. For now, I beg you to get tested. From one mother to another, I am asking for your help. It is as simple and as complicated as that.

Thank you,

Cassandra Richards.

'She has some flaming cheek. You are not doing it, I hope.'

'I understand where she is coming from. It's just a test.'

Ida didn't answer, but picked up her phone and stepped outside to the back yard. Margo couldn't hear the words, but the outraged urgent tone of Ida's voice was in the air. When she stepped back in to the kitchen, her face was flushed with excitement.

'Jack is only down by the river, he'll be here in a few minutes.'

Margo sat, afraid almost to speak. She heard Ida fidgeting, switching on the kettle, placing three mugs on the table, transferring the milk to a jug and hunting out the sugar bowl. Ida, realising how it looked, stopped. 'Even in a crisis, I like the table to look just right, though I have relented with the beakers.'

She had scoured the teapot when Jack arrived. Ida pushed the laptop towards him. When he finished reading the email, he sat back in his chair, looking at Margo.

'What are you going to do? What do you need us to do?'

'She is going to ignore this, that is what she is going to do,' Ida blustered.

Margo sipped her tea. 'I have to be tested, I don't want anything to happen to that poor girl.'

'But what if you are a match?' Ida said, her eyes wide with worry.

'I will have a bigger decision to make.'

'But you can't expose yourself to that,' Ida said, flicking crumbs off the table onto the floor in her agitation. Jack stood up and, taking his mug of tea to the kitchen sink, he threw the dregs down.

'Margo is doing the right thing. Where it will lead is another matter, but she can't not get tested.'

Ida snapped her fingers in frustration. 'I think the less you have to do with that woman the better. How do you know it's even true?'

Jack, who had lifted the latch on the back door, swung around sharply. 'Ida, it's Margo's decision, but think about it, what sort of a mother would make this thing up?'

'I'm looking at all possibilities,' Ida said, her voice high-pitched, because she was both outraged and offended. Margo, who had only heard noise and not the words aired, spoke in a low firm tone.

'I will get tested. That girl and I are tied together, whether we like it or not; if I can help her, then I will do so. It could be Elsa and if it was, I would move heaven and earth and ask the impossible to make her better.'

Jack waved at the two women as he made his way back to pulling out weeds at the far side of the river, near the bridge. Ida fiddled with her spoon, not sure of what to say next.

Margo closed the laptop and concentrated on the pattern on the kitchen table. Conor had come home with the oilcloth after a trip to Wicklow town. It was garish, a riot of red, pink and purple, clusters of flowers. Conor had called it After Monet. Margo had laughed at him, saying the great artist would surely turn in his grave.

Ida sighed loudly.

'Why don't you think I'm doing the right thing, Ida?'

Ida shuffled in the chair. 'I think to go down a road when you don't know the final destination is taking too much of a chance.'

'But if I can help this girl...' Margo got up to let the dog out, but stayed standing at the door, as if she was waiting for visitors. 'If I refuse this request and something happens to her, I will never forgive myself.'

Ida, who had been tracing the length of a hollyhock on the oilcloth, pounded the table with the side of her fist, making the dog tear back into the house and Margo jump back, bumping against the coat rack, knocking off Elsa's raincoat.

'I'm afraid for you. Don't make a hasty decision, think of Elsa who needs you so much.'

Ida's voice was shaking; Margo was not sure if she was going to burst into tears.

Ida got up, pulling her cardigan around her.

'I've said my piece, take it or leave it, but promise me you will give it more thought before you answer that email.'

'I'm not going to do anything in a rush; but I know I have to go for the test.' Before Ida had time to answer, Margo added quickly, 'Besides, I may not be a proper match. A lot has to happen before I am picked as a donor.'

Ida reached into the cupboard and pulled out the Hoover.

'I'll get on with sprucing up the front rooms,' she said, leaving the kitchen, pulling the Hoover behind her.

Margo slipped out the back door to the river. She saw Jack towards the bend, so she walked along the bank parallel to the house, until she reached the weeping beech and the bank of fuchsia.

Pushing her way past the fuchsia, she got to the wooden seat Conor had placed there for her last birthday. She loved this seat, where she could sit away from the house, watching the river flow by and the cattle nosing the grass in the far field.

Closing her eyes, she listened to the water gushing past the rocks which jutted out from the bank, slowing the flow of the river to the sea.

This girl in America was her child, hers and Conor's, a biological tie they could not ignore. Elsa was their heart and soul, but this other girl was their blood. She could not turn her back on her. If she was a donor match, she knew what the next decision was going to be. She could see the bridge from here and if she closed her eyes, she could see Conor standing, surveying the land, watching for the heron, hoping he would glide past.

These days she liked to sit here and remember. There was no sickness or cancer intruding here. When Conor was bad, she had sat on her thinking chair in the drawing room or at the kitchen table, always within calling distance. But this seat was her place to be when she did not care who was looking for her, when time had no meaning, when she could be straight with the world and not have to watch her thoughts or words. It was the only place these days where she could think with enough clarity, the sound of the water or the birds the only intruders on her thoughts. The blackbird and the thrush were nearby, one flitting between the branches, finding the highest spot before letting out a throaty call; the other like an old woman walking with her head down, surveying the ground as if it was laced with gold.

She heard Ida call out to Jack and she knew she was really looking for her. Much as she wanted to stay hidden, she knew Ida would be upset if she did not emerge, and she didn't deserve that.

Slowly, she made her way back to the house. Jack was back in the kitchen. Margo knew he had been trying to calm Ida down because she could see anxiety in her face.

Ida, her face red with stress, her hands on her hips, stood in front of Margo. 'They are nearly on top of us. Where were you?'

Margo saw Jack place a restraining hand on Ida's arm, which she shook off. 'What do you mean? I went for a walk to clear my head.'

'The new guests rang, asked if they can have lunch when they arrive. I told them they could, at twenty euros apiece. I said we will do toasted sandwiches, chips or salad and a bowl of soup for that.'

Ida's face scrunched like a crumpled bag as she continued. 'They asked was everything organic and homemade. I said it was because it usually is and now what am I going to do? They will be here in half an hour.'

Margo would have cracked up laughing, if Ida had not been so upset.

'Jack, go down to the fancy deli in town and get four portions of vegetable soup and four of tomato and basil and some nice fancy brown and white bread. I think I have enough ingredients for a salad and cheese and tuna sandwiches.'

She took a fifty euro note out of her pocket and gave it to Jack, who muttered that he had better get change out of that. Ida, who had composed herself sufficiently, patted a little water on her neck, to help her calm down further.

'I'll get on with setting the table in the dining room. We're lucky I hoovered in there earlier.'

Margo set to work getting the crockery and the condiments ready. By the time Jack came back, laden down with white bags and plastic containers of soup, the two women were standing waiting for him.

Ida tipped the soup into two saucepans she had ready on the stove, while Jack took the rubbish out to the outside bins.

'We're getting very good at this type of rushed meal,' Ida said and they laughed, sitting waiting until they heard the guests' car on the driveway.

Ida didn't mention the donor test again until the tourists had had their lunch and retired to their rooms. She was stacking the dishwasher when she quietly asked if Margo had made up her mind completely.

'You aren't going to like it, but yes. If I can help this girl, I will. We are connected.'

Ida straightened up, two plates still in her hands. 'If that's what you've decided, I'll say no more. Let me come with you, when you are having the tests.'

'It's not as though I'm being tested for cancer or something like that. I'll be fine.'

'I just want to support you, what can be wrong with that?'

Margo, noting the upset in Ida's voice, relented. 'The Americans are in a hurry, aren't they?'

'Time is the one thing which is important to them.' Ida grabbed her coat. 'I'll be back in the morning to get the breakfast ready for the guests. Are they still checking out tomorrow?'

'As far as I know.'

Ida left, flagging down Jack's Jeep in the driveway, so she could get a lift home.

Margo was glad to have the place almost to herself. She saw the tourists wandering down by the river, so she retired to Conor's study. Here, she could sit among the things he valued most and feel a part of him was still here with her.

She had expected to grow old with him, support each other as they built on their dreams at Rathmoney House. Instead she was adrift, her own plans by necessity on hold, until she could shake off this paralysis which seemed to have settled within her. What she wouldn't give to have the old days back. Sitting at his desk, she imagined he was nearby, because that was the only way she could get through each day.

Chapter Twenty

Bowling Green, Ohio.

'Mom, where will I get a kidney?' Tilly asked, her eyes filled with worry.

'Don't worry, sweetie, the doctors will sort that out.'

'Am I going to get one of yours?'

'I'm afraid I'm not a match, darling, so I can't give you one of mine.'

Tilly reached to playfully pull one of the tassels on Cassie's sleeve. 'I'm glad they aren't going to cut you open, Mom.'

'Silly goose.'

'Grandad said he's too old.'

'And slow.'

Tilly giggled. 'I think if I got some of Grandad's kidney, it'd make him even slower.'

'Your Daddy rang, said he is going to make it to see you soon.'

Tilly made a face. 'I don't want Daddy's kidney.'

'Sweetheart, why do you say that?'

'Because it might make me get mean to you and I don't want that.'

Cassie ruffled Tilly's hair. 'Having a transplant is not going to change anything about you, sweetie.'

'Do I have to have someone else's kidney?'

'Yes, darling, you do.'

'Can't they just patch up the ones already in me?'

'I wish it were that simple.'

Tilly leaned back on her pillows and looked at her mother. 'Why isn't Daddy here?'

'He says he's very busy in Baltimore.'

'Can't he get a day off?'

Cassie didn't know what to answer, but Tilly picked up on her uncertainty.

'Is he somebody else's Daddy now?'

Cassie squeezed Tilly's hand tight. 'No, sweetie, he's not.'

'It just might be the answer,' Tilly said, her face solemn. Cassie thought if it was not so sad, she would find her daughter's words of wisdom amusing.

A knock at the door made Tilly perk up, throwing her long hair behind her back. Charles's sister put her head around the door.

'I don't know if I am welcome, can I come in?'

Cassie rushed to the door, gently shoving Crystal out into the hallway.

'What are you doing here?'

'I wanted to see Tilly, I have a gift for her.'

'You know your brother has left us here to fend for ourselves. I don't want you upsetting Tilly.'

'I just want to visit, I won't say anything I shouldn't.' Her voice caught. 'Charles has asked the family to cut off contact. I wanted to give Tilly something to remember me by.'

'You won't allude to any of the other business or upset her in any way?'

'I promise.'

Cassie stood back to allow Crystal to step into Tilly's room.

Tilly, her eyes suspicious, looked at her aunt. 'Have you guys been rowing?'

'No, dear, your mom just wanted to make sure I don't stay too long and tire you out.'

'I'm not so tired,' Tilly said, throwing her mother a funny look.

Crystal, a tall, handsome woman, opened her handbag and took out a package. 'I have something for you. I know you have admired it and I wanted you to have it, because you are such a brave girl.'

Tilly became excited when she saw the aquamarine-coloured box.

'It's the bracelet, isn't it?'

Crystal opened the box and put it on the bed.

Tilly gasped. '"Please Return to Tiffany", you let me wear this that weekend when Mom and Dad were in Boston. I love it.'

'I knew you would remember it.'

Tilly beamed with delight as Crystal took the bracelet with the heart charm out of the box, slipping it onto her wrist and tying the catch.

'Look, Mommy, it's so beautiful.'

Tilly threw up her arm, so the silver of the linked beads glinted in the light.

'But isn't this the jewellery your late parents gave to you on your twenty-first?'

'It's my pleasure, this brave girl needs a pick-me-up as well as a kidney. I couldn't think of a better way.' She turned to Tilly. 'We bought the bracelet in Tiffany's, Fifth Avenue. Your Nana told me to keep it and pass it on to my daughter when she was twenty-one. You are the nearest thing I have to a daughter, Tilly.'

Tears were beginning to bulge in Crystal's eyes, so she turned away, pretending to busy herself shifting things around inside her handbag.

Cassie took Tilly's hand and examined the bracelet.

'Stunning, simply stunning,' she said.

Tilly looked earnestly at her mother. 'I wouldn't mind having Auntie Crystal's kidney, she's nice.'

Looking up from her bag, Crystal smiled. 'I have too many bad habits, you don't want anything out of this body, believe you me. Look for a clean-living teetotaller.'

'You've been too kind,' Cassie said, but Crystal brushed off her praise.

'I'm so glad Tilly likes it,' she said.

'Have you seen Daddy's new family?' Tilly's sudden question threw both women.

'Crystal doesn't want to be talking about that, Tilly,' Cassie said, a little too sharply.

Crystal stroked Tilly's hair. 'Sure, he has a girlfriend, honey, but no children.'

'Have you met her?'

'I don't think your mom would like me talking like this with you.'

Tilly sighed in resignation. 'Can you come again soon?' she asked.

Crystal hesitated. 'I'm out of town for a while, but maybe after.'

She kissed Tilly on the cheek.

'Thank you for the bracelet. Just like you told me, I'll look after it and pass it on to my own daughter when she is twenty-one or incredibly brave.'

'Like you, poppet,' Crystal replied as she walked to the door.

Cassie followed her out into the corridor.

'Thank you for stopping by, Crystal, and for the gift. It means a lot to both Tilly and me.'

'We never did see eye to eye, Cas, but for what it's worth, I think that brother of mine is a heartless fool. He should be here fighting for his daughter.'

Cassie didn't answer, but hugged her sister-in-law, whispering *thank you* in her ear.

When she got back into the room, Tilly had taken off the bracelet.

'I am going to keep it for good wear.'

'Crystal is a nice person.'

'You once called her a moany ass.'

'Well, she is a nice moany ass,' Cassie said and they both guffawed.

They were still giggling when Vince came in to the room.

'This is such a tonic, to see you two happy.'

'For us too,' Cassie said, slipping the Tiffany box into her handbag.

'I might just have something else to make you two smile,' he said, calling the person waiting outside the room to enter.

Becca Barton stepped forward, holding a huge jigsaw puzzle. 'I had to meet Tilly, and Cassie, I had to come back and give you a hug.' She kissed Tilly lightly on both cheeks before embracing Cassie tightly. 'Your grandad here smuggled me in, so I only have a few minutes before they drag me away.'

'Why don't you two go out and chat and I will open up this jigsaw for Tilly,' Vince said.

He made a big deal of placing the jigsaw on the table in front of Tilly and started pulling at the side to open it. Once he saw Becca and Cassie leave the room, he quickly got the jigsaw box and pushed it under the bed.

'That's enough of that,' he grimaced, making Tilly chortle again.

'Why did she bring me a jigsaw?'

'I guess it's been so long since she's had anything to do with a child of your age. Becca really is behind the times.'

'Even more than you, Grandad?'

'Definitely more than me.'

In the hallway, Becca Barton pulled Cassie to one side. 'Darling, how are you?'

'To be honest, it's really tough. You didn't have to come all this way, disrupt your plans.'

'As a matter of fact, I did. I keep in touch with Vince on Facebook and he sent me a message to tell me what happened to Tilly.'

'Gosh, aren't you two so connected.'

'I can't donate a kidney, I'm too old, but I want to do something to help.'

'There's no need, Becca, just being here is enough.'

Becca Barton reached into her handbag and pulled out an envelope. 'For you, to help out in whatever way you want. Don't think I have forgotten your kindness to an old woman. You opened up the possibility of fulfilling my dreams.'

'I can't take your money, Becca.'

'Of course you can and you're welcome to it. Now I must get along, my new tenants have invited me to visit.'

'Thank you, Becca, I will never forget your incredible generosity.'

'Use it to help your precious daughter and think of me from time to time.'

Cassie ripped open the envelope and saw the cheque for $10,000. Becca put her finger to Cassie's lips.

'Not a word, it's our secret.'

She scuttled off, leaving Cassie smiling in the corridor, immensely grateful her financial worries had been wiped away in one kind gesture. When she walked back into Tilly's room, she held out the cheque for her daughter and father to see.

'That's a lot of zeros, does it mean we're rich?' Tilly asked.

'We're better off than this morning, for sure,' Cassie replied, carefully folding the cheque into her purse.

'Becca was determined, you made a huge impression on her, Cassie,' Vince said.

'I was kind, that's all. It's so easy to be kind to Becca. It looks like I might not be the only one. Facebook friends, I hear.'

'She's a lovely lady, I wish I had fully realised it before she left town and took up travelling the country.'

Chapter Twenty-One

Rathmoney, County Wicklow.

From: **rathmoneyhouse@gmail.com**
To: **cassierichards@gmail.com**

Dear Cassandra,

I went for the investigations and blood tests you requested and I
am sure the results will be back soon. My gut tells me I must be a
match and what do I do then? Strange I should turn to you for some
direction, but maybe you, above all others, understand. We must
remain strong for our daughters.

You have to save your daughter, and I have to make sure if I help
you, this daughter of mine here with me does not lose her mother.

I know the doctors will say there is little risk to me, but my
mother's caution is telling me to move slowly towards my final
decision, examining all different scenarios.

You, of necessity, have to be a miracle maker. I, of necessity,
must be a cautious but generous donor.

I have never met Tilly, but I know where she came from. I feel
I'm getting to know you, my admiration for your courage in the
face of adversity is boundless. These are some of the reasons to
grant your request, but I think the deciding factor is that this girl I

brought into the world and you brought up needs our help. I won't be left wanting in this regard, now or at any time in the future.

I have not spoken to my solicitor about this, I am afraid she will try to dissuade me.

I'm not for turning; only a negative donor match will do that. I hope between the two of us, we can make the miracle happen for Tilly.

Yours,

Margo

Margo sat in bed, her iPad balanced on her lap. The fumbling in the hallway of the guests returning tipsy, the clanging of the bolt on the front door as it was pushed across, the giggling and shushing, the voice of the young woman from the Wallflower Suite when she spoke echoed through the house.

All of it brought Margo to an earlier time, when she liked to design and sew in this room, the natural light streaming in through the long windows. Even as the light faded, she had persisted. When he got in, Conor used to call out to her, softly at first as he searched the ground floor rooms. When he realised she was upstairs, his voice became louder, but the tone remained the same, a kind of enunciating and elongating of her name. She heard it now, repeating through the house, searching for her, making her brain throb and hurt.

Shaking herself so she didn't succumb to the loneliness, she banished the memory of his voice as too painful, so that it petered away, like a feather whipped up by the wind. The guests quiet now, the stillness of the house rang in her ears, the dark of the night outside this room walling in on her. She sat waiting for a reply.

Cassie was sitting in her car in the hospital car park, sipping a soda. This was her break. When Vince took over at Tilly's bedside, he told her go home, shower, change her clothes, but instead she was sitting emailing every Congressman she ever heard of, tweeting about her daughter's plight, trying to make a miracle happen, trying to find a donor.

Two days ago she had ended up in the local newspaper pleading with the townsfolk to consider becoming a living kidney donor. There were lots of messages of support and a few who labelled her an oddball pushy all-American Mom, but nothing concrete to give her even a glimmer of hope.

When she saw the email from Margo, she opened it quickly, to avoid the stress of expectation. After she scanned it, she put her head on the steering wheel and sobbed. For now, she had all the hope she needed, that she could make this miracle possible.

From: **cassierichards@gmail.com**
To: **rathmoneyhouse@gmail.com**

Dear Margo,
Thank you a thousand, no, a million times over. I will never be able to thank you enough. Now, I can only hope and pray you will be a donor match.

If that is the case, you will be the miracle maker and I, your grateful friend. My attorney, if he finds out I have made contact is going to get very cross, but it's difficult for anyone outside of us to understand the pull within us, for the girl we raised and the girl we created and nurtured in the womb.

I hope you and Elsa are well and I hope we can get to know each other better.

    Cassie xxx

My Dearest Cassie,

This is such an unusual time for both of us, but talking directly, mother to mother, is our best hope. We alone know our beautiful girls. That we are in such a ludicrous situation is heartbreaking, but by communicating, we can hopefully make sense of this terrible situation we find ourselves in.

I hope I can be a donor to Tilly. Our priority must be our two lovely twelve-year-old girls. I am so glad you found us here at Rathmoney House and yes, I hope we can be friends.

Talk soon.

Yours,

Margo

Margo set the alarm before shutting her iPad and lying down, maybe to sleep.

When Samantha Kiely rang early the next day, her voice was formal, strict even. 'I have a communication here from Cassandra Richards's US attorney saying he did not authorise his client to email you, asking you to take tests to see if you are a kidney donor match. Did you recieve such a message, Margo? Even worse, did you reply without taking my advice?'

Margo didn't answer immediately.

'How could you go and do something like that without even contacting me?'

'If the girl's life can be saved and I can be part of it, that is what I will do.'

'What if it is a deliberate ploy to get you across to the US, where you will be bound by the laws over there?'

'That didn't dawn on me. She pleaded with me mother

to mother, how could I turn my back on that young girl? In another life, she would have been *my* little girl.'

'Margo, if you don't keep me in the loop, I can't act on your behalf.'

'I didn't think I was doing anything wrong.'

'Every action has a reason, every action has a consequence. That is why you need legal representation.'

'I didn't mean to exclude you, but I would rather get on with Cassandra Richards than not. I know she feels the same. She says she doesn't want to take Elsa, and I don't want to take Tilly from her – it seems like we understand each other.'

'She has the most to gain.'

'Samantha, the ones with the most to gain and the most to lose are twelve years old – we can't lose sight of that. While I appreciate you are only looking out for me, I have to make my own decisions here. We are talking about two young girls and their future; I don't want to be the one to mess it up.'

Samantha Kiely sighed deeply. 'It's not my job to be emotionally involved, but to give sound legal advice. We will leave it at that; if you are in further contact, please let me know and under no circumstances agree to go to the US, or make promises on anything else, before consulting with me.'

Margo remembered saying she would keep the solicitor in the loop, but deep down, she knew her only loyalty was to two twelve-year-old girls. When an email arrrived from Cassandra Richards soon afterwards, she opened it immediately.

From: **cassierichards@gmail.com**
To: **rathmoneyhouse@gmail.com**

My Dearest Margo,
I am overwhelmed by your generosity and kindness in this difficult situation.

I thought you might like to know a little about the daughter you have not seen in so long.

We called her Tilly to give her a strong name and she has lived up to that description in mind, if not always in body. Truth be told, our little girl has always been the one to get sick at the drop of a hat and seems to be most susceptible to every bug that ever considered dropping in to our small town. But somehow, she is also the strongest person we know, a little girl who has had to take on a heck of a lot in her twelve years. She is bright, funny and prone to wearing very odd combinations of clothes, calling it fashion. She also loves to play practical jokes and would dearly love to own a dog. But mostly she is a kind, gentle, loving girl.

Last year for my birthday, she made a gorgeous chocolate cake. She has a gift for baking and makes the sweetest, softest pastry for pie. That is all I can think of at the moment. I would love, if you feel like it, if you were to paint a small picture for me of Elsa.

Cassie xx

From: **rathmoneyhouse@gmail.com**
To: **cassierichards@gmail.com**

Dear Cassie,

Elsa is a beautiful young girl with shiny, black hair. She likes to wear it long and loose and hates that she has to tie it up for school. Elsa loves animals and from a very young age would tramp the fields with my late husband Conor, tending to the stock on the farm.

Our Labrador, Max, grew up with her and she still often sneaks him upstairs and into her bed.

After Conor died, it was to Max she turned for comfort and sometimes even now, I often find her head sunk into his neck as he takes on the grief that is left behind.

Elsa is a stubborn girl, she did not walk until she was nearly three years of age. I was so worried, I even took her to the doctor. But Elsa being Elsa, she walked when she was good and ready. There were no cautious stumbles for her, she got up, walked across the room, turned the door handle and off she went.

She also is very good at baking, but then she spent all her young days with Conor, either tending to the farm and the animals or at the kitchen table getting dinner ready.

She misses Conor so much, they had a special bond. Elsa had been doing well at school, though at the moment, so soon after Conor's death, she is finding it hard to concentrate and I know she is questioning the big things, like the meaning of life.

We are meeting at a very strange and hard time in our lives, Cassie, but maybe there would never have been a good time.

Margo xx

From: **cassierichards@gmail.com**
To: **rathmoneyhouse@gmail.com**

Margo,

I am so sorry you lost Conor, a husband you obviously loved and still love very much. This must be a terrible time for you and Elsa. The discovery of Tilly and me must be an extra burden to bear. For that, I'm truly sorry. That Tilly will never know Conor is also a deep sadness.

You are grieving and our intrusion must appear obscene, but I know grief is a beautiful emotion too, in somehow bringing us even closer to the one we have lost. Grief is the price we pay for love and while I never knew Conor, I know his daughter and wife, that's enough to figure he was a very fine man indeed.

My apologies, if you feel I am overstepping the mark. I will understand if you don't want to reply.

Cassie xxx

Margo opened the email and downloaded the picture. Cassie sitting, Tilly standing beside her, her arm around her mother's shoulders. Margo expanded the picture, so that the girl's face almost filled the screen. Her eyes were his, kind, hazel in colour. Conor.

She had his nose too and the way his lips curled when he smiled.

She was looking at the daughter he never knew, which made her feel his loss profoundly. That this girl had not felt his love, and that Elsa would see this girl who looked so like her father made Margo want to bawl her eyes out.

She shut the iPad quickly. Walking to the window, she took in the distant blur of blue that was the sea. Conor would usually be up and about this early, feeding the animals before heading back to the house to cook breakfast for all of them. The horses still walked up the field waiting for him and his bucket.

How could she refuse a chance of a normal life for this girl? She could not look in those eyes and turn her back on her. Tilly was a sensitive girl, she could see it in her. She loved her mother too, she was sure, and she had recently lost a father to separation. There was no father anywhere to guide her now. Like Elsa, she must rely on her mother. They were two mothers trying to do the right thing; two mothers trying to do their best.

Whether their best would be enough remained to be seen. She saw Jack tramping across the fields, two buckets in his hands, feeding the Rathmoney animals before his own.

He was wearing a thick jacket with the hood up, so she knew it must be cold, an icy wind blowing in from the Irish Sea agitating the branches of the trees.

It was the same scene early every morning. If she opened the window, she could hear the birds singing. It was a perfect life here at Rathmoney, or so everybody thought.

Trailing away from the window, she opened the iPad again.

Mother and daughter were beautiful. These were good people caught up in a series of events.

She read the lines written under the photograph.

> **Margo,**
> **This is a photograph I cherish, taken only a few months ago when Tilly was in full health. I hope for your sake you see the resemblance you are looking for and I ask you to open your heart to this girl, who is kind in both heart and in spirit.**
> **May I ask that you do the same and let me look at a photograph of Elsa?**
> **Cassie xxx**

From: **rathmoneyhouse@gmail.com**
To: **cassierichards@gmail.com**

Cassie,

I am glad you wrote what you did. Yes, you know something of Conor in his daughter, like I know something of you in yours. I feel it is both the distance between us and the closeness that allows me to talk to you.

One of the hardest things, when the person you love is gone, is that after the first weeks, nobody wants to say anything. Conor became almost airbrushed out of our lives, spoken only of in hushed tones when I am not around.

Elsa is very quiet too, though sometimes I find her in his study, sitting there staring out the window, as if she expects him to walk across the fields. I know it means she is feeling the same desolation as I am, but we soldier on. How, I don't honestly know.

Tilly looks so like Conor. I know you want to see Elsa, so I am sending a recent photo of the two of us.

Margo xx

Xx

Cassie took in her face, the soft eyes, the tilt of her head, the way the wavy locks fell over her shoulders. Elsa, she guessed, liked to let her long hair fall over and hide her face so she had a barrier between herself and the world. The hair was dark, almost black in colour, much the same as Cassie's.

The photo showed mother and daughter sitting in the sunshine, holding ice creams, both smiling at the camera. Elsa was leaning in to Margo, their shoulders touching. Cassie felt a pang of jealousy at this happy scene before her.

Yet she was reassured to see this girl, her daughter, so loved.

'Mom, turn off your phone, the light is in my eyes.'

Tilly shifted on the hospital bed. Quickly, Cassie filed the photo and closed her phone.

'What were you doing? It's the middle of the night.'

'I couldn't sleep.'

She would have said more, but Tilly had already shut her eyes. Cassie did the same, happy to be able to conjure up an image of the girl who lived so far away, who probably spoke so differently and yet looked so like her.

Chapter Twenty-Two

Rathmoney, County Wicklow.

Ida was late arriving at Rathmoney. Margo had already taken the orders for breakfast and was throwing the sausages in the pan.

'Thank goodness, the guests in the Wallflower Suite want the Rathmoney granola yoghurt pot, did you bring some?'

Ida took a large tub out of her basket. 'I got caught up in the town, Mary Foster took a turn in the thrift shop. I was in the vegetable shop and next thing, there was a shout from a poor customer who had found Mary on the floor.'

'Will she be all right?'

'One of the ambulance men said something about some sort of weakness, something to do with her diabetes. You know what she did before they closed the ambulance door?'

Margo wanted to say she didn't give a hoot and that right now, she only cared about breakfast for the Wallflower Suite.

'She sat up on the trolley and called out to me: "Ida, I'm trusting you to keep the thrift shop running" and she threw the keys at me.'

'How are you going to do that?'

'Well I'm not, am I? Who the hell works for no pay? I have more than enough to be doing here anyway.'

Ida put her hand to her mouth. 'I didn't mean to imply I'm working here for nothing. You know we are glad to help out and the extra land is a huge bonus for Jack. That was a very generous offer from you.'

'Ida, we'd better get on with the breakfast.'

Ida bustled about, but Margo knew she was upset by the set of her shoulders. They got the two breakfasts out without saying another word.

When they heard the guests finish up in the dining room, Margo got down two mugs like she usually did and poured coffee from the pot.

'Maybe we should work out something between us,' Margo said.

Ida waited a few minutes before she spoke. 'Margo Clifford, do you really think I have been muttering in my chest that you are taking advantage of me? I would lay down my life for you and Elsa. Don't even think I'm looking to be paid to get this business off the ground and don't insult me by offering anything.'

Margo listened intently. 'You are so important to us Ida, you and Jack, but I don't want anyone to think we are taking advantage of you.'

'What taking advantage? If I didn't have Rathmoney House to come to every day, what do you think I would be doing? This has been a new lease of life for me and Jack too, though he would never admit it.'

Margo took down the tin where she kept the ginger cake she bought at the bakery in Greystones every Saturday.

'And where else would I get such delicious cake?'

Margo knew Ida was trying to be polite, because she usually

made a face and huffed that shop-bought ginger cake was not a patch on homemade.

'Maybe you are going too far, Ida.'

'Maybe I am,' Ida smirked. She reached over and poured a top-up on her coffee. 'Any more word from that woman in America?'

Margo noted the sharp tone of her voice, the refusal to mention Cassie's name. She fingered the piece of paper in her hand, unsure whether she should share it. She wanted to keep it to herself, but she wished too to talk about this girl who looked so like Conor, it took her breath away.

Taking out the photo printout, she placed it on the table in front of Ida.

'What's this?'

Margo pushed it closer.

Ida stared at the printout. 'It's the child.'

'No doubt.'

Ida picked up the sheet. She was smiling. 'It's like Conor is looking at me.' Ida pushed away the paper and took out a packet of tissues, slowly eased one out and wiped her eyes. 'I suppose she sent you this.'

'I sent her one of Elsa too.'

'You know what she's doing, she's twisting your arm. No, I'm wrong, you're twisting your own arm. This photograph sent to you, only a short time after you have lost your husband, she is trying to brainwash you, mark my words.'

Margo wanted to burst out laughing, but she knew by the set of Ida's mouth, she was fiercely upset. She had other news too, but now was not the time to share with Ida that she was a donor match. A small knock on the kitchen door made Margo hastily fold up the picture and stuff it back in her pocket. When the woman staying in the Wallflower Suite stuck her head around the kitchen door, both Ida and Margo were standing beside the table smiling. The visitor, slightly disconcerted at the reception, apologised profusely for the intrusion.

'I wanted to say that was the best granola I have ever had. Could I be really cheeky and ask about the yoghurt, it was so delicious.'

Ida straightened up. 'I'm so happy you enjoyed it, but I'm afraid it is a Rathmoney special recipe, which means even if you threaten me, I can't reveal it.'

The young woman giggled. 'I admit I have a vested interest. I run a small guesthouse in the UK and I would love to serve the Rathmoney granola pot.'

'Flattering and all as that is, my lips are sealed.'

The woman's laugh filled the room.

'It was worth a try, wasn't it? I just love what you're doing here.'

She said her goodbyes, but Margo waited until she heard the thud of the front door before saying anything.

'What's so special about the yoghurt anyway?' she asked Ida.

'Bugger if I know. I was a bit stuck last night and sent Jack down to Aldi, silly man came back with a spicy apple yoghurt.'

'That's what she was raving about?'

'I could hardly tell her she was eating Aldi's finest.'

'Ida, I can't keep up with you.'

Ida gave a mock bow as they cleared off the kitchen table, before going upstairs to start on the guest bedrooms. They had all the donkey work done and were dusting down the furniture when Ida asked to see Tilly's picture again. Margo pulled the paper from her pocket. Ida took it, flattening it out on the dressing table.

'She has his look, his kind eyes.'

Margo didn't answer, closing her eyes so she could remember him. Last night, she woke up in the early hours, frantically trying to call up his smile. His lips curled down at the corners, giving him a comical look, but she couldn't remember which corner curved down the most. It gave him a lopsided expression. Tilly had a slight lopsided look to her lips. Through Tilly, she would never forget the look of Conor; through Elsa she would never forget his character.

Tilly was finally well enough to be allowed home from hospital with medication, a strict diet and warnings about fluid intake as well as twice-weekly visits for dialysis. Exhausted, Cassie had been at her bedside the whole time. At first Charles came to the hospital every weekend, but Cassie thought he was distracted, always out of the room taking phone calls. Tilly became irritated at him too, constantly asking when was he going to let her visit Baltimore.

For the last two weeks, he had phoned saying he could not leave work. 'It's bad timing, but this is a new part of the business just getting off the ground, I have to stay here.'

'How do you expect me to answer that, Charles?' Cassie replied and he just said he would ring Tilly himself and explain. When she got the call, Tilly's face crumpled, but her reassuring words to her father betrayed none of her true feelings.

Cassie avoided talking to Charles as much as possible after that, often not answering his calls, in the hope it would make him rush to visit his daughter in hospital.

Just days before Tilly was discharged home, Charles turned up, a big teddy bear under his arm. Tilly at first was reticent, but soon was chatting away, glad to see her dad again. After a while, Charles asked to speak to Cassie in the corridor.

'Cas, I understand you have asked the Irish woman to be a donor and I am glad if she agrees. If the insurance company is happy, that's fine with me.'

'There's a but, isn't there?'

'I am not getting caught up in any of the other legal stuff. I have enough going on now, trying to keep the business afloat.'

'You are abandoning Tilly.'

Charles looked angry. 'I am doing no such thing. I'm taking a step back. My health insurance is paying for all this, please don't forget that.'

'Tilly needs you more than ever.'

'Please, no emotional blackmail. Do you think this is easy for me?'

'Do you think it is easy for Tilly?'

'You have this, Cassie; I will check in with Tilly from time to time, but I have to concentrate on the company right now. No business, no bills paid.'

'It's a pathetic excuse.'

Charles moved closer, so she could see the vein on his neck pulsing. 'If Baltimore goes under, it drags everything down with it, then you can forget your operation altogether,' he snapped. He stalked off, without saying goodbye to Tilly.

On Tilly's first night home, Cassie could not leave her bedside.

'Mom, I'm OK, you don't have to stay with me.'

'Hush, sweetie, I want to.'

'But I want the light off.'

'That's OK,' Cassie said as she reached and turned off the bedside light.

For a few minutes, it was quiet and still, the light from the hall throwing funny shapes across the room. The sounds of the street intensified; somebody took a trip to the garbage.

'Is it because you think I am going to die or something?' Tilly asked, her voice tense and urgent. Cassie switched the light back on.

'What?'

'Mom, am I going to die?'

'Darling, once you get the transplant, things will start looking up, you'll be back to your old self. There's no need to be worrying.'

'You didn't answer the question.'

Cassie grabbed Tilly by the shoulders.

'You are not going to die, Tilly Richards, because I won't let you. You will get better and all this will be just a bad memory.'

'Mom, you're hurting me.'

Cassie released her grip, slumping back on the chair beside the bed.

'When Nancy came to visit the other day, she said her mom said it was strange you or daddy weren't a match.'

'Not her again. If she said the world was flat would you believe her?'

'No.'

'Thank heavens for that.'

Tilly reached out to her mother. 'Do you want to get into bed beside me and we can rest together?'

'Thanks, sweetie.'

She nudged in beside Tilly and they snuggled, not needing to talk anymore. There was a long road ahead: she wished she felt as confident as she sounded. Closing her eyes, she tried to banish the doubts, thinking of happier, carefree times when Tilly could just be a kid. Tilly nuzzled into her and Cassie finally fell asleep in the close comfort of her daughter.

Part Two

Chapter Twenty-Three

Rathmoney, County Wicklow.

Margo had been up most of the night going back and forth in her head, desperately trying to find a solution. She sat in her chair by the drawing-room window looking into the still darkness around Rathmoney House. Inside was quiet; Elsa asleep upstairs, the dog stretched out at Margo's feet.

No matter which way she weighed it, she could not travel to the US. It was only a fool who would risk setting foot in that country with Elsa. She knew too, she could not travel without her little girl, who clung to her more than ever since losing her dad. Samantha Kiely was clear in her advice: Margo would be foolhardy to take Elsa to America and the solicitor was against it. Elsa was the biological daughter of Cassie and Charles Richards, the last thing Margo wanted was to be submerged in a legal quagmire in another country.

Margo felt sick, worry churning her stomach. Not only was she about to let Tilly down, but she was fearful Cassie's disappointment and distrust might ignite an unseemly tug of war over Elsa. This was all down to Charles Richards. Samantha said he was an unknown quantity and should not be trusted. She was right. That Tilly should be caught in the middle seemed so unfair, but Margo's loyalty at this juncture had to be to Elsa, the girl she knew and had raised for the last twelve years.

The darkness outside slowly receded, so that in the half light between night and dawn, she could make out the shapes of the trees, the fences around the paddocks, an animal, possibly a fox slinking past the house and down the avenue.

As the birds started to shuffle out of a dark-induced sleep, she sat down to write the email. There was only one way around this. She hoped Cassie could see beyond her initial devastation, to take the course of action she proposed.

From: **rathmoneyhouse@gmail.com**
To: **cassierichards@gmail.com**

Dear Cassie,

I want to help Tilly more than anything, but I have a major difficulty with travelling to the US. I would never travel so far without Elsa, especially since she so recently lost her dad. However, my solicitor has pointed out that if we both enter the country, I leave myself open to an application made in the courts over there in relation to Elsa. Even if it was not successful, the very thought of it is so stressful, I have to ask myself should I travel?

I have wrestled with this and I know you are depending on me, but my priority has to be Elsa. I owe it to our little family not to put her in peril in any way.

I know you are hurting reading this, but it's not you and Tilly I am afraid of, but that Charles, as birth father of Elsa may try in some way to inveigle his way into her life or place some claim over her.

I want to be a donor for Tilly and I am so glad I am a match, but I am too afraid to travel with Elsa to the United States at this time. That is the conundrum I face and I apologise that this email dashes all your hopes.

However, as I have struggled with this, I have come up with a scenario which may work for us. If you can find some way you can bring Tilly to Ireland and she can have her surgery here, I give you my word of honour, I will do everything possible to help. I assure you, I will make no legal claim on Tilly. It has always been my hope we could work something out as we get to know and trust each other.

I know what you are thinking, why should I trust you, but I can only reiterate all that I have said above and also invite you and Tilly to stay in Rathmoney House with us, before and after the transplant.

I know you will have a lot to consider and look into, so I don't expect an answer immediately.

Very kind regards,

Margo xx

Margo clicked the send button, her head pounding. What if Cassie cut off contact or took umbrage on behalf of Charles? It was more than she could bear, but she had to be true to Elsa. Everything must follow from that.

Hours later, Cassie checked her mail as she poured a cup of coffee. She heard her neighbour move his car from the driveway as she scanned down Margo's email. Pushing the cup away, she read it again. Dismay seeped through her. Anger pushed up inside her and she dialled her attorney's number. 'Dale, I know it's early, but an urgent situation has arisen with Tilly. I need to talk to you.'

She called Karen next to come and sit with Tilly, who was still asleep. She was waiting outside when she arrived. 'Tilly can call me when she wakes up, I hope not to be too long.'

She drove to the attorney's office, arriving before Dale. As she waited in the car, she dialled Charles's number. When he answered, she thought his voice was hungover hoarse. 'The medical insurance, will it cover the transplant taking place outside the US?'

'Cas, it's so early, what do you mean?'

'The other mother in this baby mess is a donor match and wants to give a kidney to Tilly, but she won't travel here.'

'Why not?'

'She's afraid of you.'

'Have you been smearing my reputation again?'

'No I haven't, I have everything to lose by her not coming here.'

'What's all this to do with me? I told you, I want to take a step back.'

'She's afraid you could make legal moves to go after her daughter.'

'That would cost big bucks I don't have. What are you going to do?'

'I may have to bring Tilly to Ireland. Can you check the health insurance?'

'It's a mad idea, but OK, if you want me to, I will.'

Dale Winters pulled up in his old Buick as she got off the phone. 'Cassie, just let me open up and we can chat.'

She waited outside, opening and closing the clasp on her handbag over and over, until Dale called her in. 'Cas, what's wrong? I hate to see you like this.'

She handed over her iPad. 'Read that email and tell me what I can do.'

Dale shifted in his seat.

'The woman has a point, Cassie. With a financial settlement in the offing, who knows what Charles would be capable of?'

'I spoke to him just now. He says he's not going to cause trouble.'

'And you believe him?'

'Charles was always good at suiting himself. Deep down, I know Margo is right.'

She stopped to check her phone as a text came in. Her face puckered, pain waved through her. She stood up, but she did not know why. She was lost, like a child who loses sight of its mother in a crowd.

'What is it, Cas?'

'Charles checked with the health insurers, they won't cover for the transplant anywhere else, only the States. Something about no need to travel outside the States. What the hell do they know?'

Dale concentrated on reading Margo's email again. 'I can't fault the legal advice to this mother. She is unlikely to change her position.'

Cassie stood in front of Dale's desk, staring past him to the wall behind. 'What am I going to do? The money I can raise will never be enough to pay for the transplant to happen in Ireland, even if we sell Vince's house along with everything I own.'

Dale leaned back in his seat. 'The French hospital has appointed a mediator; liability is not in issue. The hospital wants this sorted away from the glare of the media. Maybe we can work something out.'

'What do you mean?'

Dale cleared his throat. 'I don't want to get your hopes up, Cas, but I'm thinking if we are close to a financial settlement, maybe I can wrestle something from the French that will satisfy the Irish medics, we are good for the money.'

Cassie dropped her head, the tears forming tiny specks of grey on her shirt.

'Do you think you can do it, Dale?'

'I will do my best, Cas.'

'You are my only hope.'

He stood up as she left. She was not sure afterwards if she even said goodbye.

When she got home, she rummaged for nearly an hour in the basement, looking for the box of baby photos. She didn't know why it suddenly became so urgent that she looked through them, but she wanted to remind herself of those happy first days with Tilly.

She found the box wedged between some of Charles's old tax files. She carried it to the living room, where she sat with it on her knees. When she had carelessly chucked the photos in this shoebox, she was not to know then how important these portraits of those early days would become. The first time she'd held her daughter, Tilly was crying, her face scrunched like a cartoon character. Placed on Cassie's breast, she quietened, happy in the reassurance of her Mom's heartbeat. Charles went up close to capture those initial moments, when anxious noise gave way to peace and calm.

Peering at the photographs from when she was hours old, there was no hint of what was to follow, when the little baby with the thatch of black hair had been taken for a few hours of light therapy to sort out her jaundice. A few hours later she was back in Cassie's arms.

Exhausted by worry, Cassie had fretted that when she stroked her daughter's head, her hair appeared somehow different, but those around her had laughed.

'This baby has been through a lot, allow her not to look her best,' the nurse said gently in English.

The box was full of photographs of the first happy times with baby Tilly. Lazy days with picnics by the river, little Tilly content in her bassinet; long nights when she refused to sleep, one photograph showing Charles in his boxer shorts walking up and down the living room of their small apartment.

Another photograph showed Charles holding Tilly close, her tiny fingers wrapped around his thumb. Charles was grinning. Even now with all that was going on, Cassie treasured these records of when they were so happy. But the pleasure of revisiting those golden moments brought with it the pain of realising things were already not what they seemed, although nobody had known.

Shutting the box quickly, Cassie was cross at herself for dredging up the past.

It was several days before Dale came back with news. 'We are nearly there, Cas. They will have to examine Tilly's file and are waiting on a report from her medical team here, but it looks like it will happen and we will get an undertaking from the French about the settlement of the potential Irish hospital bill very soon.'

Cassie was hardly able to talk as relief coursed through her. 'Are you sure, Dale?'

'Nothing is certain, Cas, until it is, but once they are happy the whole transplant story is for real, it's a matter of getting the wheels in motion and the doctors on both sides liaising to start the work.'

'Tilly is so tired of it all, especially the dialysis and all the diet and drink restrictions. We both are.'

Dale did not reply for a moment. 'Cassie, do you think Charles will make any late-stage objections to you taking Tilly out of the United States?'

Alarm streaked through her, her heart began to pound.

'Dale, why would he do that? He told me he had no problem with it – as long as I wasn't expecting him to pay for it. Why would he change his mind?'

The attorney hesitated at first, but when he spoke, he was firm. 'If he thinks he can use anything – even Tilly – as leverage in your divorce, you can't rule it out. You need to talk to him, Cas, explain how vital it is you get Tilly to Ireland.'

She sat down, looking at the family photograph of the three of them, Tilly doing bunny ears behind Charles's head. It's not that she wanted to go back to those days, but more that she wanted to be free of the constant worry and the stress that filled their lives now.

'Cas, are you all right?'

'Sorry, Dale, I was thinking Tilly has a passport of her own; maybe we should just fly to Ireland.'

'No, we don't want any last-minute hitches. It's time to remind Charles that if he hadn't been so obstructive on the child support, things would be a lot different.'

'I don't understand how you're getting the French to promise to pay for everything, when they haven't made an offer to settle yet.'

'It is only a matter of time. They want a satisfactory outcome and they know by doing this, you will be on side.'

'Will there be anything left, not that I even care, if Tilly can have the transplant?'

Dale laughed.

'Cas, there will be plenty, it's my job to make sure of that. Get things sorted with Charles and we should get the go-ahead from France by the end of the week.'

When Dale rang off, Cassie remained sitting on the couch. She couldn't celebrate, not until they got the all-clear to travel. She dialled Charles's number straight away, because she was afraid if she thought too much about what she had to say, she would get too angry and mess it up.

Charles was in a hurry.

'Is Tilly OK?' he asked

'Yes, I need to talk.'

'Can it wait, I am swamped here?'

'No, it can't.'

'Cassandra, what is it? I have my own life here now.'

'I am taking Tilly to Ireland for the surgery, maybe next week or the week after.'

'You know the insurance won't cover it.'

'I have found a way to finance it, I'm still working out the details.'

'Cas, I'm glad Tilly is going to have the transplant. I wish her the best, I really do, but I'm busy here.'

Cassie took a deep breath.

'I need you to promise you won't do anything to stop Tilly leaving the US.'

'For pity's sake, what do you think I am?'

'You haven't given me your word yet.'

'You're coming back, aren't you?'

'Of course we are.'

'That's all right then.'

'Do you give your word?'

'Yes, now can I go?'

She said goodbye. Somehow, she felt no sense of relief. Charles's lack of interest in what was happening to Tilly was confirmation his new life in Baltimore was a lot more precious to him than his estranged wife and daughter.

Realising they needed to set off for dialysis, Cassie called out to Tilly. 'Time to go, sweetheart. Hopefully the friend you made last week will be there today.'

Tilly who was already dressed, shrugged her shoulders and put in her earphones, a signal she didn't want to chat. As Cassie pulled out of the driveway, a text pinged in from Dale.

'All medical reports in and French say they will get back to us to tomorrow.'

Cassie barely slept that night, staring into the darkness, afraid to hope. Best not to expect too much and have all her hopes dashed. Dale rang her early from home.

'I have an email and an arrangement has been put in place to lodge funds in lieu of payment of all medical bills re the transplant in Ireland. Get on to your medical team and tell them when they decide, you are good to go.'

'Thank you, Dale, you are a true friend.'

Afterwards, she sat for several minutes unable to move and afraid Dale would ring back to say he had got it wrong. Taking deep breaths she went over everything in her head. There were details, a lot of details to be worked out, but they were only details.

She sat down to write an email to Margo.

From: **cassierichards@gmail.com**
To: **rathmoneyhouse@gmail.com**

My Dearest Margo,

I won't pretend I wasn't devastated when I heard you could not travel to the US. However, I understand you cannot go against sound legal advice and I respect your decision, which I know was extremely difficult to make.

It is the measure of you, that at the same time you dashed my hopes, you also threw me a lifeline, which I have grabbed with both hands. I also have been lucky to get good advice from my attorney, who has brokered a deal that the transplant will be paid out of the final settlement.

We are in the happy position that Tilly will soon be cleared for travel and we hope to arrive in Ireland, maybe within the next two weeks. I hope this does not inconvenience you too much, we are already causing so much upheaval in your life.

I am so looking forward to meeting you, Margo, so I may thank you in person for the great thing you have done for my little family.

Love,

Cassie xxx

Chapter Twenty-Four

Rathmoney, County Wicklow.

Margo stood at the top of the front steps, bulging black refuse sacks all around her. When she saw the small van in the driveway, she worried they might not all fit in. The van pulled up and a young man with a tattoo down his right arm jumped out. 'I'm Mary Foster's son. Are these the bags for the thrift shop?'

Margo nodded and he began to throw them in the back.

'You've had quite a clear out,' he said.

Margo didn't know what to answer.

'My mam said to tell you this lot will go on to Bray, she does that...' he stopped, trying to find the right words.

'It's all right, I understand, she does it when someone local dies.'

The young man looked relieved and concentrated instead on throwing the remaining sacks into the back of the van.

'How is your mam?'

'Still not back in the thrift shop fully, but improving. My aunt is running things for her and I help out, when I can.'

He said he had better get along as he had more collections to do. Margo stood on the steps, watching the van go back down the avenue. So much had happened in the space of a few weeks and now the last of Conor was being taken away. The time was right, she was sure, but it still wrenched her heart.

The day before, when Elsa had been at a friend's house, Margo knew the time had come to clear away her husband's possessions. Having finished all necessary assessments and medical tests, a new chapter was about to begin with Cassie and Tilly due to arrive in Ireland.

Margo had taken a deep breath and opened his side of the wardrobe wide. It smelled of clothes locked away for too long, mustiness mingling and overpowering the memory of him. Most of the clothes didn't remind her of the man anymore, only the illness.

Slowly, she pulled shirts, cardigans and jackets from their hangers, folding them into the refuse sacks she had lined along one side of the room. She faltered only when she touched his brown corduroy jacket. She had always hated it, but he refused to throw it away. Funny now that she should dither, when she had a chance to chuck it. She held it up to her face; it smelled of the old Conor, the sweet spicy smell of his aftershave and the hint of cigar, from when he used to sneak a smoke in his little hideout in the far fields. Folding the jacket, she automatically checked the pockets, pulling out a small piece of paper. A list. There were three things on it and the date, such a significant date:

Flowers, M
Kinder egg, E
Bottle of wine

Such a simple note, a note that would be discarded by many, but she knew the significance. The day he got those tests results back from the doctor, he had not rushed home flowing with tears. He had instead brought thoughtful gifts and let Margo and Elsa enjoy the simple pleasure of being truly loved, before the next day when he broke the news of his cancer diagnosis.

Now their lives were set to change again, but she had no idea how, only that she would soon meet the girl she never had a chance to raise. Quickly she gathered up the bundles of trousers from two shelves, working feverishly, trying not to think too much about what she was doing. She filled sack after sack, until there were only a few items left in the wardrobe.

She kept just three reminders of him: the deep blue cashmere jumper he wore for so long she used to tease him it would have to be cut off; the checked tweed coat he bought the previous Christmas, saying he wanted to dress the part when the guesthouse opened; and his US college scarf, which she put in a drawer for Elsa when she got older.

When she got to the back of the wardrobe, there were only two pieces of clothing left. On hangers and wrapped in plastic, his wedding suit and her dress. His suit was an aubergine colour, her dress, off-white silk, cut on the bias. Pulling back the plastic, she pressed the silk, remembering how he told her he had never seen her look so lovely.

'Promise me you will wear it on our twentieth anniversary,' he said and she had laughed, saying she would, as long as he wore that suit, the one he'd had specially made for the wedding.

She sighed now to think how easy it had been in those days to make plans, how easy it was to think the future would be the same as the present. Would that she could see into the future now and see where she and Elsa were destined to be. Catching up the suit and dress, she placed them in a special box marked 'attic'.

Some day in the future, she or maybe even Elsa, would pull these out and wonder about the marriage of Conor and Margo. She looked around the room. With Conor cleared away, it was a different place and it was no huge hardship to move out of their bedroom for a while.

Next Margo sat Elsa down to ask her permission to share her room. 'I think if I was going to a strange place, especially if one us were poorly, I would like to have you near me, which is why I think my bedroom, with the little room off is a good idea for the Americans.'

'Why can't they be in the guest wing?'

Margo was thrown by the question, but she tried not to show it. 'We may not know them well yet, but they are distant cousins, part of our extended family, so they stay in the house with us.'

Elsa appeared satisfied with this explanation.

'I can have you to myself,' she said, running into Margo's arms for a hug.

'I am always here for you, you soft thing.'

Elsa pulled away. 'Even if you give this girl a kidney?'

'You know why I am doing it, I am a match and I can spare a kidney. I just want to help her.'

'Do they know daddy is dead?'

'Yes, they do.'

Elsa began clearing a place in her wardrobe for a few of Margo's things. They worked side by side for about ten minutes, before Elsa asked another question. 'Am I supposed to be friends with the girl?'

'I hope so, it might be nice for you to have more company around here.'

'I hope she's not too sick. What will we do if she doesn't like dogs?'

'Who doesn't like dogs? Somehow, I don't think that is going to be the case, her mum says Tilly always wanted to have a dog.'

After they had reorganised Elsa's room, they set about getting the main bedroom and annex ready for Cassie and Tilly. Elsa picked a soft blue colour and they roller painted the walls together, not caring that fine speckles of paint landed on their clothes and hair. When they were finished Elsa stood back and took the room in. 'I like this room; when they go back to America, can I move in?'

Margo reached over and flicked Elsa's hair. 'When they go back home, you can do anything you want.'

Cassie was exhausted. When word came that agreement had been reached between the US and Irish hospitals on the schedule for the final preparation towards transplant, she sank to the floor and cried. She could have curled up on that spot and stayed there, but instead she emailed Margo.

From: **cassierichards@gmail.com**
To: **rathmoneyhouse@gmail.com**

Dear Margo,

Tilly has been cleared for travel and all arrangements are made with the Irish transplant team. We can now come to Ireland.

There is a long road ahead, but at least we are now taking the steps forward. As you know, Tilly is on dialysis and will have to travel to Dublin for it two days after she arrives, but it's a small price to pay. Doctors have told me that you started your preparation work-up a while ago too, so the transplant should be good to go very soon.

I am exhausted now from all the preparation, but I feel a tremendous happiness that we will finally meet and in such amazing circumstances. I will email when I have exact dates and times.

We hope to be with you and Elsa very soon.

Cassie xxx

Chapter Twenty-Five

Rathmoney, County Wicklow.

Elsa was dawdling. She didn't want to leave, but Margo was insisting.

'There will be plenty of time to get to know them when you get home. Anyway, I'm sure they will just go to bed and try to sleep off the jetlag.'

Margo shoved Elsa's lunch box in to the knapsack.

Elsa shrugged her shoulders. 'Whatever.'

Margo bit her lip, not wanting to send her daughter away with her ears burning from a telling off. Once Elsa had been collected, Ida hurried up the driveway, so she was out of breath by the time she pushed up the latch on the back door.

'Jack just texted to say he's on his way, they should be here in just over an hour, depending on traffic.'

Ida nattered on, but Margo wasn't listening.

When Ida tugged her sleeve, to pull her to sit at the kitchen table, she allowed herself to follow.

'You need to gather your thoughts, prepare.'

'Everything is done, the rooms are ready.'

Ida reached into her basket. 'I brought some flowers to put in the mother's room.' She busied herself filling a glass vase with water and arranging the blooms. 'Are they in the Wallflower Suite?'

'I decided to give them my room at the front.'

'What?'

'It wasn't difficult to get it organised.'

'Why?'

'Because it's bigger and with the little room off, they can be close to each other.'

Ida put down the vase on the draining board. 'But what about Conor's clothes?'

'I sent them to the thrift shop.'

Ida grimaced, but made no further comment out loud. Picking up the vase, she said she would place the flowers on the chest of drawers beside the bay window. Margo heard her tramp slowly upstairs, the boards creaking in the front bedroom as she crossed the floor to the window.

When she heard Ida descending the stairs, she braced herself for criticism.

'You have done a lovely job of that room; it looks right nice.'

'I moved a single bed into Elsa's for me, she likes the idea of company and I think I will too, until this is all over.'

'Whatever suits,' Ida said, trying very hard not to cause a fuss about something which was none of her business anyway.

Margo looked at Ida oddly, but was glad not to face a cross-examination. She expected a grilling about Conor's clothes, but Ida kept her counsel.

Ida touched Margo's arm gently. 'Jack said they are turning off for Rathmoney, they will be here in five minutes or so. Do you want me to stay or go?'

Margo took Ida's hand. 'I think I need to do this on my own.'

Ida, a rigid smile on her face, said she would skedaddle out the back.

Margo stood inside the drawing-room window, waiting for the first glimpse of Jack's Jeep.

The dog, sitting at the bottom of the steps, may have heard the engine from far off, because he stood up and wagged his tail. Margo took it all in. How many times had she stood here waiting for Conor to pull up? Excited with his latest purchase, he would tell her to be out on the steps. Like a kid, he would emerge from the car beaming, with a long story and a huge shopping haul.

Here she was waiting for another American, but there was no sense of excitement, only worry swelling through her. Max, ears alert, wagged his tail fiercely, watching the bend on the avenue; the horses, familiar with the sound of Jack's Jeep, rested their heads on the fence and waited. A wagtail fluttered onto the window sill, pecking at the paint, strutting about, its tiny head flicking from side to side.

The Jeep came into view, coasting up the avenue, dipping in and out of the potholes.

The wagtail launched into the air, flying low under the wooden planks of the fence and across the fields towards the sea.

Margo's mouth was dry, her legs stiff as she made her way to the front door.

Max pranced about excitedly, giving the odd bark.

Not sure where to stand, Margo stepped down two of the steps, nervously straightening her clothes with the palm of her hands.

Jack jumped out of the Jeep when it halted, rushing around to the passenger's side to help Cassie down. Tall, with fine features framed by strands of hair from a messy bun, Margo thought Cassie looked beautiful.

On the ground, Cassie took in Rathmoney House in the sunshine.

'Awesome,' she called out, twirling around to get a better view.

Tilly refused Jack's help, getting out to stand behind her mother. Margo stared at her, a range of emotions flitting across her heart. She looked overwhelmed, a shy girl, her shoulders hunched, the long black hair falling over most of her face. She tugged at her mother's jacket like a nervous toddler, making Margo want to rush to reassure her, hug her tight.

Cassie, who was watching Tilly as she stroked the Labrador, spun around when she heard the footsteps.

'I don't know what to say, Margo.'

'No need to say anything.'

'There are no words big enough to accurately record my thanks.'

'Don't be daft, anyone would do the same.'

Cassie called to Tilly, who was leaning on the fence looking at the horses.

Reluctantly she left her post, walking slowly towards her mother. Cassie reached out, smothering her daughter in a warm embrace. She peeped through at Margo, her eyes wary. Margo saw Conor in those eyes, his reticence in a new situation, his shy demeanor. That he was not here to see this girl and welcome her to Rathmoney House made her profoundly sad.

A tinge of jealousy spiked through Margo when she saw Tilly nuzzle in, hiding her face in the folds of Cassie's blouse. Cassie picked up on her daughter's hesitancy.

'Please don't think we are rude, but maybe we can do proper introductions later.'

'Of course,' Margo said as she led the way to the front door, Jack following with the cases.

Cassie whistled under her breath when she was shown into the front bedroom.

Standing at the window, she took in the view. 'It's so peaceful here, I can feel myself cranking down a notch already. Is that the sea?'

'The Irish Sea, it will be too cold yet for swimming,' Jack said as he placed the cases to one side of the room.

'I'm going to have a dip in that sea one day soon, I'm not afraid of a bit of cold,' Cassie said.

Jack took her in; she was tall, her face was open and friendly, framed by long black hair with deep purple highlights. He saw the determination in her eyes and he wondered how she would fit in with the pace of life at Rathmoney House.

Margo beckoned Tilly to follow her to the little room.

'You can have your own space in here, if you like.'

'Thanks,' Tilly said shyly and Margo thought she had Conor's reticence as well as his gentle nature. She wanted to cuddle her, stroke her hair, ask her questions, but she kept it formal, in case she lost the grip altogether and blurted out something inappropriate which could not be unsaid.

'Is Elsa about?' Cassie asked.

Margo recognised the attempts made to downplay the request.

'She wanted to be here, but I said she should have a normal day at school, and that you guys would want to rest.'

Cassie looked disappointed.

Tilly kicked off her shoes and lay on the double bed. 'Mom, I can even see the sea from here in bed.'

Margo quickly excused herself and told Cassie to drop downstairs when she was ready. She crossed the floor in four strides, waiting until she was on the landing and had pulled the door shut behind her, before she let the tears sweep down her face.

That his daughter should pick on the one important fact about the placement of the bed was both a joy and a shock to Margo.

The very first day they viewed Rathmoney House, Conor had sat against the side wall.

'There's no point having a bed in this room, if we can't marvel at the view as we loll against the pillows,' he said.

It's why they had often slept with the curtains wide open, so they could sit up and watch the early morning sun rise, sprinkling gold across the Irish Sea and shoots of pinks into the sky. When he was ill, Conor sat for hours gazing at the sea, often calling for his binoculars in the hope of identifying the seabirds and the odd seal which slunk up on to the quiet beach early in the morning, or the cargo ships that slid across the horizon. That this American daughter of theirs should now do the same was exhilarating, joyful and poignantly sad, all at once.

Cassie followed Margo down the stairs almost straight away.

'You have such a beautiful home, I imagined something different.'

'Not as fancy, I guess. I'm glad to surprise you.'

She walked to the drinks cabinet and picked up a bottle of whiskey with one hand and a bottle of Baileys in the other.

'What's your tipple?'

'Whiskey, please.'

'Ice?'

'Have you ever met an American who doesn't?'

'Conor liked his drinks chilled, but he never let an ice cube near his whiskey.'

'Conor was American?'

'Irish American.'

Cassie walked around the drawing room, taking in the velvet couch, the heavy drapes, the table with the little boxes. 'You are a collector?'

'Conor was, he liked to buy a box everywhere we went. He said every box held a story from our lives. When we were old, we could occupy ourselves trying to remember those stories. It seemed like a good idea at the time.'

'It's a good idea, but maybe you're not ready yet to cherish those memories.'

Cassie picked up a black lacquer box.

Margo gently but firmly took the box from her.

'Another time, please.'

Cassie put her glass down.

'I have offended you, I'm sorry, the jetlag is making me do stupid things.'

'No, it's fine, it's just that sometimes, even the good memories are so painful.'

Cassie, not sure how to react, sat on the velvet armchair by the window. Margo plopped down at the end of the couch, where she could look directly at her visitor.

'Let's start over. I'm sorry if I sounded sharp.'

'Perfectly understandable; I am fidgety, nervous, I guess.'

'We have to stay friends, there's too much at stake for both of us.'

'God yes, that would be unforgivable.'

They smiled at each other, both wary, hesitant.

'How is Tilly?'

'Awfully tired, she's in bed listening to her music.'

'But she is good for the operation?'

'I hope so, we have been doing all the preparation work-up. Her bloods are good. She attends for dialysis.'

'I have done all the work-up as well.'

'I'm sorry about all the hassle you have had to go through.'

'No need to be.'

'I mean this other business; I wish I had never fought Charles so hard, this baby business would have remained secret.'

Margo took a gulp of her whiskey.

'Now, that's silly talk.'

Cassie swirled the whiskey in her tumbler, the ice cubes chinking.

'I feel so bad causing all this trouble, all the times I have wished to turn back the clock, let Charles go, let him off free.'

'You would still have ended up looking for a donor.'

Cassie looked at Margo.

'How would I have found you, then?'

Margo thought for a minute before she spoke.

'You may not have.'

Cassie put her glass down on the window sill.

'I can't bear to think about it.'

'You don't have to. At least that's going to be sorted very soon.'

'Are you afraid?' Cassie asked.

Margo shifted, pulling her feet up under her.

'Terrified.'

'Tilly is worried, but she tries to hide it from me.'

'Maybe I can talk to her; if she knows I'm not so brave, it might help.'

'That's so kind of you.'

'Maybe I just want to sit and talk to her.'

Cassie laughed. 'That's exactly how I feel about Elsa, but I don't have such an in.'

'Two of us going under the scalpel is quite enough, thank you.'

Cassie laughed again. 'How is it I find it so easy to talk to you? There are some who would say we should be at each other's throats.'

'The only people who will gain from that are the lawyers. I have something to ask you.' Margo, almost afraid to say her words out loud, leaned towards Cassie. 'Things sometimes go wrong. I need an assurance from you, in case they do.'

'But that's not going to happen.' Cassie stumbled over her words.

'I hope it doesn't, but if I don't come back from the operating theatre, I want you to promise me one thing.'

'Anything, you know I will.'

'Hear me out, before you say yes.' Margo sighed deeply. 'If something awful happens and I don't survive, I want you to walk away and leave Elsa here with Ida and Jack.'

Cassie made to speak, but Margo put up her hand to stop her.

'Elsa has only just lost her dad, to lose me would be a killer blow. She would need to be around people she knows and loves and who love her. She would also need not to be burdened by this terrible swap mess. Can you do this for me?'

Margo stopped, the emotion of what she had said too much for her. Cassie turned away to look out the window. Margo sat back on the couch, suddenly fearful.

When Cassie turned back to face Margo, tears were spilling down her face.

'I give you my word.'

'Your word is good enough for me.'

Cassie wiped her tears away with the end of her sleeve and sighed.

'We can really talk the heavy stuff.'

'Speaking of heavy stuff, have you told Tilly anything?'

'About the swap, no.'

'We have to decide if and when we tell the girls.'

'Can we wait until after surgery? Tilly needs all her strength, I want her to concentrate on recovery, not be distracted by this.'

'Exactly my thinking. To that end, I have told Elsa you're my cousin and I'm a donor match and will be donating a kidney.'

'I suppose having a long-lost American cousin is nothing unusual in these parts.'

'It should suit this situation and satisfy those who seek to pry.'

'I hadn't thought of any of that.'

'You have enough on your plate.'

Margo topped up their glasses. 'There will be plenty of time to get to know each other; this is a huge step for such a young girl, I know that.'

'And for you; you are giving her the ultimate gift.'

'I'm glad I can help.'

'You know I would do the same for Elsa.'

'I do.'

They sat, the sound of the hall clock ticking a reminder that time, for them, was now more precious.

Cassie broke into the silence.

'When is Elsa home?'

'Not until the afternoon. She's not sure yet how she feels about this.'

'Maybe when she gets to know us she'll feel less worried. I brought her a gift but I'll wait until I think she's ready.' Cassie put her glass down. 'Margo, there's nothing to measure my gratitude to you. All I can give is my word, I will do nothing to separate you and Elsa. We can work things out, I hope.'

'Me too.'

Margo got up and poked the fire so that sparks went up the chimney.

Cassie reached into her handbag for her packet of cigarettes. 'May I?'

'I don't allow smoking in the house, but just this once, because the girls are not here.'

'I went back on the cigarettes, had been off them for years, but at the moment they are the only thing that keeps me sane. Maybe when the transplant is done, I can throw them away.'

'It might help when you have to stand out in the cold every time you want a smoke,' Margo joked, handing a small saucer to Cassie to use as an ashtray.

Cassie snapped open a silver lighter and lit her cigarette, taking in a long drag before blowing the smoke up to the ceiling, where it billowed around the crystal chandelier.

'I often sit in the car in the driveway, smacking on a cigarette, wondering how I got into this terrible situation and trapped you in it too. We owe it to each other to make the best of this.'

'Now the transplant is nearly underway, I can get my solicitor to start looking towards a solution we will all be happy with.'

'And I can instruct my attorney to co-operate.' Cassie puffed some more smoke up to the chandelier. 'If your housekeeper finds any stains on the crystal, she can blame me.'

'I don't have a housekeeper, Ida and Jack are my friends and neighbours from across the way.'

'They know?'

'The only ones who do.'

Cassie got up and stubbed out the remains of her cigarette.

'I need to rest before Elsa gets back. Thank you, Margo, for everything.'

When Margo responded, Cassie enfolded her in a big hug.

Crying quietly, Cassie could barely speak before pulling away, saying she should go to Tilly. Margo stood by the window.

Outside on the stone steps, Max the Labrador surveyed the land before settling down. Jack, who had changed into his work clothes, chipped away at the moss around the main gate. Ida had offered to collect Elsa, so Margo sat and waited for her daughter to come home, to meet the new guests in Rathmoney House.

Slumping into the wingback chair, she felt exhausted, she wanted to run upstairs and hug this shy young girl, welcome her home and bore her to bits with stories about her dad. That she couldn't do any of this hurt unbelievably.

She'd only known her for a day back then, but she looked into her eyes now and she felt an enormous love for her, a love she only previously held for Elsa. Twelve years had passed and her daughter was Elsa, she would never let that go, but this Tilly, nervous and unsure to be here at Rathmoney, was every bit her child too.

The memory of her baby flooded back, the warmth of her as she'd held her close, her tiny face still scrunched as if she wanted to hide from the daylight. Her fingers were so long, her thatch of hair silken. When she was born, the chateau owner had wrapped her in a soft blue blanket, the name of the chateau monogrammed in one corner. She had held her close in the back of the ambulance, only allowing the hospital nurse to take her to weigh her and measure and check her over, before placing her in a bassinet.

Conor, frantic, had abandoned his car at the hospital door and run up two flights of stairs, arriving in the room out of breath and panting. He was afraid to hold her at first, getting down low by the cot and stroking her gently.

She had kissed each of her little fingers before she was taken away for light therapy, and whispered *I love you* to her, over and over.

Margo closed her eyes, lost in the memory, when a small voice raised her from her reverie. 'Pardon me, could I have a drink of water, please? Mom is asleep and I don't want to wake her.'

Margo looked at the young girl in the Disney pyjamas. She was so like him, Margo thought. There was a gentleness about her that was Conor. 'Of course, I should have left some in your room. Are you allowed much to drink?'

'Not really, I have to watch it.'

Margo got up and beckoned Tilly to follow her to the kitchen. She poured a glass of water from the filter jug she kept in the fridge and sat opposite Tilly as she drank. 'It must be strange for you, having to travel here.'

'Mom says it's the only way I can have a chance of getting better.'

'We all want that for you.'

'Where is your daughter?'

'Elsa is at summer camp, she should be home any minute.'

Max pushed in the back door. Tilly called him over and he approached her, wagging his tail, pushing his snout into her lap. 'He's so cute.'

'Do you have pets?'

'No, Daddy said they were too much work. I had a goldfish once, but I think I overfed him and he died. I was at a slumber party and Mom only noticed when the water went a funny colour.'

When they heard the front door opening, Margo called out. 'In here, darling.'

Elsa rushed to the kitchen. 'Mum, guess what happened today?' She stopped talking when she saw Tilly sitting at the table, and hung back at the doorway. Margo took in her watchful eyes, her cheeks slightly pink with nerves.

'Come, say hello, Elsa.'

Elsa did as she was bid, mumbling a quiet *hello*. Tilly smiled. Margo let the quiet between them linger as Elsa sat down at the table. Margo turned away, pretending to be busy pouring a drink for Elsa.

Tilly was the first to break through the silence. 'You have a lovely dog.'

Elsa smiled, calling Max over to her. Putting her fingers to her lips to tell Tilly not to say anything, she took a biscuit from her pocket. Showing it to the dog, he sat and put his paw on her lap, before gently taking it from her hand. Tilly, her eyes wide in admiration, stifled a laugh.

'What happened today?' Margo asked.

'Ava fell over and was taken to hospital, they think she's broken her ankle,' Elsa said.

She turned to Tilly. 'Do you want to come out and feed the horses some treats?'

Tilly grinned 'Do I need to get changed?'

Margo turned around. 'Best not wake your mum, I'm sure we can find socks, wellies and a coat for you.'

Elsa ran off to the coat rack, coming back with pink wellies, thick socks and a jacket. Excited, Tilly pulled on the Wellingtons, not letting on that they were a fraction too big for her.

Before they went out, Margo pulled Elsa aside. 'Tilly is jet-lagged and because of her kidney not working right, she might need to take things a bit slow, so don't run off on her.'

Margo went to the drawing-room window, where she could see them climb the fence and head to the lower field. She was glad when she saw Elsa give her hand to Tilly to help her down from the bottom rung of the fence. How quickly they had stepped in together, she thought, and it made her happy.

Cassie was on the landing, on the way back from the bathroom, when she bumped into Elsa. Elsa laughed when they practically collided and Cassie recognised Charles's loud guffaw. She wanted to run her hand down her long hair, the same colour as her own. She also had Cassie's delicate features. 'You must be Elsa.'

Elsa, feeling shy, just nodded but took Cassie's hand when it was extended.

'Have you met Tilly?'

'Yes, we went to the field to see the horses.'

'How lovely, I'm sure Tilly enjoyed that.'

'I have to go now, we're going to play Cluedo.'

Elsa pulled her hand away and skipped down the stairs. Feeling a little light-headed, Cassie returned to the bedroom. Such an ordinary encounter and yet such an extraordinary one. She was back in the birthing suite, Charles telling her their baby was a beautiful girl. Her first cry was a joy. She had held her, skin touching skin until they took her to weigh her.

Cassie had insisted her baby be in the bed beside her. She'd held her in her little nest of blankets, Charles sitting beside them beaming with pride, neither able to find the words for the extent of their happiness. When she needed light therapy the next day, Cassie had let her go and fallen into a deep sleep. Life had been so good back then.

But now, even the happy memories were tainted by the events unearthed by Charles's stupid attempt to avoid child support. Taking a cigarette from the packet, she pushed up the sash window and sitting on the ledge, she lit up. These were strange days, but they would pass, she thought as she blew the smoke out the window, letting it glide across the garden.

Chapter Twenty-Six

Rathmoney, County Wicklow.

The next morning, Ida wasn't sure if she should go over to Rathmoney House at her usual time, but she chanced it anyway.

She dithered on the avenue when she saw the curtains were still pulled across in the upstairs bedroom. Shafts of sunshine sheeted across the front of the house, but there appeared to be nobody up to welcome the morning. When she saw Max amble around the front, wagging his tail before flopping onto the gravel of the avenue, Ida knew somebody must have let him out. She stopped briefly to inspect the herb patch and thought she must remind Jack to put out beer to attract the slugs, as they had destroyed the lettuces Elsa had sowed just a while back.

At the back door, she hesitated again, waiting to peep in the kitchen window to check if Margo was up. Elsa was eating a bowl of cereal at the table. She knocked, but Elsa didn't hear it because she had her earphones in, listening to music. Ida was scrabbling around in her handbag for her keys when the door swung open.

'Ida, there's nobody else up.'

'The Americans probably have jetlag.'

'Mummy said they will be tired for a few days, because of the stress of the flight.'

'What do you think of them?'

'I don't know.' Elsa bounded off up the stairs.

Ida was scrubbing pots when Margo came into the kitchen.

'I thought I would catch up on a bit of spring cleaning.'

'Ida, it's still summer.'

Ida put down the pot.

'OK, I admit it, I'm dying to meet this Cassie woman properly.'

'I heard her wandering about late last night, I would say she is still fast asleep.'

Ida's face fell in disappointment.

'Mary Foster already rang asking about your visitors; she said everybody was saying they were supposed to be long-lost cousins.'

'At least we got that right,' Margo muttered as she spooned coffee into the machine.

'As long as you let the American in on the secret,' Ida replied.

'What secret?' Elsa called out as she scooted through the kitchen to grab a carton of juice from the fridge.

'No secret, just Ida and her talk,' Margo said quickly, but Elsa had already run off to watch television.

Ida laughed but peeked at Margo, afraid she was cross.

Margo was too tired to chastise Ida and announced she was going back to bed. Ida scrubbed the pots more fiercely, humming a tune to herself, so that when Tilly stepped into the kitchen, she didn't even notice.

Tilly sat on the floor, eye to eye with Max, patting his head. When Ida turned to hang the shining clean pots from the rail near the hob, she didn't see the girl at first and gruffly told the dog to move.

'I don't think you should talk to him like that,' Tilly said, making Ida jump.

'Where did you spring from?'

Tilly stood up, and extended her hand.

'I'm Tilly; my mom said I had to introduce myself properly today, because I was such a grump yesterday.'

Ida took her hand.

'Very pleased to meet you. Call me Ida.'

'Do you work here?'

'Yes and no. I'd like to think I care more about this place than someone just doing a job.'

'Mom says everything is old-fashioned here, but I'm not to say anything.'

'Well, you're doing a mighty fine job of that. Now, get up off that floor, we don't want your kidneys getting cold, as well as everything else.'

Tilly sat at the table.

'Are you hungry?'

'Can I have pancakes?'

'You can.'

'Can I help make them?'

Ida got a bowl from the cupboard.

'Why don't you go to the drawing room and call Elsa? She loves pancakes, we can all make them together.'

Tilly got off the chair and made to go out the door, but she turned back.

'I don't know what to say.'

Ida rubbed her hands together in mock frustration.

'How about "we are making pancakes, would you like to join us?"'

Tilly disappeared but came back almost as fast.

'She didn't answer.'

'Did she hear you OK?'

'I think so.'

'Maybe she's still a little sleepy. Why don't we just get on with it; I'm sure if Elsa wants to join us, she will.'

'What recipe are we using?'

'Ida's recipe from my head, sure all we need is butter, eggs and milk?'

'And vanilla,' a voice at the door said, and Elsa stepped in to the room.

'My dad always put in two drops of vanilla. He made the best pancakes ever.'

Tilly swung around to Elsa.

'My dad never made pancakes; was it fun?'

Elsa nodded her head enthusiastically. 'And at weekends we had a special pan for flipping.'

'Cool.'

Elsa ran to the big drawer under the sink. 'Ida, do you think we could make extra to flip?'

Ida looked at the two expectant faces; two happy girls with no idea of their past.

'It's not the weekend, but it's the first full day Tilly and her mum are here at Rathmoney House, so flipping pancakes it is.'

Both girls clapped their hands in excitement, before rolling their sleeves up to get busy cracking the eggs into the well of the flour, adding the milk and vanilla and taking turns stirring.

Ida pulled back, letting them work and chat side by side, their heads touching at the kitchen table; Max strategically positioned between them, ever hopeful of a spillage.

At one stage, Jack called at the back door, but the girls barely noticed him.

He laughed when Ida snapped at him to go home for breakfast, they were too busy.

Elsa took over flipping operations before they had even tasted a pancake.

'I'm sure your daddy left it until the end,' Ida said.

'That doesn't mean it was the best thing to do.'

'I suppose it could be a good thing to work up an appetite.'

Elsa put the frying pan on the hob and Tilly poured in some mixture.

'Not too big, we want to have lots to flip,' Elsa said.

They stood watching the pancake bubble and cook.

When it was ready, Elsa transferred it to the flipping pan.

'So we don't flip any hot burnt butter on ourselves.'

She handed the pan to Tilly.

'I don't know how.'

'Give it a go, just straight up,' Ida said.

Tilly positioned herself in the middle of the floor, her legs apart, holding the pan stiffly with her two hands.

Max moved over to stand beside her.

'On three,' Elsa said, starting to count.

Tilly flipped the pan up, the pancake shot into the air and landed half on and half off the table, breaking up on the oilcloth. Max ran to the table, pulling at the pancake until it was all on the floor and he gobbled it up. Tilly stood, her mouth open, not sure how to react.

'Don't worry, that happened to me the first few times as well. Let me show you,' Elsa said, taking the pan and transferring another pancake.

'It's in the grip, flick from the wrist and not too high at first.'

The dog, realising he may not get another pancake, lay on the floor watching.

'Try again,' Elsa said, handing the pan to Tilly.

She did, flipping low and successfully.

'Do we have to eat the flipping pancakes?' Tilly asked.

'God forbid! While you two were busy trying to wreck the joint, I cooked yours. All you have to do is decide on a topping,' Ida said, placing two plates with warm pancakes on the table.

Elsa ran to the cupboard and took out the Nutella.

'I didn't think you had that over here,' Tilly said.

'Course we do, we have everything here,' Elsa replied.

Ida worked around the girls, filling the dishwasher as they chatted at the table. As she picked up the flipping pan, Elsa called out to her.

'Can me and Tilly flip one like crazy, so Max can get it?'

Ida handed over the pan.

They got in the middle of the floor, Elsa's hand over Tilly's.

'One, two, three.'

The pancake shot across the room, making the Labrador push past Ida and catch it before it hit the ground.

'I think that's quite enough pancakes for a whole week. That dog is going to get too fat,' Ida said.

Elsa turned to Tilly.

'Do you want to come to my hiding place?'

'Yes please.'

'Come on, then.' Elsa ran off, and Tilly, feeling tired, followed slowly.

Elsa waited for her at the door of Conor's study. When Tilly caught up, Elsa took her hand.

'This was my dad's room and now it's mine, though I let my mum come in here too.' She ran and sat on the swivel chair behind the wide desk.

'Where is your dad?'

'I don't really know. He died and everybody says he is gone to heaven, but I'm not sure I believe them.'

'My dad has left us, it's just me and Mom.'

Elsa swivelled in the chair to look out the window. 'If I sit here, I can pretend everything is the way it used it be.'

'Nancy in my class says my dad is going to have a new family, that's why he didn't visit much when I was in hospital.'

'Did you mind?'

'I don't know.'

'I'll visit you in hospital. Are you afraid?'

'Afraid?'

'Yeah, worried.'

'Oh, scared. A bit.'

They heard Cassie call Tilly's name.

'Quick, let's get under the desk,' Elsa said, pushing the swivel chair over to the window.

They were stuffing their fists in their mouths, trying to stop the giggles, when Cassie stepped into the room.

She was standing, looking at the train engines on their tracks, when Max bounded around the desk. Wagging his tail, he tried to fit in beside the girls, making them squeal and kick out.

'You've met my partner in crime. I knew Max would find you scallywags.' Cassie laughed. The girls bopped up from behind the desk. She stopped to savour this moment of joy, the delight in their faces, the closeness of the two of them.

'Mom, can Elsa be with me later when I take my medicine, please?'

'I guess.'

Just then, Ida called Cassie to the kitchen for coffee, while Tilly followed Elsa upstairs.

'Thank you, Ida, for letting the girls flip pancakes. It means a lot.'

Ida got a china cup and saucer and placed them on the table.

'I won't take the praise for that, those girls got it all together by themselves.'

'I'm grateful, at any rate.'

Ida didn't answer, but busied herself getting a tray ready to bring up to Margo.

Cassie took a flower from the jug in the middle of the table.

'To make it extra special. Do you have a small vase for this?'

Ida rummaged in a top cupboard, taking down a porcelain vase.

'Conor and Margo bought it in Italy.'

Cassie took the vase and walked to the sink, where she filled it with water. Standing looking out the window, she spoke quietly to Ida.

'You don't know me, but I want to say to you as Margo's friend, I am not here to cause trouble. I'll be forever grateful to Margo for what she is doing for Tilly.'

Ida took the vase and placed it on the tray beside the mug of coffee and buttered toast.

'Words are easily bandied about; Ida Roper will give her final verdict according to actions, not empty promises,' she said, making her way upstairs.

Cassie checked she had her cigarettes and walked outside to the barn. Drawing her dressing gown around her, she pulled out the packet, tapping her pockets for her lighter, cursing when she realised she didn't have it.

Jack, who was feeding a horse in the nearby stable, watched for a few moments. She was about to walk back to the house when he called her.

Holding out his lighter, he walked towards her. 'I would prefer it if you didn't smoke in the barn; that place would go up in minutes if there was an accident.'

'I'm sorry, it's just I can't smoke in the house.'

'That makes two of us. Come on, I'll show you my favourite spot.'

He led the way and she followed to an empty stable further down the yard.

Opening the door, she saw there was a table and chairs.

'They can't see us here from the house, but if they call at the back door we can hear them.'

Cassie held out her cigarette pack to Jack and he took one, lighting hers before his own.

'Ida doesn't like you smoking?'

'Nor does Margo. This spot suits me fine.'

'What do you think of the whole situation, Jack?'

He seemed surprised she was so forthright. 'It's for you and Margo, and between you only. Young Tilly is a lovely girl.'

'And Elsa too, so smart.'

Jack stubbed out his cigarette in an ashtray he kept in the drawer of the table. 'I had better get back to work. Feel free to use my smoking shed any time.'

She smiled, reminding Jack of someone beautiful he knew a long time ago.

When Jack was gone, Cassie sat for a while, stretching out, blowing smoke rings out the stable door until she heard Tilly calling. When she got back to the house, Tilly was waiting for her, her face full of excitement. 'Ida says if it's OK with you, I can go into town with her and Elsa. Margo has gone to Bray to the bank.'

Cassie nodded, and after Ida had promised to keep a watchful eye on both girls, she waved them off.

Cassie went upstairs and got dressed, before setting off to find a quiet spot in the garden. She was perched on the stump of an old tree near the river, when Jack spied her.

'So you like the garden?'

Cassie swung around. 'Beautiful, how do you keep it so lovely?'

'I'm afraid it has a bit of a wild look. When Conor wasn't well, there wasn't anybody to tend it, so I try and do a bit now, especially the beds near the house.'

'You must never get any work done on your own place.'

'I'm lucky, I have mainly cattle, this place gives me a chance to indulge in gardening. Real farmers don't care much for flower beds; I have nice specimen trees though and Ida likes her roses.'

'Why put so much time into this garden?'

'Don't tell anyone, but I quite enjoy it and anyway, Margo isn't going to be able to do any of this, with all that is ahead.'

'You're not sure, are you, that she should have put herself forward as a donor.'

'Does it matter what I think?'

'Not really; it's all lined up now.'

Jack got the shovel and pushed it into the ground to dislodge a large dandelion. 'Tilly is a lovely girl, we all want to see her better.'

'But...?'

'It's what happens after that is a worry; Ida has sleepless nights over it.'

'Ida sounds like one of life's worriers.'

Jack bent down to wrench out the stubborn dandelion root. 'Does she have a reason to worry?'

Cassie touched Jack lightly on the arm. 'Not on my part, she doesn't.'

'I'm glad to hear that.'

'Can I help you with this?'

'I'm clearing the bed, Margo has to decide what to plant here.'

'A wild mix would be perfect.'

'We had better get all these weeds out, then.'

He began to dig and she bent down, tugging hard on those he had loosened. 'Aren't you supposed to throw over an old carpet or something?'

'I doubt Ida would allow me to deface the front beds with the old sitting-room carpet. Anyway, she wants this looking good by the end of today.'

'She is a hard taskmaster.'

'She knows what she wants, it's one of the things I admire most about her.'

'I bet you were childhood sweethearts.'

Jack snorted. 'Nothing like that, Ida wouldn't even look in my direction at school.'

Cassie stood up. 'Did you love her from afar for so long? Very romantic.'

Jack dug the shovel extra deep to unearth a large fennel plant. 'That fennel is reseeding and threatening to take over,' he said, trying to divert the conversation.

Cassie, taking the hint, worked quietly beside him, a small hill of weeds forming on the footpath.

After a while he stopped. 'Time for lunch.'

'Why don't you come into the house, I'm sure I can make us a sandwich. Everybody else is out, but I can throw a few things together,' she said, suddenly feeling nervous.

'Are you sure, because I can go home?'

'Nonsense, I've got to make something for myself, anyway. Margo told me to help myself.'

They strolled together to the back of the house and into the kitchen. Jack showed Cassie where everything was and she set about assembling tuna mayonnaise sandwiches. Jack went out and picked a small bunch of parsley from the herb patch, while Cassie arranged the sandwiches on plates. They were sitting at the kitchen table when Ida, along with Tilly and Elsa, returned from shopping in Rathmoney.

'Don't you two look cosy? And there's us rushing home in case you were falling with the hunger,' she said as she took down the sliced pan and began to make some sandwiches for the girls.

'We worked hard in the garden, getting the front bed cleared,' Cassie said, but Ida did not answer. Tilly said she was tired and Ida told her she would bring her a tray in bed.

'I was saying to Jack, wildflowers would be quite stunning in that bed,' Cassie said.

Ida turned and looked at Jack. 'You heard the boss,' she said.

Chapter Twenty-Seven

Rathmoney, County Wicklow.

'Are you really going to put wildflowers in that bed, they will look a holy show?' Ida said a few days later at breakfast.

'I think it's for Margo to decide.'

'She needs something in there that is going to look good year-round.'

Jack put down his mug of tea. 'Ida, this isn't about the flower bed, is it?'

'I'm not sure you should be so friendly with Cassandra, Jack. Any spark sets tongues wagging, you know that.'

'I doubt if anybody is much interested in who I am talking to, Ida.'

'You'd be surprised, there's a lot of talk about the American in Rathmoney. She's making quite a name for herself, going around putting talk on everyone. She just sails into the shops and starts gabbing.'

'Since when was it a crime to be friendly?'

Ida detected an angry tone in Jack's voice, so she left it at that. He said he had fences to mend and went off with his toolbox.

*

Jack was hammering in nails on the paddock fence when he saw Cassie as she walked purposefully along, a big basket under her arm and her dress flowing behind her.

He could make out the shape of her body, the long legs accentuated as the silk dress was pushed between them by the light breeze.

She slowed down when she saw the horses and he wondered should he call out to her, to reassure her.

She took a small box from her bag.

He should not let her feed them, but he wanted to see what would happen. Slowly, the chestnut nudged forward as she held out chunks of apple on the palm of her hand. The mare would not indulge, so the chestnut gobbled the lot, leaning against Cassie when it was all gone. Jack was about to call the cheeky pony off, but he saw Cassie confidently push him away, continuing on the path to the sea. This was a woman waiting for her daughter to go into hospital, possessed of a bravery only those who have sat by the bedside of a sick child would understand.

Cassie climbed the fencing at the far end, stopping to fix her hair, which had fallen out of its loose ponytail, before tramping across the rough sand-infused land. It gave way to a pebbly spit and a well-worn path brought her down to a tiny sandy crescent, cut off by a small outcrop from the public beach.

Everybody called this spot Rathmoney House strand: the land here had once been good fertile soil, now eroded, pulled back by the waves into the sea.

Cassie threw her basket on the ground, spreading her towel before sitting down and stretching out. It was midday, but the day was just beginning back home. She took her phone out. Bonnie's number flashed up on the screen.

'How are you, darling?' Bonnie sounded upbeat.

'OK, I guess.'

'What's wrong?'

'I just want this to be done. I've come out for a walk while Tilly is sleeping but I can't stop worrying. Tell me some gossip to distract me.'

'Zack says all is forgiven, come home. Last week he sent out the office junior to close a million-dollar deal and she only went and told the clients that there was a zoning problem with some of the land. You can imagine what happened.'

'Did he roar and shout?'

'He did more than that, honey, he got so mad he went stir crazy, threw a plant pot which smashed through the window, bounced off the sidewalk and landed on the hood of the sheriff's car.'

Cassie giggled.

'Don't tell me Mr Perfect was arrested.'

'Taken away and cautioned. His wife has gone and booked a trip to Europe, says the man needs a vacation.'

'Old Zack won't want to leave the United States.'

'I don't know what you are laughing at girl, he might just turn up at your door.'

'Christ, no, Bonnie, spare me that.'

Bonnie laughed heartily. 'I have to run. I'll ring again on Thursday, maybe the old guy will provide another episode of fun for us. Tell me if you get any news on a surgery date for Tilly before then, though. I know the waiting must be driving you crazy. Hang on in there!'

Cassie pushed her phone deep in the basket and pulled off her dress before picking her way carefully across the sand, afraid of stubbing her toes on a stone. The sun glanced off her shoulders and she wasn't cold but she shivered, suddenly feeling exposed. The inlet was protected on all sides by land stacked as if somebody had built it that way, but still she was nervous.

Stepping into the water, she felt the cold seep around her,

waves brushing against her legs taking her breath away. Cold crept through her, but she liked it. Wading into the water, she felt alive, the pulsing pain helping to clear her mind.

Launching herself into the depth of the water, she let it curl around her as she swam with strong strokes parallel to the shore, the rhythmic movements making her body warm up.

When she waded out, she ran across the sand, quickly towelling herself before the first exhilaration of the swim faded.

Jack waved to her as he walked across the tufted grass.

'Was the water too cold for you?'

'Invigorating.'

'I saw you walk across the fields earlier. Try not to feed the horses or they will pester you every time.'

'It's just a few apple slices.'

'Buster, the chestnut, can get a bit pushy.'

She laughed and he thought she looked younger somehow. 'Do you have your own private beach, too?' she asked.

'We're on the wrong side of the road for that, but the land is not as scraggly; swings and roundabouts.'

She bundled up her towel and stuffed it in the basket without folding it. He turned away as she slipped on her dress over her swimsuit.

'Do you mind putting the work in to somebody else's farm?'

'I want to help out, keep things ticking over for Margo, she has enough going on. Conor would have done the same for Ida.'

'Tell me about him.'

'He was a quiet man, a brilliant chef, he would have been great at running the guesthouse, but a terrible farmer.'

'But Margo said—'

Jack chortled. 'Conor couldn't help it, he wasn't made like that. The animals were his friends; you don't send your friends to the slaughterhouse.'

They started walking up through the sandy grass as far as the fence. He held her basket as she climbed over.

'How is Tilly today?'

'Good, we just have to keep her on track for surgery.'

'She and Elsa are getting on.'

'I want a friendship to grow between the two of them.'

'I don't know Tilly, but when it comes to Elsa, just give her time.'

'Time … it shouldn't be a word of any significance for girls so young, but time is something Tilly can't spare.'

She could tell he felt foolish, dropping his head and walking on. She fell into step beside him until they came upon the horses. 'If you don't mind, I have a little apple left over.'

'Buster will plague you for life.'

Shrugging his shoulders, he walked ahead, calling the horses by pursing his lips and making a strange braying noise. She was going to laugh until she saw the two animals amble from the far corner of the field towards them.

'Are you some sort of horse whisperer?'

'Nothing like that. I feed them, nothing more, nothing less.'

Buster nuzzled her and gently took the apple, pushing at her basket for more.

'See what I mean, he has you down as a soft touch.'

She giggled and he raised his hands, making the horses trot away.

'Did the Cliffords always live in this place?'

'No they bought it from Clara Hegarty; she was quite a character, loved her fancy clothes. You would see her out instructing her workers, dressed as though she should be at a tea dance. Loved her jewellery, too. Most around here thought she was a bit odd, but maybe she was right to do things her own way. It must have done her some good: she was well into her nineties when she died.'

'Sounds like my sort of woman, I want to know more about her.'

'Another time; I had better get along, check the cattle in the far field.'

He quickened his step, veering off to a gap in the hedge.

'You should come in and join me in the water some morning,' she called after him.

'Are you making it a regular thing?'

'It helped clear my head.'

'I was never one much for getting in the water, could never really find time in the day.'

'Which is why early in the morning is best.'

Jack smiled.

'Except four hours earlier is my early morning.'

She laughed, walking on, waving to him as he moved out of sight into the next field, Max chasing ahead of him. When she saw the front door open, she did not bother going around the back. Ida, tidying up the drawing room, called out to her.

'Don't tell me you were mad enough to get in the sea?'

Cassie swung around, the wide skirt of her dress swishing against the hall table.

'You should try it.'

'What nonsense! Now go and get into the shower straight away, you don't want to catch cold.'

'I'm going to try for a dip every morning.'

She laughed when she saw Ida pull a face.

'When you are sniffling, don't say I didn't warn you.'

Cassie was on the third step of the stairs when Ida spoke again.

'The previous owner of this house was just the same, a law unto herself, and she liked to swim at odd times too.'

'From what I hear, she lived to a good old age.'

Ida huffed loudly, disappearing into the kitchen.

Cassie was humming to herself as she walked to Tilly's room.

'Darling, the sea was cold, but wonderful. When you're better and the water's a little warmer, you must come in.'

Tilly, busy on her iPad, did not look up.

Elsa wandered in. 'Tilly, will you still be here for my birthday? Mum says I can have my party at Dublin Zoo.'

'When is it?'

'The thirtieth of November, you might still be here.'

Cassie looked alarmed. Ida, who had walked in with fresh towels, gasped.

'You're kidding me!' Tilly said.

'Why?'

'My birthday is the same day, thirtieth November, 2000, right, Mom?'

Cassie couldn't answer.

'We're the same age. We can have a joint birthday celebration. I'll ask Mum,' Elsa said.

She turned away but stopped at the door. 'I haven't met anyone before who has the same birthday as me.'

It was Ida who first composed herself enough to be able to speak. 'Isn't that one of life's strange and wonderful coincidences. I only ever shared a birthday with our old Border Collie back home. Aren't you two so lucky?'

Cassie mouthed *thank you* to Ida, who went downstairs to warn Margo.

Chapter Twenty-Eight

Rathmoney, County Wicklow.

'I wish I could remember you at the French hospital.'

Cassie had told Margo about the girls' discovery of their shared birthday, and the two women couldn't help but remember that day.

'Charles insisted I get a private suite.'

Margo raised her eyes to the ceiling.

'I didn't even know there was such a thing!'

'If you had the bucks.'

Margo poured two coffees and handed one to Cassie.

'What would Conor have made of all this?'

Margo had lain in bed the previous night wondering the exact same thing. Conor would have kicked against the very idea of it until he looked into Tilly's eyes; then he would never have stopped fighting for her.

'I only know he would have fought tooth and nail for Elsa.'

Cassie took a gulp of her coffee.

'I won't give up Tilly for anyone. They can put me in jail, I don't care.'

'Let them try to lock us up.'

They stood in the kitchen of Rathmoney House, realising that with those statements, important decisions had already been made.

'We need to work as a team,' Margo said.

'I'm in,' Cassie replied.

Outside, they heard the Labrador whip through the yard, scattering hens and geese in all directions. Margo ran to the back door.

'Stupid dog, he will never learn to leave the hens alone.' She flung open the door and the dog piled in, wagging his tail.

When the racket outside had died down and the flock of geese had waddled over the bridge to the far field, Margo pushed Max out the door again.

'So if we're a team, we should agree a strategy.'

'Dale says the mediator will want to interview us and the girls,' Cassie said.

'Why don't we tell them to get the hell out of our lives?' Margo motioned Cassie to sit down. 'We have to take control.'

'How?' Cassie asked, picking at the design on the tablecloth as she tried to think.

Margo put her hand out to stop her.

'First, we don't co-operate with this inquiry. We tell the mediator where to go.'

'But Dale said we have to.'

Margo shook her head.

'What can they do if we both say no? Anyway, how can an outsider know what's best for us and our girls?'

Cassie toyed with a thread on the edge of the tablecloth, twirling it around her finger.

'Will they accept that?'

'Do we care?'

'We might run the risk of our attorneys refusing to represent us, leaving us high and dry on the lawsuit.'

'I hope they have more backbone than that.'

Cassie, feeling nervous, stirred another spoon of sugar into her coffee, even though she didn't particularly like it sweet.

Agitated, Margo pulled a pile of laundry off the airing rack and began to fold the clothes into different piles.

'We should email our attorneys straight away, but also outline exactly what we want.'

Margo pushed the clothes to one side.

'I want to have the two girls in my life, but the girl I raised as my daughter to remain my daughter.'

'Snap.'

'We just have to get it set in stone and make it legal.'

'Our attorneys can do that, we need to make all the rest go away.'

Margo shook her head.

'When it comes down to it, I doubt if we really matter at all in this scenario. The hospital will be trying to cover its tracks. It will blame a minion or try to make out we were careless.'

'How could it do that?' Cassie's voice wavered. 'Tilly was only gone a few hours. I keep going back over it: when Tilly was brought back to me, Charles was carrying her. Why didn't he notice? Why didn't I notice? Neither of us did.'

'Elsa was only out of my sight for a very short time. She was tagged on her foot and she still had a tag on when she came back. I said that Elsa's hair was not as thick and said it was lighter somehow but they laughed at me, saying *black is black*. I thought I was strange in the head. I laughed with them.'

'I want it all to go away. I'm so tired,' Cassie said.

Margo barely heard her next words, spoken from behind her fingers.

'There are no winners, only losers: us four. Even if they give us millions, the two of us and our daughters, we will have lost out big-time. No amount of money will compensate us for the lost years. Money is only paper.'

'The legal people are the winners. They will get their big fat cheques at the end of all this, but you're right that we will never get back the lost years.'

'You paint a bad picture, Margo.'

'It's what I feel.'

'So we want everything to stay as it is?'

'Yes.'

Cassie began to weep, her shoulders shaking, her body rocking with the power of emotion pumping through her. 'I just don't understand how it happened.'

'We need answers,' Margo said as she went to the door to call the dog. 'You know they are getting off scot free, because we are not going public, they are hiding behind that. Our only hope is to get as much money as possible out of them, so these two girls of ours will never want for anything.'

'There is something we haven't mentioned in all this today,' Cassie ventured.

'What?'

'Our decision not to tell the girls; can that last longer than Tilly's recovery? I want to get to know Elsa and you to get to know Tilly, but on our terms, not because we have to try and forge a kind of mother-daughter relationship.'

Margo tipped some food in a bowl for the dog, placing it on the floor.

'We are calling the shots, Cassie, we decide when the girls are told and nobody else.'

'Agreed. Although we need to get clever about it. When they found out they shared a birthday earlier, I felt it was all going to unravel.' Cassie paused and reached into her pocket for a pack of cigarettes.

'I know you smoke by the open window in your room, but it has to be outside, down here,' Margo said. 'That first day was a one-off.'

'I'm desperate for a cigarette.'

'I asked Jack to put a bench to the right of the kitchen door, it should be a nice spot for you and if it rains, you can hide in the stables.'

Cassie took out her lighter and made for the door.

She didn't bother to sit on the bench, but wandered around the yard, puffing on her cigarette.

Margo watched her for a few moments, before busying herself getting the dry laundry sorted. When Tilly strolled into the room, she didn't notice at first.

'Is Mom having a smoke?'

Margo wasn't sure how to answer.

'I know she smokes, she started back after Daddy left us.' Tilly looked around for the dog.

'Max is out and about exploring. Did you hear the geese chasing him earlier?'

'Will it happen again?' Tilly's eyes opened wide with excitement.

Margo shook her head.

'I think he's learned his lesson, for now anyway. It won't happen again until he forgets what it's like to be chased by a gaggle of geese.'

Tilly giggled.

'Where's Ida?'

'She's not here this morning.'

Tilly looked disappointed. Nervously, she danced from one leg to the other, before she spoke again.

'Do you mind giving me a kidney?'

Margo took in her anxious face.

'Of course I don't.'

'Why are you doing it?'

'I'm a match, you need help.'

Elsa bounded down the stairs.

'Mummy, can we go somewhere today?'

'I'm not sure if Tilly will be allowed take a road trip.'

'My mom says I need to take it easy.'

It was Elsa's turn to look disappointed.

'We could take a picnic down to the sea. The four of us,' Margo said.

'But it's not sunny,' Tilly said, staring out the window.

'Nobody waits for the sun to shine around these parts,' Margo laughed.

Elsa pulled at Margo's hand.

'Can we bring buckets and spades and our wetsuits?'

'If Cassie says yes, why not. We can find a wetsuit for Tilly.'

Tilly tugged at the back door and shouted to her mother.

'Can we all go for a picnic by the sea, pretty please?'

Cassie, hiding the last of her cigarette behind her back, shouted she would come in a minute. When she got as far as the kitchen, she was still reeking of smoke.

'It's cold, we'll need our coats and hats.'

'And wetsuits,' Tilly said.

Cassie grimaced.

'I'm sorry, hon, but I'll have to veto a dip in the sea for you.'

'Mom, why?'

'Just not at the moment, darling. When you have fully recovered after surgery it'll be different. I can't risk you picking up a bug, you know that.'

Elsa walked over and took Tilly's hand.

'I won't get in either, we can fish in the rock pools instead.'

Margo started making sandwiches as Cassie and Tilly went upstairs to change into their warm clothes. Elsa got a packet of Jaffa Cakes and put them in the basket.

'I like Tilly, don't you?' she asked Margo.

'Lucky I do, considering I'm giving her a kidney.'

'Can I ask a question?'

Margo wrapped the sandwiches in foil.

'I suppose you girls want fizzy drinks?'

'What's going to happen if I need a kidney, like Tilly does?'

Margo looked at her daughter.

'We would find you one, like Cassie found one for Tilly. It's all about matching you to the right person.'

'But I could match with you, you're my mum.'

Margo put down the roll of tinfoil. Was this the way it was to be from now on, a worry in the pit of her stomach, that somehow Elsa would find out she was a fraud and an interloper?

'Yeah, sure; now let's get our coats on, because they will be downstairs any minute.'

'Do you think Tilly will be allowed to play football?'

Margo shrugged her shoulders.

'Let's just see what happens.'

Chapter Twenty-Nine

Rathmoney, County Wicklow.

Will my mum die if she gives away a kidney? Margo could not believe what she was reading in the Google search. Elsa had borrowed her laptop earlier that evening, to watch her favourite programme on Netflix. How worried she must be. Margo could not bear it. She felt guilty, she had thought everything was going well on the countdown to the transplant.

They had got into a routine at Rathmoney House. Margo and Tilly kept up with all their check-ups and tests, Tilly had dialysis twice a week in Dublin. Elsa sometimes went along with her friend and they played cards or games on the iPad to pass the time. Cassie went for a dip each morning in the sea because she said it helped her to focus on the positive. Margo pretended that everything was all right, until they were very close to the day which was ringed in red on the calendar: 'Hospital Admission Margo and Tilly.'

There was so much concentration on Tilly, Margo realised now she might not have appreciated the full effect this was having on Elsa. But after seeing Elsa's Google search, she couldn't sleep, worrying that maybe even volunteering for the transplant had been unfair on her daughter, unfair too to dredge up the fear of losing her remaining parent so soon after Conor's passing. She sat in the drawing room for hours but could find no answers.

Feeling defeated, once daylight broke through she pulled on a warm cardigan and stole out of the house, afraid of waking Elsa. She set off walking across the fields, pushing the horses out of the way when they nudged at her pockets. The sun was shining, but a fresh breeze whipping in across the sea made her shiver. Conor had liked to walk by the shore, he said it helped him think clearly, which is what she was hoping for this morning. She was worried about the transplant. She was not going to back out, but a fear simmered in her heart, that this was all too much. Elsa was afraid, she knew that now too.

She crossed over the last fence and walked across the shore to the water's edge. Wave upon wave broke in front of her; a seal popped up its head, eyeing her curiously. She thought if anybody could see her, she must look odd, the sea water practically on top of her, so she turned away to walk parallel to the shore, her head bowed against the wind.

Conor would never have approved of her risking her life. The doctors did not deny it was major surgery, but for her they said the risk was less than the recipient. For Tilly, the risks were different, the risk of rejection, terrifying. Would her relation-ship with Tilly be any stronger when this daughter who had her whole make-up also took her kidney? It wouldn't make Tilly love her. She felt guilty and selfish, but what if something went terribly wrong, what would Elsa do? How would she feel, abandoned by both her father and mother within such a short time? Was the gift of a kidney a reckless decision; should she reconsider?

Bending down, she picked up the biggest stone she could carry, staggered to the water and dumped it in. The seal disappeared, the waves broke up and she, somehow, for that brief moment felt a little better.

She heard somebody calling her name, the word elongated in the wind.

Sweeping around, she saw Cassie climb the last fence. When she got as far as Margo, Cassie was out of breath and coughing. Margo slapped her on the back, until she could compose herself. 'You should go to the doctor about that.'

'I will, when I have time. It's probably just a smoker's cough.'

Cassie detected a shadow flit across Margo's face. 'Am I intruding?'

Margo didn't answer but began to walk towards the spit of land jutting into the sea, which gave Rathmoney House strand such privacy.

'I saw you from the bedroom window.'

Margo ignored her.

'What's wrong?' Cassie asked nervously.

Margo shook her head, stamping across the sand, not slowing her pace.

Still not quite over her coughing fit, Cassie tried to keep up. 'Come off it, you surely don't usually walk like this.'

Margo didn't answer, but pushed her hands deep into her pockets and carried on. Cassie trotted beside her. Margo made to turn away, mumbling she needed some space, but Cassie reached out, tugging at her cardigan. 'If this is about Tilly and the transplant, you have to tell me.'

Margo pulled away, quickening her pace, stumbling over the clumps of seaweed at the tide line. Cassie followed.

'I need time to think, this is such a big thing in all of our lives,' Margo said, her words whipped away by the sound of the waves and the breeze, blowing in over the Irish Sea.

'Are you having second thoughts?'

Margo walked faster.

Cassie managed to step in front, forcing Margo to stop.

'You're not pulling out, are you?'

Tears rolled down Margo's face. 'What will Elsa do if it all goes wrong and I die on the operating table?'

Cassie turned away towards the sea, her shoulders hunched. 'I can't give guarantees, there are none to give.'

Cassie moved a short distance away. Margo saw her clench her fists as if steeling herself for the next round, before turning back to face her again.

'What has changed? Has something happened?'

'I'm afraid, Cassie; so afraid.'

In a few paces Cassie was back by her side.

'So am I.'

'What about Elsa?'

'I understand, but what about Tilly, too? You are her only chance to have a normal life.'

'But Elsa is so afraid of losing me. You know what she googled?'

'What?'

'*Will my mum die if she gives away a kidney?*' Margo gripped Cassie's shoulders. 'What did we ever do to deserve this?'

Cassie shook her head. 'If you can't go ahead, I won't blame you.'

Margo looked out to sea, where a small fishing boat was bobbing on the water. 'If I can't go ahead with it, I will never forgive my cowardice.'

'It's not cowardly to want to protect your daughter from further pain.'

Margo didn't say anything, but began to sob some more, the tears strangling in her throat making her breathing ragged. Cassie put her arm around Margo's shoulders.

'I understand your fear and I can only confirm my earlier promise. If this is last minute jitters, just think, the surgeon is as

252

confident as he can be of a good outcome. That is all any of us can hold on to.' Cassie shivered with the cold. She wanted Becca Barton's warm Pacific Ocean, not this cold, grey, unwelcoming sea. 'I have no definite answers, Margo; there is no contract between us. You don't owe us anything.' Cassie's voice was flat, defeated.

'I was awake most of the night. I came down here to clear my head,' Margo said.

'I should leave you alone, I'm not going to put pressure on you, it's a huge decision for you and for Elsa.'

Margo caught a fistful of stones and threw them, watching them rain on the water.

'The three of us loved to come and skip stones. Conor was so good at it, he could get nine skips in one throw. Once, when Elsa was very young and when they were not looking, I threw a bunch of stones all at the same time. Elsa was so impressed and after that, she asked Conor, why couldn't he be as good as Mummy?'

Margo leaned against Cassie. 'Those were simpler days.'

'For me too.'

After a few moments, Cassie made to disentangle herself, but Margo pulled her back. 'Conor is gone and I have to accept that. I have to stop torturing myself trying to figure out what he would do.'

'You are under enormous strain, I understand.'

'Every fibre of my being says I should help Tilly.'

Margo fell silent, afraid she would back out and equally fearful of her commitment to a surgery which, if it went wrong, would tear them all apart.

When Cassie spoke, her tone was gentle. 'Margo, if it helps, if something happened to you and...'

She stopped, trying to find the right words. 'I don't for a

minute think anything bad will happen, but if it did, I would help look after Elsa.'

'Would you, with Jack and Ida?'

'I promise.'

Margo watched the waves making towards the shore. How often had she stood here, watching Elsa paddling, Max ploughing into the waves, Conor lying on a rug examining the clouds. What she wouldn't give for even half a moment like that now.

She had brought Cassie and Tilly to Rathmoney; how could she back out? Margo Clifford was a woman of her word, she thought, but she muttered a silent prayer to whoever cared to listen, to help both herself and Tilly share in their doctors' faith that there would be a successful outcome for all.

She turned to Cassie. 'Can you keep your promise?'

'I will do everything to keep that promise.'

'I will not waver again.'

She saw Cassie's face relax. 'Are you doubly sure, Margo? I have to know.'

'I am.'

Cassie stared at Margo. 'You had me so scared.'

'I had myself scared. Please, you must never tell Tilly I almost faltered at the last hurdle.'

'I won't,' Cassie said, as the two women turned to walk across the fields together to Rathmoney House.

'We need to do something to take our minds off all this medical stuff,' Cassie said as they neared the house.

'I know the exact thing,' Margo said, a spring in her step suddenly.

Cassie, trying to keep up, began to cough and Margo slowed down.

'Elsa has been asking for so long to see the Rathmoney designer dress collection, maybe the four of us could have a fashion show in the drawing room.'

'Who is this designer?'

'French, Jacques Heim, romantic with a capital R. I will ask Jack to get the collection down from the attic.'

'That's a funny place to keep it.'

'Not when you see how they are packed in their original boxes, wrapped with tissue with sprays of dried lavender to deter the insects and moths. They came with the house, belonged to the previous owner.'

When they got as far as the kitchen, Tilly and Elsa were sitting eating chocolate brownies.

'You spoil her, Ida,' Cassie said.

'Nothing wrong with a bit of TLC,' she replied, telling the two girls to run along.

'Mommy, Ida says she will show me how and I will be able to bake you a cake for your birthday.'

Ida put her hand to her lips. 'Shush now, I thought we agreed it was going to be a surprise, you funny thing.'

Tilly giggled, marching after the dog to the drawing room. Elsa followed as the two girls tried to get the best spot at the sofa.

'Those girls,' Cassie said. She turned to Ida. 'Thank you for being so kind, I know the circumstances are not ideal,' she said as Ida carried a tray through for the children.

Margo went in search of Jack to help get the designer boxes down from the attic.

When Ida got back to the kitchen, she sat opposite Cassie at the table. 'Cassandra, now that we are on our own, I wanted to have a quick word.'

Cassie reached for the cookie jar and opened it, sniggering when the sound of a cockerel echoed about them.

Ida tapped her foot impatiently. 'Tilly is a beautiful girl, there is a lot of her father in her.'

'That's nice to hear.'

'I have to tell you, and Jack will back me up on this, we are worried.'

'I don't understand.'

'What happens after the operation?'

'Margo and I have been through all this, there are months of recuperation ahead for Tilly.'

'Stop beating about the bush, you know exactly what I mean.'

'Ida, the transplant surgery is my priority now and getting the best outcome for Tilly.'

'Afterwards, are you going to be happy to go back to the States with Tilly and leave Margo and Elsa be?'

'I want what is right for all of us.'

Ida jumped up so quickly, the chair fell back. 'What sort of answer is that?'

Cassie pushed her head into her hands. 'Ida, I don't want to talk about this anymore.'

'All I know is nobody is thinking of Margo and Elsa. You waltz into their lives and you get what you want, but who is thinking of what all this is doing to them?'

'Ida, I wish you would respect what I have said and stop trying to read more in to it. Margo knows me better than you think.'

'She does not know you a wet week, for all she knows you have plans to take both Tilly and Elsa. It will happen over my dead body.'

Cassie stood up slowly, leaning over the table, so she was almost eye to eye with Ida.

'I know you think the worst of me. I can't change that, but I would appreciate it if you kept your wild accusations to yourself.'

'What wild accusations?'

Margo walked into the kitchen, looking from one woman to the other.

Cassie grabbed her basket. 'Ida can fill you in. Do you mind if we leave the fashion show for another time, I need to get some air.'

'That's OK, I can't find Jack anyway.'

Muttering a tight *thank you*, Cassie swept out of the back door as Margo looked to Ida, who was making a fuss of putting the chair back in its place.

'What has happened?'

'Nothing to be worried about.'

'Let me be the judge of that.'

Ida flopped down on the chair.

'I just spoke my mind, asked what her plans are for after the transplant.'

'Ida, we are all feeling the stress of this waiting, we just have to get through the hospital stuff, before we plan anything else.'

Ida thumped the table.

'And what are the rest of us supposed to do, not care what happens to you all? I'm not a robot, Margo, I worry about you and Elsa. Elsa is like my own grandchild. I can't stand idly by.'

'Ida, this is something you are going to have to let us work out by ourselves.'

She would have said more, and could have because she felt so cross and angry, but she saw Ida's face crumple and big wet tears spill down her cheeks.

'I'm sorry, but I could not bear to lose Elsa. She means the world to me.'

Margo felt herself soften towards Ida and patted her on the shoulder.

'Elsa adores you Ida, both you and Jack. None of that is going to change.'

Cassie stalked down the driveway, her indignation steaming her on, so she almost stumbled into the biggest pothole. At the gate she slowed down, stopping to catch her breath. She was tired today because she'd got up several times during the night to check on Tilly.

The horses spotted her, cantering over. She patted them lightly. Buster reached over, pushing at her pockets looking for treats. She forced the chestnut pony away, resuming her walk at a brisk pace. She had no idea what the future held, only that this operation could give a better life to Tilly. How could she even consider anything beyond that? Right now, she was just glad to escape from Ida and her persistent concern. She set off again at a brisk march. Would that she had somebody such as her in her own corner.

In the town, she stopped to look in the butcher's window. She hadn't realised she'd walked so far. Deep in thought, she must have stood there too long, because the butcher sent a boy out to ask if she needed help. Shaking her head, she moved off, wandering aimlessly down the main street past the newsagents, the post office and the thrift shop. She was about to turn back, when Jack spotted her.

'I guess Rathmoney can't compete with an average American town,' he said.

'It's fine.'

He shuffled, not sure what to say next.

'I was looking for somewhere to have a coffee.'

'McLysaghts is not bad. Come on, I'll treat you to a coffee and cake.'

He led the way three doors up to the bright café with tables outside. When Jack came back holding a tray with two caramel lattes and two slices of chocolate cake, she tried to smile.

'Is there something wrong?'

'Why do you ask?'

'You seem different. Has there been bad news?' When she didn't answer, he busied himself stirring sugar into his coffee.

'Your Ida thinks I am going to run off with Tilly and Elsa, once the operation is done,' Cassie blurted out.

Jack spluttered into his latte.

'Why does Ida hate me so much?' Cassie continued.

'Ida doesn't hate you, but she is protective of Margo and Elsa. We both are.'

'Is that what you think as well?'

'It's hard not to. You have bounced into their lives when they are at their most vulnerable, we are only watching out for them.'

'I give you my word I'm not going to do anything to hurt Margo and Elsa.'

'I'm glad to hear that.'

They sat beside each other, quietly sipping the coffee, Jack tearing into his chocolate cake. A few people passing on the street saluted Jack, slowing down to take in the beautiful woman beside him. Others whispered about Jack Roper and the tall American, commenting that Jack and Ida appeared to like the window seat at McLysaghts.

When they had finished, Jack offered Cassie a lift back to Rathmoney House. As they got in the Jeep, Cassie started to laugh.

'What's so funny?' he asked.

'Did you see the looks we got?'

'I can't say I did.'

'Oh come on, Jack.'

He chuckled and she noticed for the first time laughter lines around his eyes.

'It sounds like you may need a break from Rathmoney,' he said.

'I wish.'

'If you have the time, I would be glad to run you into the mountains. It's a great place to clear the head, works every time for me.'

Cassie agreed and Jack turned the car in the opposite direction to Rathmoney House.

They didn't talk as he negotiated the narrow roads leading up to the Sally Gap. She felt the stress melt away as they headed for the clouds, the heather scenting the air. Every now and again, he pulled over, so they could take in the panorama. Before the Sally Gap, he parked the car.

'There's a nice path here we can take, if you are up to the walk.'

They walked single file, Jack leading the way. When he heard her breath shorten, he stopped. 'Take time out, look at the mountains tipping against the sky, the eagle soaring above us.'

'It's so quiet.'

'Even the rabbits are hiding, because of our high-flying friend.'

She twirled around, taking in the vista from all sides. Suddenly, she felt dizzy and Jack had to put a hand out to steady her. She fell against him and he noticed how light she was. She apologised and he laughed it off. When they had to go back to the car, he offered her his hand, for fear she would fall on the slippery stones flung across the path in places. She liked the comfort of his grip, he liked the lightness of her touch. They did not need to talk much on the way home but were happy to just be.

When the Jeep got as far as Rathmoney House, Cassie said she would walk up the avenue on her own. 'Ida will be wondering where you got to,' she said and he agreed, turning into his own driveway once he saw Cassie had gone through the gates to the house.

When he got inside, Jack found Ida upstairs in the small bedroom which had once been set aside for Elizabeth. Ida was sitting in the rocking chair they had placed by the window all those years ago.

'I have been thinking of her a lot,' Ida said. She was holding a small red gingham dress she had bought in Gorey just a month before the birth, and had kept pristine ever since. 'I wonder did I jinx the birth by buying this dress? At the time I hadn't a clue whether it was going to be a boy or a girl.'

'Ida, we have been through all this. It is nothing you did or anyone did. Elizabeth died and there was nothing we could do to change that.'

'I know, the sane part of me knows that.' She sighed. 'It is still so hard after all these years.'

'I know.'

He took the dress from Ida and folded it back into the chest of drawers with the few other baby things she had never quite been able to let go of. 'Come on, let's have a pot of Earl Grey.'

She let him lead her out of the room and downstairs to the kitchen.

'I was thinking maybe we could go out for dinner Thursday evening, spend a bit of time together, have a good chat.'

'I would like that,' she said.

Chapter Thirty

Rathmoney, County Wicklow.

Margo was waiting in the kitchen when Ida arrived at the door, carrying two big glass jars.

'Peanut butter; Tilly was saying how much she missed it. Our shop-bought stuff just isn't the same as she has back home apparently, so I thought maybe homemade would be good.'

'How on earth did you make peanut butter?' Margo asked as she took a spoon and scooped a taste from one of the jars.

'Got the recipe on the internet.'

'I'm impressed, it tastes great. Tilly will love it.'

Margo closed the jar. 'While we are on our own, I wanted to talk to you about the guesthouse, Ida.'

'You are giving it up, aren't you?'

'How did you know?'

'Because it makes sense, you have enough on your mind right now.'

'I thought if we closed for a month or two, just until we can get the operation and recovery out of the way, that would be best.'

'What, close and lose any chance of future business? We can mark it fully booked, but take down the sign at the gate.'

'Trust you to come up with an idea like that.'

Ida sighed. 'It was fun while it lasted,' she said and Margo thought she detected a tremor in her friend's voice.

'We will reopen, Ida. I want to, I love having different people at Rathmoney.'

'If you say so,' Ida said, taking off her jacket and reaching for the kettle.

'It keeps me busy and has kept my mind off things, but really we need the whole of Rathmoney House to ourselves, so we can concentrate on recovery after the surgery,' Margo said.

Ida put two mugs on the table 'You're right. I suppose you won't want me annoying you every morning, either.'

'Oh, Ida, we'd be lost here without you.'

'As long as I'm not in the way.'

Margo wanted to laugh, but she knew the hurt in Ida was real. 'You belong in Rathmoney House; you are family, Ida.'

Satisfied, Ida concentrated on making the tea and Margo got on with scrambling eggs for breakfast.

Cassie stuck her head round the kitchen door and said she was off for a swim and would eat later.

When Ida was sure Cassie was out of earshot, she turned to Margo. 'What do you make of her and Jack?'

'They are friends, what's wrong with that?'

'Nothing, if that's all they are.'

Margo scraped the scrambled eggs into a bowl.

'Ida, don't be so silly.'

Jack saw Cassie close the front door and climb the fence to cross the fields to the sea. When he caught her eye, she waved and said something, but he didn't catch it. Turning away, he grabbed a hammer and a box of nails from his Jeep, before heading to the bench at the weeping beech. Margo was worried the rickety seat might collapse, so she had asked him to repair it.

'Another Conor special,' he joked. 'His legacy is all around us!'

Margo smiled, making Jack realise how long it had been since her eyes had lit up.

He was about to fight his way around the bank of fuchsias, when Ida called him from the front steps. He stood waiting for her to shout out again, but she beckoned him furiously to join her.

Strolling back up the avenue, he noted an agitation in her as she waited for him.

'Jack, Margo needs a bit of time out to herself so she's asked me to stay on here and look after the girls today.'

'Can't Cassie do that?'

'She can, but I reckon she is busy enough.'

'We were meant to have some time out ourselves, or had you forgotten?'

Ida's face fell. 'I already said yes to Margo.'

He didn't respond, shuffling the gravel on the driveway with his boot.

'You understand, don't you?'

Ida's voice was high-pitched with worry, so he nodded, saying it didn't matter.

'Maybe we will get a bit of time to ourselves when everything is back to normal.'

Jack swung to face Ida. 'With all that is happening around here, nothing will ever be back to the old normal. It's a new type of normal we can hope for from now on.'

Ida, disconcerted by her husband's attitude, huffed loudly before disappearing back indoors. Jack wandered down to the river, his eyes on the reedy bank, where he knew the heron was nesting. When she rose up, gliding so close he heard the whining swish of her wings, he stepped back to watch her negotiate and dip under the arch of the bridge, her smooth flight entrancing and distracting him, so he followed her for a few moments before losing his bearings on the nest.

Walking onto the bridge, he leaned his weight on it, shaking and checking it. Margo was nervous about such things, now that Rathmoney House had visitors. She wanted everything to be safe and in good working order. Quickly, he walked back up the avenue to the fuchsia patch. Leading with his shoulder, he pushed his way past the bank of red and purple flowers to the grove. When he heard the sobbing, he thought it might be Margo. He was about to retreat when he saw Cassie's basket on the ground as if it had been carelessly thrown to one side.

Cassie had not swum this morning, put off by the biting cold wind blowing across the waves, churning up the salt water. Unsure of her strength in the face of an angry sea, she had turned away, crossing the field to the avenue, seeking out the bench where she could take a quiet moment, far away from everyone at Rathmoney House.

When Vince rang, she was glad to hear his voice and hurried to sit down.

'Cas, I'm afraid I have sad news about Becca Barton.'

Cassie felt her chest tighten. 'What?'

'She got as far as San Francisco, but then she had some sort of weakness, and I'm afraid that within two days she was dead.'

Tears ran down Cassie's face as she thought of Becca and of the last time she saw her. She wanted to remember her at home, loitering on her porch, sipping her coffee, watching the world on her doorstep. Vince's words faded away and she was drinking an ice-cold drink, not needing to say anything, sitting with Becca.

'Cas, are you still there?'

Cassie attempted to pull herself together. 'Sorry, it's just a shock.'

'I was talking to Todd; he managed to fly out to be with her before she died.'

'I'm glad of that. Did she get to see the ocean?'

'Funny you should ask, you know what Todd did? He rented one of those houses on the water's edge. He even had a nursing team with him. They carried her bed down to the shore; she died looking out at and listening to the Pacific Ocean.'

Cassie bawled. 'All her life she wanted to be there.'

'Well, she made it, in her last few hours.'

Cassie shook herself, the warm glow of happy memories returning. She was suddenly happy that her dear friend had achieved her dream, not only to sit by the Pacific Ocean, but to do so with her son, who clearly had finally listened to her wishes, and made them a reality.

'Maybe I shouldn't have told you.' Vince sounded worried.

'I'm glad you did, I was very fond of Becca.'

'I wish I was there to give you a hug, darling.'

'I know.'

'Cas, how is Tilly?'

'The doctors are happy for surgery to go ahead. It won't be long now.'

'I've sent a gift, she should get it before she goes in. I've decided to come over for a week or so, once she's out of hospital. I may be of more use to you then.'

'Really? Tilly will love it. Me too, I really need a friendly face right now.' Cassie sighed.

'Sweetheart, you will get through all this.'

'I know. I just want it to be done.'

After Vince rang off, Cassie sat in the quiet glade, sobbing. A robin perched on a fuchsia branch watching her as she let go the worry of the last few months. She let the tears flow, for her daughter about to undergo life-saving surgery; for the woman prepared to save her and for the old lady who only got to feel the sea breeze on her face in her last hours on earth.

A thrush hopped around the undergrowth, tipping its head from side to side.

Cassie wanted to scream, to shout that life was so unfair, but did not want to draw attention to herself.

Hunched over, her shoulders shaking, her long hair spilling over her face, she was unaware that Jack was observing her. Afraid to turn away, afraid to move forward, he berated himself for standing idly by in the face of such blistering pain.

Shaking any doubts from his head, he marched across to Cassie. 'What's the matter?' he asked, reaching the bench in three strides.

Skimming her hands over her face, she saw Jack through a blur of tears.

'Cassie, I can't see you like this, is it about the transplant?'

'I just learned that I've lost a good friend, Jack.'

'I'm sorry to hear that, Cassie.'

She looked directly at him. 'I always seem to bring bad luck; stay away from me, Jack.'

'I can look after myself.'

'What will I do if it doesn't work, Jack? I will watch Tilly die and I will have compromised Margo's health for nothing.'

'That's not going to happen.'

'How do you know?'

'I don't, but I don't think we can go into this any other way. That and a prayer, maybe, if you believe in that sort of thing.'

'How can there be a God, when there is so much bad in the world? If this is a test, I'm failing miserably.'

Jack sat down beside her, the seat shifting with the additional weight. He put his arm around her, letting her lean into him. 'Cassie, there are no answers for any of this. We just have to muddle through.'

'Muddling through is not enough, Jack. I have to make a miracle happen, I can't fail.'

'You're not on your own. You're at Rathmoney House now; we're all with you, every step of the way.'

He kissed the top of her head lightly.

'Thank you,' she said gently

'Best get you back to the house; Ida will have a search party out looking for us.'

'Do you think?'

'I know, and she'd better not see you crying or she'll ask questions.'

'How am I going to get past her?'

'I'll distract her, ask her advice on the new flower bed. Ida loves to be asked for her counsel.'

Cassie chuckled.

'That's better, nice to hear you laugh,' he said, brushing a leaf from her hair.

Taking out his handkerchief, he walked to the river and, bending down, he dipped the hankie in the water. Squeezing it out, he handed the damp cloth to Cassie. 'Wipe your face before going near the house.'

Ida was in the guest quarters with Margo giving them the once over before Cassie's father took up residence. 'I hope he realises he has to pay the going rate: the price is not going down, just because you are going in to hospital for a major operation.'

Margo smiled. 'Don't be daft. He could be here quite a while, I told him to make himself at home. We are closed after all, so there is no charge.'

'Do you think that's wise? He might stay on for months.'

Margo laughed out loud. 'Ida, he's as good as family.'

Ida did not hear Margo's reply; she was too busy watching Jack and Cassie as they pushed past the fuchsia bank, Cassie laughing when her basket got stuck and Jack had to tug it out. They were chatting as they strolled towards the house. Ida, wondering what they could be talking about, felt a twinge of jealousy.

Would Jack tell her he had laughed and chatted with the tall American?

All the times they had lingered by the river, she and Jack, swapping stories, sometimes strolling hand in hand, other times so close the top of their arms rubbed against each other. Seeing him with Cassie now, she realised they had not gone by the river together in a long time, though she could not remember when exactly they'd stopped.

She'd caught Jack's hand last Thursday. He had cupped hers in his, but it was an awkward holding and she wasn't sure he had even noticed when she slipped away.

Turning away from the window, Ida looked at Margo. 'Are you still sure you want to go through with the surgery?'

'Not that again, Ida, please.'

Ida sat on the bed. 'I'm worried.'

'You must be, sitting on a perfectly made guest bed.'

Ida jumped up. 'No one will think badly of you, if you want to pull out.'

'I'm not going to pull out.'

Ida would have said more, but her phone beeped. She smiled and, shaking her head as she read the message, she turned to Margo.

'That soft husband of mine says can I come down and advise him on what to do in the new flower bed. He's acting like we live at Rathmoney House.' She bustled about, fixing the cushions on the bed. 'I'll make him wait a few minutes. It's only good for him to have to wait a bit.'

'Jack has a well of love and patience for you.'

'As long as it doesn't run dry.'

269

'I could never imagine that happening.'

'He's very friendly with Cassie. Have you noticed?'

'Ida, don't be daft Yes, I have seen him with Cassie, but that man loves you. I have no doubt of that.'

'He took her out for a spin to see the mountains, the other day. What was that about?'

'Cassie needed a break. She said the two hours helped her a lot; she was quite stressed by everything. She just needed time out, that's all.'

'I wish I could be so sure,' Ida replied, before she bustled out of the room, closing the door behind her. Once on the landing, she stopped to gather herself, leaning against the wall, pushing her forehead onto the cool plaster.

After a few moments, she straightened up, making her way down the stairs to meet her husband. Jack was tinkering with the tractor trailer.

'You took your time.'

'I was busy working, don't you know. Some of us don't have all the time in the world to be sauntering and chatting.'

Jack looked at his wife oddly, but he could not make out from her face what was wrong with her.

'I was wondering, do you want me to put some roses in this flower bed?'

'It's not for me to say, have you asked Margo?'

He didn't answer.

'Hasn't the American decided on wildflowers?'

'Ida, what's eating you?'

Ida swung around to Jack. 'Coffee in town, taking a spin into the mountains and now lingering beside the river. I don't like it, Jack Roper.'

Jack shook his head. 'We are friends, we talk, that's all.' He reached over, pulling Ida to him, so her head was on his chest.

'There's nothing in this world that can come between the two of us.'

She nodded, her chin digging in to his fleece. 'She's a beautiful woman. You like her?'

'Of course I do, but Ida, you are my life.'

'Even when I'm blathering on?'

'Especially then.'

'Go with the wildflowers, I hear she really likes them. She's going through enough not to be upset over this trifle.'

He pretended to tip his cap to Ida. 'Certainly, madam, whatever you say, madam.'

She pushed him away gently, telling him to get back to work.

Chapter Thirty-One

Rathmoney, County Wicklow.

'A woman's marriage goes up in smoke and our lives are turned upside down forever, is that what you are saying?'

Margo's voice was high-pitched, tense. She beckoned Cassie to join her as she put the solicitor on speakerphone. 'They know how the babies were swapped,' Margo hissed as Cassie approached.

Samantha Kiely's voice was loud and clear. 'There is nothing fair about this account and no comfort for either of you, but these facts indicate compensation will have to be high. With this inquiry report and conclusions, we can push towards final settlement.'

Margo sat in her wingback chair, telling Samantha she was on speakerphone and Cassie had joined the conversation.

'You should really discuss this with your own attorney, Ms Kading, I'm sure Mr Winters has got the same communication and will be on to you at the start of business.'

'We are in this together. I want Cassie to hear what is in this letter; we can't expect her to wait at least five hours,' Margo said.

'As long as Cassie knows she must take her own advice from her attorney.'

'I understand, but please tell me what is going on,' Cassie asked quietly.

The solicitor cleared her throat. 'As I have just told Margo, the results of the French inquiry are in. I have got a brief email, but the gist is a nurse looking after both babies who had been sent for light therapy took off their name tags, but later got confused and took a guess as to which tag should be on which baby.'

'As simple as that?' Cassie blurted out.

'There is more: she'd been drinking. She's admitted that she'd had four or five shots of cognac before coming on duty.'

'Jesus Christ,' Cassie said.

'It gets better, or I suppose worse,' Margo interjected.

Samantha cleared her throat. 'Yes, it turns out the woman's husband had walked out on her two days before and she was an emotional mess.'

Cassie sighed loudly. Whipping a tissue from the box on the coffee table, she blotted beads of sweat from her brow. 'Some drunken bitch is having marriage problems and she ruins our lives.'

'I don't know whether to laugh or cry,' Margo said, her voice curiously emotionless.

'Why didn't she ring in sick, stay at home and drink a bottle or two of wine? Why didn't she do that? Why did she have to take off the tags anyway? Oh God, why didn't we notice?'

'It's not our fault. None of this is.'

Cassie kicked at the edge of the Persian rug. 'I hate that woman and what she has done to us, what she stole from us. She didn't give a damn who she hurt with her drinking.'

The solicitor coughed in case she had been forgotten. 'I will read out the two relevant paragraphs of the letter. The rest is in an email to you.'

Cassie sat back down beside Margo.

'The relief nurse, who no longer works at the hospital or is on the register of nurses, admitted when interviewed that she had taken the tag from each baby's foot when both babies were receiving light treatment for their jaundice. The nurse, who had drunk cognac before reporting for work, admitted she had problems in her marriage and was depressed. She also admitted she took the tags off both babies, but after the treatment could not remember which tag went on which child and decided to guess. She was unclear as to why she took off the identity tags, when there was no requirement in the first place to do so. The woman is no longer working as a nurse anywhere in the French health system.'

'I will never forgive that woman,' Cassie said.

'Me neither,' Margo replied, her voice so low Cassie could barely hear her.

Margo sat unable to speak further. It was a brief explanation, but it was both devastating and insulting.

When the French hospital finished its inquiry, she expected a long, drawn-out explanation as to why their children were swapped. It should be a complex story, which would give them some comfort that there was nothing they could have done to prevent losing their babies. Instead there was a terse paragraph in a legal letter, designed to close the sad episode. What really hurt was the lack of apology, or even any recognition of the pain and heartache the mistake had caused.

Samantha Kiely spoke quietly. 'You do realise this is good news all round? There's an end in sight. I expect a first offer very soon.' She rang off, promising she would call back as soon as she heard anything from the hospital side.

Margo remembered the narrow plastic tag, because Conor had worried it would mark Elsa's foot. She heard herself mocking him, saying he would have to learn to lighten up as a dad. How she wished she could have that time back, when life was just the three of them.

Margo took down a photograph of Conor and Elsa from the mantelpiece. 'I'm so angry on his behalf, he never got an opportunity to love Tilly as much as he loved Elsa.'

Cassie stood at the window watching Tilly and Elsa playing ball with Max. 'We have all lost out. I look at Elsa and see myself when I was a little girl. Sometimes I look at her face and I want to hug her so tight.' She looked at Margo. 'Don't worry, I won't, just being here is enough. But I do worry one day it won't be.'

Margo sighed loudly. 'I'm the same. Tilly reminds me so much of Conor, I'm amazed Elsa doesn't see the similarity; but then, she has no reason to suspect. She tells me she finds it easy being around Tilly, but she doesn't question why. Why would she? For her, it's good to have a companion after losing the one person she adored. Last night, she asked me did I think Conor knew you were here. I told her quite honestly, I hoped he did.'

Cassie shook her head. 'We are in a mess, yet maybe we've found something greater here between us.'

'I hope so,' Margo said.

Cassie moved across the room. 'I can't talk anymore, I'm going for a smoke.'

She walked out of the room, leaving Margo sitting in her chair by the window.

When Cassie got to the stables, Jack was already sitting in a chair blowing smoke rings. 'I'll have one of yours, I forgot mine,' she said.

He held out the pack, waiting until she had picked her cigarette and put it in her mouth, before stretching across with the lighter. She took a long drag, releasing the smoke slowly.

'Do you want to talk about it?' he asked gently.

'I don't know, Jack, it's like I have lost twelve years out of my life, like somebody has just come along and erased it. I'm finding it hard to get my head around it.'

'I think you have to look forward now. There is too much pain looking back.'

'I can't help it, I'm so angry. It turns out a drunken nurse swapped the name tags on each baby. What she did in a minute has changed our lives forever.'

Jack stood up. 'Come on, I want to show you something.'

He extended his hand to help her up. Pulling her gently, when she stood up he held her close. 'Let me introduce you to Dinah.'

Releasing Cassie, he walked ahead of her across the yard to the river. They went over to the bridge, Jack leading the way to a small kennel he had specially built.

'Little Dinah is a duckling we rescued. She got separated from the mother and the other ducklings as they went down-river. Bess the cat found her. I don't know what came over her, but suddenly, they were as thick as thieves. That duckling treats Bess like her mama, she is an old cat and maybe she likes the attention, but it works for them.'

Unhitching the clasps, he lifted the roof off. The long haired black cat stirred, stretched her paws and went back to sleep, the tiny duckling nuzzled into her belly.

Cassie gasped.

'The cat seems to like the company and we feed them both at the same time. There is a bond there, that's all that matters. Look at how content they are. Look at the bond you have with Tilly, the one you can forge with Elsa.'

'I like you, Jack, and I like this story. It's a funny way to put everything in perspective, thank you.' She hesitated before tentatively reaching out and kissing him gently on the lips. As quickly, she pulled away.

'I'm sorry, I don't know what came over me.'

He didn't say anything, but pulled her close, planting a kiss on the top of her head.

They stood for a moment, her head on his chest before separating. 'I'd better get back to the house,' she said.

He put the roof back on and closed the clasps.

He called after her. 'I will take a dip in the sea with you in the morning.'

She turned around beaming. 'I would like that very much.'

Jack was already in the water, swimming parallel to the shore when Cassie arrived at the beach the next morning. She threw off her clothes and ran into the sea in her bikini, faltering and tripping as the highest wave hit her. Jack caught her and kissed her.

She kissed him back, before shoving him away roughly.

'What's wrong?'

'Jack, I really like you and in a different time, who knows, but we risk hurting too many people.'

He didn't say anything but pulled away, looking out to sea. He swam away and she followed, coughing when she finally caught up with him.

He patted her on the back, when she turned away, embarrassed.

'It might be time to get you to a doctor, Cas.'

'I will, soon.'

He caught her by the shoulders.

'No, get it sorted now, you are no good to Tilly if you're sick.' Tears brimmed up in her eyes. Gently, he rubbed her arm. 'I should not have kissed you just now, I'm sorry.'

'I have so much on my mind, Jack, I have to be there a hundred per cent for Tilly. I'll be honest, I don't have time for any distractions.' She laughed. 'It's a poor choice of words, you are a lot more than a distraction. I am so fond of you.'

'And me, you.'

'I couldn't bear either to hurt Ida. Margo, I imagine, would have something to say as well.'

'Wrong time, wrong place,' he said quietly.

She nodded.

'Jack, I feel a real connection, I don't even care about the difference in our ages, but there are so many reasons why we shouldn't let this go further.'

'As long as we can stay good friends.'

She smiled and he noticed a glimmer of tears in her eyes.

'I can't get through this without you, Jack.'

'I am there every step of the way, make no mistake about that.'

They swam a short distance together, before she started to get too cold and they got out.

They stood side by side as they dried down. Jack bundled up his clothes and threw his towel over his shoulder. 'I'm going to head home, I might see you later.'

Cassie smiled. Pulling on her dress, she walked slowly back to Rathmoney House. She was exhausted.

When Cassie walked in the front door, Margo was on the phone, but she motioned Cassie to watch as she drew two match stick figures on a small scrap of paper, followed by €1million.

'It does not take into account that Conor was deprived of meeting his daughter and never knew the truth,' Margo said.

Samantha Kiely did not immediately respond but when she did, she spoke slowly, her tone firm. 'Margo, they didn't just pick a number out of a hat, this followed a lot of back and forth between all sides. Frankly, I think it is a very good offer. I'm not sure a court would give you more.'

'Can I have a little time to think about it?'

'I told them we would get back to them by the end of the week, so go away, think about it, talk it over with Ms Kading.

I'm sure her attorney will be on to her at start of business in the States. Try to get back to me by Thursday,' she said, before ending the call.

'Do you think they have offered me the same?' Cassie asked.

'I hope they aren't differentiating our pain. That would be grossly unfair.'

'I'm sure Dale will make contact as soon as he can,' Cassie said, sinking into the couch, because she really did not feel well.

'It's obscene someone can put a price on our loss. What price do you put on that loss for Tilly, who lost out in a chance to meet her dad?'

'Elsa has lost her father too, to divorce.'

'I know.'

They sat quietly for a moment, each caught up in their own thoughts. Margo thought of Conor and how he always insisted Elsa had his grandmother's eyes. What did he know. Cassie, feeling queasy, closed her eyes and her mind lingered on Jack's kiss. Her time with Jack was the only brightness in her life right now and even that was tinged with guilt.

'When we accept this settlement, it will be all over in the eyes of the law, but for us, it will go on,' Margo said.

'Because we can never get back the lost years.'

Margo pushed Max out of her way with her foot.

'We're going to have to work so hard to forge meaningful relationships with our daughters, when we have no foundations. Nobody has even mentioned an apology, as if they're afraid a show of compassion would harm their case.'

Cassie needed to be alone. She didn't say so, but Margo understood.

Cassie went straight to the smoking shed. She was glad Jack wasn't there. Lighting up her cigarette, she sat down, sprawling her long legs out in front of her. She heard Tilly and Elsa down by the river; she knew by the lilt of their voices they were happy. It was very early in the United States, but she dialled Dale's number anyway.

'I'm sorry, Dale, I couldn't wait. Can you check your email?'

'OK, give me a few minutes, I'll ring you back.'

Ten minutes later, as she worried Dale might have been sidetracked, he rang back.

'Cas, they have offered an immediate transfer of one million euros in full settlement of the case.'

'What do you think I should do?'

'It all depends on how you want to play it. We can refuse this offer, hoping to hold out for a bigger one. That's a strategy we can adopt, but we have to ask what is best for you and Tilly. Tilly goes for her transplant in a few days and to have this finalised would be a good thing. If we hold out for more, we will have to start preparing the case in full, briefing certain attorneys and getting expert reports prepared, all of which will cost a lot and require input from both yourself and Tilly.'

'You mean she would have to be assessed.'

'Yes and a lot of these reports will be looking back at the last twelve years in detail, trying to establish if there was any lasting trauma suffered as a result of the swap.'

'Instinctively, I want to take the one million, but I should discuss it with Margo first.'

'Take your time, I don't want you to rush in to a decision.'

'Neither Tilly nor Elsa knows about the swap yet. We were going to wait until Tilly was fully recovered. If we hold out for a larger settlement, the girls will have to be told. That decision has got to be mine and Margo's. One million euros is a hell of a lot and it also buys us peace of mind.'

'Take a step back, figure out if it is fair and enough. Either way, I can get the ball rolling once you let me know.'

Cassie swallowed hard.

'Thanks, Dale.'

'Cassie, we will be praying for Tilly.'

'I know.'

'Get in touch when you are ready, Cas.'

Cassie could have told Dale there and then, but she owed it to Margo to discuss it with her first. Stubbing out her cigarette, she made for the house. Margo wasn't in either the kitchen or the drawing room. Cassie hesitated outside Conor's study. Knocking softly, she waited until Margo opened the door. 'Is there something wrong?' Margo asked.

'I know you want space, Margo, but I have to tell you something that may help you make your decision on the settlement.'

Margo stepped out into the hall, gesturing to Cassie to follow her to the drawing room.

'Is it about the girls? My solicitor rang back to say there may be a possibility Elsa and Tilly would be required to be interviewed, if we push for a bigger offer.'

'I want to keep the girls out of this.'

'Me too.'

'They are holding it like a stick over our heads,' Cassie said.

'One million each will make an enormous difference to our lives. I want to get rid of this.'

'I feel the same.'

'That stick is only there to beat us if we let it. We should do what suits us, which is accept the offer and get these people gone, once and for all.'

'I agree.'

Once the decision had been made, there was no point in waiting. Margo phoned Samantha Kiely, Cassie sent Dale an email.

'Some part of me wants to celebrate, but mainly I feel no great joy, only relief this part has come to an end,' Cassie said.

Margo took a bottle of Baileys and two glasses from the bookshelf. She poured a small drink for herself and a normal size for Cassie.

'To the millionaire swap-kids and their mothers.'

They clinked glasses, not with joy but with relief that something had been done to right the wrong and this part of the battle was over.

'Soon, I hope to be able to hold up my glass and toast the successful transplant.'

Cassie held up her glass, but before they could clink, she pulled away.

'Margo, I'm terrified something will go wrong. I don't want to tempt fate.'

'The toast will be better after the transplant and when we know it has been a success.'

'Thank you.'

'You're welcome. Just don't let on to Ida that I had a small sip of Baileys. If she had her way, she would have me on bread and water to get me in top shape for surgery.'

They giggled, Cassie sitting on the couch, Margo in her velvet chair. They waited together for their daughters to return, hungry and happy.

Chapter Thirty-Two

Rathmoney, County Wicklow.

Cassie could not sleep. She had a funny feeling in her throat and a pain around the neck. She pulled at her pillows and plumped them up several times, but at five o'clock she gave up. Stealing downstairs, she moved to the drawing room so she could curl up on the couch and look at the TV. She was surprised to see Margo half-dozing in the wingback chair by the window. Quickly reversing, she made to go to the kitchen, but Margo called her back.

'You couldn't sleep either?'

'Sleep does not come easily to me these days.'

'Come in, join me please, we can chat now that nobody else is about.'

'You mean Ida.'

Margo laughed. 'Ida is the best friend anybody could have, but I wouldn't like to be her enemy.' Cassie pulled up a leather tub chair beside the wingback. 'It's beautiful here.'

'From this spot, I can see all that I love about Rathmoney: the granite steps leading to the front door, the horses in the field, the avenue that curls towards the house, the bank of fuchsia and the river, a backdrop to everything. When things are bad, I sit here and the vista reminds me of all that is right in my life.'

'You must find yourself wanting to sit here a lot lately.'

'Yes, this house, this landscape is my security blanket.' Margo reached out to grasp Cassie's hand. 'Here I am, a grown woman afraid of going into hospital. Poor Tilly must be so scared.'

Cassie shook her head. 'I don't even know if I should have pushed everyone and everything so hard to achieve this. What if it all goes wrong for either of you?'

Margo patted her gently. 'We will not give that any further thought. We will breathe deeply and take in the Rathmoney House vista and we will hope and pray that everything will go right and that the next time we are all under the same roof again, it will be a cause for celebration.'

'I have no words, Margo.'

'None needed.'

They sat, a calm descending on the room, the birds calling out the first sounds of dawn. The sun rose over the sea, sending its rays to flash across the fields and sparkle on the windows. The hens in the barn cackled, the dog still in the kitchen whined and scraped at the back door.

Margo and Cassie watched Jack come up the avenue, his Jeep dipping in and out of the big pothole nobody had bothered to get filled.

'You and Jack get on well,' Margo said quietly.

'I like him.'

'Ida has noticed too.'

'What do you mean?'

Cassie made to get up, but Margo put a hand out to stop her. 'I just want you to know, that's all.'

'Know what, exactly?'

'There has been talk – you have been seen out and about with Jack.'

'We're friends.'

'I guess Ida is worried that people are talking.'

Cassie jumped up. 'Don't any of you think I have enough going on in my life without trying to break up a rock-solid marriage as well. Jack is a good friend and that's all I'm looking for right now. Ida would be better off minding her own relationship than listening to hurtful gossip.'

She began to cough and splutter. Annoyed at herself, she ran to the kitchen for a drink. Margo followed.

'Are you all right?'

'I can't seem to get rid of this stupid cough,' she said, gulping down a glass of water.

'Maybe you should go to a doctor. I can make an appointment with mine, if you like.'

'I'm all right, it's probably from all those years when I smoked like a chimney. I was off the cigarettes for ages, but now it's like I never stopped.'

'Best get it checked. You don't want Tilly to pick up any virus.'

'I wouldn't put Tilly at risk in any way.'

'I know. I didn't mean to upset you.'

Cassie smiled. 'I flew off the handle. I think I will get a walk in before Tilly wakes up.' She stopped at the door. 'I could go to the doctor later if they have an appointment.'

'I'll ring the surgery,' Margo said.

Cassie went out by the back door, Max running ahead of her. She walked over the bridge to the far fields. Keeping to the side of the field where the cattle were, she headed for the stile, where she could sit and think, far enough away from Rathmoney House. When she heard her name being called, she didn't look back. After a few minutes, Jack came up beside her, panting and out of breath.

'Where are you off to in such a hurry?'

'Careful, no further; somebody might be watching.'

'What?'

'You heard, I wouldn't want to be feeding any more choice tidbits to the gossips.'

'Cassie, what has happened? Has Ida said something?'

'No, but everybody else has. Don't they have anything better to do than comment on us two, the way we walk, the way we stand and the way we talk?'

'What stupidity is this?'

Cassie looked at Jack. He could see she had been crying, because the tip of her nose was red.

'My husband has left me; my daughter is not my daughter; my Tilly has to have a transplant; haven't I enough going down without this?'

'Ignore them. If anyone bothers to ask Ida's opinion, she will tell them pretty sharpish what she thinks.'

'Jack, I have feelings for you, but I don't want to hurt Ida, she has been a brick and such a support to Tilly who adores her.'

'Cassie, we are friends, let the others think what they want.'

She sat on the stile. 'Trouble is, I want to be more than your friend,' she said softly.

'Me too.'

'It's too complicated, Jack.'

'Let's just see how we go. Tilly has to be your priority now.'

They stayed beside each other, each staring out to sea, neither wanting to break the feeling of warm companionship between them.

Two brown rabbits scampered into the middle of the field and began to munch on clover.

'So cute, I must tell Tilly.' Cassie's voice was hoarse.

Jack reached into his pocket and took out a box of cough sweets.

'It might be that you're not used to our damp air.'

She pushed out a lozenge, making the rabbits stop and twitch their noses, on alert as the sound of the packaging punctured the stillness.

'Jack, could you ever imagine living anywhere else?'

He laughed. 'I did once, when I was nineteen.'

He stopped as if thinking back to a different time.

'Tell me, I need a distraction right now.'

He laughed again. 'I seem to be expert at providing a distraction.'

'Why don't you tell me your story and I will be the judge,' she said, shoving him gently.

He climbed up onto the stile to sit beside her.

'I spent a year in Salamanca, Spain. I was in teacher training college and managed to pick up a summer job working in a bar. The pay wasn't great, but I loved the town and a girl, Maria. She was my first love; it was heady, sweet and impossible. Her mother and father were set against us, I had no prospects according to them, and even if I returned to Ireland and teacher training, where would that get me?

'We were pretty sure of each other, but life got in the way. My father had a terrible accident on the farm; I was called home. He lasted two weeks before he passed away. Maybe you can guess the rest. My mother was in bits, so I stayed on with her. I had to take over the running of the farm, talk of returning to Spain disappeared, I never went back to college, either.'

When he had finished, Jack shifted on the stile, jumping down to kick at dandelions bunched around the base.

'What happened to Maria?'

'I kept writing to her, asking for more time, never able to commit to a date when I could return. She got tired of me and I don't blame her. Later she wrote me a short note to say she was now married and wishing me well for the future.'

Jack reached into his pocket again and took out the lozenges, popping one in his mouth.

'I met Ida not long after that. She has her own story to tell, but we recognised something in one another, decided to make a go of it. My mother died two months later and I was left the farm. It's a good productive farm, we do well. Around these parts, I'm known as one of the wealthy guys. Funny, the way things pan out, isn't it?'

'Did you ever hear from Maria again or try to make contact?' Cassie asked gently.

'There was no point, what was done was done.'

'But you and Ida are good?'

Jack nodded.

'Ida is my rock and I am hers. We understand each other... Your turn now.'

'My story is no grand romance. We met in High School. Charles Richards was the big guy and I was the funny fish beside him, always experimenting with different hairstyles and outfits. I got pregnant just as Charles graduated and got a job. We got married and when he was sent to Paris, I went along as well. That's how Tilly ended up being born in France. Once we had Tilly, we wanted to go home to our folks, so we went back to our hometown and Charles joined his daddy in the car business. I stayed home, looking after Tilly until she was about six years old.'

'I bet you never expected to end up anywhere like Rathmoney.'

'I'm small town, I like Rathmoney. I guess you didn't expect to spend all of your life here?'

'I didn't, but it doesn't mean I'm not happy.'

She made to get off the stile, he put his hand out to help and she accepted.

She got down, standing so close to him he could breathe in her perfume.

Reaching up, she pulled him towards her, kissing him firmly on the lips. 'Let the gossips go to hell.'

She turned and walked quickly back towards the house.

Jack went in the opposite direction, to round up the horses.

Cassie was about to cross the bridge, when Bonnie rang.

'Cas, I've got news. I've been dying to tell you but I know you've already got so much to think about. But it's official now. I'm leaving Bowling Green. It's goodbye, Ohio. Greg has a posting in Hawaii. We're off at the end of the week. Can you believe it?'

'Wow, I'm jealous.' Cassie smiled, hearing the excitement in her friend's voice.

'Zack says I'll miss the buzz of real estate.'

Cassie laughed. 'Like a hole in the head. What are your plans?'

Bonnie spoke in a low voice. 'It might be time to start a family.'

Cassie whooped loudly and Bonnie laughed.

'I just hope I can be as good a mom as you, Cas.'

'Be your own kind of mom, Bonnie, you'll be great.'

'Greg doesn't start the new job for a month, so we'll vacation first. Give us a bit of time to get settled and I'll ring you about meeting up. Maybe you and Tilly can come to us, a holiday in Hawaii might be just the tonic after all you've been through.'

Cassie smiled. 'That's a lovely thought, it'll sustain me through the next while.'

'Give me a month or so, there's a lot going on in the run-up to the move and after.'

'I'll be in a better mood to plan when Tilly is done with the medical stuff. Tell me: how did Zack take your news?'

'He blames you for starting a trend.'

Somebody behind Bonnie called her.

'Got to go, babe. Talk soon.'

Cassie trudged back to Rathmoney House. When Margo saw her, she waved and waited, standing at the front steps, to greet her.

'I'm glad you're back, the doctor has a cancellation and can take you in half an hour.'

'Let me get changed quickly,' Cassie said as she hurried inside and upstairs.

When she came back down, Margo was already in the car.

'I'm sorry about earlier,' she said.

'Don't worry, the tension is getting to all of us,' Cassie replied.

Chapter Thirty-Three

Rathmoney, County Wicklow.

They all gathered early in the hallway of Rathmoney House. After weeks of preparation, medication and worry, the time for the kidney transplant had arrived. Margo, with Elsa by her side, was trying to stay calm and smiling too much. Ida was fussing, telling Jack to bring the bags to the cars. 'The red case is Margo's, the one with the stickers, Tilly's.'

'Ida, I think I guessed that already,' Jack said and Elsa giggled.

When Cassie came downstairs with Tilly, Ida began to fire out instructions.

'You aren't listening, are you?' Ida said at the top of her voice. Nobody answered, so she followed Jack out onto the top steps.

'Poor Ida, she's only like this because she's so nervous,' Margo whispered to Cassie.

Cassie turned to Margo and Elsa. 'Tilly and I wanted to say something to you both, can we go to the drawing room for a minute?'

They trooped in behind Cassie and sat on the couch. Cassie took a deep breath.

'There were days I honestly thought we would never get to the stage where Tilly would have the chance of a kidney transplant.'

She put her hand out to Tilly, who snuggled in to her. 'So this is a big day and you two, Margo and Elsa, have made it possible.' She held out her hand to Elsa. 'The day I came here, I told your mum I had a gift for you. Now is a good time to give it to you.'

She held out a long box. Elsa opened it and took out a silver necklace.

'It's a friendship necklace, it links to mine,' Tilly said, showing her the chain.

'Because we are the best of friends,' Elsa laughed.

Cassie pulled another box from her handbag and handed it to Margo. Embarrassed, Margo took the box and opened it. Inside was a small butterfly-shaped brooch, its wings sparkling with cobalt blue and deep green stones.

'Nana used to wear that brooch. She liked to put it on with her navy silk dress,' Tilly said.

'I am honoured. I shall have to buy a navy dress to best show it off,' Margo said, making Tilly beam.

'My mother always loved Weiss jewellery, she gave me that brooch when Tilly was born. We pass it on to you now, as you, in turn, give her new life,' Cassie said.

'I will treasure it,' Margo replied.

Ida loitered at the drawing room door. 'I don't want to rush you, but we need to get going.'

Suddenly, Tilly held back as the others bustled to the cars.

'What's wrong?' Elsa asked.

'Why can't we all go to the same hospital?'

'It's just the way it's done here, kids one place, adults the other,' Margo said.

Cassie hugged her daughter tight. 'Margo will come to see you in a few days, when she has recovered and you both feel much better.'

'Don't you worry, you lot, Jack and Ida Roper will be back and forth between the two,' Ida said as she ushered them outside.

They all laughed, Cassie and Margo relieved Ida had managed to lighten the mood before they travelled off to separate hospitals in two cars, Jack driving one, Ida the other.

Jack and Elsa sat with Margo until she was taken down to surgery. Before she left, she spoke to Tilly on FaceTime. 'Darling, don't be worried, soon the kidney will be on its way by ambulance to your hospital and to you.'

'Mom says we'll both be very sore, but I will have loads of energy in a few days.'

'There'll be no stopping you, Max will be thrilled.'

Margo saw Tilly smile. 'Think of all the things you'll be able to do and don't worry, you won't end up talking like me,' Margo joked.

Tilly laughed. Cassie made to say something, but Margo put her hand up to stop her.

'See you at the other side, Cas.'

Elsa kissed her mum, making every effort to appear brave. As Margo was taken down to surgery, she stood clutching Jack's hand tight.

'Come on, kiddo. We'll go back to Rathmoney for a bit and come back later, when your mum is back on the ward,' he said.

Over at the other hospital, Cassie was told she could go home, it would take another two to three hours. She didn't want to leave, so she sat waiting.

Before they took Tilly down, they reported that everything had gone well for Margo.

Tilly was nervous and quiet.

'I'll be right here waiting for you. Remember, it won't be long before you can race across the fields to the sea,' Cassie whispered.

Tilly nodded and Cassie knew she had her brave face on.

When they wheeled Tilly away, Cassie sat in the hospital room on her own. Afraid even to go for a coffee, despite the numerous reassurances there wouldn't be any news for at least three hours, she sat waiting. When she heard a bustle in the corridor and her name being mentioned, she opened the door.

Ida was standing, a large Tesco shopping bag in her hand. 'They say I can't visit, but I told them you could do with the company,' Ida said, her voice unnecessarily loud.

'Please can she stay? She is family to all of us. I could do with a shoulder to lean on.'

The nurse relented, letting Ida bustle past.

'How are you doing, Cassie? It's the hardest thing, waiting for news.'

'They told me I could come back in a few hours. I know they would ring, but somehow, I can't explain it, I just can't leave.'

'Of course you can't, which is why I'm here.'

Ida opened up the shopping bag, taking out a flask of coffee.

'I've left it black, exactly the way you like it, and no sugar. It's poison, but, so be it.'

'That's so kind of you, but what about yourself?'

'I have a nice flask of sweet, milky tea.'

Dipping into the bag, Ida produced a packet of fig rolls.

'They are good for dunking and the figs fool me into thinking I am eating healthily,' she said, blathering on because she was nervous.

Cassie poured out a coffee and sipped it. 'When they came to bring Tilly down, they said things were going well with Margo.'

'Thank God, and it will go well with Tilly too.'

They sat for a while, not saying much, listening to the hospital sounds: people walking by, the odd conversation outside the door, trolleys trundling past, greetings called down the corridor.

After a while, Ida got up and stretched.

'We were reading the stairs will be difficult for the two of them, especially for Tilly, for a little while after their operations. Jack was wondering if we should convert one of the downstairs rooms at Rathmoney, to make a temporary bedroom for you and Tilly.'

'What does Margo think?'

'Jack talked to her last night about it and she said maybe the dining room, because it's beside the downstairs bathroom. We can store the dining-room furniture in the barn. It will be OK there for a short time.'

'I hadn't thought of any of this.'

'Why would you? You have had enough to deal with. As we speak, Jack is setting up a bed for Margo in Conor's office, though her recovery will be a lot easier.'

Cassie joined Ida at the window overlooking the car park.

'What will I do if Tilly's system doesn't accept Margo's kidney? They said back in the States that if she had been brought in even weeks later, it would have been an awful lot worse.' The words caught in her throat. 'If this doesn't work, Ida, Tilly is in serious trouble and even with dialysis, she will be a very sick girl.'

'We're not even going to consider this. How in God's name is her body going to kick against her mother's kidney? That would be unthinkable.'

Cassie started to sob.

'Jesus, I have done it again, opened my big mouth. I'm sorry.'

'There's no need to apologise, Margo and I are good with all this.'

Ida put her arm around Cassie's shoulders. 'I know it has taken me a while to come around, but as far as I am concerned those two girls have two mothers each and they are the best mums in the world.'

Cassie smiled through her tears.

'That means a lot coming from you, Ida.'

'I know, considering I was such a cow when you first arrived.'

They sat down, Ida reaching into the Tesco bag again, taking out a plate covered in foil.

'I have a bit of lunch for you here, your favourite, wild salmon, new potatoes and asparagus. I'm sure the nurses have a microwave we can use.'

'I don't think they'll be too happy about that.'

'Nonsense, sure you have to keep your strength up. I brought a nice chocolate mousse for dessert as well.'

Ida went off in search of the nurses' station. Cassie rang Vince.

'I'll be with you very soon, sweetie, and will help every way I can.' Her father's voice was steady and soothing.

'Just having you here will be enough.'

'Is there anybody sitting with you at the hospital?'

'I am being overwhelmed by kindness, but until this whole thing is over and we are out the other side, I'm not going to relax.'

'Have you let Charles know?'

'He's not in our lives anymore, but he does know. I rang him before we left.'

'I've heard they may have to pull out of Baltimore, that sales are not as good as expected.'

Cassie felt suddenly afraid. 'Vince, please don't tell anyone about the French settlement or he will try and take it from us.'

'Don't take me for a fool, Cassandra. My lips are sealed.'

'I'm sorry, I just don't want any more hassle.'

'I'll be over for a few weeks, so we'll have plenty of time to chat. You just concentrate on what is happening there today. I'll see you soon.'

'OK.'

'And, darling, everything will be fine with Tilly and Margo. It's a new beginning.'

'I hope you're right.'

Ida came back into the room, holding the plate with a tea towel.

'You get this food inside you while it's still hot,' she said, also producing a small bottle of wine from her bag.

'There's nothing wrong with a sip of fine wine either,' she said, but Cassie shook her head.

Ida took out a magazine and began to flick through it.

'That bag is like a treasure trove, Ida.'

Ida looked out over the reading glasses she had slipped on to catch up with the latest news about the royal family.

'We haven't seen eye to eye, you and me, since you came to Rathmoney and I wanted to make it up to you.'

'I understand how much you care for Margo and Elsa.'

Ida pulled off her glasses and placed them in a case. 'And Tilly. And yourself too, I only want the best for you.'

'We just have to get through all of this, then we can work out how the four of us can continue.'

Ida looked a little alarmed. 'Margo told me you guys had talked and decided more or less to leave things as they are.'

'We have, but once Tilly's recuperation is over in a few months, we'll be returning to the States. I guess we will have to be back and forth, visiting each other.'

'Won't Elsa love that, jet-setting to the US.'

'You and Jack will have to come too.'

'That would be nice, but with two farms to run, highly unlikely.'

'You two are so lucky, Ida. Jack thinks the world of you. He told me how he used to love you from afar and how happy he was when he finally got to ask you out.'

'That Jack Roper is a fool; I wouldn't be listening to him, if I were you.'

A nurse stuck her head in to say everything was going fine,

Margo was in recovery and they would have news from Tilly's team in an hour or so.

Ida reached over and grasped Cassie's arm. 'We are halfway there.'

When the nurse left the room Ida allowed herself a little clap.

'That's a very good sign that everything went so well at Margo's end. I must ring Jack, make sure they've told Elsa. She will be on pins to find out, too.' She turned, before stepping out in to the corridor. 'All the prayers are going to Tilly now, don't you worry about that.'

Alone, Cassie paced the room. It wasn't just the surgery she feared, it was the days and weeks afterwards, but particularly the hours after the transplant when they would get early indications of whether or not Tilly's system was accepting the new kidney. This had to work out, because she had no Plan B for Tilly's future if it didn't. She hoped too that her plans for Tilly's recovery would not be affected by the fact that she herself had to have a series of tests: the doctor had ordered them to take place this week.

The door opened. The surgeon stood with a smile on his face.

'Everything went well, Ms Kading. Tilly is in recovery and will be brought back to the room shortly. Margo is also doing well, I hear. The next hours are crucial for Tilly, she will be monitored closely. She will be sore and tired, so no need to talk much, just be a reassuring presence. They will both need to rest.'

As the surgeon made to leave, Cassie put a hand on his arm. 'Thank you so much. I will be forever grateful.'

'Let's see how it goes. The surgery went well. Now it is up to Tilly and that kidney.'

Chapter Thirty-Four

Rathmoney, County Wicklow.

Margo was sore, but she could walk short distances. When she was discharged, Elsa helped her into the lift and Jack followed with her bag.

'Jack, I want to visit Tilly, can we go there first?'

'I was in yesterday, we played Cluedo and she is walking around and drinking loads. Cassie keeps offering her really nice drinks, but she only wants water,' Elsa said. 'Do you want to know what Ida did?'

'She won't be happy about you telling tales, young lady,' Jack said kindly.

'You have to tell. This is going to be good.'

Elsa giggled. 'She went to McDonalds.'

'Has Ida ever been in any sort of burger joint before?' Margo asked.

Jack laughed heartily. 'She must love you girls, she always swore she would never darken the door.'

Elsa, bursting with excitement, continued. 'She went to McDonalds on O'Connell Street and ordered two double cheeseburgers, fries and ice creams. She even got curly fries for herself and Cassie. Then she put it all in her basket and smuggled it into Tilly's room.'

Margo laughed.

'And that's not all. When she saw the ice cream was melting and we were only halfway through our meals, she called in the nurse and asked if she could store the ice creams in the kitchen fridge.'

'What did the nurse say?'

'*Yes*, of course. Nobody says no to Ida.'

'She really is something,' Margo said.

'One in a million, I have never met anyone with a bigger heart,' Jack said, though Margo thought she detected a sadness about him. As if picking up on Margo's concern, Jack continued, 'She would have been the best mother in the world, just the right mix of compassion, fun and firmness.'

'I think she is getting a second chance with Elsa and Tilly,' Margo said gently.

Jack nodded, pulling in to a parking space at the children's hospital. Ida was waiting at the entrance.

'I thought of going to Smyths toy shop to buy something for the girls, would Elsa like to come along? She might be better at picking something appropriate. Otherwise, I might come back with Barbie dolls.'

Margo smiled as Elsa hopped out to join Ida and took her hand. She watched as they set off down the street, chatting happily.

'Your wife is amazing, none of us should forget that,' Margo said to Jack.

He looked troubled. 'I love Ida, I hope you know that, Margo.'

'It doesn't matter about me, Ida needs to know.'

Jack couldn't look directly at her. 'Can you manage the lift up to the second floor on your own?'

'I can.'

'Right, see you up in Tilly's room in a while. I reckon Ida and Elsa could do with a bit of help, carrying back all they intend to buy.'

Margo thought he ran like a teenage boy down the street to catch up with his wife.

By the time Margo reached Tilly's room, she was weary. Stopping to sit in the ward corridor outside, she saw Cassie chatting to Tilly, who was sitting up in bed, the colour returned to her cheeks, her eyes brighter. They were connected forever now, this girl and she.

She had not only given life to her once, but now a second time. A glow of satisfaction coursed through her; but sadness, too, that Tilly still did not know how much she really meant to her.

Cassie got up to close the door and spotted Margo. 'Margo, what are you doing out there on your own? Where is Jack?'

'I'm fine, can I come in?'

'You don't even have to ask.' She turned around and called to Tilly. 'Look who's here.'

Tilly squealed, holding out her two hands to Margo.

'Just an air kiss, otherwise it will hurt too much,' Margo said as she perched as near as possible to Tilly.

'Do you hurt too?' Tilly asked.

'Yeah, but that's all right.'

She saw Cassie back out of the room and she was grateful. Her Tilly, the little girl who loved to drink slushies and to wear her hair in a ponytail. She had given her not just a kidney, but a path for the future and the means to take on life, full of zest and energy.

'You look a bit tired, Margo.'

'That's because I am.'

'Do you feel different?'

'Tired, but incredibly happy.'

She saw Tilly was holding back the tears. 'I'm sore and I have a pump to use to get the painkillers in. Mom says I have to thank you, but I'm not sure she understands. Thank you is not enough.'

'Silly girl, all you need to do is just get better.'

'Do you miss it?'

'I decided a while back it was your kidney and I was looking after it for you. Now, it's where it belongs.'

Margo looked at Tilly, propped up against her hospital pillows, her eyes glistening, her hair scraped back from her face. Lovely, gentle Tilly. She was back in that moment in another hospital twelve years ago, when she'd pledged to this beautiful baby girl to look after her always. She had made that pledge with all her heart; at least now she had honoured some of that promise. At least now they had a bond that did not hark back to the past. Maybe, too, they could start afresh, forge a relationship from a shared experience.

She saw Cassie hovering at the door and beckoned her to come in.

'Tilly will soon be running marathons.'

'Thanks to you, I hope so. She's being monitored all the time, but so far everything is fine, she walks about already.'

'All will be well. It just has to be,' Margo said firmly. They heard Elsa's voice in the corridor. She ran in with two Build-A-Bears in her arms. 'Look what Jack and Ida got us.'

She handed a bear to Tilly. 'It will be nice and soft for you to cuddle, until you are feeling better.'

She turned to Margo. 'You can have mine, until the pain goes away.'

Margo reached out and kissed her daughter. 'Thank you, darling.'

Ida said they had better not crowd around Tilly. 'We need to get you home, Margo, you look a wreck, no offence.'

Margo let Ida help her downstairs and in to the car.

It was a quiet but lovely homecoming for Margo to Rathmoney House. Elsa caught her mother by the hand and brought her straight to the study, where Conor's desk had been moved to the side and a single bed placed by the window.

'I asked Jack to put the bed there, so you can see the fields and the sea,' she said, helping her mother to sit down.

'Where are you going to sleep, sweetie?'

'Ida says I have to stay upstairs, because we have to keep the place as sterile as possible and I am a normal child, who naturally has a lot of bugs.'

'What a load of nonsense.'

'I thought so too, but I didn't say anything.'

'I'll talk to Jack. There is a comfy camp bed in the attic, I think it will fit in right beside me.'

Elsa beamed at her mother.

'Tilly won't be home for a few days, so it can be like old times, just you and me.'

Elsa flung herself into her mother's arms, but Margo didn't tell her it hurt as they hugged tight.

'Mummy, can I ask a question?'

'Shoot.'

'Now she has a part of you inside her, does it mean you'll love Tilly more than you love me?'

Margo pulled her daughter to her.

'Elsa, nothing will change or replace the bond between us. You are my girl and that's that.'

'But you did a big thing together.'

'A strange, shared experience, you mean, and yes, Tilly has

my kidney; we're lucky everything has gone well, but you are my girl, Elsa.'

Elsa, happy with the reassurance offered by her mother, asked how long they would have to sleep in the study.

'I don't think for very long, we'll have to wait and see.'

'Ida says Tilly won't be able to play for months, but Cassie says that's nuts and once she gets over the surgery, she'll have even more energy than me.'

'Well, let's hope that happens soon.'

'Yeah, because then Max can come home.'

'Why, where is Max?'

'Ida said he couldn't be here, because of germs or in case he jumped up on you or Tilly or tripped you up. He's at Ida and Jack's, but he's not happy.'

'Poor old Max, he has not jumped up on anyone since he was a puppy. I'll talk to Jack, maybe he can come home, but he won't be allowed past the kitchen for a while.'

There was a knock at the door and Ida came in with a tray.

'Thanks, Ida, but can I take that in the drawing room? The doctors said to try to get back to a normal routine as soon as possible, walking and sitting out are very important.'

Ida walked ahead to the drawing room, pulling the coffee table beside Margo's favourite chair, so she could place the tray on it.

'You can't do too much, you need to rest.'

'This velvet chair is all I need right now, Ida.'

Elsa rushed into the room.

'Mummy, Ava's mum is on the phone. She says can I go swimming with Ava please?' She handed the phone to Margo.

'Elsa is delighted, thank you so much. Yes, she can be ready in fifteen minutes, no bother.'

Ida made to say something, but Margo tapped her gently on the hand.

'Run off and find your swimming gear, Elsa, they will be here to collect you very soon,' she said. Margo waited to talk to Ida until Elsa was out of the room.

'I know you think she should stay and keep me company, but letting her off is the best signal that everything is as it should be. Besides, I'm going to get a better rest this way.'

'When you put it like that, I understand.'

'Ida, you and Jack have been so fantastic these past weeks. Do you think Jack could run Max back? We can ban him from everywhere in the house but the kitchen. Rathmoney House is just not the same without him.'

'God yes, we just did it as a precaution,' Ida said, placing a cushion behind Margo's back.

Margo sat back against the cushion. She had missed Rathmoney House when she was in hospital, found herself drawing up images of the view from this chair, the fields, the slick of sea sparkling now in the warm sunshine. When she saw a car come up the avenue, she called Elsa.

Elsa thundered down the stairs.

'Have you put on your sunblock?' she called out.

Elsa said she had and when she reached down for a kiss, Margo could smell it.

'Jack will drop Max home shortly,' Margo whispered in Elsa's ear.

'Yippee, poor Max must have been so sad.'

When the car pulled in at the front, Rita got out, holding a big bunch of flowers.

'They must be for you, Mummy.'

'Ida is on top of all that. You run along and enjoy yourself,' Margo said.

Elsa waved to her as the car swept away and Margo wondered if Rita had spotted her inside the window.

Once the car disappeared out of view and Ida had gone back

to the kitchen, Margo was left to sip her tea, sitting in her favourite spot.

The medical team had judged the transplant as a success and before long, Tilly should be back to more than her normal self. The settlement meant they would no longer have money worries. How life had changed for them. But there would be more changes to come. When Tilly was back on her feet, she and Cassie intended to work out a plan for the school holidays, so they could alternate between Rathmoney and the US. Samantha Kiely insisted they draw up a contract signed by all parties, but Margo and Cassie had still to discuss that. Even more importantly, they still hadn't agreed what or when to tell their girls.

But just as a knot of anxiety was forming in her chest, she saw Max bounding up the avenue and Margo laughed out loud. Rathmoney House really wasn't the same without the golden Labrador flopped out the front.

Part Three

Chapter Thirty-Five

Rathmoney, County Wicklow.

Vince Kading arrived at the front door of Rathmoney House when everybody but Elsa was still in bed.

'Mummy, there's a strange man at the door,' she said, shaking Margo gently.

Margo pulled on her dressing gown and opened the door a few inches. 'I'm afraid we are not taking paying guests at the moment,' she said.

'My apologies my flight got in so early. I'm Cassie's dad.'

Margo pulled back the door. Vince extended his hand to Elsa.

'And you must be the lovely Elsa. My granddaughter has been telling me about you.'

Elsa nodded, shrinking back a little from the tall man with the grey hair.

'I don't think Cassie is expecting you until tomorrow.'

Vince grinned. 'The airline was overbooked tomorrow, so they offered me first class a day early instead and said they would pay for a taxi to my final destination. I'm not sure they reckoned on it being in the next county.'

Cassie was dozing when she heard the familiar loud tones of her father. Jumping out of bed, she started to cough and had to take a drink before making her way downstairs. Vince was already chatting to Margo and Elsa in the kitchen.

When he saw Cassie he got to his feet. 'Sweetheart, come here. You look so tired.'

'Tilly is coming home today. She is doing fine, Daddy.'

'And we have baked a cake, we'll have a party,' Elsa piped up.

Vince took her in. If it was true that traits skip a generation, it certainly came out in this young girl, he thought. She looked just like Cassie's mum at that age, the way she shook her head and that shy to wide smile.

'Tilly has told me all about your dog, where is he?'

Elsa called Max at the top of her voice and he came bounding across the yard, pushing the back door in.

'I brought this fellow a nice chewy toy,' Vince said, producing a squeaky stuffed toy from his cabin bag.

Vince threw the toy in the air and the dog jumped and caught it, making Elsa laugh.

'You two will have to take that play outside,' Cassie said, and Vince followed Elsa and the dog out into the back yard.

Cassie stood inside the kitchen window, watching them playing with Max, who on every occasion brought back the ball and dropped it at Elsa's feet. 'I so wish my mother could have met Elsa. It's special, isn't it, the relationship between grandchildren and grandparents.'

Margo joined her at the window. 'For Elsa this is her first experience of a grandparent; she's loving it and she doesn't even know why.'

They already had balloons and bunting out the front and a Welcome Home sign Elsa had coloured in. When it was time for Jack and Cassie to collect Tilly, Max was kept in the barn, in case he lost the run of himself and got too boisterous.

Everyone waited until they heard the sound of the Jeep

returning. Jack drove around the back, so Tilly did not have to negotiate the front steps.

Vince was waiting in the kitchen to surprise his grand-daughter. When she saw him, Tilly quickened her pace until she was beside him.

Vince picked up her hand and gently kissed it.

'Grandad, I knew you would come.'

'And I plan to stay for weeks. I want to get to know you and your pal, Elsa here.'

'Elsa made me a sign.'

'And a special Welcome Home cake,' Ida said, as she placed a triple-layer chocolate cake on the table.

Vince pulled out his phone.

'Tilly, Elsa, get in beside the cake, I must have a photo of this fine creation,' he said as the girls giggled, their heads touching.

Margo heard Cassie cough and leave the room. She followed her to the drawing room. 'You must be exhausted Cassie, it's time for you to get some rest now.'

'I don't feel very well, but the relief that we have got this far is huge.'

'In a few months' time, it will all be just a memory and Tilly will have energy to burn.'

'Already, she seems like a different girl.' Cassie began to cry.

'What is it, what's the matter?'

'I just feel so overwhelmed, I can never repay you, Margo, for what you have done for Tilly.'

'You are not fighting me for Elsa or preventing me from get-ting to know Tilly. That is all the thanks I need.'

Cassie walked over to the table with the boxes on it. Reach-ing into her handbag, she took out a small wooden box. It was roughly made and out of keeping with the others on the table.

'Tilly made this at school. Everyone else made picture frames but she insisted she had to do it. It belongs here with all the other boxes Conor loved,' she said, slipping the box on to the table.

Margo picked up the little box, rubbing it lightly between her hands. 'I will treasure it. Thank you. But how did you get it?'

'Dad had to pack up our things because Charles is selling our house. I asked him to bring the box.'

'Won't Tilly mind if we have the box at Rathmoney?'

'We talked about it last night, she is quite honoured that it be included in Conor's collection. That is if you are happy.'

'I am more than happy, it's my new favourite box.'

'That American is really a bit much, don't you think?' Ida said as she walked in to the drawing room. She stopped when she saw Cassie. 'I'm sorry, I thought you were inspecting the new bedroom.'

Cassie just laughed. 'I suppose my father is a bit much. You can always hear him coming, and he loves his phone and recording every moment.'

'I wasn't meaning to be rude, I like your father, we had a lovely chat just now, but I didn't want him wearing Tilly out,' Ida blustered.

Cassie smiled. 'I know, Ida. I think he's happy his daughter and granddaughter have found their feet here at Rathmoney; maybe we should get back to the kitchen and cut the cake.'

'He is full of it. But this is a happy day for all of us.'

Chapter Thirty-Six

Rathmoney, County Wicklow.

Margo got up early, tiptoeing into the kitchen in case she woke Cassie and Tilly. These days she liked to pour herself a coffee and wander down to her bench by the river. She was about to slip out the back door when Tilly came into the kitchen.

'Where are you going, can I come too?'

'Honey, don't you have to take your medicine?'

'Mom says she has to be here when I take it, so I'll wait until she gets up.'

'I'm just going to my bench by the river to have my coffee. Do you want to bring a drink?'

Tilly went to the fridge and grabbed a mini carton of orange juice. They walked side by side, Max following on behind.

'You're looking very good, Tilly, the kidney is working well.'

'I guess. I have a lot of energy now. Sometimes, Elsa tells me to slow down.'

'That must be a nice feeling.'

'I say to her she should get a kidney from my mom and then we will be even more related,' Tilly laughed as they pushed past the fuchsia to the glade by the river.

They sat down, sipping their drinks while they watched the dog try to take a rock from the river.

'My mom's birthday is tomorrow. Do you think if I ask Ida nicely she will help me bake a cake?'

'Ida loves an excuse to make a cake, we must get you going on that this morning.'

'I've made a card and I thought the cake could be a gift.'

Max got out of the river, shaking himself fiercely, making Margo and Tilly scream.

'I guess I have Lab coffee now,' Margo said, throwing out the last from her mug onto the grass.

'Can I ask you something?'

'Sure.'

'When I was in hospital, Mom told me you were meant to show her lots of lovely designer dresses, but she never got to see them.'

'I had forgotten about that.'

'Mom loves beautiful clothes.'

Margo laughed. 'What a great idea, we can have a fashion show, the four of us, well five with Ida, and birthday cake and I'm sure we have champagne somewhere.'

Tilly clapped in delight.

'It's going to be the best birthday ever. We can get Grandad to take photos of Mom in beautiful dresses.'

'I will get Jack to get the boxes down from the attic tonight, once you and your mum have gone to bed.'

Margo phoned Ida to ask about the cake.

'Ida says it might be best if you and Elsa went to her house to do the cake; no chance of Cassie finding out that way.'

When the two of them walked back to the house, both Elsa and Cassie were eating breakfast in the kitchen.

'The wanderers have returned. Where were you two?'

'Down by the river, Max got in, he's a silly dog.'

Tilly and Margo smiled.

The rest of the day went in a blur of secret activity. Ida had supervised the baking of a sponge cake with vanilla cream filling and a frosted cream icing with the words 'Happy Birthday Cassie' on top. Vince had stocked up on delicious snacks and champagne. That night, Jack got the boxes of dresses down and laid them out behind the couch.

The next morning, Tilly and Elsa woke Cassie. She went to wrap her kimono around her, but Tilly told her to get dressed and put on some make-up.

Cassie, a little nervous at what might be planned, picked the light-green silk dress she'd bought in Arklow the previous month and swept her long hair into a bun. Tilly and Elsa watched her intently as she put on a little foundation with a slick of nude lipstick.

'You look lovely,' Elsa said.

Tilly produced a long scarf. 'You're going to have to trust us. We are going to blindfold you and bring you somewhere.'

Cassie allowed them to tie the scarf over her eyes, Tilly guiding her from the front, Elsa from behind as they walked slowly to the drawing room.

They walked her as far as the mantelpiece, with Tilly untying the mask as the others shouted Happy Birthday.

Cassie was so surprised and delighted she almost started to cry, telling her dad to hold off on photos. She cut the cake, giving the first slices to Tilly and Elsa. 'Cake for breakfast! I think you girls had a lot of help,' she said, winking at Ida. 'Thank you all, this has got to be the best birthday yet.'

'And it is only beginning,' Tilly said as she motioned to Margo to bring out the boxes.

'We thought it was a perfect day for a fashion show,' Elsa said.

'Are these your old designer dresses?' Cassie asked.

'And you get to pick out your favourite one,' Margo said as they lined up the boxes along the length of the Persian rug.

'That's our cue to get out of the ladies' way, Jack. I'll be in the kitchen, reading the *Seattle Times* online. Let me know when it's safe to come out,' Vince said.

He and Jack left, but the women hardly noticed as they tore into the boxes, carefully lifting the dresses, some heavy taffeta and satin embroidered, others silk and lace, a confection of colour in the drawing room.

Cassie pulled out a cerise pink silk organza ball gown. It rustled as she shook it out, the aroma of lavender encircling her. Holding it up to her, she twirled around the room, the dress fabric and the light-pink organza lining swishing in the morning sunshine spilling in to the room.

'I adore this dress.'

'You have the legs for it. Mrs Hegarty, the previous owner, often wore it, around the house would you believe. She said her legs weren't good enough to be seen in public, but you have a nice set of pins,' Ida said.

'Did you know her?'

'My mother was a dressmaker and often adjusted these gowns for her. She was once married to a very rich French man, Claude Devereaux. That's how she came by all these Jacques Heim dresses. The French man bought this house, intending it to be their holiday home. Unfortunately, he was killed in a horse-riding accident in France soon after.

'Poor Clara got thrown out on her ear by his French family. They were very wealthy and were afraid she would inherit it all. She told my mother she was thrown the keys of Rathmoney House and told to leave for Ireland immediately. She arrived here with barely a word of English and all her ballgowns in boxes.'

Margo, who was examining a blue tulle and lace evening

gown, stopped what she was doing. 'She must have been in shock, moving from Parisian high society to Rathmoney.'

Cassie pulled off her green silk dress and stepped into the pink organza gown with the simple square neckline. When she moved from behind the couch, Tilly and Elsa gasped.

'You look so beautiful, Mom,' Tilly said, rubbing her hand along the length of the skirt.

'I love that it is shorter at the front. You could wear runners with it,' Elsa said and they all laughed.

'I think it's a brilliant idea, Elsa, I'm tall enough already,' Cassie said and Elsa beamed with pride.

Cassie turned to Ida. 'This Mrs Hegarty, how on earth did she manage here?'

'Her name wasn't Hegarty then. Clara Devereaux married a local farmer, John Hegarty. She never talked about him much; he died after five years, but she was left his farm and she sold it and was able to make Rathmoney House and farm viable after that. She had one son, he lived in Dublin and never came back to see her, but he was the first in the gate when she was dead. He had a For Sale sign up before the funeral.'

'It looks like Rathmoney House has always been about strong women,' Cassie said.

'Well this strong woman loves the delicate blue dress with the frills.' Margo held up a strapless gown with a delicate powder-blue ruched bodice, leading to layers and layers of organza frills edged in Chantilly lace.

Margo slipped the dress on over her head, using the voluminous skirt to give her some privacy while she took off her top and jeans.

She twirled beside Cassie, the delicate blue gown a direct contrast to the deep pink dress.

Ida picked out a shiny satin blue gown. 'Can I use your bedroom, Cassie, to change? I'm not as modern as the rest of you.'

Cassie nodded, helping Tilly to lift out another dress from a box.

'It's a mermaid dress. Can I try it on?'

Cassie looked at Margo.

'I don't see why not,' she said.

Tilly tore off her tracksuit, stepping into the strapless beaded dress with a fishtail of ruffles.

'I'm going to have to sit down, because I have nothing that will hold it up,' she said, rolling on to the couch, lounging like a pink sparkling mermaid on a rock.

Elsa picked a royal-blue sleeveless glittering gown which was far too long for her, so she hitched it up, using Cassie's scarf as a belt.

Margo and Cassie were admiring their daughters when Ida stepped back into the room.

'Well, is nobody going to pass verdict on how I look?' she said in mock agitation.

In crisp shiny satin with a gathered waist and folds of fabric in the skirt, Ida had never looked so different.

'It really suits you,' Cassie said.

'We will have to find an event where you can wear it,' Margo said.

'I remember this dress. My mother turned it up for Mrs Hegarty once. Little did I know that some day, I would be able to try it on.'

Elsa ran to get Vince and Jack.

Jack stopped in his tracks when he saw his wife. 'Ida, it's like our wedding day all over again, mesmerising.'

She blushed. 'Jack, you stop with that talk,' she said and everybody laughed, because they knew Ida was secretly delighted.

Jack poured more champagne while Vince gave his daughter the small gift he had carried all the way from the US.

When she opened it, there were two drop pearl earrings.

'They will go beautifully with that dress. Your mother always kept them for best, which meant she rarely got a chance to wear them. Don't you make that mistake.'

Sensing a sadness in her father, she hugged him tight before putting on the earrings. She couldn't help but think of the Chanel necklace Becca had given her. It still lay in its box, Cassie torn over what to do with it. She didn't know if her father would be delighted if she told him she had it – or ashamed that she must know about his gambling.

They popped some more champagne along with fizzy drinks for the girls and they all ate more cake. Vince took photographs, until everybody began to make funny faces.

At one stage, Cassie fell onto the couch, a wave of tiredness snaking through her and the others joked it was good to see her let go, after the terrible stress of the last few months.

Ida ran her hand across Cassie's forehead and said she might have a temperature.

'She has been through so much, surely there is nothing wrong with some overindulgence on her birthday?' Margo said, and Ida nodded in agreement.

When Cassie woke up much later and said she had better get out of the ballgown, Margo said to keep it.

'It's my birthday gift to you. You look like a model in it. That dress may have been designed decades ago, but it was created with you in mind, Cassie.'

'Here I am thanking you again, Margo. At the rate I'm going, I will forever be in your debt.'

Chapter Thirty-Seven

Rathmoney, County Wicklow.

Two days later Jack was out and about in the farm when Cassie rang him.

'Jack, I need a favour.'

'Go ahead.'

'I need a lift to Dublin, I have an appointment in an hour with a consultant.'

'What's wrong? Is it something with Tilly?'

'Jack, I don't want anyone to know, but I have to collect the results of my own tests. I had an MRI scan a while back, when Tilly was still in hospital. There was no point telling everybody at the time, there really was enough going on.'

'What MRI, why?'

'I can't face going in on my own, Jack.'

'Shouldn't Margo know about this?'

'Margo knew I had a doctor's appointment – she booked it for me – but I didn't tell her about the scan. I don't want to worry her.'

'Of course I'll come with you.'

'I'm afraid, Jack.'

'Cassie, don't be worrying until you have to. I can pick you up in ten.'

She knew she had to get dressed. What was a bad news outfit? The blue dress with the silver shimmer hem winked at her; she didn't even know she had brought it from the States. Slipping it over her head, she found it ridiculous that she was checking how she looked in the mirror, swinging the skirt so the reflection of the silver skittered across the room.

Tying her hair up, she applied a little light foundation and her favourite pink lipstick to give herself a lift. Her mother's words rang in her ears. Never give in to the bad times, fight with whatever you've got.

Maybe she could stay here, pretend she was just this tall woman in the blue dress, the mother of a child recovering from a kidney transplant, the American staying at Rathmoney House. She saw Jack's Jeep come up the avenue and she hurriedly put on her sandals. There could be no pretending.

Running down the stairs, she pulled back the front door, startling Max, who was lying across the top step.

Jack, who had arrived at the top of the avenue, saw her stepping over the dog as she pulled the door shut behind her, the dress shimmering in the soft sunshine. At that moment, he thought he had never seen her look so beautiful.

'Thanks for doing this, Jack.'

'You look lovely, blue is your colour.'

'It's my bad news dress.'

'Don't talk like that.'

In the waiting room, she sat primly at the edge of her seat, waiting while others were called in. Twice she went up to the nurse to remind her she was there.

'There are people going in ahead of me. Why is it taking so long?'

'Mr O'Meara has his own way of organising things, you haven't been forgotten.'

When her name was eventually called, Jack walked into the consultant's office with her.

The consultant put his hands on the desk in front of him. 'I'm glad you have somebody with you, Cassandra, it's not good news.' He waited a few seconds to let his words sink in. 'You have a Stage Four cancerous tumour. It is terminal, I am afraid, and not only is it inoperable, but it is spreading.' He waited when he heard her sharp intake of breath. 'It's time, Cassandra, to get your affairs in order.'

'I can't die, my daughter is only twelve and she just had a kidney transplant.'

The doctor examined his hands, Jack leaned forward, wrapping Cassie in his arms.

'Jack, tell him about Tilly.'

The consultant looked directly at Cassie. 'I am very sorry, if there was anything we could do, we would do it. The only thing we can offer is palliative chemotherapy, but that of itself is very hard on the body. Many feel the harsh side effects are not worth the extra weeks and they would rather spend their last days with their family in a more meaningful way.'

'Last days? I can't do this. What about Tilly?' She pushed against Jack, fisting punches into his chest.

'Will I leave you alone so you can talk?' the doctor asked Jack and he nodded, tears flowing down his face.

The consultant stepped away from his desk and through a door that Jack later thought he must have had installed for precisely this reason.

Cassie burrowed into him. 'How am I going to tell Tilly?'

He held her tighter, knowing at the moment there were no answers.

Cassie pushed her head up, so she could see Jack. 'And Elsa, what am I going to do?'

'Sssh, ssh,' he said, aware his words were hopelessly inadequate and doing nothing to calm Cassie's fear. Wiping away his own tears, he gripped Cassie hard. 'We will make one decision at a time. First, we will ask the doctor what else we can do to prolong your life, fight this cruel disease.' He wasn't sure if she could hear him. Gently he touched her face. 'Cassie, I'm here for you.' Blotting her tears with his hankie, he kissed her lightly on the head. 'All of us at Rathmoney are here for you.'

A nurse came into the room. 'A glass of water in case you need it. Take your time.'

Cassie took the glass, gulping down the water. 'Take me home, Jack, I'm so weary.'

'As soon as the consultant finishes with us.'

'What more is there to say?'

Jack got up and knocked on the door. 'We're ready for you now.'

The consultant returned from the back room.

Cassie straightened up in her seat. 'I just want to know if I was at home in the States, would the prognosis be the same?'

The consultant sighed loudly. 'It has gone too far, Cassandra, there's nothing anybody can do, anywhere. As I said, with palliative chemotherapy you can possibly buy more time, but you have to consider the side effects.'

He was halfway through the list, when Cassie put her hand up. 'Without the chemo, what is it looking like?'

'Pain management; two, maybe three weeks, tops; maybe shorter.'

This time there was no gasp from Cassie. Instead she had a faraway look, as if she was calculating something. 'I can be at home?'

'If you wish, or you can have hospice care.'

Cassie turned to Jack. 'I want to go now.' She stood up. 'I apologise for my behaviour earlier, I'm sure your job is hard enough without my histrionics.'

The consultant stood up and extended his hand to Cassie. 'Please don't apologise, go home and if you have any further questions – either of you – don't hesitate to get in touch. We will be in contact with your GP about pain management and get a special team in place to help you. Good luck, Cassandra.'

Jack shook his hand and they walked out of the room as another person's name was called.

'I don't want to face Tilly yet or even go to Rathmoney. Can you take me somewhere else?' Cassie's voice quavered. Suddenly she felt cold and so weak.

'It's time to go back to the mountains,' he said, opening the Jeep door, almost lifting her into the seat.

'Will I phone Ida and tell her we will be late back?'

'Please, but don't tell her why, I have to decide how I'm going to tell the others.'

Jack walked away from the Jeep to make the call.

'What do you mean you could be late? What is she doing?' Ida asked impatiently.

'Something has come up for her, she just needs time to think.'

'Does she now?'

'Ida, I will explain later.'

'Is there something wrong?'

'Yes, but I'm not allowed to say; trust me and leave it for now.'

Ida heard the shake in his voice. 'Jack, are you all right?'

'Yeah.'

'Tell me, what is it?'

'Ida, later.'

'Tell her I will stay with Tilly as long as she wants. I'm not going anywhere, and Jack...?'

Jack felt tears rise up in him again.

'Look after her and look after yourself, I love you.'

'I love you too.'

He rang off before she had time to say anything else. Pushing his phone into his pocket, he wiped his face with his sleeve.

'I made it difficult for you, I'm sorry.'

'Ida is fine, she told me to look after you.'

He swung out into the traffic, heading for the mountains. They had only gone a few miles when Cassie slipped down on the seat, asleep. He glanced at her curled up like a young child. Anger coursed through him that she should have this cancer. He passed all the favourite viewing spots for tourists and pulled into the road where there was a narrow path up the mountain through the heather. Quietly, making sure not to bang the Jeep door in case he woke her, Jack stepped onto the path.

With the determination of a man who knows where he is going, he beetled along the path and around the bend so the Jeep was out of sight. Here in the midst of the heather, he threw back his head and stared at the sky. The clouds loitered overhead, the sun warmed his face.

He wanted to scream, but could not, afraid to upset the perfect calm. Instead, he fell to his knees, praying fervently that things could be different. When he was finished, he got up, straightened his shoulders and walked back to the Jeep.

Cassie stirred as he approached. 'Where have you taken me?'

'Deep in the mountains. You won't have anybody bothering you here.'

'Can I get out and walk?'

'Stick to the path, it's bog out there, you could sink deep.'

'I have already fallen too deep to be saved.'

She set off down the road; he wasn't sure if he should follow, so he leaned against the Jeep watching her. She climbed up on the rocks. He followed her with his eyes as she threw her arms in the air, shouting loud to the sky. Jack could only vaguely make out the words.

When she came back, Cassie was smiling. 'I tried to bargain, but whoever is up there wasn't taking callers today.'

'Maybe you should go for a second opinion.'

'And waste my time, building up false hope, to have it cruelly dashed again and again?' She bent down, pulling at the purple heather, crushing the tiny flowers between her fingers. 'If this is the price I have to pay for Tilly's life, so be it, but if this is just an indication of how shitty life can be, then I will fight it with every ounce of energy I have. This cruel enemy has a grip on me, but for the days I have left, I intend to live life and surround myself with all that is good and kind.'

'What about Tilly?' Jack asked gently.

Cassie turned away, her head bowed.

He followed her, placing his hands on her shoulders.

'What am I going to do, Jack, how do I tell her?'

She was shaking, so he wrapped his arms around her, letting her lean back into him. 'Tell her the truth, it's all you can do.'

'I'm bailing out, time to paddle your own canoe, sweetie?'

'The words will come, you will know when is the best time.'

'As if there will ever be a best time.'

'Hush, one thing at a time, Cassandra.'

Suddenly, Cassie began to laugh, loud hysterical laughing, which made Jack feel very uncomfortable.

'What is it?'

'All these years I have scrimped and scraped. Now when I finally have enough to have a decent lifestyle, this cancer robs me of it. It has wormed its way into my life and now it takes away every good thing that could ever happen to me. It takes away the daughter I adore and the little Irish girl I am only getting to know. It's an unfair enemy, grabbing all the advantages for its side, leaving me helpless, weak and lonely. I am pathetic.'

'You are not.'

Cassie walked across the road to take in the view. 'This cancer takes away any chance I had with you, Jack. Tilly is going to hate me for abandoning her and Elsa, I'm never going to get to know them grow up.' She kicked the heather plant until the bruised browned flowers fell off.

'You're jumping too far ahead, Cassie, remember: small steps.'

'No steps, I refuse to co-operate with this fucking disease. Let's get back to Rathmoney.'

'Will you tell the others?'

'When I'm ready.'

Jack drove beside the mountain bog, concentrating on the winding road, so he did not have to think of what the next days and weeks would bring.

Chapter Thirty-Eight

Rathmoney, County Wicklow.

Cassie waited until the girls were in bed before she invited Vince, Margo, Ida and Jack to the drawing room.

Ida wasn't in the mood to visit Rathmoney after ten at night, muttering that it had better be worth it. 'Do you think she is going to thank us, give us a gift or something; they must be nearly ready to go back to the States?' she asked her husband as she touched up her make-up.

Jack didn't answer, but waited patiently for his wife.

They arrived at Rathmoney as the others gathered in the drawing room.

'I turned down an invitation to meet one of my new pals in the pub. This better be good, honey,' Vince said as he walked into the room.

When they all had gathered, Cassie, who had pulled the velvet wingback to the centre of the floor, asked Jack to close the door.

'Well, come on, the suspense is killing me,' Vince laughed.

Cassie took a deep breath. 'I'm afraid I have called you here tonight to ask your help and advice. I have bad news.'

Margo perched at the edge of the couch, her heart pounding. 'What bad news?'

Cassie looked from one to the other. 'I have just learned that I am dying. It's cancer, I have only weeks to live.'

Ida shook her head. Jack took her hand.

Vince got up and went to his daughter. 'No, Cas. How can this be?'

'I have had problems with my throat: the coughing, you've all heard it. The cancer has spread all over. I am so weary.'

'There must be something we can do, bring you back to the States. Get you on some trials.'

'I've thought of all that. It's too far gone. I have maybe two to three weeks at most.' She looked at Margo. 'Here I am, turning your life upside down again.'

Margo stared at her, unable to answer.

Vince stayed by his daughter, unable to speak further. Jack said he would go and make tea for everybody.

Ida moved over on the couch beside Margo. 'How can we help?' she asked, her voice so low, Cassie barely heard her.

'Ida, by just being yourself, you have been such a friend to me and Tilly.'

Ida reached into her handbag, taking out a packet of tissues, which she offered around. 'I wish I could stand in for you, this is so unfair.'

'I know,' Cassie said quietly.

Vince grabbed Cassie's two hands. 'I will bring you back to the States, I don't care what it costs. There must be something we can do, something, somewhere in the world.'

'I know you mean well, Daddy, and if I thought there was anything which could zap this disease, I'd be first in line, but there's no hope. I want to spend time now with Tilly and with Elsa and you guys, not waste time looking for cures I'll never find.'

Cassie turned to Margo. 'I have huge favours to ask.'

'Anything,' Margo whispered.

'Think carefully, before you agree to either of these; they are big decisions.'

Margo steeled herself for what she was about to hear.

'Tilly is so happy here. Vince is moving to Seattle. Charles has already checked out of her life. There's nothing back in Ohio for Tilly. Could she stay, grow up here at Rathmoney?'

There was a sharp intake of breath from Ida, which she tried to disguise.

'I can honestly say this time at Rathmoney had been the happiest in my entire life. I see Tilly so happy here too, which is why I ask this enormous favour. What I want is for Tilly to be surrounded by those she loves as she lets me go, and as she tries to pick up the pieces afterwards.'

Margo, silent, shifted on the couch. She could hardly fathom that death was calling again to Rathmoney.

Standing up, she struggled to draw out the words, but when they came they spewed out so fast, she hardly knew what she said. The pain of loss consumed her again and anger that Tilly and Elsa should have to endure so much, so young.

'I feel Rathmoney is your home as well as mine, of course you will be here. This is Tilly's home as much as it is Elsa's. Where else would she be, this is settled.'

'Thank you,' Cassie said quietly.

Jack brought in a tray of tea and put it on the coffee table. 'I laced it with brandy,' he said, handing out the mugs.

'Does Tills know?'

Cassie shook her head. She gulped her drink, before replacing the mug on the coffee table. Tears shone in her eyes. 'That is why I need you all, those who are dearest to me, to advise me on how I should tell her, when I should tell her and how I map out the future for her.'

Everybody fell quiet, not because they didn't want to have an input, but the stark reality of a young child, without either her mother or father, gripped all their hearts.

'You know I will take and look after Tilly, but it's your decision,' Vince said.

Ida made to say something, but Jack squeezed her hand to stop her.

Cassie looked at Margo, who was bawling now. 'Margo?'

Margo, still unable to speak, threw herself at Cassie. They cried in each other's arms. When the convulsions of tears gave way to quiet sobbing, Margo pulled away.

'If Tilly wants to stay here, I will love her and care for her to the end of my days. I will never let the memory of you fade.'

Cassie reached out and gripped Margo's hand tight. 'I know you will love her.' She turned to Ida and Jack. 'You are such good friends and Tilly adores you both. It makes me so happy to think you'll be in her life.'

Next she walked over to Vince. 'Do you think it could work for you? Maybe you could visit and when both girls are old enough and if Margo agrees, they could vacation with you.'

Vince sighed. 'If this is what you want, Cassie, and what Tilly wants, I won't stand in your way, but will give it my full support. For Tilly to grow up having the equivalent of a sister in Elsa and role models in Margo, Ida and Jack would be a fine thing.'

Cassie, feeling suddenly light-headed, sat down. 'Margo, I have asked your solicitor to come out to Rathmoney tomorrow afternoon. All this must be set down in my will, so Charles – if he turns up – is not able to challenge it or cause any trouble.'

'You are going to have to build a strong firewall in case that drunkard raises his ugly head,' Vince said.

'Whatever you put in, that will be carried out in full, never you fear,' Jack said.

'Which is why I am asking you to be executor, Jack.'

Jack reached over and shook Cassie's hand. 'I would be honoured, Cassie, anything I can do to help.'

'There was another thing, Margo. I wonder could I move back upstairs? I like being able to see the fields and sea from there.'

'We will have to do a rota, so you have somebody with you all the time,' Ida said.

'A palliative care team starts the day after tomorrow.'

'What can they do for you, that we can't do?' Ida asked.

'Pain management mostly, tonight is probably my last night to be able to engage as much as this.'

'When are you going to tell Tilly?' Margo asked.

'Tomorrow morning.'

They all fell quiet, the silence of the night seeping around them.

Margo was the first to speak. 'I will tell Elsa at the same time.'

Nobody knew what to say next, so Cassie said she was tired and asked Vince to help her from the chair to her bedroom.

'Thanks for being here, Dad.'

'Where else would I be?' he said.

Chapter Thirty-Nine

Rathmoney, County Wicklow.

When Tilly opened her eyes the next morning, Cassie was already awake. 'Come over here, we will snuggle up for a while,' Cassie said, but Tilly jumped out of bed.

'Ida said I could show her how to make waffles in the new waffle maker. Do you want some?'

Cassie shook her head. 'You can go to Ida in a while, there's something I need to tell you first.'

Tilly sighed loudly and sat on the edge of Cassie's bed. 'Is it about Ohio? I don't want to go back to the States; can't we stay here?'

'That's one of the things I want to talk to you about.'

Tilly clapped her hands and Cassie felt a huge pang of guilt, that within minutes she would shatter this happy innocence.

'Tilly, I haven't been feeling well for a while, I'm afraid I have bad news. I have cancer and I am dying.' She saw alarm shadow across Tilly's face. 'The doctors aren't able to do anything for me, I'm going to die very soon.'

Tilly looked directly in to Cassie's eyes. 'What do you mean, going to die very soon?'

'In a few weeks. The cancer is very bad. That's why I've been so tired.'

'Can't you get a transplant or something, like me?'

'I'm afraid not.'

Tilly looked directly at her mother. 'I don't want you to die, Mommy.'

'I know.'

'Isn't there medicine or something?'

'They can give me stuff for the pain, but I am going to die.'

Tilly threw herself at her mother. She didn't cry, that would come later. They held each other, the familiar sounds of Rathmoney House all around them. Ida was in the kitchen, getting breakfast ready; Max was outside barking at the geese as they waddled down the river bank. They could hear Jack's tractor coming up the avenue and Elsa arguing with her mother upstairs.

'I don't want you to die, Mommy.'

'I know, sweetheart.'

'Where will I go?'

'We can talk about that another time.'

'I'm not living with Daddy. I want to stay here with everyone. Can I stay here?' Tilly looked at her mother. 'I like it here, it feels like home.'

'I'll talk to Margo,' Cassie said, not wanting to tell Tilly until she was certain Margo wouldn't change her mind.

'Will Grandad visit if I stay here?'

'Of course.'

'Can I go make the waffles now?'

Cassie nodded, feeling fatigue wash over her.

After a few minutes, there was a tap on the door. Margo peered in.

'I'm going to tell Elsa. Tilly said you told her.'

'I'm not sure how she took it. She's gone off to make waffles with Ida now.'

'I know when I told Elsa about Conor, she was much the same, desperate to carry on doing normal stuff, in the hope life could be different.'

'I'm afraid I've messed it up.'

'You've been honest, it's all you can do now.'

Cassie looked directly at Margo. 'Are you being truthful with me, when you say Tilly can grow up here? I need to know you won't change your mind, before I tell her.'

'Yes, I am. More than anything, I want to look after Tilly. Please ask the solicitor about appointing me guardian. I want to lock it in legally.'

'I know, in case Charles bursts on the scene looking to get my money and using Tilly to do it.'

'You know I neither want nor need your money; put it in trust for Tilly.'

'There's something else we need to discuss,' Cassie said, shifting in the bed, trying to find a comfortable spot. She took a deep breath. 'We have to decide if we tell the girls about the swap before—'

Margo interrupted. 'They're too young, and already dealing with your illness, Cas. Maybe now isn't the time.'

Cassie nodded. 'I couldn't bear the look on Tilly's face, or on Elsa's; but am I leaving too much for you to handle?'

'As long as you let me decide when is best.'

'I trust you will know when is right.'

'I'll do my best. That's settled then,' Margo said, her voice shaking.

Later that evening, when the solicitor had left, Cassie sat with Margo in the drawing room.

'She says I can appoint you as a testamentary guardian in my will.'

'That will be binding, will it?'

'Yes. If Charles decides to turn up, there will be little he can do.'

'I will never have Tilly want for anything, you know that.'

'That is one thing I'm very sure of. In my will, I leave everything to Tilly, but the funds in my bank accounts, including the settlement money, will be put in trust until she is twenty-one. There will be a provision that once she reaches college age, you can apply for her fees and accommodation costs.'

Margo made to speak, but Cassie put her hand up to hush her.

'I've decided on that age because it's so far away and knowing Charles, he won't want to hang around that long to take her money. Also she will, I hope, be a mature young woman able to handle such a large amount of money.'

'It's a wise decision, Cassie.'

'Margo, promise me, if Charles does turn up, you'll try and keep him out of Tilly's life. He is bad news.'

'I promise.'

Margo saw Cassie was flagging, so without asking, she lifted her feet onto the couch for her and placed a cushion behind her head.

She tiptoed out of the drawing room as she knew Cassie needed to rest. Gently, she opened the front door and went down the steps to lean on the paddock fence. Cassie had put a burden on her shoulders and she was willing to carry it, though she dreaded how she would ever be able to tell the girls about their past in such a way that they didn't feel massively let down.

Chapter Forty

Rathmoney, County Wicklow.

Cassie got the best of care at Rathmoney House with the specially trained team on hand at key times during the day and at night. Margo and Ida divided up the day between them, so that Cassie always had somebody there to help. Tilly went to school with Elsa, tearing up the stairs when she got home to sit beside her mother and chat.

Every now and again Jack called in and sat beside Cassie, sometimes talking, other times letting the silence between them say what they couldn't. During these quiet times, they held hands, Jack on edge in case Ida or Margo walked in.

One night when he came home, Ida had tea ready for him. 'Jack, I have something to say and I want you to hear me out.'

He knew by the precise way she said the words, it was serious. 'Go ahead.'

'For the last week or so, you have been running yourself ragged, trying to keep two farms going and trying to spend time with Cassie.'

'Ida, you know the situation, she has not long left.'

Ida shook her head. 'You have me all wrong Jack. I love you, I know you.'

'But...?'

'For God's sake, man, will you let me talk. I'm not a teenager. A woman knows when she sees love between two people.'

'Ida, I don't want anything to come between us.'

'And it's not going to.'

'I don't understand.'

'I have asked Patrick Donnelly to take over the feeding of the animals and other jobs that need to be done around the farm until further notice. He is charging a pretty penny, but he is a solid worker, so the farms are in good hands.'

'What do you mean, Ida?'

Ida looked at her husband, the dark circles under his eyes, the worry lines on his forehead. 'She needs you, Jack, she needs you at her side. I am telling you to go to her and when you are ready, come home.' She sat on the couch beside him. 'I don't know if I ever thanked you, for what you did for me all those years ago.'

'You never had to thank me, Ida. I loved you then and I love you now.'

She rapped him on the knee. 'I know that and I know how you care for Cassie and she you. I have seen her these last days, the way her face lights up when you come in to the room.'

Jack, unable to speak, nodded in agreement. 'I'm sorry, Ida.'

'Let's not waste time on that nonsense, you took on a lot with me, I have always known that.'

'But what will people say, and what about Margo?'

'Jack, I will say what you said to me when I was noticeably pregnant with another man's child, and you asked me to marry you. Who cares what people say; we know the truth and that is all that matters.'

'Ida, I don't deserve you.'

She slapped him gently again. 'You do deserve me and I will be here, when you are ready to come home. I spoke quite candidly to Margo about this and we put the camp bed in Cassie's room for you.'

'I don't know what to say.'

'Don't say anything. Go back now to Rathmoney House and I will see you there in the morning, I will include you in the breakfast round.'

He gave her his hand and she leaned on him to get up off the couch. When she was standing, he did not let her go, but instead pulled her close. 'Thank you,' he whispered in her ear.

'Just come back, Jack, when it's the right time.'

He reached down, kissing the top of her head gently.

When he left, Ida poured herself a whiskey and sat at the kitchen table, their old dog at her feet. She gulped the alcohol, grimacing when it burned down her throat. She loved Jack Roper with all her heart, but she was worried that maybe she had come to that realisation too late.

He was in pain, she could see that. Before this, he had been wrestling with the love he undoubtedly held for the American. She couldn't bear to see him like this, steeling himself against the inevitable, when he would lose Cassie.

She hated that he loved Cassie, his eyes brightened when he saw her, he listened intently when she spoke. For God's sake, he even got in to the Irish Sea to swim with her.

She tried to hate Cassie, but she couldn't. She saw how she fought her feelings for him, often in the last week giving him the harsh word, in a misguided attempt to insulate him from the terrible grief of her passing.

Ida downed the last of the whiskey in one. This situation had been thrust in her lap and she was dealing with it the only way she knew how. She hoped Jack would come home to her when it was all over and maybe, just maybe, when he had nursed his grieving heart, they could start again.

She pushed away the whiskey bottle. She should go to bed,

but she could not face getting into their bed without Jack. She went back to the sitting room and lay on the couch, praying she had done the right thing.

When Jack got back to Rathmoney, Margo told him to go quietly upstairs as Cassie was asleep. 'It will be a nice surprise for her to see you, when she wakes up.'

'Thanks, Margo.'

'It was all Ida's idea.'

When he went upstairs, he sat on the camp bed beside Cassie, watching her sleep. He did not know how long he had sat there studying her face, when she stirred.

She smiled when she saw him. 'I thought you'd gone home.'

'Ida told me to come back. I'm staying.'

She moved over in her bed. 'Will you lie with me, Jack?'

He got in beside her and held her gently, her head resting on his chest. 'Isn't Ida worried about what people will say?'

'She isn't and neither am I.'

He kissed her softly and they lay quietly, until Cassie fell asleep and he was able to climb in to the camp bed and get some sleep until the care nurse came in near dawn.

When Ida came up after Tilly and Elsa had gone to school, Cassie asked Jack to give them a little time on their own. 'I wanted to say thanks, Ida.'

'Nonsense, you have nothing to thank me for.'

Cassie smiled at Ida, who was fussing, making up the camp bed. 'I have everything to thank you for. I'm not sure if I was in the same position, I would be so generous.'

Ida stopped what she was doing. 'Don't call me generous, Cassie, because I am not. I am merely selfish, trying to save my own marriage, so the man I love will be happy to come back to me. That you are the beneficiary of my selfishness gives me a great deal of satisfaction.'

'He loves you, Ida, so much.'

Ida sat on the camp bed. 'And I love him. And because I love him beyond anything, I have to be realistic and acknowledge he loves you, too. I can't stand in the way of this, he would never forgive me.'

Cassie put out her hand to Ida, who grasped it. 'You're a good and kind person, Ida, the last thing I wanted to do was hurt you.'

'I know.'

'Jack made it clear from the start, he loves you and I respect that. Let me borrow him, nobody expects it to be for long.'

Ida pulled away her hand and walked to the window. 'I am going to miss you, Cassandra.'

'I know. And me you.'

'I want you to know that I am glad Jack is here with you. God knows you deserve some love and comfort, after all you've been through.'

Cassie was about to answer when Ida told her to stop.

'I have said my piece, Cassie, and I give you my blessing. The more we talk about this, the more likely we may say something to hurt the other.'

Cassie, who pulled herself higher up in her pillows nodded in agreement. 'Can I say one last thing, Ida? I want to say when I met you, I judged you all wrong, I apologise for that. There aren't many like you, Ida, I'm very glad to have got to know you.'

'And I got the measure of you wrong, Cassandra, totally wrong. I'm sorry too for the hard words. Now, enough of that, we won't say anything more about all this. I will send Jack back up.'

*

Jack was having a cup of tea with Margo in the kitchen.

'You can go up,' Ida said.

Margo tipped her tea down the sink and said she just remembered she'd better tidy up Conor's office.

'Not very subtle,' Jack said as he walked over to Ida.

'Just so you know, Cassie and I made our peace.'

'I worried about you last night.'

'I slept on the couch.'

'I was talking to Margo, maybe you could move in here.'

'Don't you be worrying about me, there will be time enough for that.'

He reached out and she stepped into his arms. 'I love you, Ida, don't forget that.'

'I won't, if you won't; now get out of here.'

He released her, kissing her gently on the cheek before going upstairs to Cassie. When Margo came back in to the kitchen, she hugged Ida tight.

After that, Jack never left Cassie's side. When she wanted to put on her make-up, he drew in her eyebrows with a steady hand; he picked out silk pyjamas for her to wear and when she could not walk anymore, he carried her down the stairs, so she could sit in the garden listening to the gurgling of the river and the fall of the waves further away. Tilly and Elsa never asked why Jack was always by her side and Ida remained attentive to Cassie, trying to find new soft foods she could eat which would not rip at her throat.

Cassie's fine features had shrivelled and her voice was croaky hoarse by the time she told Jack to prepare her for her heart to heart with Tilly. Jack picked out her clothes: turquoise pyjamas and a matching silk dressing gown.

'Hold on, I have a present for you,' he said, dipping into his inside pocket and pulling out a beautifully wrapped package.

'Another bar of chocolate? You know I have to watch my weight.'

They laughed and she ripped open the paper. A silk scarf tumbled out in a profusion of colours – blues, pinks and purples.

'It's so beautiful, like a rainbow.'

'It reminds me of the joy, the shot of technicolour you brought to all our lives and especially me.'

She draped the scarf over her shoulders. 'It will give me courage talking to Tilly.'

She reached out and ruffled his hair. 'You spoil me,' she said.

'Why wouldn't I? I love you, Cassie.'

He saw a pink colour rise up her neck and make her face glow. 'I love you too, Jack.'

They heard Tilly and Elsa in the hall downstairs. Tilly must have been told to come upstairs alone, because they only heard one set of feet on the stairs. Tilly burst in, anxiety set across her face.

'Mom, what's wrong?'

Cassie put her hands out to her daughter and told her to sit on the bed.

Jack sidled out the door, leaving the two of them together.

'I'm very ill now, Tills, and soon I'm going to die.'

Tilly sat, her face crumpling in tears.

'There are a few things I need to say. I've never met anyone who wants to die and I'm no different: if I could, I would be beside you forever. But, Tilly, we have a lot of lovely memories together and in that way, I will be with you forever. When things are bad and you feel down I want you to remember good times, snuggly times and funny times.'

'Like when we stole into the locked playground in Bowling Green and got on the swings?' Tilly said, her voice shaking.

'Exactly. Let those times make you strong. I also want you, as you get older, to ask yourself what would Mom do and say about this, let it guide you.'

'I don't want you to die, Mom.'

'I don't want to baby, but this is out of my hands.'

'And can I stay here in Rathmoney?'

'Is that what you really want?'

'If you're not here, it's the only place I want to be.'

'Luckily, we've done a lot of work on that. Margo is going to be your guardian, which means she will be the boss of you, until you are eighteen years old and nobody else.'

Tilly looked at her mother. 'I don't want to go with Daddy, I don't like him anymore.'

'Strong words, Tilly, you might change your mind on that. I am making it clear in my will that Margo is to be your guardian.'

'I wish you could be here too, Mommy, I love this place so much.'

'We have good memories here and there isn't a place in the house and in the garden and down by the sea where you don't have a memory of me.'

'Remember when Ida thought there were mice, because we were scratching our nails against the wallpaper and she got a brush and started hitting the wall to scare the mice away.'

They laughed, their laughter turning to tears as they hugged each other tight. When Cassie pulled away, she looked directly at her daughter. 'Ida is a very good person and she loves you. You treat her right when you are a teenager. Margo and Jack too.'

'I will.'

'Now, off you go downstairs and get some food,' Cassie said, trying to keep her voice upbeat.

After Tilly left the room, Cassie lay back against the pillows, watching the sun glint on the sea and she wept, silent tears.

When Margo stuck her head around the door, Cassie's face brightened. 'I need your company right now to cheer me up,' she said.

Margo flopped on the camp bed. 'We all love you so much,

Cassie. Elsa bawled her eyes out when I told her. If love could keep you here, you would have a free pass.'

'Margo, I am depending on you to be strong, as strong as you've been all along and even stronger. Be strong for our girls, please.'

Margo pushed the camp bed beside Cassie, slipped her head onto Cassie's pile of pillows. 'I will, don't worry on that score.'

'And for God's sake, will you light up a cigarette so I can have a drag?'

Margo reached into the bedside locker and took out a packet. 'Where is your oxygen tank?'

'Jack moved it into the annex when we had a puff earlier.'

Margo took out two cigarettes and lit them, handing one to Cassie.

'Why are you smoking?' Cassie asked.

'I used to years ago, and I thought I might just have one.'

'As long as it is only that; you have two girls to get to adulthood, Margo.'

'You sound like Ida.'

'If Ida could only see us now.'

'You know she came in last week and I was finishing off a ciggie and she said, "Why are you smoking, that could kill you!"'

Margo smiled.

'And even when I pointed out to her the absurdity of that statement, she couldn't see the funny side of it.'

'If she only knew it was Jack who smuggled them in for you.'

Cassie giggled, pulling the silk scarf around her. 'He gave this to me this morning.'

Margo ran her hand along the softness of the silk. 'Jack never struck me as a man who bought beautiful gifts for a woman.'

'Jack is a real romantic.'

Margo blew a ring of smoke to the ceiling. 'Cassie, we are all going to miss you,' she said quietly.

Chapter Forty-One

Rathmoney, County Wicklow.

Cassie woke up in the middle of the night as she did most nights. The dark silence walled in around her, the rain against the window, a symphony it felt as though only she could hear. The stillness and quiet of the night was something she'd hated when she first came to Rathmoney, but now she welcomed it.

She pulled the duvet up around her neck to shut out the bleakness of the damp cold, but her toes still felt the pinch of chill. Grappling for the switch of the electric blanket, it slipped onto the floor. She could ask Jack for help, puncture this wall of black, but she didn't want to disturb him if she could avoid it.

She pushed out with her hand to reach the light, but missed and hit the glass of water, making the liquid shake, misting over her fingers. She leaned further out of the bed, afraid she would tumble onto the cold floor. Skimming her hand across the floorboards, there was nothing. Jack was fast asleep on the camp bed. She could hear his breathing and it comforted her.

The quiet exaggerated everything. Her ears strained for something to break the silent monotony; the wind had squalled away, only ruffling about the house now, no more stories to tell.

Closing her eyes, Cassie allowed herself to float to a different time long before all this. There was no comfort in the memories, just a sweet type of torture. To find contentment and peace would mean roving back too far.

If she could pull up the sash windows, she would do so, invite the breeze, billowing about the house to come in and stay, keep her company. The wind was a friend, reflecting the mood, the turmoil of her thoughts.

Riding across the sea, whipping across the land, hitting against the house like a monster or pushing gently through the grass, tickling the cattle and the horses, whistling between the loose bits of wood at the top of the window, this wind was her nightly companion.

She could shout, let her voice punch a hole in the blackness, but they would come running, fussing. Jack would wake, she didn't want that, not yet.

They all needed to rest. She saw it in their faces, clouded with lines for smiles. This is what cancer had done to all of them. These hours were the only times she truly had to herself to ponder the past.

A stranger who walked in would never believe that life had once been different; to think that she'd once worn tight clothes, worried about her roots, filled colour through her eyebrows with a special pencil.

These days, she had to ask somebody if they could spare the time or had a steady hand to draw a line, where once an eyebrow grew.

It depended on the person and it was the strangest of things that it was Jack, more used to inking sheep and handling horses, who had the steadiest, gentlest hand to draw where her eyebrows should be.

For the others, it was too much of a reminder of what had been and what was to come, so that the line wavered, shivering to the tremble of the hand and the intensity of the memory.

She thought back to the loveliest day. It was a few days ago, such a beautiful day, different to any before this, different to the days of necessary routine which had evolved around this intermission for her between life and death.

The letters had been dictated, the legal documents drawn up and the will signed. Now, her strength, weak as it was, could divert to her loved ones and this brutal act of dying.

She'd been propped against the pillows, waiting for the morphine to take hold. Listening and taking comfort in the familiar sounds of the house, the girls playing hide and seek, Ida sweeping the front steps, Margo stacking the dishwasher. She heard Jack step into the hall. Ida must have whispered, she couldn't make out what she said, but Jack was not a man who could lower his voice.

'I'll go upstairs and have a little word,' he said.

Jack had tapped lightly on the bedroom door. 'Cassie, do you want some company?'

'It depends, Jack. I have a pretty tight schedule, the board members will be expecting to hear from me soon. And there's a video call to the US sometime this a.m., but consult my PA, I may be able to squeeze in five minutes for you.'

Jack pushed open the door. 'Aren't you the right comedian today?'

'Better to be laughing than crying.'

'Unless the laughing is really crying.'

He walked across to the bed and sat in the big armchair, where he could reach out and hold her hand. 'What is eating you, sweetheart?'

'Dumb question, Jack, there is only one thing eating me, this bloody cancer.'

He'd got up and, walking across to the sash windows, he pulled them up, one by one. Fresh chilled air had seeped in to the room.

'You know I can't afford to get cold, Jack, what are you doing?'

'There's only one way to get rid of this maudlin mood, chase it away. Where are your clothes? You'll need a coat, scarf, hat and gloves. The sun is shining, it's a beautiful day out there.'

'Everybody is fed up because I'm so grumpy, aren't they?'

'My lips are sealed.'

Margo walked in, a big coat over her arm, hats and gloves in her hands.

Tilly rushed in behind. 'Mom, you can wear the pink dress.'

'The ball gown? I don't think so.'

Tilly's face fell. 'But it makes you feel better and you look so beautiful in it.'

Margo pulled out a pair of leggings and thick socks.

'You can wear these underneath and I'm sure I have a thermal vest in a nice colour.'

'How can I refuse? Now will somebody tell me where we are going?'

'To the beach, for a picnic.'

'But how? What about the oxygen tank?'

'Sandra, the nurse, is coming too and we have managed to get a smaller portable oxygen tank. You will be well looked after,' Jack said.

The women had ushered him out of the room as they got Cassie dressed, letting the silk organza gown slip over her head, Ida bunching the fabric in with a pin at the back, so Cassie did not realise how much weight she had lost.

Tilly clapped in excitement; nobody commented on Cassie's collarbones accentuated further by the simple square neckline, her pale features strangely enchanting against the cerise pink backdrop.

Elsa ran off to her room, returning with a knitted pink hat.

'Ida knitted it for me, it matches your dress.'

Cassie put on the hat, pulling Elsa and Tilly to her for a photograph.

Ida had prepared a picnic basket with flasks of tea and coffee, champagne with proper flutes to drink from, china cups and saucers for the hot drinks. Ida outdid herself on the food with mini quiches, sandwiches, apple tart, mini cupcakes and brownies.

Vince had been down to the sea earlier and set up the wind breaker, a small tent, a rug and loungers.

Margo was about to call Jack to carry Cassie down the stairs, when Ida told her to wait and fished a bottle of Chanel No. 5 perfume from her bag, spraying everybody liberally. Cassie coughed, but she told Ida not to stop.

'How did you know it's my favourite?' she said, making Ida beam with pleasure.

'I keep it for special occasions.'

'And this is certainly one,' Cassie said, calling Margo, Ida and the girls together for a selfie.

Jack picked Cassie up gingerly, remarking she was as light as a feather, before making his way downstairs, through the kitchen to the back yard. 'Your chariot awaits,' he said, showing her the pony and trap, festooned with ribbons.

'He has taken down the fences so we can bring you all the way to the sea in comfort,' Ida said, her face full of pride.

Tilly and Elsa joined Cassie in the trap, Jack holding the reins. The others walked behind as the happy procession went to the sea.

Cassie tried to call up the joy of that afternoon now, the laughter, the photographs, the tender moment when Vince carried her down to the water's edge and held her, while she dangled her fingers through the waves. Tilly and Elsa in Wellingtons splashing, the dog barking and wagging his tail; Margo and Ida getting tipsy on champagne, Jack singing softly to her as the waves followed each other to shore. Her heart burst with joy to think the sun had come out, so she could throw off her hat and gloves and step with Tilly on one side and Elsa the other along the sand.

It was a perfect day.

Chapter Forty-Two

Rathmoney, County Wicklow.

The town of Rathmoney was quiet, the shops closed. The iron gates at Rathmoney House were dragged across. A man gripped the thick round bars and shook hard. Shudders of frustration pulsed through him as the gate refused to give way. Cursing loudly, he kicked the tufts of grass clustered around the base, before swivelling about as if he expected a crowd to be watching.

A blackbird flitted by, bouncing over the top of the gate. The man changed his plan and stepped over the stile, tugging his holdall bag roughly after him. Stepping onto the avenue, he stood, listening as if he expected to be admonished for trespassing. A robin hopped onto the stile, its head cocked to one side, joining in the listening. Taking a handkerchief out of his pocket, the man mopped his forehead, then dropped his bag on the ground and unbuttoned his coat.

He stood quietly perspiring for a while, dithering over whether he should continue up the avenue. Feeling tired, he decided against hauling the bag with him, instead pushing it under the briars and nettles to collect on the way out.

On the avenue he stepped out smartly, hoping to cover as much ground as possible before he was detected. Moving forward, he put his hands in his pockets. If anybody had seen him, they would have thought he was a welcome visitor, his stride long, his coat swinging as he moved. They would not know his fists were clenched, his nails digging into the skin on the palms of his hands, because he had read somewhere if a dog smelled fear, he was sure to attack. The cows in the first field moseyed over to the fence when they saw him; two horses watched from the shade of an oak tree at the far end of the paddock. As he rounded the rhododendron, the Labrador sitting on the front steps stood up and barked. The man stopped as the deep barking echoed around the estate and somewhere nearby, another dog answered.

Rathmoney House looked closed up, the only sign of life the dog, who was advancing, his tail wagging. The man dug the nails in deeper as the dog woofed, prancing, pushing against him.

As he drew closer to the house, he saw the shutters were drawn across, a black bow, two long tails floating in the breeze, tied to the door. The dog ambled off, leaving the man standing in front of the house wondering what to do.

Slumping down on the stone steps, he waited, but nobody came to check the intrusion. Kicking a few pebbles under the fuchsia, he climbed up to the front door. Reaching for the doorbell, he brushed against the velvet bow. His hand stopped mid-reach. Suddenly he felt out of place, fearful he was intruding on their grief.

Turning, he quickly ran down the steps, watching the windows, afraid the door would open. Agitated he would be found out, he rushed past the front of the house so that the dog ran around from the back and barked again. It was his grief too, not that anyone would acknowledge that. Beetling back down the avenue, he cursed he had let the cab go. His mouth dried up when he saw a car coming towards him. Standing to one side, he hoped it would pass, but the car slowed.

Jack rolled down the window. When the man was close enough he called out to him.

'Are you looking for somebody?'

'I was hoping to visit, I know the family.'

Jack turned off the engine and stepped out of the car. 'There has been a bereavement. Rathmoney House is closed, the gates were across to stop strangers wandering through.'

'I am Charles Richards, Cassandra's ex-husband. Have I missed the service?'

Jack took the man in, his pinstripe suit, a heavy coat swinging open, a college scarf around his neck. 'Nobody knew you intended to come.'

'A last-minute decision.'

'The service is over, everybody is gathering at McLysaght's Hotel. I have to collect something at the house first, but I'm going back there, do you want a lift?'

'A lift?'

Jack stared hard at the American. 'A ride in the car.'

'Will I be welcome?'

'You won't be made unwelcome, if that's what you're worried about.'

As Charles got in to the car, Jack called out to him. 'Is that your bag I saw stuffed under the bushes near the gate?'

'Yes.'

'Remind me to stop and pick it up on the way out.'

Charles sat in the front seat, pushing the seat back so he could stretch his legs. Jack drove around to the back door, saying he would not be long as he got out of the car.

Unlocking the back door, Jack stopped in the kitchen to quickly feed Max, before making his way upstairs. Standing on the landing, he paused outside her bedroom door. If she was there, she would have called out to him, because she always recognised his step.

Slowly, he turned the brass doorknob and stepped into the darkened room. The Chanel perfume lingered still in the air; he breathed her in, his heart hurting, his sadness flowing to every corner of the room.

He didn't even know why he was here. One minute he was standing outside the graveyard watching the huddle of people still at the graveside, queueing up to offer sympathy to Margo and Ida; the next minute he was whispering in Ida's ear he would go home for a bit and feed the animals, meet them back at the hotel. Ida told him to take his time, a softness of understanding in her eyes.

Moving to her chair by the window, he pulled the shutter back a little, a chink of light bursting in to the room. He wanted to read her letter again in this room; this and the sea were the two places he most associated with Cas.

Rathmoney House,
County Wicklow.

Jack,

I am sitting in the chair you put by the window for me. It is such a peaceful place to write this letter. I can see you tramping across the dewy wet grass to find the horses. I saw you look up once, but I didn't wave. I don't want you to expect me to be here, I can't bear to think you might be lonely when I'm gone.

Jack, it doesn't mean I don't want you to miss me. Miss the chats, the laughs, the arguments we had, the fun we had, miss the quiet times together or Ida's huffing and puffing, when she saw us in the sea.

Don't let the loneliness take hold, let Ida love you now, Jack, she deserves that. You deserve it.

I know you know how much I love you. Know too this quiet love of ours has sustained me in the worst of times.

I have regrets, mostly because I won't see Tilly grow up to be a fine young woman and to see her and Elsa keep their friendship as the years go on.

There is also a regret that you and I did not meet at a different time or at least when I was without disease and carefree. I wonder how it would have been for us?

Maybe we wouldn't have got on at all; maybe this enemy of a disease, which has seeped into me, stealing everything including my dignity, gave me at the end the finest gift of all: your love.

Jack, even at the worst moments, I have never been lonely; your enduring love has given me strength and the courage to face this final mountain I must climb.

As you know, I have asked Margo to be Tilly's guardian and to raise the two girls as her own. Jack, promise me to watch over Tilly and Elsa and to make sure they stay at Rathmoney, where I know they are happiest.

As executor of my will, you know I want Tilly to be here, where she is loved. Vince agrees with this. Promise me, if there is any attempt by anybody to do or say differently, you will act according to the wishes of my will.

The other afternoon, when I was resting, I peeked at you as you sat by my bed. Your head was bowed, your chin resting on your chest. These days have made you so tired. I wanted to console you, but could not reach you. I moved in the bed, letting out a small sigh. Straight away you were beside me. I knew you would come to me and I know all that I ask, you will do.

When I look in your eyes, I forget all the bad bits. I don't feel like a woman ravaged by cancer anymore, I feel like a beautiful woman again, a woman in love.

It is a great thing you have done for me. Thank you, I will love you always.

Your Cassandra xx

Jack folded the letter and placed it in the inside pocket of his jacket. All the days he'd rushed up the stairs, pulling a chair close to the bed to chat to her, carrying her downstairs when she wanted to see the flower beds at the side of the house where they had planted the wildflowers. The time he put her in the pony and trap and brought her to the sea.

Ida had gone along with it all because she wanted Cassie to feel some joy. Dear Ida, she even gave her the bottle of her treasured Chanel No. 5, so they could spray it around the room, in the hope of creating small moments of happiness for Cassie as she waited for death.

Getting up from the chair, he saw Cassie's silk scarf draped over the bedpost. Sliding it off, he buried his face in its softness.

Curling up the silk, he pushed it into his inside pocket as he left the room quickly. He had to think of Ida now. Cassandra was right; she had been so patient, never once confronting him, never once the bad word. For Ida, that said so much and he knew it.

Downstairs, he stood in the hall to compose himself before heading back out to the car. Charles Richards, who was leaning against the bonnet dragging on a cigarette, threw it on the ground and stamped on it when he saw Jack coming out the back door.

He got into the front seat as Jack started up the car. 'You don't look too good, man, are you OK?'

Jack didn't answer.

Charles, sensing his driver's discomfort, shut his mouth, filling the void between them by humming a tune to himself.

When they pulled into the car park of the small seaside hotel, Jack parked away from the door. 'I thought if you stayed in the car for a few moments, I could alert Margo as to your presence. We have to think of Tilly; she has been through so much.'

'I didn't come all this way to be hidden, Jack.'

'It's a difficult time, especially for Tilly.'

'I rather hoped my daughter would be glad to see me, especially now.'

Charles jumped out of the car. Striding out, he made for the front door, Jack fumbling to lock the car as he followed quickly behind.

Ida, walking through the foyer, saw her husband gesticulating frantically, pointing at Charles's back.

Moving into the American's path, she grabbed hold of one of his hands. 'Who have we here? One of Cassie's friends?'

Pulling his hand smartly away, Charles made to walk around Ida, but she deftly sidestepped, this time placing a hand on his chest.

'May I be of assistance?'

'I don't think so, mam, I am here to see my daughter.'

'Who is...?'

'Tilly,' Jack said.

'You are the ex-husband?'

'My reputation precedes me.'

'It certainly does, Mr Richards, and it is nothing to crow about.'

Charles turned his back on Ida and walked into the noisy Parnell Room. Tilly and Elsa were sitting eating their soup when Tilly saw her father push through the swell of people at the free bar.

Elsa, sensing the change in Tilly, put her hand on her knee. 'What's wrong?'

Tilly did not reply at first, but shrank in to her friend as Charles pushed his way towards her.

Charles looked at the girl beside Tilly, eyeing him up and down, the same soft blue eyes as Cassie, the long slender nose, the hair falling into her face.

He stopped in his tracks. He bet she was tall too and able to speak up for herself. Every bit of her was Cassie.

Shaking his shoulders, ignoring the crowd now beginning to stare at him, he walked up to the table. 'Baby doll, how much you've grown. Aren't you going to give your daddy a hug?'

Tilly stayed where she was.

'She's upset, she doesn't want to hug,' Elsa answered for her and Charles noticed a glint of fight in her eye.

Margo came up behind him. 'Mr Richards, I am Margo Clifford. Thank you for coming.' Conscious that people were listening and watching, she extended her hand.

'I didn't mean to miss the service.'

'She had a nice send-off; we all got to know Cassie in the time she lived here, she was much loved in these parts.'

'She was a mighty fine lady.'

'We're glad you think so. Maybe we can go and talk somewhere more private.'

Charles turned to Tilly. 'Come here, baby doll.'

Tilly got out from behind the table and this time she threw herself at her father. She said nothing but he felt the power of the sobs pumping through her.

Pushing her back, he reached for his handkerchief and wiped the lapel of his suit jacket, before dabbing her face. 'Sweetheart, Daddy is here now; there is nothing to worry about.' He handed her the handkerchief and told her to dry her eyes.

Elsa got up and pulled Tilly gently by the hand. 'Will we go outside to the sea?'

Tilly nodded and the two girls walked off, hand in hand.

'They get on well,' Margo said, taking Charles gently by the arm and guiding him to the lobby.

'Jack has arranged for us to use a little office here. You don't mind if he stands in with us, he is a trusted friend.'

Charles shrugged his shoulders, pulling off his coat and throwing it over the arm of a chair when they got to the room.

Margo stood at the window looking out over the sea. She could see the girls running on the sand, the faint sound of their squeals reaching her.

'Is that really my Tilly?' Charles asked, coming up behind her.

'Yes, she loves the sea as much as Cassie did.'

Margo turned around sharply. 'Mr Richards, why are you here?'

Her direct question took him by surprise. 'I've come to comfort my daughter on the loss of her mother. Why else would I be here?'

'You didn't come when Cassie was ill. You didn't come when Tilly was recovering from her transplant. Contact has been nil this past while, why now?'

'I don't have to answer to you.'

Jack stepped forward. 'You abandoned Cassie when she needed the most help for Tilly. Why should any of us believe that you now have her interests at heart?'

Charles clapped his hands in frustration. 'I never intended any of this to blow up, that's the truth. I got tested to see if I could be a donor. What more could I do?'

'You could have stayed away, rather than create such confusion for Tilly,' Jack said.

Charles turned swiftly around to Jack. 'So were you sweet on Cassie, is that what this was about? Cassie could always turn a man's head with her lovely looks.'

Jack turned away, anger making red rush up his neck, a nerve in his cheek twitching.

'I imagine even allowing for the loss of hair, old Cas was still a looker.'

Jack reached him in one stride. Catching him by the throat, he pushed Charles Richards up against the wall.

'How dare you come in here talking this filth about a woman who is not even cold in the grave. Cassie was a fine person and mother. How dare you attempt to sully her good name. The whole of the town is here to pay their respects to a fine woman.'

Margo pulled at Jack. 'Don't, Jack, he's not worth it.'

Jack tightened his grip on Charles, pressing his fingers into his skin, before dropping his hand and marching out of the room.

Margo sat down in one of the two chairs, while Charles flopped into the other, rubbing his neck.

'Thanks for calling off the Rottweiler.'

'Why don't you tell us why you are here?'

'Tilly needs me right now.'

'She needed you long before this.'

Charles Richards stood up. 'You people are fine and mighty, aren't you? Tilly is my daughter. I brought her up for the first twelve years. Right now, she needs the stabilising influence of that person who has known her all her life, not people she just met in the last few months.'

'First, Mr Richards, Tilly is not your daughter, as you well know. Secondly, Cassie has all this sorted in her will. We have to respect her wishes.'

'So you want to take my daughter from me and expect me to stand idly by?'

'You'll need to wait to hear what's in Cassie's will, until the reading tomorrow. Can you wait until then?'

'I guess I'll have to.'

Margo stood up. 'We got off to a bad start. Why don't you stay at Rathmoney House?'

'I don't think I could afford your prices.'

'I didn't mean as a paying guest; the solicitor is coming to the house at ten in the morning.'

'I think I would rather book in here. I'll get a cab and be at the house. Don't start without me.'

Charles walked out the door, where a number of people were waiting to introduce themselves and offer their sympathies.

Outside, Tilly sat on the rocks looking out to the sea, Elsa at her feet turning over pebbles between her fingers. 'What does he want?'

'I don't know.'

'Will you have to go back to America?'

Tilly didn't answer.

Chapter Forty-Three

Rathmoney, County Wicklow.

Margo watched Charles sitting at the bar caressing a whiskey. Cassie had warned her this might happen.

'He's an asshole. Vince said the Baltimore move was a mess and the company has lost a shitload of money. They had to close down the car lot in Baltimore and the other one's not doing well now either. You watch your back, one day he could just turn up.'

'I think we're able to deal with Charles, don't you worry,' Margo said as she gently brushed the wig, before handing it to Cassie to put on.

Cassie deftly fitted it. 'Is it straight?'

Margo had nodded, handing Cassie her powder compact and lipstick next.

'Please heed the warning about my ex-husband. If he thinks he can get his hands on Tilly's settlement money, he will do whatever it takes to achieve that. We may finally be divorced, but he will try to get to it through Tilly.'

'That money is held in trust.'

'Yes, but we don't want him worming his way into her affections in the meantime.'

Margo watched him gulping back the whiskey and calling for another.

Ida stood beside her. 'I sent Jack out to the girls. That man is a ball of trouble. It's going to take everything we've got to bounce him away.'

Mary Foster came up to say her goodbyes. 'I liked the American, she spoke her mind, but she had a good heart, I'm sure.'

When she was out of earshot, Ida giggled.

'What was all that about? Am I missing something?' Margo asked.

Ida cackled out loud, so that a few still standing at the bar hoping for another free drink turned around to stare at them. Ida didn't seem to care. 'I thought Cas told you about their run-in?'

'No.'

'She might have thought back then you would not approve. Mary Foster is such a gossip. It was at the start, when we hadn't said anything about the kidney transplant and people were speculating about your hospital stay. Cassie was in the thrift shop, she bought a lovely handbag there. Mary started to quiz her about you and the sudden illness. At first Cas batted all queries away quite nicely.' Ida stepped closer to Margo. 'I will use her exact words, but I don't want anyone else to hear.' She leaned closer, so Margo felt the warmth of Ida's breath on her ear. 'You know what she said?' Ida paused for dramatic effect. '"Honey, you go find yourself a man and get laid. Then you might not be so interested in other people's business."'

Margo guffawed. 'What did Mary do?'

'I'm told she gave Cassie her change, followed her to the door and when Cas left, she closed up the shop for the day.'

'Poor Mary, Cassie could have a very sharp tongue.'

Ida looked at Margo. 'She told her straight; it's what I liked about Cas.'

363

'She liked you too, Ida.'

'I know, and she liked Jack even more.'

Margo made to say something, but Dan McCarthy came to pay his respects. 'She was a breath of fresh air in Rathmoney. I loved when she called in to chat, always carrying that basket of hers.'

'Not that she ever bought anything,' his wife interjected, a little too severely.

Mr McCarthy shook the hands of both Margo and Ida, before gently ushering his wife away.

'The secret life of Cassie,' Ida said.

'Connie McCarthy has no idea, but she got off lightly,' Margo joked.

Vince was next to say his goodbyes. 'I'm not going to talk to Charles Richards, the last thing you need is a brawl.'

'You will be back soon, I hope.'

'As soon as I get settled in Seattle, I'll be in touch. Maybe I'll pop over around Christmas.'

'We look forward to that.'

Vince held back his emotions until Margo gave him a hug.

'You were all so good to Cas, I know Tilly is in very good hands,' he said through tears.

'Have you said goodbye to Tilly?'

'I have and I promised to FaceTime,' he laughed.

Charles Richards, hearing the sound of their laughter, left the bar stool, arriving beside them as Vince slipped out a side door. 'You all certainly held Cassandra in high regard.'

'We loved her very much. Cassie and Tilly coming to Rathmoney were like rays of sunshine warming your face on a damp day. Judging by the flowers sent by friends in the States, including her former boss, Zack, there were many across the water who held Cassie in equally high regard.'

'Cassie was always good at getting people on side.'

Margo straightened up, because when she did so, she was almost as tall as he was. 'Mr Richards, you will kindly not insult a woman we all loved dearly.'

The next morning Charles Richards was dropped off at the gate of Rathmoney House and walked up the avenue in the rain, arriving at the same time as Samantha Kiely.

'I don't want to talk to you, you made Mom cry a lot,' Tilly said, when she saw Charles in the drawing room of Rathmoney House.

'He's just here for the reading of your mum's will and the legal stuff,' Margo said, before Ida distracted the two girls with the promise of a baking session.

Before she went into the kitchen, Tilly pulled at Margo's hand. 'Tell him my mom arranged for me to live here and please tell him to go away.'

When Margo returned to the drawing room, she closed the door behind her.

Charles Richards sat stony-faced as the solicitor outlined the last wishes of Cassandra Kading.

When she had finished reading the will, Samantha Kiely turned to Charles. 'In summation, Mr Richards, we have offered you the courtesy of allowing you to sit in on the reading of the will. It was the last wish of Cassandra Kading that Margo Clifford be appointed as the testamentary guardian to Tilly Richards. This means Margo Clifford is responsible for the girl's welfare. Cassandra Kading left everything she possessed at the time of her death to Tilly Richards and any funds will be kept in trust for her.'

Margo stood up. 'I will ask you now to leave Rathmoney House. If you would like to say goodbye to Tilly, you may do so, if she wishes.'

Charles got up, looking around the room. 'Cassandra gets

the last laugh from beyond the grave, but you people have not heard the end of this. I brought up that child for twelve years, I deserve to be compensated. You live fancy, you can afford it.'

Jack stood up as Margo's eyes flashed with fury. 'Tell him to go away and leave us alone,' she shouted.

Jack moved towards Charles. 'You heard the lady, it's time to go.'

'If you think by throwing me out, I am finished with this, you're wrong.'

Samantha Kiely looked over her glasses. 'You have no rights here, Mr Richards. You can make all the empty threats you like, but that is the reality. You are of course free to seek your own independent legal advice.'

Jack went to push Charles, but the American shoved his hands away.

'I'm leaving. Please tell Tilly that Daddy had to rush off.' He turned to Margo. 'Make no mistake, you will be hearing from me.'

With that, Charles stalked out of the house, walking quickly as the rain pelted down.

Samantha Kiely packed up her files. 'Let's hope it was a lot of bluster from Mr Richards, the last thing you want is expensive litigation,' she said.

Margo watched the solicitor dash through the rain to her car. There was a big storm approaching and Jack would soon have to go out to bring the horses in from the fields, tidy up the back yard and secure all the outhouses. The rain began to really sheet down as she made her way to the kitchen, where she could hear the happy chat of Tilly and Elsa, busy making cupcakes with Ida.

Chapter Forty-Four

Rathmoney, County Wicklow.

All night it rained with no let-up, thundering down, pelting onto the roof as if it was trying to knock the house down.

Streams and lakes swelled by the rainwater crept across the land, water bubbled up from nowhere. Margo, unable to get back to sleep in the early morning, was wiping down the worktops in the kitchen. All the time she listened to the storm blowing against the house, the rain drumming down, the barn door rattling as if sending out a signal. She stopped to look at a breaking news report on television, a severe red weather warning flashing on the screen.

The dog whined to go out. She pressed up the latch, the wind pushing against the door invading the room, making the clothes billow out on the air rack over the stove. She expected Max to lift his leg at the nearest rose bush before returning inside, but he galloped off instead, barking into the wind, making the hens locked in the barn cackle up a racket. Shouting after Max, the force of rain and wind in her face wetting the top of her pyjamas, she rattled his bowl.

She could still hear the dog, but she couldn't see him. Pushing the door shut, she wiped the rain from her face and hair.

When her phone rang, she jumped.

'I'm off down to check on the sheep in the far fields. Are you all right up at the house?' Jack said, the wind howling into his phone.

'Max ran off barking, I don't know what's wrong with him.'

'I'll call him when I drive into the yard and if I find him, I'll throw him in the kitchen door, he might just be spooked.'

She was worried, so she turned back to tidy up the kitchen, spraying and wiping down the counter tops again. She heard Jack park the Jeep and she waved to him, but he didn't see her. Standing at the sink, she saw him pull the barn door shut and place a lock on it, so that all she was left with was the sound of the wind and the rain, water dripping from overflowing gutters onto the kitchen windowsill.

Their first paying guests after Cassie's death were due later today, but she had no idea if they would bother even making the journey out of the city to Rathmoney. It was a booking made from before she closed the guesthouse, but she felt she should honour it.

Her phone rang again.

'I can't see Max, I'll go down the river a bit, just in case the stupid dog fell in.'

'Christ, how could that happen?'

'The river is the worst I have ever seen it; keep the girls in when they wake, it's not safe. And if those people come, tell them to stay off the bridge and steer clear of the water.'

'I'm not sure that they will, who would venture out by choice in this weather anyway?'

'Fools from the city, who have nothing better to do.'

He rang off and she went to the front door in case she could see the dog.

When she pulled back the door, the wind slapped it, forcing its way past her into the hall, lifting the mirror from the wall.

The vase of flowers on the hall table tipped over and water poured over the marble top onto the floor. She called out for Max, but her words were plucked out of the air and whirled away.

Using all her strength, she managed to push the front door shut and went back to the kitchen to await news of the dog.

She was folding teacloths in a bid to pass time, when the kitchen door swung open with a bang.

Thinking it was Jack with Max, she spun around with a smile on her face. 'So where did that stupid mutt get to . . . ?'

Margo stiffened, unable to continue.

'Sorry to barge in; dreadful weather, isn't it, or maybe this is what you folks call normal?'

Charles Richards, his coat sodden on his back, pulled out a chair at the kitchen table and sat down.

'What are you doing back here?'

The wind howled through the room, the rain spitting in to the kitchen. Margo walked over to the door and pushed it shut, automatically checking outside for the dog before she did so.

'What do you want?'

Charles Richards stretched out his legs. 'Isn't that a fine welcome for a man who braved the atrocious weather to walk out from the town to Rathmoney House?'

A pool of water formed on the floor where he sat. 'I've been thinking about the will.'

'Why are you here?' She turned her back, concentrating on the hob.

'I'm Tilly's father of twelve years, you can't just airbrush me out.'

Margo turned around. 'I don't have to, you did that all by yourself.'

'What is it with you people, you think you can take my daughter without a fight?'

369

'She's not your daughter.'

Charles stood and leaned towards her across the table. Even from there she could smell stale whiskey on his breath. His eyes narrowed. 'But Elsa is my daughter.'

'What are you implying?'

'Let's be clear, I'm not implying anything. I am telling you to start playing the game my way or you could lose that precious sweetpea you call your daughter.'

'You have no claim on her.'

'The DNA test doesn't lie, does it?'

Panic surged through her. 'Is that why you came back, to threaten me?'

In an effort to appear calm, she put the cleaning cloth and spray away and took a box of cornflakes from the cupboard, placing it in the centre of the table. Charles sat back down watching her.

'What happened, cat caught your tongue?'

'Mr Richards, you have been Tilly's father for twelve years and I don't want to fall out with you, but if you continue down this road and try to take my Elsa, I will fight you every step of the way. Don't underestimate me or the funds I have for such a battle either side of the Atlantic.'

Charles threw his head back and guffawed loudly. 'Yes, I forgot the millionaire widow. Hasn't this mess turned out well for you; you get millions in compensation and Cassie has ensured that you are in charge of the two girls and their stash of cash.'

'There's no need to be like that.'

Charles slapped his knee as if she had cracked another good joke. 'Now, if you considered sharing the pot of money, then I could decide to leave and not bother you anymore.'

'You want money to go away?'

'Can we do a deal?'

'Does your flesh and blood mean so little to you?'

Charles stood up. 'On the contrary, my daughter means exactly one million dollars to me.'

Margo thumped the worktop, the intensity of her hand hitting the wood causing pain to shoot up her arm.

'I know my rights: if I apply to a judge for guardianship of both girls, I will get a hearing and what will you do then? Do you want to risk losing those beautiful daughters?'

'Cassie warned me this might happen. I thought she was being overly harsh; now I realise she wasn't harsh enough.'

'Cassandra was no saint either.'

'Cassie was a good person and a mother who would do anything for her daughter, I won't have the likes of you throwing dirt around now.'

'Darling Cas had you all fooled, I have to admire that woman.'

'Get out, get out.' Margo roared the words.

'Quiet, you don't want to wake the girls.' Charles Richards put his hands out, attempting to grab Margo. 'We can be civilised about this, it's just a matter of how much money.'

Margo heard the dog barking in the yard, a sound that brought a vague sense of comfort. At least Max was safe. 'Just go. How can you do this at a time like this, when we are all grieving? Crawl back into the woodwork, Charles.'

He laughed out loud. 'Never going to happen.'

'The will says the girls stay here, that's what is happening.'

'Neat and tidy and without consultation with the biological father of one and the daddy of twelve years to the other.'

'But a good parent to neither.' Once Margo threw out the words, she immediately regretted them.

'Keep your harsh words to yourself. If you want, you can do this the hard way, spend years bogged down in expensive litigation as those girls grow towards adulthood.'

'You're such a bastard.'

'I prefer to be called a businessman, but you lash out whatever way you want. It will come down to the bucks in the end.'

'I told you to get out.'

Margo marched across to the door and pulled it open. The wind skittered past, throwing rain across them.

Charles Richards shrugged his shoulders. 'You thought I'd gone quietly; well thanks to this bad weather and a flight delay here, I've been nosing around and the little birds tell me you are sitting on millions.'

'That's none of your business.'

Charles leaned in to Margo. 'It is very much my business. You pay up, I leave and never bother you or the girls again, and you don't drown in a swamp hole of litigation.'

'I won't let you threaten me like this.'

'You have until noon tomorrow to come up with the one million. Otherwise, it's bye bye, Elsa. Remember sharing is caring.'

He laughed again and she thought if she plunged a knife into his gut, it would not be good enough for him.

He pushed past her, turning when he got to the yard. 'Tomorrow at noon it is.'

Pain flashed across her temple, her hand hurt as she held on to the door handle, despite the wind battering her, attempting to wrench the door from her grip.

Anger festered in her stomach, rising up through her, until she expelled it by banging the door shut behind him. She stood, tears streaming down her face, every part of her wanting to follow him, attack him, make him get out of their lives. Relief at his departure gave way to panic. She had no idea where he had gone and this suddenly made her afraid. She picked up her phone to ring Jack, but she had no signal.

Thundering up the stairs to the landing window, she waited to see Charles Richards step out onto the avenue. He was there, his pace slow, his shoulder against the wind, huddling against the rain, tramping down the avenue thick with mud, water ponding in the potholes. She saw him reach into his pocket and take out a naggin of whiskey. Holding his back to the wind and rain, turning towards the house, he raised the naggin to slug the whiskey. She shrank back from the window, her heart beating fast. When she dared look out again, she saw Charles shove the bottle deep into his inside pocket on the right side of his coat.

Max ran out from the side of the house, barking loudly and wagging his tail. Charles kicked out at the dog, turning down the path by the river.

Transfixed, she stood watching him, tripping over a tree root, a foot slipping on the river bank. There was a dangerous reticence in her: what if she was not here, did not know he was walking by the water. Maybe he would sway away from it, maybe he would turn back to the house. She should go about her business. He was not her responsibility. Margo remained rooted; the rain grew heavier still, sheeting across from the west, the wind pushing the water down the river, making it rise up and break against the lower branches of the trees. At the bridge, the river surged through, swirling where it was at its widest and deepest.

At the top of the stairs, her eyes followed Charles's every move, every tremor from this man who threatened to take Elsa.

She felt tired and afraid. The rain blasted against the window, she lost sight of Charles. Panic surged through her; she turned to go down the stairs, but abruptly stopped.

What was she doing? She hadn't asked him to drink himself stupid, she was not responsible for this man.

When she got to the kitchen, Jack was shaking out his raincoat. 'Who is the idiot I saw by the river? You should have told the guests to stay away from the water, I've never seen it so swollen.'

'It's Charles.'

Jack dropped his raincoat on the table. 'Why has he come back?'

'To cause trouble. We had words; he said he is going to lodge a claim on Elsa.'

'Holy Jesus, I hope you put a flea in his ear.'

Margo leaned against the table. 'I think I'm going to have to pay him off.'

Jack looked at her directly. 'Over my dead body.'

'He knows we got a million in settlement. He's been drinking in the pubs in town; he must have heard talk there.'

Jack shook his head. 'You give in to him today, he will be back tomorrow looking for more. No, you hold tough, we will wear him down and he'll go home with his tail between his legs.'

'He won't, Jack. What am I going to do?'

'Nothing.'

'Do you think I should go after him? He's in no fit state to be wandering near the river.'

'Why would you, and leave yourself open to a lot of abuse from a drunkard. I'll find him.'

'And when you do?'

'I'll tell him to go to hell, run him off the place.'

Jack pulled on his rain jacket and whistling for his own dog, he walked out the back door without saying another word. The wind and rain blasted into the house, making Margo feel uneasy.

She busied herself getting toast and Nutella and two cups of hot chocolate for the girls. Placing it all on a tray, she put a smile on her face as she walked upstairs to where Tilly and Elsa were curled up in bed, watching their favourite TV programme.

When she leaned to place the tray between them, they barely noticed, Tilly nodding thank you, Elsa almost annoyed at the interruption.

At the landing window, she peered out, but there was nothing to see, only the rain blotting out her view. Making her way downstairs, she decided to read the letter in an effort to distract herself. Taking the envelope from the desk in Conor's study, she crossed to the drawing room and her velvet chair.

Today was the day Cassie had asked her to open her last letter to her. It was exactly seven days since she died.

'Seven days after I am gone, please wait until then. I want you to take time out, open it and read my final words to you,' she said, when she'd handed it to Margo nearly two months ago.

Rathmoney House,
County Wicklow.

My Dearest Margo,

Today is the day to get back to normal. I am no more and no amount of sadness will change my situation. The hardest thing has been leaving you all. But I do, in the sure knowledge that as I exit this world, I have achieved the greatest miracle, the gift of life for my lovely Tilly.

Margo, I thank you and Jack and Ida for enriching these last days for me. As this disease reduced me to a shadow of my former self, your strength and friendship sustained me.

The time has come now for you to concentrate on staying strong for our two girls. How I envy you, but the thought equally brings a comfort.

Stay strong, Margo. Stay stubborn and stay kind. Take comfort in the fact that you have done a good thing, not only in giving a life to your daughter, but also now a home.

The best thing for our girls is to grow up at Rathmoney and when they are ready, they can spread their wings to many farther shores, returning always to the place which took them in and kept them safe, Rathmoney House.

Margo, you must live life now for the two of us, make every decision out of love for our girls and I know you will be on the right road.

I have utmost faith in you to be a loving and supportive mother to our daughters. I thank you for the friendship, the laughs, the advice but mostly for the gift of life to Tilly and the gift of friendship to us both when you were at your lowest.

It's time now Margo to soar, enjoy life and the precious gift of Elsa and Tilly.

Love,

Cas xxxx

Cassie was such a part of Rathmoney, she had left her mark, without even trying. Margo could hardly remember back to the time before she arrived, before she had brought a rainbow of colour into their lives. What Conor would have made of this, she hardly knew. She was through to the other side with the two daughters she treasured more than anything. Where they went from here, she didn't know, but she was not going to let Charles Richards interfere.

When the rain outside got even heavier, the water coming down in never-ending sheets, she moved away from the window.

Cassie was right. It was time now for Margo to be strong and the first thing she should do is stand up for her girls.

Pulling on her raincoat and stepping into her Wellington boots, Margo walked out into the back yard, her head bent against the wind and rain. The river was roaring like the sea. The rain was dancing on the corrugated iron shed roof, heightening the fear in her heart. The bed of hollyhocks had been flattened by the wind into a sea of mud; tree branches were strewn everywhere.

The dog ran towards her, wagging his tail and barking, leading the way to the river.

Jack, coming across the bridge, told Margo to go back. 'It's not safe just now, I'm going to have to block it off.'

'Is he gone?'

'I hope so.'

Jack told her again to get back in the house, so she moved towards the yard. At first she didn't hear Jack and Charles arguing, only stray words in the wind. When she turned around, Charles Richards was on the other side of the bridge, shouting.

Jack motioned at him to stay where he was, shouting to be careful, but Charles ignored him, stepping onto the wooden bridge, holding on to the handrail at one side. The wind howled louder, making the dog cower down afraid.

Margo made to shout at Charles to get off her property when a squall of wind pushed her sideways, knocking her to the ground. Jack ran to her, helping her to her feet, holding her by the shoulders as they pushed forward towards the house, every step taking all their energy, their breath laboured, pain spiking through her. A branch sheared off the oak tree. When she looked back, she saw Charles midway across the bridge. The water in the river roared now. He shouted something, but the wind snatched away his words. She stumbled again and fell.

Jack wrestled her to her feet, pushing her towards the back door. Looking back as the wind howled at its loudest, she saw the bridge give way to the wrecking-ball wind, crashing and groaning into the river. She thought she saw Charles in the water.

Jack forced her on, shouting at her to get to the house. The wind whipped around them, punching them, making them dip their heads low, like boxers defeated in the ring.

When they got to the house, Max jumped at the back door, flinging it open as they fell into the kitchen.

On the television, the presenter was saying a new weather warning had just been issued. 'This is probably our worst storm in decades, with winds of 150 kilometres per hour and gusts of 180 kilometres per hour in places predicted. It is extremely dangerous and everybody is directed to stay indoors until this intense phase of the storm passes, which is expected to be about midday.'

Margo couldn't think straight. 'Charles – I think he was on the bridge when it gave way. I thought I saw him in the water,' she shouted, making to go back out.

Jack pulled at her, standing in front of her to stop her.

'We have to try and help him,' Margo shrieked. She was cold and shivering.

'You are not going out there again. It's too dangerous, I won't let you.'

Margo picked up her mobile, but there still was no signal.

'What are you doing?' Jack asked.

'We have to do something to help.'

Jack grabbed her roughly by the arms. 'Margo, see sense, if he was pulled away by all that water, there's nothing anyone can do for him. I won't let you risk your life for that piece of shit. Think of Tilly and Elsa.'

Shivering, unable to speak, Margo collapsed into the chair by the stove.

Jack opened the cupboards, pushing things around until he found a bottle of brandy.

Pouring out two glasses he handed one to Margo.

'That Mr Richards is very good at looking after himself. If anyone can survive, he can. He will turn up tomorrow, no fear of that.'

'Shouldn't we check?'

'I will, but when this part of the storm passes. It's still too dangerous out there. We still have no phone signal either – mobile or landline.'

They sat with tumblers of brandy in their hands. Margo went upstairs to check on the girls, but they were preoccupied now looking at a movie on the iPad. The wind howled around the house, rattling the back door, knocking down the guttering at the front, lifting slates off the roof and making them crash into smithereens across the garden, upending the half-full water barrel and hurling it across the yard.

'What did Charles say to you out there?' Margo asked.

'Nothing that made sense; he's an angry, bitter man.'

'About Cassie and you?'

Jack ran his hand along his brow. 'If he came back thinking he could blackmail me, he's very wrong. Ida is the one who has been holding me up since Cas passed.' Jack shook his head in an attempt to preempt the tears. 'I don't mind saying, I miss her terribly. Ida and me, we're finding our way. You know our story, she understands. I don't need that excuse of a man throwing dirt on what was a beautiful and honest friendship.'

'She loved you too.'

'I know.'

They did not speak again, the storm howling around them, invading their thoughts, mirroring the anger in their hearts that Charles Richards should return to stir up trouble.

When the wind slowed down, its fury sated, they did not move for fear it would rise up again.

On the television, there were images of devastation across the country: flooding on low ground, trees down everywhere and whole towns and villages cut off by rising water.

After a while, Jack got up from the table, his chair screeching across the tiles. 'I'll have a look outside on the way home. If there is anything, I will ring you. Otherwise, I'll be back to greet him tomorrow.'

Margo nodded and stood up, ready to shut and lock the door after him.

Chapter Forty-Five

Rathmoney, County Wicklow.

Jack and Margo sat in the kitchen waiting. It was after the noon deadline but there was no sign of Charles Richards.

Ida had taken the girls to her house for the day, so they had no idea Charles was due at Rathmoney House.

Jack had searched for hours straight after the worst of the storm, but there was no sign of the American. When the wind finally dropped down, he walked the length of the river on the Rathmoney land twice, but there was nothing. He searched the field and where the old oak tree had given way in the high wind halfway up the avenue.

Margo had watched from the landing and front bedroom until the light went, afraid Charles Richards would make another burst for the house.

'Maybe he got away in the storm and had a rethink of his position?' Jack said when by ten minutes past twelve there was no contact.

'Or he is making us suffer and wait; or perhaps he is dead, swept out to sea.' Margo began to pace the kitchen.

'If he had drowned in that river, I would surely have found him.'

'This not knowing is the worst: I will spend my whole life wondering, is he going to barge in here again to take Elsa.'

'Hold tough, we will wait until one and if he still doesn't show, we'll leave it at that.'

'Except we might never know what happened.'

'Either he had a change of heart or something has happened to him. He did go out in the worst of the storm.'

'Shouldn't we get people out looking for him?'

'And put a spotlight on Rathmoney House, just when those two girls are trying to recover from the loss of Cas?'

Margo wasn't entirely sure if she agreed, but she was too exhausted to argue.

'We have done nothing wrong, have we?'

Jack shook his head.

'I told him to get in out of the storm and he told me to go to hell. I never saw him after that.'

'Still, he is linked to the girls.'

Jack clenched his fists, banging down on the table, making it shake. 'If that bastard is gone from their lives, it can only be a good thing,' he said, adding that he was off to check on the storm damage.

'If he makes contact, let me know,' he said as he reached for his jacket.

Margo went to her chair by the drawing-room window. With Charles disappeared, who knew what was going to happen next. He had already walked out of Tilly's life once before, now they faced the prospect he could turn up at any time. She honestly did not know which was worse.

She was now the key person left in both their lives. The responsibility was heavy on Margo's shoulders, her abiding fear that she might buckle under the weight.

The sun broke through, picking out the buds of the red hot poker, still standing as all around it, the purple and pink of hollyhocks peeped from a sea of mud. Tilly and Elsa had earlier found a small fish thrown up in Cassie's flower bed, where the rose bushes were bald without their summer blooms, the petals once in shining pink, yellow and red, now brown and battered into the gravel of the avenue. All around her, the gardens of Rathmoney looked sad and dejected, the plants and trees that survived displaying the scars of both wind and rain.

Max snuffled about the avenue wagging his tail, busy sniffing the flotsam and jetsam of the big storm. Rathmoney House and gardens would recover in time, she knew that, but she worried that the mystery of Charles Richards's whereabouts would come back to haunt them all.

Within two days, the mystery was solved, when a farmer searching for a lost calf found the body of the American caught in the undergrowth on the banks of the river, where it fed into the sea.

'Jo Sheppard told me after he rang and reported it. It is him, I identified him at the location,' Jack said.

Margo held on to the hall table, as her head began to reel. 'I never wished him dead.'

Jack motioned her to follow him in to Conor's office.

'Will they come asking questions?' she asked, her throat caked dry.

'I don't think so. I told them who he was and kept Rathmoney House out of it. I said we had seen him last two days before, and that he had agreed to leave the parenting of Tilly to you and not interfere with the provisions of Cassie's will.'

Margo felt tears rise up inside her.

'They asked me about family,' Jack hesitated. 'I told them about Cassie and that you were now the legal guardian. I said they could check with you, but you may prefer not to burden Tilly with this news right now, considering he has already told her he was taking a step back from her life. I'm sorry I didn't consult you, I was thinking on my feet.'

'You said the truth; the only decent thing he did was to reject Tilly.'

'Will the rest of the family come looking for Tilly?'

'I doubt that, Cassie said they wanted nothing to do with her, once she was not his. She mentioned his sister once – but she would have no contact point. Vince has sold the house in Bowling Green and moved away. I'm sure the police will find his family, though.'

'It's hard to hear, but that man only wanted the money, a father-daughter relationship wasn't his priority.' Jack took Margo's hands. 'He is gone forever and it's good riddance. It can be our secret he came to Rathmoney, threatening to bring all sorts in on top of you. Nobody needs to know and especially not the two girls. He walked out of their lives a few days ago, we will leave it at that.'

Margo nodded. 'I can't get it out of my mind that we should have done more.'

Jack sighed. 'Margo, there was nothing we could do. You have to let it rest now, for the sake of the future for Tilly and Elsa.'

'I suppose.'

'I'm off, Ida will get cross if I don't sort out the slates on our own roof.'

Margo went to the kitchen and sat at the table, her head in her hands. If she told the truth, she was glad Charles was out of their lives; maybe now everybody at Rathmoney House could get back to normal.

Chapter Forty-Six

Rathmoney, County Wicklow.

It was a crisp day in autumn when they decided to bring the ashes that were once Cassie to the sea.

'We should dress up for Mom,' Tilly said.

'What we need are coats, it's going to be cold on the shore,' Ida said, making Tilly and Elsa laugh.

'No, can we dress up in the lovely designer dresses? Mom would love that.'

'And catch cold? Those dresses were not meant for the Irish Sea, but for sophisticated Parisian soirées,' Ida huffed, looking to Margo for support.

'I don't know, Ida, I think Cassie would love the idea of us in satin and silk making our way to the sea.'

'It looks like I'm outnumbered,' Ida said, pretending to be annoyed.

Tilly and Elsa clapped with excitement and ran off to find Jack and ask him to get the boxes from the attic.

'If I had known it would make those two so happy, I would never have objected,' Ida said.

'It gives them a different focus from death and Cassie would have loved the idea,' Margo said.

'At least we are on Rathmoney House land, there are very few who will see us.'

'You're not worried what people will say, surely?'

'Old habits die hard,' Ida said, throwing her eyes up at her own stupidity.

They heard a clatter in the hall as Jack put up the ladder and opened the attic.

Tilly ran in to Margo. 'Can I wear the pink dress Mom wore the last time?'

'You can, but it's still upstairs. Because your mom liked to have it hanging on the outside of the wardrobe, where she could see it. I left it there.'

Ida said she would go up and get it while Jack got down the last of the boxes. She hesitated on the top landing outside the front bedroom. None of them, until now, had had the inclination to enter this room. Slowly, Ida turned the handle. The room was dark, the shutters still across. The bed was stripped bare, the locker, which had once held so much of Cassie's medication, had been cleared. Ida saw a packet of cigarettes on top of the locker and she clicked her tongue in frustration. The cerise dress was where she had hung it when Cassie had asked her to put it on show. 'It reminds me of that lovely time we all laughed together,' she said, and Ida had to hold back her tears.

Ida lightly touched the silk, the folds of fabric slipping across her hands. Stretching up to unhook it from the hanger, she let it bundle down, until she could drape it over her arm, the rustle of the silk organza loud in the gloomy quietness of the room. She didn't know if Margo would ever move back to this bedroom, which had hosted the death of two loved ones.

When she got downstairs, Tilly and Elsa already had the boxes open.

'Ida, what do you think?' Elsa asked as she twirled across the drawing room, in the blue, sleeveless, sparkling gown she had hitched up with a long scarf of deep purple.

'I hope you are going to wear your coat young lady or you will get a nasty cold,' Ida grumbled as she handed the pink dress to Tilly.

Tilly hesitated.

'What's wrong, darling?' Margo asked.

'It's so beautiful, I don't want to ruin it, trailing it across the beach,'

Margo laughed. 'Tilly, you are beginning to sound too much like Ida,' she said as she pulled the powder-blue flouncy dress over her jeans.

Ida, rummaging for the satin dress she favoured, pulled Tilly over beside her. 'Your mum would be so honoured if you wore this dress she loved, why don't I hitch it up in a bundle at the back, a bustle, and then it won't trail on the sand.'

Tilly nodded enthusiastically and Ida set to work, catching up the silk skirt and lining and securing it with thick elastic bands and ribbon.

Nobody noticed Jack was missing until they heard his Jeep pull in to the back yard. Ida had gone off to change, so when he walked through to the drawing room, it was only Margo and the girls who were there.

'Jack you look so ...'

Margo stopped.

'Like a gentleman farmer,' Ida said from the hall. She walked over and straightened his bow tie and picked a little speck of fluff off his suit jacket.

'You look beautiful,' he said, making her flush pink.

'Do a twirl, Ida,' Elsa said.

Ida swung around, the folds of the satin skirt sweeping across the Persian rug while the others clapped. Jack held Ida's coat for her and they all wrapped up for a walk in the autumn sunshine down to the sea.

The horses walked with the group as they crossed the far fields, almost as if they were escorting Cassie to the sea, a place where she had found peace. Max ran on ahead, waiting on shore for the group, Margo carrying the urn.

The shore was different, battered by the storm waves, seaweed and rubbish deposited on the tideline, higher than they'd ever seen before.

Tilly and Elsa ran about picking up shells and examining the remains of starfish and tiny crabs.

'Should we say something?' Ida asked.

'Maybe Tilly would like to say a few words, before we scatter the ashes,' Margo said.

Tilly took a scoop of the ashes. 'Thanks, Mom, for bringing me here. I will always come to visit you on the beach.' She leaned as far as she could and threw the ashes, watching as they rode a wave.

'Can I do it as well?' Elsa asked. 'I want to say thank you for bringing Tilly to Rathmoney,' she said, throwing the ashes high, so they speckled across the water. Margo watched, her heart thumping as Elsa danced across the sand, oblivious to the full significance of her participation.

Margo gave the urn to Jack. 'Scatter them, the rest of us can say our silent prayers.'

Jack, who had slipped off his shoes and socks and rolled up his trousers, stepped into the water to empty the urn, letting the ashes be pulled out far, before returning to shore.

'Goodbye, dear friend,' Margo whispered.

Ida dipped her head in prayer.

They stood and watched for a while. Walking back across the fields to Rathmoney House, Tilly and Elsa scampered ahead with the dog.

'You'd better fix the bridge today,' Margo said to Jack.

'I will,' he replied. He took Ida's hand. 'I will be home in an hour or so.'

'I know,' she said, her voice light, the look in her eyes warm.

Chapter Forty-Seven

Rathmoney, County Wicklow.

Margo tiptoed down the stairs, stepping over the loose balloons, picking up three half-empty bottles of beer from the hall table on the way. In the kitchen, the table was covered in streamers, from where they had popped several the night before, the remains too of the birthday cake in plastic plates across the worktops. Pouring the last of the beer from the bottles down the sink, before throwing them into the recycling box, Margo next let Max out the back door. The dog pissed in his usual spot in the flower bed under the kitchen window, before heading around to the front of the house, where he liked to sit with a full view of the avenue.

Margo made her way to the drawing room, sighing when she saw popcorn strewn across the Persian rug. Picking her way through, trying not to squish the kernels into the carpet, she saw her velvet chair had been pulled across to the fireplace, so the band's sound equipment could fit by the window. Pushing a speaker out of the way, she had enough room to manoeuvre her favourite chair back into its place.

Here she could sit, her back to the mess of last night's eighteenth birthday party. The house was quiet, Tilly and

Elsa crashed upstairs after stealing up to bed some time as dawn peeped through and the last guests wandered down the avenue.

She was glad of this quiet time in her thinking chair. She had had years to think of how to do it, but now she must tell the girls, regardless of the consequences.

She had intended to do it last Thursday when they returned from the city, but the sight of Tilly and Elsa laden down with shopping bags, chatting happily, full of the upcoming party and their eighteenth birthdays stopped her, for fear of spoiling things.

She could hardly understand herself why she hadn't told the girls before now, only she was afraid of losing these two daughters she loved more than anything. Would it count that she had been mother and father to both of them, there to pick them up when life went wrong, to cheer at the good times. She was the one who had held their hands all these years.

She loved them so deeply; they were a team, but now she was afraid that even the strength of the team could not withstand the assault of this news.

Before they cut their joint birthday cake, Tilly had stopped to remember her mom, who had not only ensured she had a new lease of life, but had also left her with a home here at Rathmoney. Margo had let her tears fall. Those around her comforted her, offering words of support, but they had no idea the tears were those welling up from a spring of fear she had no hope of stopping.

When Ida held her tight around the shoulders, she leaned into her. Ida didn't say anything, but each time Margo convulsed with tears, she tightened her grip, until Margo finally felt the strength to pull away.

My Dearest Margo,

I have asked Jack to take a note of this letter because my mind is tired and my hand can't grip as it should.

I know we talked about not telling the girls the true story, but as I lie here I'm worried that to keep it from them for all time would be a terrible injustice.

At this stage you will have brought up our two girls, guided them through the difficult years and Tilly through the maze of grief. I hesitate to place a heavier burden on your shoulders, but it weighs heavily on my mind that we may be keeping this important information from Tilly and Elsa.

There is no doubt it will cause some ructions, but I wondered once the girls reach eighteen, shouldn't they be entitled to know? I am a coward, Margo, placing this huge weight on your shoulders, while I bow out.

There is nothing new there, I guess. Since I first came into your life, all I have done is lean on you and you have not once complained. I know when you started this, it was your love for Elsa that kept you going and now I know it is the love you hold in your heart for both our girls.

That will help you to make the right decision here.

So, yes, we talked of not telling the girls, letting them resume their childhood, but now all these years on, maybe it is time. To be honest, I have not had the energy to properly discuss this with you. Instead, in these last days I must keep the little energy I have for Tilly and Elsa, though I fear they may be a little afraid of me and I don't blame them, this disease robs me of everything, leaving nothing but the smile I have to force on my face.

Margo, I leave this letter with Jack, but the decision is in your hands; think about it and do as you see fit. If you decide not to tell Tilly and Elsa, so be it. You have my support in whatever you do.

Neither do I mind if you want to explain away Tilly's trust fund as a gift from her grandfather. Vince will never go against anything you say, you know that.

If you do decide to tell them, I have enclosed a letter here I want you to open and read to them. Please no opening beforehand and if your decision is not to tell them, I ask you to destroy it, let the words melt away.

I know you will have brought up our girls to be fine young women. I respect any decision such a good mother makes.

With my gratitude and love always.

Cas Xxxx

Margo sat at the drawing-room window holding the letter. Hours may have passed, but her opinion remained resolute. She saw Jack arrive in his tractor, the horses canter across the field to greet him. The heron swooped low for the length of the river. Max, now old and slow, lay out in the avenue, reluctantly moving when the tractor came near. Soon Tilly and Elsa would be up, full of chat about the party. Taking Cassie's letter and the separate sealed envelope to Tilly and Elsa, she carefully folded them together; next in to two and four, before she pulled at the bulk of paper with her fingers, digging at it, until it tore into tiny pieces.

Meticulously, she gathered any stray shreds, before compacting it into a tight ball. Pushing the ball into her pocket, she walked out the front door to the path by the river. Strolling by the river, the ferns spilling water into her slippers, she stepped onto the bridge, standing when she reached the middle, mesmerised by the slow flow of the water. The level of the water was so low, rocks protruded above the surface in places. The heron glided past and down the river; a robin stopped on one rock mid-stream. Max followed Margo onto the bridge, flopping at her feet.

Slowly she took out the ball of paper from her pocket and let it drop over the side of the bridge. It landed in the water, bobbing for a moment until, saturated, it broke apart, disintegrating, the ink of the words diluted by the river water. She stood as the pieces of paper drifted away, some clinging to the reeds beside the bank, other parts drifting downriver to the sea.

When she was sure it had all disappeared, dissipated by the water current, she turned and walked back to Rathmoney House, the dog following slowly behind.

Acknowledgements

Writing is a solitary endeavour, but I am very lucky to have a great team behind me which ensures that germ of an idea way back when, becomes a novel available to readers worldwide.

Thanks seems such a small word for the support offered by my family and best friends, John Roshan and Zia. They are there on all the writing days, especially when the words don't come easy, cheering me on to the finish line. One million thanks guys!

My literary agent Jenny Brown is the first person to thrown an eye over the early drafts and her advice and encouragement is invaluable. Thank you for your unstinting support for my writing Jenny!

Huge thanks to my wonderful editor at Orion, Clare Hey, for her guidance, wise words and constant good humour and to all the team at Orion Publishing for their warm welcome and support.

There were many who assisted me greatly with the fine details in this, my fourth novel, and I am very grateful for the help and support of Doireann O'Mahony BL, Vivienne Traynor, Bernie Osgood and renal nurse, Mairead Kinlough, Children's University Hospital, Temple Street, Dublin.

Finally, to all the readers who have taken my books to their hearts, thanks a million for your support. To those new readers who happen on this novel, welcome to Rathmoney House and it is my wish you enjoy reading it as much as I enjoyed writing it.